I0629583

HALFDAN SAGA
THE BATTLE OF EDGE KEEP

By R. Adrian Kolosso

First American Edition, 2024

Amazon Paperback Edition, 2024

Published by R. Adrian Kolosso

Distributed by Kindle Direct Publishing

North Charleston, SC: 4900 Lacross Rd., North Charleston, SC 29406-6558

Seattle, WA: 410 Terry Ave N., Seattle, WA 98109

kdp.amazon.com

Text and Illustrations Copyright © R. Adrian Kolosso, 2024

All rights reserved.

Without limiting the rights under the copyright reserved above, no part of this publication may be reproduced, stored in or introduced into a retrieval system, or transmitted, in any form or by any means (electronic, mechanical, photocopying, recording, or otherwise), without prior written permission of the copyright owner. R. Adrian Kolosso P.O. Box 412 Burlington, WI 53105

A catalog record for this book is available from the Library of Congress.

ISBN 979-8-9920393-1-3

This is a work of fiction. Names, characters, places, and incidents either are the product of the author's imagination or are used fictitiously, and any resemblance to actual persons, living or dead, business establishments, events, or locales is entirely coincidental.

Edited by

Candace Kolosso

&

Michael Crowley

Illustrated by

Candace Kolosso

Digitally Illustrated

Emily Chapman

Appendix in back to reference Asterisked words

***

Mercenary, by the name of Halfdan, is making his way through an ancient *Norvegr forest. He is a rugged man with long dark brown hair, wearing a vibrant blue tunic that matches his eyes. His pants are tucked in his tall boots, causing the pants to puff out where the two meet. His nose is slightly off kilter from it being broken in a fight years ago. Over the years, Halfdan has learned to put on a stern face to hide his kind heart. With him he carries a forged bearded axe, worn from battle. Halfdan is followed by a *seidmadr, a man of magic. The seidmadr went by many names, but was known to Halfdan as Frode. Frode's long white hair swayed in the wind, along with his beard which is adorned with braids and dark wooden beads. He wears a long black cloak with a collar made of wolf fur. His face is worn from age but that doesn't prevent him from looking gentle, due to his perpetual smile. Frode was known throughout the towns and rural villages for his herbal medicine and affiliation with spirits and magic.

What makes a woman a *seidr, or a man a seidmadr, was their ability to see or even shape the future. Frode has told Halfdan many times that seeing the future wasn't much of a gift, but more of a nuisance. Seeing things that you weren't able to change was frustrating and trying to shape the future often ends with things going horribly wrong. Many years ago Frode had told a *Jarl that his son would be killed by a dog; in response the Jarl killed all the dogs in his farming community. In the end the villagers got new dogs and sent them out to kill the Jarl's son. After, Frode would only tell people the joyful parts of their future.

Frode has paid Halfdan to escort him to Thwaite, because it is said that the villagers there had found new gem stones. Since crystals and gems are the bones of the earth, they have some magical properties. To the untrained, they do not hold much value other than

1

decoration or status. But for those who practice magic, crystals and gems can do wondrous things. Frode has hired Halfdan many times as a guide and for protection. They have a rapport with each other and together look for a remedy to a village's plague. The mysterious illness started out harmless enough, a mild cough and fatigue. Days later a fever would grow and soon the victims would no longer respond. This caused the village to fall into deep despair and isolation. Wondering why the Gods and Goddesses have forsaken them.

Halfdan looked down as he walked; frowning as he thought. Stepping over moss covered stones and branches as he contemplated. Halfdan took deep breaths, tasting the cold earthy air as it rhythmically rushed to fill his lungs. He picked leaves along the way to preoccupy his nerves, taking in the textures and sensations each one had to offer.

"What troubles you, my friend? I can tell that something is on your mind?" Frode asked, concerned for Halfdan. Despite his naturally deep tone Frode often tried to carry it as gently as he could. "Did you hear me?"

"Oh, sorry Frode. It's Liv. I know we already talked about this. But is there anything else you can do for her? I've heard of other seidrs performing spells to give the dying new life and-"

"I am sorry." said Frode interrupting Halfdan before he could say more. "The magic you speak about is dangerous. Especially to a child. You know I am bound by oaths to limited magic by my predecessor. All of the cunning in the area are working on a cure for Liv's plagued village. Have faith in *Eir. With the herbs I gave her, along with plenty of water and sunlight Liv will be able to hang on until there is a cure."

Halfdan kept walking with a heavy aura still frowning, dropping and picking new leaves repetitively. Frode can tell that Halfdan wasn't happy with him. Both could see that Liv was showing no signs of recovery. Knowing that her younger brother and father have recently passed from the same plague only made their doubts grow.

Halfdan had grown very fond of the young Liv in the short time he came to know her. Frode knew Halfdan wouldn't be able to cope with the loss. He would talk fondly of Liv and it was apparent Halfdan enjoyed her company. It was a shame that her time was short, but thus is death. For it cares not for age or status.

Frode and Halfdan kept walking in silence. Time passes when you are focused. Frode picked plants and herbs along the way, making their trip take longer than it should. In hopes of sparking a conversation, Frode would discuss the names of plants and explain their healing properties. Rather than engaging in conversation Halfdan made grunts of acknowledgement.

Halfdan slowly led Frode into a small clearing, both appreciating at having to no longer move around tree branches. Frode began to notice that Halfdan's steps became slower and slower. He was puzzled as Frode slowly walked behind Halfdan, examining him. But once they were in the middle of the clearing Frode could tell that something was wrong, dreadfully wrong.

Halfdan abruptly stopped. For a moment Frode was unsure if Halfdan saw something, uncertainty soon grew into uneasiness. When the sound of horses running through the forest and their riders yelling reached Frode's ears his heart dropped. Seconds after making their presence known, men on their steeds rode out into the clearing, a premeditated plan to surround Halfdan and Frode. The men were dirty from living a rugged life and wore leather armor. Their horses were painted with blue jagged patterns, despite the paint being old and flaking off it was still intimidating.

"I'm sorry." Halfdan said heavily as he hung his head in shame. "I need the money to hire a seidr that will do any type of magic needed to save Liv."

"Blackhare gives her regards." said a man on a horse. It was obvious he led the team of bandits. He was rough looking with cold eyes and a blood curdling smile that showed his plaque ridden teeth.

The name Blackhare rang in Frode's mind. Blackhare is a seidr who was mad with power. She is known for her long white hair and never aging looks. Blackhare got her name for her fluffle of black

3

rabbits that she kept and adored. Despite her young looks and her affinity for animals she was bluntly envious of others magical prowess. If you did not join her, you were against her. Something that Frode has been weary of. Blackhare was not known to common men as an enemy, but to lone magical individuals she was dangerous. Meticulously working to overrule the other cunning, something that has never happened before. She promises unity, but others knew there was a different agenda. What Blackhare is planning has been weighing on Frode's mind for some time.

"We can do this the easy way, or the hard way." said the leader with an oddly joyful grin. "I personally prefer the hard way. It makes things interesting. Blackhare will like to hear about you struggling for your life."

Halfdan straightened up and looked around confused at what the bandit leader said. "We agreed that we wouldn't hurt him! You were going to deliver him to Blackhare, unharmed!" exclaimed Halfdan, trying to sound mean but there was a crack of fear in his voice.

The leader's grin grew larger. "I said I was going to deliver him to Blackhare. Just not all of him. Sorry for the confusion."

With a simple nod of his head one of the leader's men lifted a bow, his arrow already drawn and ready. Halfdan was hit in the chest before he could realize what was happening. Halfdan staggered for a split second before he hit the ground. Yelling in pain as blood began to drool out of his mouth as his lungs began to fill with blood.

"Sorry, friend." Said the bandit leader in a condescending tone as he adjusted himself on his horse to get more comfortable. "But I'm not very good at sharing silver. Especially to a traitor such as you. Giving up your one ally for a favor and a handful of silver from Blackhare. Well, let me tell you something. Blackhare doesn't like to owe anyone any favors. So she pays me to take care of any loose ends."

The bandits begin to laugh as another man draws an arrow aimed at Halfdan. All in a game to make Halfdan yell in pain for amusement. Similar to a cat playing with a wounded mouse for fun, a sad end to ones life.

As the men were tormenting Halfdan, Frode picked up a twig off the ground and closed his eyes. He closed his mind off from the chaos and encompassed into the trees surrounding him. He felt their strength, grace, and peacefulness. Frode tightened his grasp on the twig, snapping it. Suddenly the trees surrounding them, both young and old, burst from the bottom and fell as if giants were kicking the trees to the ground. The men and their horses were suddenly startled. Most weren't able to react fast enough and met their end by fallen trees. Despite the thunderous deafening sound of the trees meeting the ground you could still hear bones being crushed. It sounded similar to pumpkins being thrown and cracking open but instead screams would abruptly stop.

The bandit leader held his ground as trees fell around him. His horse was panicking and pranced in place with fear. The man aimed his bow at Frode, focusing his aim and steadily breathing. Before he could take the shot a branch knocked him off his horse. The snapping of wood and the yelling caused his horse to begin to buck and kick in terror, trampling his master under his hooves. The horse was unsure as to where to go and was quickly hit by a falling tree.

Frode stood still in the middle of the clearing as he slowly opened his eyes. He was an arm's reach away from all the trees he dismembered. There was no way to avoid hearing the sounds of pain and death that surrounded him. Frode slowly made his way to Halfdan; only stopping once more to look at the carnage around him. On the ground was a nest with dead baby birds which that had been flung out of a fallen tree. Sorrow went through Frode's body as his eyes grew heavy. As he looked around he could see horses crushed by heavy limbs with their riders pinned beneath them. Blood was running out from under the fallen trees and cascading over the green leaves turning them crimson. So many innocent animals died just to save himself.

Frode heard Halfdan moan. Surprised and pleased Frode made his way to his friend, moving branches and climbing over logs and limbs. Halfdan was spared by the trees, but arrows still pierced through him. Frode examined the arrows that were in his shoulder, chest and upper leg. The arrow in Halfdan's leg had severed an artery, causing blood to run profusely out of the wound. Each time Halfdan opened his mouth to cough, blood would spatter out in thick droplets. Frode sat next to Halfdan who reached out to him. Halfdan wasn't able to talk due to pain, but his eyes said what he wasn't able to express.

Frode held Halfdan's hand and smiled. "I forgive you."

Halfdan's eyes became distant as he began to gasp for air. Frode squeezed Halfdan's hand before putting it down. Frode exhaled and focused his energy. He pressed his index and middle finger on his forehead. Then placed his hand over his heart. Focusing all of his energy into his hand. Frode's hand felt cold, tingly but yet strong. Slowly, he placed his hand over Halfdan's heart. Frode used all his might to expel his energy into Halfdan.

Halfdan's body jolted, hit with adrenalin. He felt his heart pound rapidly with life as sweat encased his body. Halfdan felt anxious and fearful, unsure as to what was happening.

As Halfdan sat up, Frode used this opportunity to push the arrow deeper into Halfdan's body. Frode ignored Halfdan's screams as he broke the tip of the arrow off. With the arrow head removed Frode could pull the remainder of the arrow out the entry wound. Halfdan's body shook from the odd sensation of a foreign object being pulled through his body. The arrow in the leg was impaled in the bone, so Frode had no choice but to pull it out. Frode knew it was going to be more painful than pushing it through. Frode applied pressure and swiftly pulled the arrow out. Halfdan yelled with vigor as sweat began to drip down his face. Feeling the arrow rip its way out of his body was gut-wrenchingly painful.

"Use this gift to save your beloved Liv. You are not bound by oaths as I." Frode took a moment to gaze upon Halfdan, who was still shaking and looking around with glossy eyes. "Farewell for now, my friend." said Frode sincerely as he took off his cloak to cover Halfdan. Frode slowly laid down next to Halfdan and closed his eyes. Already gone from this world, Frode did not have a last exhale, for his spirit and energy was already within Halfdan.

Halfdan's eyes were still dazed as he began to collect himself and attempted to comprehend what had happened. Slowly Halfdan's heart began to slow to a regular beat and his blurry vision cleared. Halfdan pushed through the pain to sit over Frode, he could tell something was wrong. The muscles in Frode's face were relaxed and his eyes and mouth were slightly open. It was as if Frode was sleeping but eerily still.

"Frode?" Halfdan asked, placing his hand onto Frode's chest and gently shoving him. "No, oh-no." Was all Halfdan was able to say as Frode's head fell limply to one side. With his hand balled into a fist Halfdan began hitting Frode's chest, tears falling down and wetting the dead man's tunic with each blow. "You can't leave me like this! Take it back! Take it back!... Take it back."

Halfdan cried alone in the still forest as he sat near his deceased friend, not ready to accept that Frode was gone. The smell of upturned earth and blood lingered in the air. The forest birds began to sing again, as if the spirit of the woods was unaffected by the carnage. Halfdan could feel the blood on his clothes begin to cool, an unsettling sensation.

The word traitor repeated itself within Halfdan's head. He betrayed his friend for a favor and a handful of silver. With the realization that Frode still went against his own oaths and code to perform magic to save his friend, Halfdan began to dry heave and shake, overwhelmed with emotion and energy. Like a child, Halfdan began to wish that this was all a dream and that he would wake up soon. Frode would still be alive and Halfdan would finally be able to tell him how important their friendship was to him.

CHAPTER 2

FROM DEATH COMES LIFE

It took some effort and strain, but Halfdan was able to drag Frode over the mess of fallen trees and limbs. The thought of wild animals desecrating Frode's corps motivated Halfdan to find a decent place to lay his friend. A simple burial wasn't customary for Frode's beliefs; however, Halfdan wouldn't be able to drag his body all the way back to the village. Halfdan kept telling himself that he would come back and build a pyre to cremate him, that was a lie. Deep down Halfdan knew he never wanted to come back to this place.

There was some daylight left, enough time to make a campfire if Halfdan hurried. Satisfied with the area Halfdan laid Frode's body down upon a grassy area, put small rocks over his eyes to keep them closed and tried to make him look at peace. Halfdan went out to collect wood and when he came back he saw a fly hovering around Frode's body. Stomach purge began to run down Frode's face, it was brown and thick. Sadness and defeat washed over Halfdan, he wasn't ready to see Frode's body in such a state. A campfire will have to wait.

Halfdan dragged Frode's corpse some more until he found a river. Gently, as if Frode was still alive, Halfdan placed a log under his friend's head to elevate it to try and keep the purge down. With rigor mortis set it was easier to move Frode. Halfdan was able to find decent rocks in the river to cover Frode's body. He figured a spot next to a river under an oak tree would be fitting for Frode's body to rest. Oak trees symbolized wisdom and a river simply seemed peaceful. For years to come the oak tree should still be standing and the river flowing.

Humming a somber dirge, Halfdan continued to collect rocks from the river until twilight. There wasn't enough sunlight left to make a fire and the bugs were beginning to be a nuisance. Halfdan had a good collection of rocks and had three different piles separated by size. With the last bit of sunlight Halfdan covered Frode with leaves, dirt and rocks. Meticulously placing the rocks to make sure Frode was covered.

Halfdan laid reeds upon Frode's *cairn, trying his best to make his resting place look more pleasing. The familiar smell of death and upturned soil was filling the air. Halfdan strategically laid Frode's cloak that was gifted to him on the ground to keeping the earth from absorbing his heat, feeling the dirt and moving it around with his hands to make a flat surface to sleep. Halfdan put his hands behind his head and watched as the last bit of sun faded away. It was easy to deal with the loss of his friend as he was collecting rocks and erecting the cairn. Now that Halfdan was able to rest the emotions began to flood back in.

Traitor. That's what he was now. He betrayed someone that considered him a friend. No one was supposed to get hurt, that was the plan. Halfdan felt guilty, he knew the idea of no one getting hurt was never going to happen, it only eased his mind at the moment. Besides being tired, Halfdan's body felt claustrophobic, as if there wasn't enough room for him. Halfdan assumed Frode gave him his life's energy. The thought of Frode using his spirit to give him more life made Halfdan feel sick. Why would Frode want to be a part of him, a traitor, after what happened? Halfdan wondered if a friend betrayed him would he have enough forgiveness and compassion to save their life. Grimacing at the thought he knew the answer would have been no, most likely he would have felt exuberant watching a traitor suffer. Halfdan closed his eyes, pushing the thoughts away from his mind and focused on the sounds of the river. Rhythmically turning and tumbling over the rocks as fish traveled against the river's current.

Halfdan was startled awake by the sound of footsteps, unable to recall falling asleep. Fear froze his body and Halfdan had to build

9

up the courage to look for his axe. Heavy clouds covered the moon, plunging the land into a deep darkness. Halfdan widened his eyes desperate to see. He slowly moved his hand away from his side and felt the ground for his axe. Barely touching the tips of the grass in his search. He could hear the unknown entity was examining the cairn. The movement abruptly stopped, Halfdan had to catch his breath. Worried that maybe this creature heard him moving. Halfdan heard the footsteps quickly running in the other direction. Halfdan continued to feel around for his axe, brushing his hand slowly upon the earth. He was relieved when he felt the familiar handle. Halfdan grabbed the axe and held it close to him. The slight comfort from having a weapon on him helped, but he couldn't shake the feeling of being watched in every direction, exposed and unable to see. Halfdan began pleading for the sun to rise, unsure if it was still late in the night or nearing dawn. Never before did Halfdan feel that the sunrise took too long to appear. He was more accustomed to cursing the morning light for making his hangover worse.

At the first sliver of light Halfdan sat up. He placed his hand upon Frode's cairn, an intricate mound of rocks and earth. Halfdan was sad to leave Frode's corpse, but he knew that he couldn't stay for long. Since the stars were covered by clouds all night Halfdan had to guess in what direction to go. Despite essentially being lost, Halfdan made his way through the forest relying on his instincts to guide him. His clothes were stiff from dried blood which made each movement of his body uncomfortable. Halfdan made his way slowly. It was difficult to move without a trail as nature was an obstacle all around him. From the shrubbery, streams and branches all presented a challenge.

Despite all of this Halfdan felt safer than being on a trail, worried about more bandits lingering around. Halfdan wasn't sure if all of them had perished by the fallen trees. Never before did he see Frode use magic in such a violent way. What else had his friend been capable of?

The sun was beginning to set again when Halfdan stumbled out of the forest and found a road. The road was familiar. It was a relief to him to see something he recognized, even if it was a dirt road. The road led to the village of Dragekall, where Liv and her mother lived. The village is said to be protected by a lindwrum. Villagers would see the lindwrum now and then, but descriptions of the beast would change each time. The only description that stayed consistent was the creature's long serpent like body being pulled by two front legs, the iconic description of a lindwrum. Those who wanted to hunt the elusive beast would be severely punished. Even if the lindwrum was fictional. The villagers relied on it for a sense of protection. Halfdan figured the ancients purposely spread rumors that the beast protected the village and surrounding forest. If the beast was real the villagers themselves were unsure. However to outsiders it seemed to be as real as the sun. Occasionally, unexplained sounds would rumble through the forest frightening people away.

It was dark by the time Halfdan arrived at the house that Liv and her mother resided. It was on the outskirt of the village and was modest but well maintained. Liv's late father worked hard to provide for his family and built it with his own hands. It seems like the good men always die too soon, leaving the world more heartless.

Halfdan loudly knocked on the door. Liv's mother, Linna, slowly answered. After her late husband and son had passed Linna used the last bit of money she had to send someone to retrieve Halfdan. With other relatives too busy to tend to their own problems she didn't have anyone else to turn to. The first time Halfdan met Linna again after years of separation she did not look like her former self. No longer wearing masculine clothes, long flowing blond hair and outgoing, she was now dressed modestly and tied her hair up tight behind her head. Linna's face was no longer full of life but looked drained from pain and worry. Each time he visited Halfdan could see Linna become more and more strained from burden.

When Linna answered, she looked Halfdan up and down with her jaw dropped open. "What happened to you? You look awful."

"Thanks, Linna." said Halfdan stern and sarcastically as he walked in and sat at the table. The weight of worry ran from his body and exhaustion set in.

"Where is Frode?" Linna asked quietly.

Halfdan's body stiffened up by the question. "Is Liv asleep? She usually comes out to greet me." Halfdan asked while looking in the direction of the bedroom, purposely avoiding Linna's question.

Linna sat at the table with Halfdan, she looked Halfdan in the face but he kept looking away, his eyes searching for Liv.

"I fear her body is being taken by the illness. She has not woken in days." Linna's eyes begins to water. "All I can do is sit by her side."

Halfdan turned to look at Linna. After a short pause he reached out to grab Linna's hand to comfort her. Ever since Halfdan arrived to help Linna there was an awkwardness that lingered in the air.

Slowly Linna pulled her hand away to wipe away a tear. "I'll give you some of my husband's clothes to wear while I fix you up."

Halfdan wasn't excited to wear her late husband's clothes, but he didn't want to sit exposed to Linna and Liv. Linna got up and placed a pot over the fireplace to heat up water, then handed a bucket and wash cloth to Halfdan. She quickly had clothes on the table for Halfdan, as if she still had them prepared for her husband's return. With there only being two rooms in the house, kitchen and bedroom, Linna went into the bedroom to let Halfdan clean up. Halfdan took off his clothes and put them aside. He began to wash the blood off his body when he noticed the wound on his leg was no longer open. He checked his chest and shoulder. Both healed as well. Halfdan felt relief with the knowledge he would not have to stitch himself up. Amazement grew with the thought of what Frode had done for him. Ease quickly turned to disgust, angry at himself in a way for feeling joy after his betrayal to Frode.

After Halfdan was cleaned up he hesitantly put on the late husband's clothes. They were worn from hard labor and threadbare. He went to find Linna. As he entered bedroom he saw Liv sleeping on the big family bed. With faint candle light he could see the damage the plague had inflected on Liv's body. Her skin was pale. Darkness circled her eyes and labored with each breath. The young woman who was once full of life now laid still. Her once blonde wavy hair was slick from sweat. Liv had a crescent moon shaped scar on her forehead from a past fight, but it didn't take away from her beauty. Linna sat next to Liv, stroking her hair. Linna raised her head and meet Halfdan's gaze with a look of despair. Liv was dying.

Halfdan left the room, grabbed his axe and walked out of the house. Linna's concern was for Liv and she would not be chasing after Halfdan. He had a habit of leaving without saying anything to her and Linna usually relied on Liv for details regarding what Halfdan was up to.

Halfdan headed to the village inn, The Singing Boar, which was once a longhouse that was converted into an inn, and the patrons were not accustomed to outsiders. Walking through the door Halfdan surveyed the room with hooded eyes. Despite the plague there were still plenty of customers filling their emptiness with mead and ale. Halfdan wasn't used to the inn being so somber as he watched people drink their sorrows away. With the plague lingering in the village no one was able to leave Dragekall, unwelcomed elsewhere. Other than tending to the sick or dead, there was not much else to do.

Halfdan pushed people out of the way to get to the counter. "Inn keep! I need to talk to you!" He boomed over a few rowdy patrons who were arguing over something but their slurred words were far from understandable.

The brawly inn keep wasn't fazed as he cleaned some wooden mugs. "You'll need to wait your turn! Just like everyone else!" He said without turning to look at Halfdan.

Halfdan grabbed a handful of silver from his leather pouch and dropped them on the counter. The inn keep recognized the familiar sound of silver hitting the counter and eagerly turned around to help Halfdan.

"What can I do for you, my good man?" The inn keep said eagerly.

"Tell me everything you know about the lindwurm, I need to know where it slumbers." Halfdan demanded.

"You know you could get your hands cut off asking those questions about our great beast." said the inn keep sternly, smile gone from his face.

"I wouldn't be able to pay you without hands, now would I?" Halfdan said angrily and fought to put on a smile as he's pushing the silver closer to the inn keep.

The inn keep stared at the silver then back at Halfdan for a second before responding. "The rumors are that it lives in a cave, hidden deep in the forest to the west of the village. I don't know the specifics because no one is willing to hunt in that area. There is something about burning alive that bothers people." The inn keep said with a slight chuckle. Then in a serious tone stated. "There is less game in the area now as well. People think its nesting. I'm not sure what your plan is, but that lindwurm is going to be more aggressive than usual if it is nesting. You need to think about your life before doing anything stupid."

"Thanks for the advice." Halfdan said while glaring at the inn keep. Halfdan turned away to leave. As he walked out of the inn he grabbed a torch off the wall and slammed the door closed. Villagers stood clear and gawked as Halfdan ran into the forest, knowing better than to stop a man that was acting out of the norm, especially a stranger.

Halfdan made his way through the trees and underbrush as quickly as he could. He was skeptical if the lindwrum of Dragekall was real, but he had to look for it. Halfdan felt his body grow weary, but he knew that Liv didn't have time for him to rest. The image of Liv's frail body gave him the energy he needed to keep moving deeper into the thick forest.

After an hour Halfdan found a trail that, he imagined, was wide and big enough for a lindwrum to traverse. Halfdan's gamble on the beast payed off. Halfdan followed the trail that was leading deeper into the forest. Halfdan could see the moon's light between the leaves, his beacon of hope. As Halfdan kept moving he could smell ember and brimstone. It didn't take long to find the lindwrum's cave. Unlike dragons and wyverns who rely on natural cave formations in the mountains, lindwrums dug burrow like caves anywhere there is dirt.

Halfdan could see a glow within the cave. He took a deep breath and held his axe in one hand and the torch in the other. He never faced a lindwrum before, nor ever seen one. Including dragons and wyverns. Halfdan was so eager to find the lindwrum that he realized he was ill prepared, so he'll have to catch the beast off guard. An axe is a poor choice of weapon to kill a lindwurm. He squatted outside the cave, listening to see if the lindwurm was within. The heat coming out of the cave was unexpected along with the light. Halfdan didn't hear any movement. If the lindwurm was inside it must be sleeping, ideal for an ambush. Halfdan slowly made his way inside the cave and followed against its sides, stepping on the ball of his feet first and then his heel to minimize his sound. There were also rocks, he had to be careful to not kick them to give him away. He slowly made his way into the belly of the cave. No lindwurm in sight but he could see the warmth coming from hot coals surrounding a large egg. To his surprise the egg was more than half his size and speckled blue and white. The egg rested on a mud pedestal to keep it from laying directly on the heat.

Frode had a theory as to why all breeds of dragons make scorching nests. He believed it was because they have to maintain the same temperature for the egg at the same temperature of the inside of the beast before it was laid. This is also the reason Frode postulated that dragons breathe fire, to make ember nests such as this. Frode had a wild idea that dragons didn't need a partner to bear young. This prevents a pair dragons from eating every living creature in their territory.

Stopping for a moment, Halfdan closed his eyes and pushed away a memory. When Frode agreed to help the people of Dragekall he asked about the village's peculiar name. After Halfdan explained

15

it was named after a supposed lindwrum Frode was ecstatic, learning everything possible about such beasts and even sea serpents. Making plans to try and study such a creature with Halfdan after the plague subsided. Plans Halfdan sadly knew would never happen.

Thinking of Frode, Halfdan wanted to admire the dragons work but he had to hurry before the lindwurm came back. An egg is much easier to deal with than an adult lindwurm, who must be out currently hunting. Halfdan put his axe away in its leather holster and with the torch he moved the red coals away to make a small opening. Heat began to make sweat roll down into Halfdan's eyes causing him to blink often. The ground was still hot even with the embers gone. Halfdan put the torch down and used his hands to put cool dirt over his path. Once the small path was tolerable, he made his way to the egg. Halfdan placed both hands on the egg and closed his eyes. He focused on the energy of the egg and honed in. Halfdan had never used magic before, but he hoped that the gift Frode gave him will make him capable of performing the magic he needed. Frode was able to do spells without saying anything, but he remembered a time that Frode had to say spells out loud, it helped him focus on his intent.

"Life is the beginning and death is the end. Your life is now mine and have the right to spend. Cut it short and give your spirit onto me."

Halfdan focused on pulling the eggs youth and liveliness, feeling the energy from the egg joining his. As the energy began to enter Halfdan's hands they began to burn and bubble. Ignoring the pain he held his focus, compelled to finish what he started. Soon the egg became cold to the touch. Halfdan could now focus on the burning pain that the energy was creating in his body, along with the surrounding embers burning his leather boots. Halfdan already had two souls in him, a third is proven to be overwhelming. His palms and fingers burned with the unborn lindwurm's energy and resembled blue flames. Wanting to yell in pain but was in shock as he stood there looking at what was becoming of his body as his hands trembled.

Suddenly, Halfdan heard rocks rolling down into the cave followed by heavy footsteps that vibrated his body. A great monstrous shadow was casted into the cave as the adult lindwurm drug its body into the cave. Halfdan hid behind the egg as the lindwurm made its way in. It was magnificent. It had shiny grey scales that reflected a brilliant blue when hit with light from the flickering coals. Its long thin legs dragged the rest of its serpent like body. Between the gaps of the scales there were black pin feathers. On its spine there was long black feathers that draped over its body. In its mouth was a bear, limp from being the lindwurm's pray. The great beast took a moment to look at its egg and made a deep cooing sound, happy to see it's unborn. Soon the lindwurm turned away to focus on its meal. The beast held the bear down with its massive claws and started to pull at its limbs.

Halfdan began to move slowly away from behind the egg, looking back at the lindwurm to see if it would notice him. All dragons are notorious for being far sighted, or so that's what Frode told him once. As long as Halfdan moved slowly he hoped to be unnoticed.

Halfdan decided to leave the torch behind as his hands began to throb with pain with its burning blue light. Building up the courage he slowly made his way out of the cave. Luckily for Halfdan, the lindwurm's back was facing the entrance of the cave. The only problem was that the beast was so long its tail ran all the way up the wall of the cave. The tail would twitch and would swoop past Halfdan each time the beast adjusted its body. Halfdan took a deep breath to calm himself for he had no choice but to keep moving forward. As Halfdan was close to exiting the cave the lindwurm shifted it body once more, sending the tail towards Halfdan one last time. The tip of the tail brushed up against him almost knocking Halfdan over. He caught himself and froze, quickly turning his head to look upon the lindwurm. The beast didn't notice for it was focused on its meal. Hearing the lindwurm effortlessly ripping the bear apart, it sounded wet and tough as the smell of iron was filling the cave. The thought of the lindwurm doing that to Halfdan made him more

17

eager to leave the cave. Halfdan picked up his pace, taking one step at a time and made it out of the cave.

As soon as his boots touched grass he bolted. With Halfdan's hands burning with energy he was able to see as he made his way through the dark forest. He did his best to ignore the pain, but he could see that the flames started to make their way up his arms. Smoke from his sleeves and flesh burning was making it difficult to breathe and burned his eyes.

By the time Halfdan made his way back to the village the blue flame was almost past his forearm. He ran though the village, his heavy breathing and echoes of his footsteps was the only sound. Halfdan kept pushing his body. The sight of Linna's house made Halfdan relieved, the ordeal was almost done. Once at the door Halfdan used his shoulder to push open the door. Despite being inside Halfdan still felt like he couldn't get to Liv fast enough. The pain was so great that Halfdan could hear himself grunting and his vision was beginning to blur. He made his way around the bed to Liv, next to her was Linna laying asleep. Candles were still lit in the room, showing how weak Liv has grown, she looked even closer to death. Halfdan put one hand on Liv's forehead and the other over her heart.

"What is mine is mine no more. You will be with life now forth. So mote it be."

It took little effort for Halfdan to transfer the unborn lindwurm's life into Liv. Halfdan's body could barely contain the energy and Liv's body was grasping for life, or so it seemed. The fire that once was burning Halfdan's hands faded as he watched Liv with anticipation. After all of that, Liv continued to lay still. Halfdan fell to his knees, spent and defeated as a whisper of a breeze moved the tall grass about outside the window.

CHAPTER 3

NOT ALL THAT FLOWS IS GOLD.
NORSE PROVERB ~ UNKNOWN

Halfdan stood outside of Liv's house and looked upon the burning village. Red hot ash flew high in the air as the great lindwurm lifted its head towards the sky and roared, filling the void with its mighty lungs. Houses began to crumble around the lindwurm as they were engulfed in flames. The delayed sounds of villagers screaming began to fill Halfdan's ears, making his heart pound in fear.

"Halfdan?" he heard faintly.

Halfdan woke from his dream, collecting his bearings. The light of dawn was filling the bedroom. He collapsed next to Liv, knees on the floor and his upper body lying on the bed.

He felt a soft hand on his shoulder. Halfdan looked upon Liv, who was sitting up looking back at him. She looked anew, face was a healthy color and there was life in her eyes.

"Why are you wearing my dad's clothes?" Liv asked, quietly.

Halfdan sprung up to embrace Liv as glee rushed through his body. Liv didn't even have time to embrace Halfdan back when he suddenly stepped back, wincing in pain. They both noticed how blistered and raw his hands and forearms were. Liv looked upon his hands in disgust then looked upon the bed. Where Halfdan's arms were lying was a large wet stain from the oozing blisters.

"Ew, Halfdan, what happened to you?"

Liv looked at Halfdan who was in slight shock, finally able to take in the trauma his arms went through.

"Come on," said Liv, softly "let's get up."

Halfdan stood up so Liv could get out of the bed. She slowly slipped out from under the covers as to not wake her mother. Together, they made their way into the kitchen.

Halfdan used his foot to pull out a chair from the table as Liv looked for dish rags. She dipped the rags into the water bucket, rang them out and gently placed the rags on Halfdan's arms. The cool, wet rags instantly relieved the pain, but the coolness didn't last long due to the extreme heat of the burns. Halfdan watched as Liv used the ladle in the water bucket to drink. She was obnoxiously trying to get as much down her as possible, spilling water as she moved the ladle to and from the bucket.

"Ugh, why is water so good! It feels like I've been asleep forever." Liv said as she used her sleeve to wipe the water from her face and began foraging in the kitchen for food.

"You have been." Halfdan said, concerned. "Do you remember anything?"

Liv looked around the cupboard she opened at Halfdan. The happiness in her face drained away and so did the sparkle of her eyes. She turned her head back into the opened cupboard and grabbed a full loaf of bread. "I remember my dad and brother lying in bed together, we were all sick." Liv said as she stepped back to close the cupboard door. "Then men came in to take them away." Liv ripped a chunk of bread off and examined it. "They're dead, aren't they?"

Halfdan watched Liv as she sat down next to him. Her eyes never leaving the bread. Halfdan felt like he shouldn't be the one to tell her, but she needed to know.

"Yes, they are. They passed a few days ago." Halfdan said quietly.

"Where are they?" Liv said as she shoved a chunk of bread in her mouth.

"I don't know." Halfdan said, looking down at the table. "We'll look for them today."

Liv broke the bread and placed half next to Halfdan. Both continued to look at the table unsure what to say. Liv continued pulling off chunks of bread and eating it. Halfdan pulled off the wet rags and laid them on the table. He carefully picked up the bread with his disfigured hand and started to eat. Both sat at the table, listening to the morning birds. Sitting next to each other was comforting.

Liv put the last bit of her bread on the table and looked at Halfdan's wounds. "What happened?"

"You wouldn't believe me if I told you."

"Tell me." said Liv, unamused.

"I got into a predicament with a lindwurm." Halfdan said between bites of the dry stale bread.

"If you don't want to tell me what happened that's fine." Liv said thinking that Halfdan was lying. She knew that Halfdan works with unsavory people, anything could have happened.

Before Halfdan could reply, Linna walked into the room shocked to see Liv out of bed. Liv quickly got up and ran to her mother. Embracing one another.

"I thought I was going to lose you." Linna said between tears.

Halfdan watched their long hug with a smile on his face. Liv and Linna broke their embrace to look at each other. Linna placed her hands on Liv's shoulders not wanting to let go.

"Where did they take them?" Liv asked.

"I don't know, I didn't want to know. I just wanted to focus on you." Linna said, wiping away her tears. "Are you hungry? Can I make you anything to eat?"

"I already ate, I want to go to the pond and clean up. I feel all gross and sweaty. You need to look at Halfdan's hands, they're grotesque."

Linna and Liv took a few footsteps towards Halfdan to gawk upon him, who reluctantly held his hands out.

Linna gasped in disgust. "What happened?"

"It's not that serious." Halfdan replied.

"It looks serious." Linna retorted.

"He wouldn't tell me either." Liv said mockingly. "I am going to the pond to clean off. I'll be right back." Liv ran to the bedroom to grab her clothes and began to run out the door.

"You need to take it easy!" Linna shouted.

"I feel great, love you!" Liv shouted back before the door slammed.

"I can't believe it, she was on her death bed. Now it's almost like nothing happened. Whatever Frode gave her must have worked." said Linna, and she kept looking at the door for a moment before turning her attention towards Halfdan. "Let me fix you up."

As Linna was busy looking in the cupboards and around the house for honey and bandages. Halfdan could hear her talking, but he was in a trance looking at his disfigured hands without a thought in his head.

After being bandaged Halfdan went outside to talk amongst villagers to find Liv's father and brother. When he was done he walked back to the house. Instead of going inside he stood outside where he had his dream. The village wasn't burning and there was no lindwurm in the middle of it. Instead the survivors of the plague were working together to make a large pyre. They decided to do one large pyre for each household. He found out they were waiting for Liv to die to cremate her along with her father and brother. Now that Liv was well they are going to build a pyre for them today. Halfdan continued to watch, the villagers could use his help but with his hands burned he couldn't do much.

Liv ran up behind Halfdan, cleaned up with fresh clothes on. She was wearing a brown apron dress, yellow underneath and with the apron decorated with colorful beads strung on the front. Her yellow hair in multiple braids going back. With several small ones on the side and a large loose one on top. A hair style traditionally worn by shield maidens. Liv incorporated light blue ribbon in her hair as decoration.

"Mom is going to wash the sheets you got all mucked up." Liv informed Halfdan.

"Sorry about that, hope I didn't get any on you."

"Only a little. Mom didn't want me to go. I told her yes, but I still want to see them. Did you find them?"

"Yeah." Halfdan said amused that Liv was going against her mother's wishes. "They are keeping them in a barn while they make the pyre."

Halfdan and Liv walked past the able bodied men and women who were building the pyre. The barn was old and was along the tree line. They could smell the sickening sweet aroma of decay before reaching the barn. Halfdan found someone earlier to help him place Liv's father and brother outside the barn, away from the rest of the dead within. Halfdan stood back as Liv walked up between her father and brother. They were able to wrap a white ribbon under their chins and up their heads to keep their mouths closed for Liv. There was nothing they could do to fix their sunken eyes. Their lips, fingertips and ears were discolored and dry. The rest of their skin was pale and moist looking.

Liv sat down between her father and brother. She reached for her father's hand and placed it upon her cheek and began to quietly sob. His hand was cold, limp and clammy. After a moment Liv gently placed her father's hand back onto his chest and turned to her brother. She ran her fingers through his greasy hair and placed her hand upon his cheek. Liv slowly stood up, turned and reached out to Halfdan who embraced her. She shoved her face into his chest as she began to cry harder. All Halfdan could do was hold her tight. The bandages covering his hands and forearm making it easier to hold Liv this time.

Liv insisted that she help build the pyre. Linna's wish was for Liv to simply rest, but she worked on the pyre regardless. Halfdan tried to help when he could, but spent some time in the inn drinking mead. The inn keep had to put Halfdan's mead in a soup bowl so he could hold it better without bending his fingers. Using both hands to bring the mead to his lips. The buzz made it easier for Halfdan to deal with the pain. The inn keep didn't ask about Halfdan's hands and figured it was best to keep his nose out of trouble, and Halfdan reeked of trouble.

Halfdan spent more time in the inn than he wanted to. The inn keep had to take coins out of Halfdan's leather pouch that rested around his waist before leaving. When Halfdan found Liv, again she was helping move her father and brother to the pyre. It took four people to move her father and two to move her brother. Liv went to Linna to let her know that the ceremony was about to begin. Linna refused to go, but gave Liv things to place with her father and brother. Blankets, flowers, and her father's favorite mug and her brother's crude fishing net that he often used. Liv placed everything with them with care and when she was ready she used a torch to light the pyre.

Slowly other villagers used their torches as well. It didn't take long for her father and brother to become engulfed in flames. The smoke from the pyre was black and thick, covering the village with a sickly odor. Periodically Liv and other villagers would add more wood, the hotter the fire got more of the black smoke subsided. Halfdan couldn't help but overhear some of the villagers talk about taking down now abandoned houses and using them for firewood. After all the residents of a house passed from the plague no one wanted to move in. Others complained about building pyres day after day and recommended creating a large burial mound. However, when brought up to the village elders they protested, they believed that burning the bodies is a way to release the soul within. Like smoke floating away into the air. Burying them would rob them of this tradition.

The villagers predicted that the pyre would require the remaining daylight and late into the night to burn. Liv wanted to stay until the process was complete. Halfdan left for a bit and brought out an old hefty blanket from the house for Liv and him to sit on. Both sat there silently watching Liv's father and brother as their bodies burned and bubbled while the flames danced above them.

"Your father was a good man." Halfdan said to Liv as they both watched the flames.

"You don't have to give me the typical words people say to those who are grieving." Liv said, keeping her eyes on the flame. "Thank you, though."

"You brother liked to fish a lot?" Halfdan asked, remembering the fishing net that was placed with her brother.

"Yeah." Liv said with a smile. "But he wasn't very good at it. I think he just liked to get out of the house." Liv's smile didn't last long. After a short pause she spoke again. "Few of my friends died as well."

"I'm sorry." Halfdan said. Knowing his words held no value. There is nothing you can say to comfort someone who has lost so many, other than being there to listen. That is what Halfdan wanted to do. Just listen.

"It feels unfair." Liv said picking a blade of grass and playing with it in her hands. "Why did I get to live? I didn't even get to tell anyone goodbye. If I would have known, I would have told them how much I loved them. We were trying to catch frogs in the rain… that was the last thing we all did together. It didn't seem like something special at the moment. The last thing my brother talked to me about was how he almost caught a big catfish. I knew he was embellishing the size but I didn't tell him. He told me it slipped out of his grasp when he untangled it out of his net. The first thing he was going to do when he got better was to try and catch that dumb fish again."

"I noticed that you didn't want any prayers said." Halfdan commented.

"Blind faith makes me angry. Why would gods and goddesses make a world like this? Is it to test us or for their amusement? I don't understand how I'm supposed to be grateful for any of this. We never had any alters or talismans like everyone else. My dad would go out and pray in the woods to Odin for wisdom at times, but never taught me anything. And it's not like saying prayers right now is going to change anything." Liv said with distaste.

"What do you believe then?" Halfdan asked, it was obvious how much Liv has been thinking about everything. It is coming out of her mouth as if she has been reciting it in her head over and over.

"I want to believe that they are still out there. That I will be able to see them again. That I'll get that chance to tell them how much

25

I love them and how important they are. Another part of me thinks there is nothing. Just nothingness. It makes me afraid but it just seems more… right. It's hard to explain."

"I understand what you are saying." Halfdan said, reassuring Liv's emotions. Despite him beginning to believe in something greater ever since his incident with Frode he didn't want to bring up his opinions. Right now he just wanted to listen to Liv. "Maybe we can try catching that catfish for your brother tomorrow."

"I'd like that. It's hard to sit still. That's when you start thinking."

"Yeah, thinking can be quite the nuisance." Halfdan took his cloak off and rolled it into a long pillow for both him and Liv.

Laying down and watching the sky turn from dusk to night. Adding wood to the pyre as needed. Halfdan and Liv stayed up watching the stars and listening to the sounds of the forest that surrounds them. The village dog wandered out to them and laid down next to them. The dog was medium sized with long copper red fur and floppy ears. Bringing much needed joy to Liv. The dog's fur was dusty and coarse, yet soft and fluffy. Something about stroking an animal's fur that calms the mind.

CHAPTER 4

A MAN SHOULD NOT CARVE RUNES, UNLESS HE WELL KNOWS HOW TO CONTROL THEM.
EGILL SKALLAGRÍMSSON ~ NORSE PROVERB

Liv woke up outside to the sound of the village beginning its morning. She saw that the dog and Halfdan were gone. This made Liv upset, she didn't like waking up alone. She then noticed the area that was once the great pyre now smoldering with small flames hanging on to life. Liv began to cry against her best wishes. The combination of suppressed emotion and waking up alone broke something inside her. She became angry with herself. Liv didn't want to cry anymore. She wanted to be strong, yet her eyes and tears keep giving her away.

In the distance Liv could hear the distinctive sounds of Halfdan's feet, slow and heavy, moving through the grass. Liv quickly tried to wipe her tears away.

"I was hoping to be back before you woke up." Halfdan said, sitting down next to Liv. Handing her a cup of water and a plate of bread and old berries.

"You could have woke me before you left." Liv said angrily.

"I'm sorry, I figured you needed to rest. Your mother washed and mended my clothing, so I'm not wearing your father's clothes anymore."

"Yeah, that was kind of creepy." Liv said before shoving food into her mouth.

"Would you have me walking around in my underwear?" Halfdan said, jokingly.

"Yes." Liv said, trying to get a rise out of Halfdan.

"Now you're being creepy. After this you need to return home. Your mom keeps asking about you and she isn't comfortable coming out here to you. I'll stay here." Halfdan knew that Liv didn't want to leave the fire unattended until they were able to get her father's and brother's bones out. Worried that the villagers would begin building another pyre before she could look through the ashes.

Halfdan watched Liv grow irritated as she got up and headed back to her house. In the other direction Halfdan could see villagers begin to pull apart a house. Proper firewood was beginning to dwindle so the villagers were turning towards the vacant houses. The plague was able to kill whole households and cut the population of the village in half.

Halfdan then saw movement in the corner of his eye, it was the dog that was with them last night lumbering towards him. Halfdan offered the dog some bread which he had saved anticipating the dog's return. The dog didn't chew the bread, just swallowed it whole. Halfdan reached out to pet the dog but it became more interested in Halfdan's bandages.

The dog began to lick them, possibly smelling the honey. Halfdan was nervous about looking at his wounds, but was also intrigued. Curiosity got the best of him, along with wanting the tight bandages off, he began to pick at the knot keeping the bandages together. It took a bit but he was able to get it started. As Halfdan began to peel the bandages off he was amazed to see how quickly his skin healed. As more and more of the skin was revealed Halfdan got more and more discouraged. Despite his arms and hands healing quickly they were severely disfigured. It didn't heal perfectly like the arrow wounds. As Halfdan kept looking at his arm the dog began to lick the honey off. Even though Halfdan found it somewhat disturbing that the dog would want honey used to heal burns. Despite the disgust, Halfdan understood hunger and let the dog continue until it was satisfied. He then took off the bandages on the other arm, repeating the process.

It didn't take long for the dog to turn its interest onto a rabbit that was running around in the forest. The dog took off after it, its tail high up in the air in excitement. Halfdan could hear the rustling go deeper into the forest until he couldn't hear it anymore. He then looked at his hands and arm, disgusted in what they looked like. The color was inconsistent and the skin was wavy and resembled flesh colored frost flowers on a window pane. He moved his fingers and clenched his hands, happy that he was still able to use them. Halfdan was eager to wash the stickiness off his arms and hands, but he had to wait for Liv to return.

Halfdan grew more eager and looked around the tree line for sticks to use to sift through the ashes. He wasn't sure if he should start without Liv. After collecting five good stick's Halfdan got more eager. Not wanting to sit down, anymore he began circling around the ashes.

Halfdan froze when he heard rustling in the woods, working its way to him. The dog leaped out of the bushes, mouth open and panting with glee and its fur was covered with burs. Halfdan was relieved that it was just the dog and not the lindwurm. He kneeled down and the dog knew it was a sign to come over. Halfdan tried to pick some of the burs out of the dog's fur, but his sticky fingers just collected loose fur.

Halfdan then thought about trying to see if he could use some magic to possibly get the burs out. He put his hands close together and focused his energy on his hands. Halfdan could feel some pressure as energy collected between his hands. The dog, unaware of what Halfdan was doing, tried to nudge Halfdan's hand with its wet nose in an attempt to get more attention. Halfdan felt a painful jolt and heard a snap between his hand and the dog's nose. The dog yelped in shock and ran off with its tail between its legs. Halfdan's lips pulled back and his face cringed, feeling bad for the dog. He could smell dog fur on his hands that had burned off. Halfdan's ego took a step back, realizing he isn't quite sure how to control his powers.

"What did you do that for?" Liv said, standing closely behind Halfdan.

He gasped and fell over. Quickly standing up in embarrassment. "Why?! Why are you always sneaking up on me?!"

"What were you doing?"

Halfdan panicked for a moment, unsure of how long Liv was standing behind him. "Frode has been teaching me magic." He lied.

"Can you teach me?" Liv asked in excitement.

"Maybe, when I figure out what I'm actually doing."

"Well, you need to hurry up and figure out what you're doing." Liv said jokingly then switching her tone "You ready?"

"Yes." Halfdan said, knowing she was talking about going through the ashes.

Halfdan and Liv used the sticks to sift through the ashes. It was more difficult to go through than they had expected. Tossing what they thought is bone onto the old blanket they had been sitting on. The bone fragments were still hot to the touch and blackened. The air lingered with the heavy smell of burnt flesh. It didn't take long for Halfdan's hands and arms to get black with soot sticking to his tacky skin. Other villagers began to help sift through the ashes, eager to start another pyre. After some time the villagers told Liv that they picked all the burned bone fragments, but she didn't let them pressure her from sifting through the ashes once more.

Once Liv was confident they got all the bones, she and Halfdan folded the blanket and gently pressed down on it, breaking up larger bone fragments. Liv held a simple clay urn that the elders made as the cremains were transferred. Slowly Halfdan and Liv began to make their way to the valley where all the residents of Dragekall were buried. When no one was looking the two quickly made their way back to the house.

Halfdan and Liv saw Linna digging a hole next to the house where she wanted to place the cremains. She wanted her husband and son close to home and knew the elders would not have approved of this. Halfdan figured that when Linna was ready they could move the urn into the valley, but as he looked at her Halfdan knew that she would never be ready. Linna didn't want to see the urn and retreated inside, leaving it up to Liv to place them. Liv's eyes began to water as they began to bury the urn with soil.

"At first it didn't seem real." Liv said, filled with great sorrow. "It feels real now. They are really gone."

CHAPTER 5

It had been two weeks since Liv put her father and brother to rest. Halfdan has been helping Liv take care of chores around the house, tending to the garden, feeding the chickens and helping the remaining villagers with their pyres. Linna has not been able to summon the strength to help. Instead she spends her days lying in bed or decorating her husband's and son's grave. Barely eating and making limited eye contact with Halfdan and her daughter. Halfdan and Liv try to comfort her, but there is nothing they can do to get her to open up.

One of the neighbors came over to talk to Linna after seeing her sitting outside. Unknown to the neighbor, Linna was grieving over the secret burial plot of her late husband and son. The neighbor tried to sympathize with Linna and tell her that her husband and son are no longer suffering and are in a better place. That was the first time Liv saw her mother punch someone. It didn't even faze Linna that she fractured her hand. Since then, neighbors have avoided Linna.

There have been no more deaths since Liv has been healed. Liv was the only one to catch the plague and survive to tell about it. Nearly half of the residents of Dragekall had died from a mysterious illness that seemed to only affect their village. In their eyes, the cunning have failed them. Not one household was spared loss and the survivors were all bereaved. Building the pyres together has been an opportunity for the villagers to support one another. During the process they have been able to share stories and comfort one another.

The long nights of keeping the pyres lit have given those not able to sleep something to do.

Halfdan was beginning to worry about Liv. She has been working her days away. Her stamina seems to have no end and she was able to collect and build pyres with ease. At first the other villagers would joke, asking Liv what she has been eating or where she has been getting her energy from. Now they stay out of Liv's way while she is working.

Today was the last day for the pyres and the villagers were eager to be freed from the constant smell of burning flesh. The only one left to cremate was a couple's first born baby. The mother wanted to hold on to her child, but it was time to let the baby go. The father asked to build the pyre alone.

Halfdan took this opportunity to try and get Liv to relax and focus on herself. That was short lived and it wasn't long until Liv wanted to occupy herself with trivial things. She noticed that the last bit of lingonberries they had were about to go bad. Liv decided that she wanted to make some bread with the lingonberries in it, something special for the three of them.

Halfdan didn't want to get in Liv's way, so he went outside to build a shelter for a brown dairy goat that they obtained. The elders have been taking objects, tools and livestock from the deceased with no relatives. Then the elders divvy out everything accordingly and Liv and Linna were provided a goat.

Liv occupied herself with making the lingonberry bread. Making sure to not knead the bread too many times to make it tough. She let the bread bake slowly and checked it often. It was finally done when the house was filled with a warm sweet aroma. Liv cut the heel of the bread off and cut another piece for her mother. Slowly, Liv walked into the bedroom where her mother was sitting on the bed. Linna's eyes were distant as she smelled the clothing that her brother once wore.

"Here you go mom. I made us some bread! I added-"

"I'm not hungry." Linna interrupted as her eyes remained unfocused towards the wall.

Liv's face became flushed and hot with anger. She threw the bread onto the bed and heatedly walked out of the house and slammed the door behind her. Outside Halfdan was still working on the shelter for the goat, it was his third attempt at getting it to stay together. He was still getting used to using his hands now that the sensation in his fingers were damaged. Halfdan saw Liv and stood up to talk to her. He noticed her face was red and she walked quickly with her hands balled into fists. Until now Halfdan had never seen Liv this angry and was taken aback by the rage.

Before Liv could say anything the dairy goat head-butted Liv in the back. The goat saw an opportunity and it took it, knowing that Liv was unaware of its position. Liv yelled profanity as she stumbled. Before Halfdan could interfere, Liv turned around and kicked the goat in the head. Liv didn't hold back and took all her anger out on the goat.

For Liv, it almost happened in slow motion. She saw her foot make contact with the goat. Its head flung back and its eyes became wide, followed by a snapping sound. Its skin around its neck ripped open, starting from the front and making its way back. The goat's head became free from its body and flew in the air. Blood squirted from the goat's ripped arteries as it dropped to the ground. The head hit the earth with a solid thud. Liv covered her open mouth with her hands, shocked at what she had done. Both Halfdan and Liv stood for a moment in astonishment.

"Do you feel better at least?" Halfdan said, breaking the silence.

"Little bit. I didn't mean to kick it that hard." Liv said, watching the goat's leg twitch.

Halfdan walked over to Liv and grabbed her hand. "Let's go for a walk."

"No." Liv said, breaking away from Halfdan's grasp. "I just want to be alone."

"No." Halfdan said sternly. "Talk to me."

Liv broke down in tears, covering her face to hide herself from Halfdan. "It's feels like I lost my mom as well." Liv said before she started to cry harder. "I can't stop moving, as soon as I stop working all I can think about is my brother. He is... was the only one who understood me. I'm also worried about you leaving. I'm starting to think my mother will never be back to her regular self. I can't support myself without my father. I can't do this by myself."

Halfdan could see heavy tears running down Liv's face, her hands unable to conceal everything. Hearing Liv say 'I'm worried about you leaving' and 'I can't do this by myself' stung at his heart. He didn't plan on leaving, but he also didn't anticipate staying forever. Halfdan averted his eyes and stood next to Liv, reaching his hand over to shoulder hug her. Then he began to use that hand to rub Liv's back as she leaned into him. Halfdan could feel the tension in Liv's back, her body hasn't been able to relax for some time now.

"I promise, I'm not going anywhere. Here," Halfdan said as he took off his cloak and wrapped it around Liv. "I'm going to pay for a room at the inn for you. I'll also give you some money for some food and mead. I think you just need to focus on yourself for a bit." He then untied his leather pouch from his waist and attached it to Liv's belt. "There is silver in there. I'll keep an eye on your mom."

"Thank you." Liv said as she sniffled her nose. "I didn't mean to kill the goat."

"I know, it's ok." Halfdan said as he watched Liv walk away as thoughts of grief filled his head. Once Liv was out of sight he walked over to his shelter and gave it a gentle shove. The shelter gave in and fell to the ground.

"Sometimes, things turn out for the best." He said to himself.

Liv kept her head down as she made her way through the village. She didn't want anyone to notice her eyes were red and puffy from crying. Wandering around the village was the copper colored dog, who noticed Liv and lumbered towards her for attention. Liv obliged, smiling at the dog's face. The dog's mouth was wide open and tongue laid to the side as Liv scratched behind its ears.

"Half-wit" Liv called the dog, mocking the dumb and blissful look it was making. "Come with me."

The dog obeyed Liv as she walked toward a merchant who was standing next to the inn and purchased some dried fish and bread. The dog eagerly followed Liv as she made her way through the village and out the other side making her way toward a river. Liv sat down on the damp grass next to the river's edge so she could watch the shimmering water move about.

"Here you go, Half-wit." Liv said, giving the dog small pieces of bread and fish. She intentionally rationed out the food to keep the dog from losing interest in her. Despite the fish being dried it still left a greasy film on Liv's fingers. Liv sat contently as she continued to feed the dog, listening to the river with the sounds of village life behind her.

Deep within the forest, the lindwurm was examining its egg. The egg was still on its dirt mound, surrounded by hot embers. The great beast made short and quiet cooing sounds between deep sniffs. The lindwurm could sense something was wrong. No matter how much heat it added to the nest the egg continues to get colder. Desperate to see signs of life, the beast nudged the egg off of its pillar. The egg broke open and the den was instantly hit with the putrid smell of rotten egg. Around the exposed dragon fetus was egg protein green from rot.

The lindwurm stood still, taking in what it was seeing. Then gently the beast rubbed its face against the dead fetus. Still making its cooing sounds as if its baby was still alive. As the lindwurm moved in closer to its offspring its talons bumped into something foreign. The creature picked it up and held it close to its eyes to examine it. It was a torch. The lindwurm knew that this was made by human hands.

Deep pain ran through the lindwurm and quickly turned into anger and resentment. The great beast dropped the torch and dragged its body out of its den and through the forest. The lindwurm moved with such fury and haste that it made a deafening noise as it pushed trees over and tumbled large stones. The once cautious lindwurm was leaving a path of destruction behind it.

The villagers of Dragekall looked around in confusion. The sounds of uprooted trees and crumbling nature were becoming louder. Village animals began to panic; chickens were jumping and running, horses huffed as they ran, goats and pigs yelled as they tried to get out of their pens. Half-wit's ears perked up and before the hairs on his back could stand up the dog turned around and ran. Liv stood up, looking into the direction of the sound of destruction. Almost in a daze, Liv began to step closer to the sound.

Once the villagers began to collect themselves, the lindwurm emerged from the forest. Standing tall, its head towered over the village. The great beast let out a deafening roar, making the sounds of the screaming villagers sound weak and small.

Halfdan and Linna quickly stepped out of the house. They both could see the mighty lindwurm lower its head and breathe fire upon the houses. Moving its head back and forth to spread as much of its heavy fiery breath as it could. The familiar smell of fire filled the air. Red ash began to float down upon the village like hot snow. Animals and people were running in every direction. The lindwurm raised its head to roar again, its head fully extended towards the sky as if it was preparing to yell at the gods. You could hear the beast take in air before it could release its thunderous roar. Villagers had to cover their ears to prevent them from ringing in pain.

"Run!" Halfdan yelled at Linna "I'll get Liv!"

Linna nodded at him before joining the crowd of those fleeing.

Halfdan ran back into the house, grabbed hold of his battle axe which was resting next to the fireplace, and ran back out. Pushing and dodging his way through those escaping the lindwurm's wrath. As he got closer the larger the beast looked with its feathers and scales puffed out in agitation. Smoke and ash continued to burn Halfdan's eyes as he forced them to remain open, looking for Liv.

On the other side of the village Liv continued to slowly make her way towards the great beast. Houses began to crumble as they were engulfed in flame. Between the smoke Liv could see the lindwurm making its way to the middle of the village. The beast

37

continued to move its large head back and forth, covering all it could see with fire. People were running away aimlessly, unable to extinguish themselves as they flailed their arms about. Their faces and gender were no longer visible, but their screams of pain told everything. A single armed man came running out of the flames, yelling in anger while maintaining his target, the lindwrum's chest. The beast took the warrior down with a single swoop of its massive claws. Liv watched as the man's lifeless body flew into the side of a burning building. Liv wasn't able to get a good look of the fallen man, for the lindwurm locked eyes with her. Both stood still, looking at one another. Slowly, the lindwurm dragged its long body closer to Liv. She stood still, feeling exposed as if the lindwurm was looking right through her.

Both Liv and the great beast were motionless for what felt like an eternity. The lindwurm broke the standstill by lowering its head to get a closer look at Liv. She could make out each individual scale on the creature's head. Each breath it took was hot and heavy, moving Liv's blond hair with each exhale. What captivated her the most was the lindwurm's eyes, so big and brown. Even though the beast couldn't talk, Liv could see the complicated emotions and thoughts through the lindwurm's eyes.

Liv saw the lindwurm's throat vibrate as it made a gentle cooing sound at her. Liv began to reach her hand out to touch the creature but the beast suddenly yelped in pain as it began to thrash its body around. Another armed man had emerged, saw the lindwurm was distracted and plunged his sword into the beast's neck. Liv was broken from her trance as she watched the man pull his sword back out of the great beast. Blood flowed out in rhythm with the lindwurm's heartbeat.

"Stop! What are you doing?!" Liv screamed as she ran and grabbed the man's arms, preventing him from striking the beast again.

The man pushed her down onto the ground with anger and raised his sword at her. "Whose side are you on, woman?"

With watery eyes Liv ignored the man and ran up to the still and dying lindwurm. She threw herself upon the beast and held it close and began to cry into its slowly cooling body. Some of the villagers walked back to the center of the village to see the spectacle. Halfdan made his way to Liv, lifting her up and leading her away from the lindwurm. The villagers moved out of their way as if Halfdan and Liv themselves were the plague. Silently watching the two leave with only the sound of fire around them.

Halfdan was holding Liv's hand and pulling her along past their house and into the direction of where Linna evacuated. Frustrated with how Liv was slowing them down he turned to her. "I need you to stop and help me look for your mother, we can't stay here."

Liv began to cry harder and tried to hide her face with her hands. Halfdan had a hard time looking at her with snot running down her face. He couldn't help but wish that Frode was here. Frode had a way with words and knew what to say. Instead it was just him pulling a poor girl around. Halfdan calmed himself and spoke to Liv gently. "Ok, I want you to go to the pond where your brother would go fishing. I need you to hide and wait until I get back. I'll find your mother."

Without saying anything Liv ran into the forest toward the pond. The thought of being alone at the moment sounded like a good idea. As Liv ran deeper and deeper into the forest she slowed down and stopped. Liv thought about how weak she felt at the moment. Running and hiding seemed like the easy way out. Anger grew within her as she began to hate herself for being emotional. For a moment Liv thought about turning around and helping Halfdan look for her mother, but she knew that it was best to stick with the plan.

CHAPTER 6

GOOD TO LOVE GOOD THINGS WHEN ALL GOES ACCORDING TO THY HEART'S DESIRE.
VÖLSUNGA SAGA – NORSE PROVERB

As Liv ran and navigated the woods she thought about how this all seemed unreal. The great lindwurm of Dragekall attacked the village that it was said to protect. Now all the familiar houses were engulfed in flames. Liv pushed those thoughts away and eventually found the pond then immediately looked for a good place to hide. Sitting in the tall grass it didn't take long for Liv to become bored. Searching through Halfdan's leather pouch she counted the rest of his unmarked silver, four pieces. Liv also found a flint and steel to start a fire. That was all that Halfdan had but it was enough to give Liv something to do. She searched the surrounding area for small sticks and branches before breaking them into smaller parts. Pulling some ribbon from her hair she placed it upon the flint and with a smooth motion she began to make some sparks by striking the steel upon the flint's edge. It took her a bit to finally get an ember to last long enough to ignite some dried grass and small twigs.

In Liv's effort to start a fire she was making a lot of smoke, unknowingly giving away her location. Eventually Halfdan, Linna and Half-wit emerged from the forest. Liv was so focused that she didn't hear them. After a brief startle, happily got up and ran to greet them. Half-wit seemed happier to see Liv than Linna, but Liv was just happy to no longer be alone. Halfdan was not happy and showed Liv how to build a fire that didn't make so much smoke. Her mistake was feeding the fire grass to keep it going. In the distance the only visible smoke was from their village of Dragekall as it burned to the ground.

"Why did you put yourself in danger?" Halfdan said abruptly after successfully building a small fire for the night.

Liv looked down in embarrassment. "I don't know. I'm sorry... I was being dumb."

"No Liv, I was. I should have..." Halfdan looked up and scanned the area. "Where is Linna?"

Liv began to look around as well. Only to see Half-wit walk out of the forest with his nose to the ground.

"We need to find Linna." said Halfdan, expecting the worst.

"Mom!" yelled Liv. "Half-wit, where's mom?" hopeful that the dog would show them. All Half-wit did was look at Liv happily and waged his tail before returning to sniffing the ground.

"Where did she go?" Liv asked Halfdan as an overshadowing feeling of defeat grew inside her. "Can you make Half-wit talk or understand us or something?"

Halfdan could feel his cheeks warm up. "Um... Let me try. I don't really know how. I'm supposed to say some words or do some hand movements to try and focus my intent but I feel silly doing it in front of you. Let me think."

Halfdan kneeled down to look into Half-wit's eyes. Using his hands to hold the dog's head still, Half-wit uncomfortably looked back at Halfdan.

"Speak!" yelled Halfdan, making Liv jump. "You will speak as I do!"

Half-wit freed his head from Halfdan and lunged to bite him. Before Halfdan could react Half-wit's legs gave out. The dog fell to the ground and began to drool and convulse. Liv wanted to hold Half-wit to console him but knew better than to touch a convulsing animal. Both Liv and Halfdan stood there watching Half-wit in horror.

Slowly Half-wit began to change in physical appearance. Gruesomely losing his copper red fur, paws turned into hands, tail shrinking to nothing, snout turning into nose. In front of Halfdan and Liv is no longer a canine but a naked man. Liv couldn't help but catch a glance of the man's genitals and they swayed about as the dog man rolled around on the grass in pain. The man soon steadied himself, holding his body up on his hands and knees as he threw up his last meal of fish.

"What did you do to me?!" shrieked the man as he stood up. Holding his head in pain as human guilt, fear and greed filled his new consciousness.

Halfdan and Liv went from shock to disgust as a dirty, lengthy redheaded man stood naked in front of them. Both of them averted their eyes towards the sky as to not look at the man's fully exposed manhood. Realizing what the two were doing, the naked man uncomfortably covered himself with his hands.

"We just wanted you to be able to talk to show us where my mom went." Liv said as she took off Halfdan's cloak to hand to the man.

Halfdan ripped the cloak out of Liv's hands. "I do not want my cloak to touch this man's nakedness."

"What? Do you want to look at his naked body?" Liv said in a snarky tone followed by a grin and raised eyebrows.

Halfdan sighed and extended his cloak to the man who shamefully took it and covered himself.

"Your mother was the other lady that was with us?" asked the man.

"Yes, do you know where she went?" Liv said in excitement.

"Follow me!" said the man, matching Liv's excitement.

Halfdan and Liv followed the man as he went running through the woods. Halfdan was huffing and catching his breath trying to keep up with the two. It didn't take long until they ended up standing atop a cliff's edge. The man looked down the cliff holding his cloak tight as to keep it from blowing in the wind. Halfdan watched as Liv turned around to walk back to camp. Confused, Halfdan walked up and stood next to the man and looked down upon Linna's twisted body.

"She seemed relieved at the moment, I didn't realize..." the man said realizing what he actually witnessed not too long ago.

"You didn't know." said Halfdan consoling the man.

There was an uncomfortable silence back at camp. Liv sat quietly and watched the fire dance upon the burning wood. Short bursts of irritation would rise every time the wind would blow smoke into her eyes, reminding her of the burning village.

All Halfdan could do was feel bad for Liv. She would now consider herself an orphan. Without saying anything the man walked over and sat down next to Liv resting his head upon her shoulder. Going back to his animal instincts as to how to console a person.

"I'm sorry, nice food girl. I didn't realize what actually happened."

Liv couldn't help but burst into laughter. "Food girl? My name is Liv. And it's ok, really. She was already gone. She is with my dad and brother now. Even if I wanted to cry right now I can't. I don't think I have any tears left."

"My name is Halfdan." Halfdan said as he sat down across from Liv and the man. "I'm sorry for turning you into a human. I'll figure out how to turn you back if you want."

"You better... curse giver." said the man frowning at Halfdan before turning his attention towards Liv. "Do I have a name? I remember you calling me something."

"Ah yes we called you Ulv." said Liv quickly as to not offend their new companion.

"Yes, it's Ulv." Halfdan said continuing the lie.

"How am I supposed to clean myself?" Ulv said concerned. "I can't reach."

"By the gods I can't handle this." said Halfdan as he looked up into the sky and listened to Liv's laughter.

Before nightfall the trio were lying around the campfire for warmth. Ulv was fast asleep and snoring. Halfdan could sense that Liv was still awake but he was unsure on what to say to bring his young friend solace. Before long Halfdan was fast asleep, taking in the warmth and false feeling of security that a fire brings.

The same was not true for Liv. The sounds of the forest kept her awake and the ground was stealing the heat from her body. She shifted toward the heat of the fire to get more comfortable but getting too close to the flames was dangerous. Starting herself on fire was a possibility, and that train of thought brought back images of people on fire back in Dragekall. Liv didn't like being the only one awake and alone with her thoughts. After a long time of tossing and turning exhaustion got to her and Liv fell into a deep sleep.

Halfdan was startled awake in the early morning by Liv's muffled screaming. He quickly sat up only to see that he was surrounded by men. Before he could act on his feet the men were upon him restraining his arms and covering his head with a fabric bag. Halfdan tried to fight back but he was overpowered. He yelled out to Liv, but there was no answer. Only the sound of commotion and shuffling feet surrounded him. Halfdan stopped resisting and let the men bind his hands behind him. Once secured the men began to lead him away.

Each step was uncertain and the old bag made it difficult for Halfdan to breathe. He was panicked and couldn't think about escaping, only thoughts of what was about to happen filled his mind. Soon the familiar smell of burning wood revealed itself to Halfdan. He could hear the footsteps of the men leading him stop. Before Halfdan could adjust himself, someone pushed him over. With his hands bound behind him Halfdan could only turn his head as his body hit the ground. Pain stung Halfdan's chest and head, but that went away when he felt a hard sole of a boot press into his back. The pressure behind that boot only created new pain. While Halfdan was pinned to the ground someone ripped the bag off of his head.

The sudden flash of sunlight hurt Halfdan's eyes as he fought to adjust his vision. Before him stood three men in matching black and garnet robes, their faces were concealed by oversize hoods leaving the only visible skin of their hands. Halfdan's gaze couldn't help but be drawn to the hands before him. They were bony, covered in green and blue spots and dry looking. Behind Halfdan were his captors, the remaining villagers of Dragekall. Halfdan looked beside him and there was Liv and Ulv. They were sitting on their knees, their hands bound behind them and mouths gaged with fabric. All the three could do was look at each other in fear. Halfdan was relieved that Liv was ok, for now.

"We will pay you for the man, you can do what you wish with the woman and the exposed one." exclaimed one of the robed men as another exchanging money to what Halfdan imagined was the new village leader, who angrily counted the gold he received.

"If we weren't in such a disaster I would have rather killed him. You magic freaks are not welcome here anymore. Now go." bellowed the new village leader.

The young man was familiar to Halfdan, probably saw him at the inn but never caught his name. He was wearing clothing that a farmer would wear, but darkened from ash. He had a semblance of superiority that was part obvious and obnoxious. His neck was thicker than his head and he didn't appear all too bright. The once peaceful village was run by the elders and most likely after lindwurm attack the elders were either dead or the young man must have overpowered the frail leaders. The young man was strong looking and that's all it takes to be a leader sometimes.

"Let them go! They didn't do anything!" protested Halfdan as two of the robed men lifted him to his feet.

The new leader didn't like what he had to say and got right up to Halfdan's face to talk.

"You come here to our village and then disaster happens. The lindwurm came and destroyed our homes and you two run into the forest to kill Linna with this strange naked man. Count yourself lucky for your friends will be getting the blood eagle." The village leader ended the conversation with a punch to Halfdan's face, knocking him unconscious.

CHAPTER 7

A TREE DOES NOT FALL WITH THE FIRST BLOW. NJÁLS SAGA ~ ICELANDIC PROVERB

Halfdan awoke to find himself lying face down in a dark, musty smelling room. The only thing in the cramped quarters was a small table and two chairs that took up most of the room. Only a small candle on the table to light up the area for there were no windows. The stone wall and heavy wood door made the room feel even smaller. Halfdan had seen rooms like these before but has never been held in one until now. They were meant to make you claustrophobic and unaware as to what day and time it was.

Halfdan sat up with a moan. His face hurt and he was cold and hungry. Slowly he lifted his body up off the hard floor and tried to push the door open. Locked. He began to pound on the door, hoping to get someone's attention. Halfdan's body was shaking and he was unsure if it was from the cold or the fear of not knowing Liv's fate.

The blood eagle was not a punishment people took lightly. They would tie the victim face down to expose their back. With a spear they cut away the skin around the ribs. Then break the ribs along the spine and pull them outward to resemble wings. Finally the lungs are pulled out. It was not a fast process, and mostly reserved as a gruesome punishment for captured enemy war leaders. Wars that haven't happened in years. For them to do such a thing to Liv was truly a sign of how much they blame her for the destruction caused by the lindwurm. So much has happened to the villagers that they need someone to blame.

Halfdan kept pounding on the door and pushing through the pain. He needed answers. He needed to go find Liv, hoping that there was enough time for him to save her. Even if that meant taking her place.

With the noise Halfdan was making he didn't hear footsteps coming and the sound of someone unlocking the door. He stopped pounding and stepped back to see a man wearing a white robe. The man had a long grey beard, bushy white eyebrows and held a wood staff that held a glass ball. Behind him were two women wearing the similar black and garnet robes as the others Halfdan has seen before. Their hair was long but this close up he could see their eyes were grey and cloudy, void of thought and staring unfocused of the events before them.

"My name is Magnus. I am the Master of the underground Rossvatnet School of Alchemy and Magic in union with the order of Blackhare. Now, I'd appreciate it if you'd sit down so we can talk."

"No." said Halfdan sternly. He was not about to take orders from anyone.

Magnus showed the palm of his hand and quickly extended it forward in the direction of Halfdan. A gust of air threw Halfdan backward, pinning him against the wall.

"I don't think you quite understand the situation. Every time you use magic it's like throwing a stone in a still lake. It creates ripples to where others can sense it. Now, we can't have people going out using magic however they please." Magnus said, stepping uncomfortably close to Halfdan and tapping him on the forehead with this staff. "I'm going to make an example out of you. As I thought, you have no idea how to use magic correctly. It's pathetic and quite childish. You're going to stay here until you learn some manners. I don't want someone like you meeting with Blackhare till you can behave." Magnus turned and stepped out of the room, closing the door behind him.

As soon as Halfdan heard the door lock he was freed from Magnus' spell and fell to the floor. He was shaking in anger, he was used to insults but never felt so trapped before. Halfdan sighed and remembered agreeing to help Blackhare in capturing Frode. The irony of Halfdan being in the same situation again, but this time

Blackhare wanted him. If Magnus was working for Blackhare then he can't be trusted. Halfdan couldn't shake off the creepy feeling of the lifeless grey eyes of Magnus' two female companions. They showed no expression, just stood behind Magnus waiting for orders.

Soon the candle burnt out and Halfdan was left alone in the dark for what felt like weeks on end. The pain from hunger and dehydration came quickly. He would lean himself against the door to try and hear any footsteps but heard nothing. The stone floor would seep the heat away from Halfdan as he tried to sleep. It reminded Halfdan of when he was a child suffering with a cold. The only thing he looked forward to was sleep. When you're sleeping you aren't hungry or in pain. When he was awake he would stretch out the stiffness of his bones and muscles then quietly sing songs to himself. The longer he was alone, the more he would hear phantom whispers often calling his name. Halfdan was nervous to acknowledge these whispers, worried that it would be a step closer to madness.

Much to his displeasure, the only thing Halfdan could think about was Liv, Ulv and Linna. What was Liv and Ulv's death like? Was it painful? Was there any way that they could have escaped? Unlikely. Halfdan would get upset with himself about the situation he got Liv into. The image of Linna lying motionless at the bottom of the cliff was stuck in his head. It's different seeing death when it's someone you know. Halfdan shook his head thinking how Linna left the group and he didn't notice. He could have stopped her. It was impossible not to feel responsible for all their deaths.

Once Halfdan woke up and could hear water dripping. The sound broke the eerie silence and brought a smile to his face. He sat and listened, figuring it must be raining outside. Slowly the dripping slowed down and the silence returned.

The next time Halfdan woke up because he could feel a mouse crawling on him. Normally he would have shooed the mouse away but the feeling of something else alive in the room with him was oddly comforting. Halfdan could sense the mouse was as hungry as he was, or it was possible he was pushing his own feelings onto this creature.

"Hunger is a horrible feeling. If I had any food I'd share with you." Halfdan said to the mouse.

"Why don't we leave and find food." replied the mouse with a quiet voice that still carried some sass. Sassiness you would expect from an aunt that left her husband and wasn't afraid to speak her mind.

"It feels too soon to go insane." replied Halfdan in a flat, unamused tone.

"I didn't know you were locked in here for being a not so funny jester." said the mouse, unimpressed with Halfdan. "Are you done being pathetic? Because I was waiting in here, with you, to open the door."

Halfdan stayed laying on the floor with a mouse on his chest for a moment. Unsure of what to make of the mouse and what it was saying.

"I'm confused." Halfdan said, breaking the silence.

"You know magic, yes?" The mouse said in a condescending tone. "Then use it. To open. The door!"

"I don't know how." Halfdan proclaimed in a defeated tone.

"You don't need to know how." The mouse said. "You didn't even try. It's pathetic."

"Look," Halfdan said as he sat up, tumbling the mouse off of him who protested with profanity. "Every time I use magic something bad happens. I severely burned myself, caused a lindwurm to take out its frustration on a village and made a dog into a human. It wasn't pleasant to see the last one."

"Maybe you should start out with something small. Like unlocking a door. I'll show you how. But, I'm only going to help you unlock a door once. So pay attention. I'd do it myself but it's not easy in this… form." Mouse said slowly losing her assertiveness.

"So you're not a very smart magic mouse?" Halfdan said, amused.

"What? No! I'm not a mouse! I possessed a mouse, my name is Elora. The girl you saw with the long brown hair to the right of Magnus, that's me. I can't do magic or really alchemy in this body. But I needed to hide when Blackhare got her claws into Magnus. Magnus is one of the few that Blackhare is working with. That's why you're here. That's also why I thought you could help me escape." Replied Elora with little enthusiasm, displeased that she needed Halfdan to escape.

"So what is wrong with your body now?" Halfdan asked concerned. Remembering how off-putting the grey eyes were.

"Ok." Elora said followed with a big exhale. "You could have volunteered to surrender your power, or you were killed and reanimated to be his slave. So everyone that is still here, other than Magnus, is dead. Now, we've been in here long enough. I know my way around the academy. After you open up this door, I'll show you the way out… any more questions?"

"No, just tell me how to get out." Halfdan lied and was filled with questions.

"Magnus didn't put any spells or inscriptions on the door. It seems like he thinks little of you. So I'm going to teach you how to push the air around you. If it's strong enough to push you back, it can do the same to the door. Remember when Magnus pushed you back? I want you to do that but with both hands. It will make it easier for you. As you extend your hands, quickly exhale. Got it?" Elora said with little enthusiasm again.

"Ok." Halfdan said as he got up. Feeling around in the dark, Halfdan made sure he was far enough away from the door to not accidently hurt himself and punch the door.

Showing the palms of his hands he quickly extended them forward in the direction of the door. Nothing. Halfdan let out a big sigh. He could hear Elora's little voice filling the air around him, but he wasn't listening. Accepting defeat Halfdan laid down, ready for the fate that Magnus has set for him. With all of Halfdan's loss there wasn't much left for him to care about. Weak and exhausted, he closed his heavy eyelids and fell asleep.

"Halfdan, we'll find you. Just hang on."

Halfdan woke up to see that the darkness had been broken by the light of a full moon. The door to his prison was wide open revealing a magnificent and proud buck standing at attention. The buck had a thirty point rack, on each point was a lit candle. Halfdan could feel the beast staring at him, beckoning him to come forth. Halfdan slowly made his way to the buck, feeling small and weak compared to the size of the creature.

Stillness swept the area, as if the trees and grass stopped moving to allow the buck to speak. This unnatural stillness caused a shiver to run down Halfdan's spine.

"I've been watching you, Halfdan." said the buck without opening its mouth to speak. It was as if the air around the beast was talking for him. "I go by many names, but you may call me Jovi. Tell me, what do I look like to you?"

It took a moment for Halfdan to summon the courage to speak before he murmured "a deer."

"I see." said Jovi. "Even as a deer you are still afraid of me. Do not be afraid. Throughout my lifetime I have helped many gods and goddesses' become who they are. I have always been there when their reign of power was ending. They call me a friend when I help them and at the end of their influence they call me an enemy. The time of gods and goddesses is over. That is why you human's never see the gods walk on the same soil as you today. All that is left are tales of old. To have human's rule themselves is a true test of judgment. However, there is a new goddess in the making. Her name is Hilda, but you know her by Blackhare."

"Blackhare?"

"Yes. She is killing everyone who can control what you call magic. Hilda is going to take it all. She will be as strong as a goddess and will rule as one, a goddess that craves power and destruction. That is why I need you, I am no longer able to walk on this earth. If you agree, I will give you some of my power. If you disagree... I will take your eyes."

"My eyes?" Halfdan asked, flabbergasted.

"Yes, your eyes." Jovi said with glee. "I have always wanted to see how the world looks through human eyes."

"How am I supposed to stop her?" Halfdan asked, trying to understand what was happening.

"Through the carnage you bring into this world. I know everything you've done. You are responsible for not one, not two but three villages to be burned to the ground. Through your acts you know how horrible destruction is. You know how to do it, so you will know how to stop it." The candles on Jovi's antlers blew out and just like that he was gone.

Halfdan awoke back into his holding room that was void of light. He was not sure if he was dreaming or hallucinating.

"Halfdan, are you awake?" Elora said, breaking the silence.

"Yeah." Halfdan said sadly. "I had an odd dream. This buck with candles on it was talking to me. I saw moonlight. It was nice to see moonlight even though it was-"

"I hear footsteps." said Elora, urgently.

The door to the room was unlocked and pushed open. The light from the torches were bright enough to hurt Halfdan's eyes which had grown accustomed to darkness. It was Magnus and his two undead slaves from before.

"I'm sure you've learned some manners by now." Magnus said with a demeaning tone.

Magnus showed the palm of his hand and quickly extended it forward in the direction of Halfdan who was struggling to get up off the floor. Unlike before, Magnus was affected by his own spell, pushing him back and pinning him against the wall along with his reanimated slaves.

"What have you done?!" Exclaimed Magnus with pure anger as he squirmed to free himself.

Halfdan scooped up Elora and began to run.

"Keep running Halfdan! Don't stop!" yelled Elora. "Go into the room at the end of the hall!"

Halfdan ran and was afraid to look back. It felt as if Magnus or his slaves were right behind them. As sore as Halfdan's body was it felt good to run. Halfdan ran past many doors but soon got to a door that was at the end of the hall. Halfdan pushed the door open. In the room was a ladder leading up to a trap door in the ceiling, there was also a reanimated slave in the room looking back at Halfdan.

The slave charged at Halfdan with a sword. He stepped out of the room back into the hall and closed the door. As soon as the reanimated slave went to open the door Halfdan kicked it in, knocking the slave on the ground. Halfdan let out a curse. Kicking the door twisted his ankle but the pain wasn't enough to make him give up. The undead slave was trying to get up when Halfdan stomped on the deceased head, causing blood and bits of hair to scatter across the floor, before stepping towards the ladder.

Halfdan put Elora on his shoulder so he could use both hands to get up the ladder. His injured ankle caused him to slip when he was half way up but he was able to catch himself. The thought of dead hands reaching up and pulling him down made him move faster. When he pushed the trap door open he saw the inside of a chicken coop. The chickens flapped their wings and clucked in excitement as Halfdan scampered out of the coop.

As the sun warmed Halfdan's skin he never thought that the sight of grass and trees would make him feel so much joy. The fresh crisp air filled his lungs with life. Halfdan followed a trail leading away from the coop and ran the whole way. Fear gave Halfdan the strength to keep running, pushing through the pain. There was a comforting tingling sensation running down his spine the farther he ran. He could feel Elora's tail bouncing up and down the faster he went. It felt like Halfdan was running for hours until he heard the bustling sound of a village.

Once Halfdan got in sight of a watering trough he pushed the horses out of the way and drank the water with little care about the hay and dirt that was floating about. At that moment the water tasted like it was from the purest spring and better than any water that he has had before in his life. Some of the villagers pointed and laughed as others stared. Halfdan didn't care, until he heard a familiar voice.

"Halfdan?"

Halfdan turned around to see Liv, her hair cut short and wearing Frode's cloak. Behind her was Ulv wearing nothing but pants and holding Halfdan's axe. Halfdan began crying, not hiding his tears from the world as he got up from his knees and gave Liv a hug. Ulv shortly followed, giving off a big grin as he third wheeled in the hug.

"Careful, mutt, don't cut me with my own axe." Halfdan said, breaking the embrace and pushing Ulv back. "Liv, your hair?"

"Let's find somewhere more private to talk." Liv said, looking around at the people watching them.

The reunited group made their way to a small inn with a few patrons. Halfdan took a deep inhale to smell food cooking and his stomach grumbled in response. Elora moved about and her soft fur brushed against his neck, Halfdan thought that she must be smelling the food too. Liv led the group upstairs to a private room.

"The villagers here are not fond of the cult and won't let them in this building, so we are safe here." said Ulv proudly.

Halfdan sat on the comfy bed and sighed in delight. He could feel Elora hiding in his hair. Whatever her reason, Halfdan was happy to be in a warm room. The smell of food distracted him and he could feel his mouth watering.

"Ulv and I followed you here through tips. I guess a lot of people dislike the cult that took you so people were more than happy to tell us where they went. But no one knew exactly where." Liv said, sitting next to Halfdan.

"I felt like I was there forever. But I'm here now. I thought you two were..." Halfdan stopped not wanting to complete his sentence.

"They cut Liv's hair to make her feel bad." Ulv blurted out. Unaware of how embarrassed Liv was of it. "Then they couldn't decide how they wanted to kill us. They didn't want to do the blood seagull" Ulv said incorrectly. "because no one could remember how to do it anymore. Then they were going to cut our heads off but some thought that it was too humane. Then someone said the same thing about hanging. Then Liv told them that I was an innocent traveler

54

and that she was the reason why so many people died. That she should face the same fate as those who faced the lindwurm. To be burned alive. Right before Liv was going to be burned I left to get something to eat. I really didn't want to watch and food always makes me feel better. Then, boom! Everyone else was on fire and Liv came to find me."

Halfdan looked at Liv, she was looking down and nervously playing with her fingers.

Ulv looked like he was going to say more, but instead sniffed the air. "I'm going to go get some food for all of us."

Halfdan and Liv watch as Ulv left without a care in the world, slamming the door behind him.

"I should have told you sooner." Halfdan said avoiding making eye contact with Liv. "The lindwurm had an egg. I took its energy and gave it to you, burning my hands in the process." Halfdan paused to look at his scarred hands. "It seems it didn't only cure your illness, but gave you strength."

"Frode did the same to you, didn't he?"

Halfdan felt his heart drop. "I didn't want you to think less of me. Frode was your friend as well. He sacrificed himself for me, even though I was responsible for his death. I was afraid that I was responsible for your death as well."

"I don't know what to do anymore." Liv said with a heavy heart. "When my neighbors tied me up and went to light the wood beneath my feet I could hear them laughing. The people I grew up with and cared for were reveling in the thought of my painful demise. Then I just exploded in a fury. I'm just happy that Ulv wasn't around... and found pants. The house is gone. Ulv and I could only find and sell enough goods for silver to last a little longer."

Halfdan thought for a moment. As much as he wanted to learn more about what Liv did to end her village it was best to let her reveal it in her own time. However, was a nomadic life and dangerous mercenary work good for Liv? "We will go to the town of Kibera. There is an inn where I stay. It's a safe place for mercenaries and we can find work. We will collect enough silver and gold to build our own home. What do you think?"

"I'm back!" Ulv said while kicking the door open with armfuls of drinking horns. "The inn keep is warming up some bread to go with our stew and will bring it up to us."

Halfdan and Liv took a horn. Before Liv could make a toast Halfdan drank from the horn with great enthusiasm.

"How long was I gone?" Halfdan asked, genuinely curious how long Liv and Ulv were looking for him.

"Three days." Liv replied before drinking more of her mead.

"What! Only three days? It felt like weeks." Halfdan let out a long groan before changing the topic. "Is it alright that I'm here? If that cult finds me again they might take you too." He said, shivering at the thought of going back to that prison of a school.

"I'm sure! The inn keep said so!" Ulv said with no concept of secrecy.

Halfdan tried his best to inform Ulv of how he can't trust everyone. Before long the inn keep came in to give stew to the group and asked questions about what happened to Halfdan. Halfdan obliged but kept his story brief. It wasn't long before sunlight was replaced by moonlight and the group decided to sleep. There were only two beds so Halfdan had to share a bed with Ulv, but he didn't mind. Halfdan didn't care about how small the bed was for two. It was warm and soft, much better than sleeping on a stone floor. And he knew Liv was safe and that was enough.

Elora waited silently, now that everyone was quiet she thought the time to make her leave was nigh. She slowly made her way out of Halfdan's hair when she was snatched up by a large hand. Elora bit down but the hand didn't loosen its grasp. Elora stopped to look and see who was manhandling her, it was Ulv. She figured that if Ulv was going to kill her he would have done it by now. She remained silent and hoped that the fool was going to let her go outside. Ulv slowly made his way out of the room and quietly closed the door behind him. He continued down the stairs and past drunkards until he was out of the building. Ulv walked on a cool dirt path and then into the woods, his bare feet exposed to the nature beneath them as dirt didn't bother him.

Before talking Ulv looked around to make sure he was alone. Only the moon light to brighten the cold night air and the sound of the inn in the distance.

"Why is a shapeshifter hiding in my friend's hair?" He asked sternly to the mouse, tightening his grip on her. Watching as Elora's black mouse eyes bulge out of her head.

"How did you know?" Elora peeped.

"You smell like no mouse I've smelled before." Ulv said, thinking himself very clever.

"What... oh, you were a dog before."

"I don't know how you know that, you trickster. But I will not let you hurt my friends." Ulv said feeling red in the face.

"Please! I didn't want to hurt anyone." Elora pleaded. "I told Halfdan that I was a student at the academy that possessed a mouse. I lied, but I only did that because no one trusts a shapeshifter. Not even my parents. I only transformed as a mouse to get away from Magnus. I went to the school to learn how to use magic and alchemy to heal the sick. I just wanted to help people. I don't know why Halfdan didn't introduce me." Elora said, hoping to get Ulv to feel bad for her.

"We will ask Halfdan then." Ulv said, turning to make his way back to the inn.

"I don't want anyone to know! Please! I don't want to be treated like a monster again. I was born like this. My parents even kicked me out when I was still a child. I even had to name myself. It's Elora."

"Well what do you want to do then, Elora? Stick around our group or go your own way?" Ulv asked sympathizing with Elora relaxing his grip on her.

"You'd let me stay in the group? Even knowing what I am?" Elora said with hope, unsure if Ulv was trying to mislead her.

"Well I don't see why not. I don't think you're a monster. If I could turn back into a dog I would. But why stay a mouse?"

"I can't turn back to who I was." Elora said sadly. "I don't remember how I originally looked. But maybe I can show Halfdan how to turn you back into a dog. I can't do any magic other than shapeshifting but I still have knowledge."

"Would you? I miss being a dog. Is there a way I can help you shape into something else less... small?"

"I need hair or fur in order to transform into something else. If you could get me cat fur that would be good. I think slowly making my way up to bigger animals will make an easy transition so I don't take long to shift. When I'm transforming I am at my most vulnerable... and get ravenously hungry afterwards."

"Don't worry Elora! I'm a pro at chasing cats so this will be easy!" Ulv said proudly.

Ulv gently put Elora on the ground then promptly turned around and ran off. Elora watched Ulv run off when a sleek black cat came out of the bushes. The cat licked its chops as its yellow eye's lock on to Elora.

Elora stood still and called out. "Ulv!... Ulv?... shit..."

CHAPTER 8

IGNIS

Halfdan woke up to the sound of Ulv and Liv whispering, a welcoming change to his recent ordeal. The early morning sun lit up the room. Liv must have opened the window for fresh air and the distant sounds of birds singing made Halfdan smile. Much better than waking up in the cold, stuffy, dark room that once held him. Halfdan sat up to look at Liv and Ulv. Liv smiled back at him while she was sitting on the edge of the bed, consoling Ulv who had deep red scratches covering his arms and torso. Ulv did not look happy and was sulking with his arms crossed.

"What happened to you?" Halfdan asked Ulv with a lack of compassion.

"Why don't you ask Elora?" Ulv said with an attitude.

A black cat jumped onto Halfdan's bed. Halfdan startled a little, not expecting a cat. Only until the cat spoke did he know it was Elora. "Ulv is upset because a cat scratched him up."

"Being human is dumb! How can you catch anything with two legs?" Ulv said in defense.

"If you wore a shirt you wouldn't have gotten scratched so badly." Halfdan replied with no sympathy. "Why were you trying to catch a cat anyway?"

"Clothing is uncomfortable. Boots make my feet sweaty. Sweating is more than unpleasant. I don't understand why humans do that." Exclaimed Ulv. The words came out so quickly it was apparent he thought them on a daily basis.

"It's my fault. I asked him to catch a cat so I could have a new form. However, all of Ulv's efforts were in vain because I was able to get a cat myself. It wasn't easy being a mouse trying to catch a cat." Elora admitted with a speck of a lie.

"Will you ever get your human body back?" Liv asked with a sympathetic frown. "It's unfortunate that you have to possess animals."

Ulv sighed. He didn't like telling lies. They make his head hurt trying to keep stories straight. But he was willing to keep Elora's true identity as a shapeshifter a secret.

"My body has been deceased for some time now." Elora said pretending to sound sad. "I don't think it's possible."

"Will you be coming with us to Kibera? It will be safer for us to go in a group." Liv asked Elora.

"You really want me to go with you?" Elora asked, surprised with a hint of skepticism.

"I don't see why not?" Liv said with a gentle and kind smile, seeing a gleam of joy in Elora's yellow cat eyes.

"We should take advantage of the daylight and get moving. We will have to ask for directions. How much silver do you have, Liv?" Halfdan asked while getting out of bed already dressed and ready to go.

"Twelve." Liv replied.

"We will have to use them wisely. Let's talk to the inn keeper for directions." Halfdan said while walking to the door. Picking up his axe from a table, thanking the gods that it wasn't lost in the fire. Liv put on Frode's cloak and crinkled her nose at how musty smelling it was as Elora jumped on her shoulders for a ride.

The group started to make their way out of the inn. Downstairs they could see its keep. Still dirty from working the night before, bent over cleaning spilled ale off the floor.

"Good morning to you three! Heading out already?" The inn keep said as he straightened himself up. "I was hoping to talk to you before you left. You see, some of the villagers wanted you to show them where this secret coop door is. We're going to break up the cultists. Free our lands from their filth."

Halfdan's face went white. The thought of voluntarily going back made every nerve in his body scream no. He could feel Liv, Ulv and Elora looking at him waiting for an answer.

Liv decided to speak for Halfdan after noticing his visible discomfort. "We must be going. Halfdan did tell you everything he knows. We wish you luck on your endeavors. Can you tell us how to get to Kibera?"

The inn keeper gave a big sly smile. "Towards the rising sun, where you came from. So you can show us how to get to the cult, Halfdan. It is along the way after all."

"Okay. We are going to get supplies and will return." Halfdan said to the inn keeper as he led his friends out the door and onto a bustling main street. The villagers were busy trading goods to start their day. Halfdan walked up to the nearest villager who was making their way to the village square. "Can you direct me to Kibera?"

The villager nodded and pointed to the west. "You will reach the village of Rivinnsjo within a day's walk before arriving at Kibera."

Halfdan thanked the man and turned to his friends. "I've been through Rivinnsjo before. We will collect supplies there."

Ulv pondered for a moment. "But the inn keep said Kibera was towards the setting sun, not the rising sun?"

"He lied to us." Replied Liv, displeased.

"Don't trust people's advice when they want something from you." Halfdan said, more angrily than displeased.

"It's for the best." Elora said quietly as for no strangers to hear. "Magnus isn't someone you want to stop by for a quick hello. Not anymore at least, now that Blackhare has her claws in him."

The group started to make their way west. Maneuvering their way around the occasional villager and their cart.

"How did you even get involved with that cult anyway?" Liv asked Elora.

"It's not a cult! Those were uniforms. They were meant to make us equal. To be part of the school you have to give away your worldly possessions. Not sell them, give them away to those in need.

Some students were looking for recruits when they found me and I really needed a place to live, so it worked out... for a while. I was told that I was gifted with herbal medicine and Latin." Elora gave off a quick smug look that complemented her feline form. "The school itself is located underground and is big and elaborate. Magnus hid the school underground out of concern that the surrounding villages would be fearful of our magic and attack. Despite the school being secretive, students leave once they are skilled enough. Helping those in need including chieftains and even kings and queens. We were taught to heal, deescalate situations, see into the future and to protect those in need. Then Blackhare came and now everything has changed. She convinced Magnus to break his oaths. The oath at Rossvatnet was to never use dark magic. Any magic used to hurt someone is considered dark magic." Elora continued. "He hurt every student and teacher at our school. Even reaching outside of the school to lure in the cunning just to trap them."

"What is Blackhare having Magnus do for her?" Halfdan asked, still not convinced Elora's school wasn't a cult.

"If only I knew." Elora said sadly as she looked behind her in the direction of Rossvatnet. "Maybe I could have saved the school. It was my home after all."

In an act of compassion Liv reached up and scratched Elora behind her ears. "We lots our home too."

"Don't touch me." Elora said, coldly.

Liv retracted her hand and grimaced. "Sorry."

"I find it amusing that Magnus captured Halfdan in the first place. He couldn't even use magic to open a door." Elora said with a smirk while side eyeing Halfdan.

Halfdan spat on the ground in distaste and glared back at Elora.

"It's ok, Halfdan. Doors are hard. I just recently figured out that you have to use your thumb." Ulv wiggled his thumbs at Halfdan who responded by rolling his eyes.

The group started out energetic but as they made their way to the village of Rivinnsjo they realized it was a push to keep moving forward. Silly conversations soon turned into groaning sounds from foot pains. The group walked the path that took them through farm fields and forest. A cool late summer breeze relieving their warm bodies.

Two little red squirrels rustled through the fallen leaves and chirped at one another. Halfdan looked back half expecting Ulv to chase after them. To his surprise the pair didn't catch Ulv's attention. Either he was too tired or becoming more of a man than a dog after all.

Ulv noticed Halfdan looking at him and decided to take this opportunity to complain. "All we got to eat was a handful of chanterelle mushrooms. All we got to drink was some river water. If we don't get something decent to eat and drink I'll shrivel up and die."

"Chanterelle mushrooms are a sign that fall is starting. Too bad you all had to eat them raw. I think they would be best pan fried with butter." Elora said, cutting off Ulv's complaints.

Ulv let out a whine as he thought about butter.

"I'm happy you know what mushrooms are edible. I'm always fearful of poisoning myself." Liv complemented Elora.

"Well I was guessing they were edible." replied Elora with no emotion. "I didn't eat any."

"I'm so happy you are with our group." Halfdan rolled his eyes again. "Look up ahead, you can see some smoke above the trees. We must be close to Rivinnsjo."

The group picked up the pace, eager to reach their destination and rest.

"Seem to remember that the wealthy merchants that live in Kibera send their families here. Kibera doesn't smell so good in the summer." Halfdan said with his nose flared, remembering the smell. "The inn here will be well over twelve silver. We will have to rest and camp outside. The silver we have will be best used for food and blankets, if we can get a good price."

"If these people have money why don't they live in large houses in the middle of the forest?" Liv asked, confused.

"They grow up in a busy city. The silence, isolation and self-reliance drives them back. So a small wealthy community would work best." Halfdan shrugged. "That's what I think anyway. Plus, safety in numbers."

The group stopped talking as they stepped out of the forest and into a clearing. In the middle of the vast clearing was a wall. A tall wall and made of trees cut from the surrounding forest. Just the wall alone was enough to make the group feel small like ants. The path that they have been following lead to a large wooden door within the wall. As they got closer they could see there were no handles on the door, it could only be opened from the inside.

Bam, bam, bam.

Halfdan pounded on the door, waiting silently for a response.

Bam, bam, bam!

Again no response. Halfdan could hear people on the other side, but none wanted to open the door.

"The sun is out. I don't understand why no one is manning the door." Halfdan asked, confused.

"Ugh. I was so excited to see Rivinnsjo too." Liv said sadly and disappointed as she leaned her ear against the door to listen, then gave up.

"Maybe it's dinner time?" Ulv said excitedly. "Throw Elora over the wall! She can tell them to open the door."

Liv could feel Elora's claws dig into her skin. Not wanting to see a dog and cat fight Liv spoke up. "I don't think sending a talking cat over the wall will work. They would either panic or think it's a trap." Liv let out a quiet sigh of relief as Elora retracted her claws.

"Let's not stand here and wait until nightfall. Whatever the reason, I feel that they aren't going to be opening the door soon. If there is a village then there has to be a clean body of water nearby. We will make camp there. I'll make the fire while you three look for food." Halfdan said as he made his way left, following along the great wooden wall.

"I'm so tired that I don't care about food anymore." Liv said pathetically.

"Shut your mouth." Ulv replied angrily. "I'm not resting until I eat."

"You ate already, remember the mushrooms?" Elora asked Ulv.

"That's not food!" Ulv exclaimed with great passion.

"This is why I want to make the fire by myself." Halfdan told the group as he turn around and glared at them as they laughed. "Let's all keep a lookout for water, just because I'm leading doesn't mean I know where I'm going."

"Let's walk along the perimeter of the wall to get an idea of what the surrounding area looks like." Elora ordered rather than suggested.

It wasn't long for the tired group to find another door within the wall. It didn't seem like an official door but rather a door of necessity. Rather than knocking on this door Halfdan suggested to follow the dirt trail into the tree line. Liv, Ulv and Elora obliged and soon the smell of lake water was filling the air. There was a small clearing around the large lake. The water was clear and the forest was close to the water's edge. Some water reeds were filling in the shore, but the water was easily accessible. Ease filled the travelers bodies, they knew that they would soon be able to rest and hopefully eat.

"I'm surprised we're the only ones here. The weather is fair and the sun is warming. No one is bathing or fishing." Elora spoke openly to the group.

"Everything about this situation is odd. Perhaps the plague arrived here as well?" Halfdan was puzzled. "I've only been here a few times and the guards always opened the door. Most of the time the door was just left open for people to come and go as they please." Halfdan stopped for a moment to look around. "We won't camp in the open, you three look around for food and I'll look for a spot to camp somewhere around the water's edge, ok? We might be able to hear voices travel across the lake so we will know if people are coming."

"Best to be safe." Liv said, affirming Halfdan's concerns.

Liv grabbed the flint and stone from the leather pouch that rested on her hip and handed it to Halfdan. He took the flint and stone in his left hand as he carried his axe with his right. He nodded his head to the group and went his separate way.

Deep down Halfdan wanted to stay with Liv, but he needed to make the best of what sunlight he had left. Fire didn't just keep them warm but also kept the wolves away. Halfdan collected sticks of all sizes as he looked around for a good spot to camp. It was obvious that people and animals made small trails along the lake, so it didn't take long to find an old camp fire. The ash was old and cold, the stones that made a circle had moss growing on them. There was a fallen tree that was placed as a seat by the fire pit. Halfdan couldn't help but think about what other people have used this place. Were they villagers who were fishing or were they children enjoying a little bit of freedom. Either way, no one was using it tonight. There was no sign of recent activity, nothing lying about that someone might come back for.

Halfdan put his sticks down and looked around for any decent sized logs. There were none, but he could cut some later perhaps. Halfdan grabbed a handful of thick dried grass and worked the grass apart. Trying to make the grass soft and frayed to be better tinder. He did the same to a thin dried stick, breaking it apart and fraying it. He knew that if he tried to start the fire with too much dried grass he would just make smoke, signaling to unwanted visitors. He would only use a little grass to get a spark going. Slowly he would add bigger sticks, then bigger branches and then logs if Halfdan could find some dry wood.

Halfdan could hear some splashing around followed by Liv playfully scolding Ulv for scaring the fish. Halfdan smiled and sighed as he kept working the flint. Ulv, when he was a dog, wasn't helpful with hunting or herding or protecting any livestock. He was a dog that would blissfully wander around the village trying to make friends with every person he met. Ulv wasn't any one person's dog but rather a dog of the village that everyone would feed, so it wasn't a surprise that he wouldn't be good at finding food as a human.

Halfdan frowned and shook his head. He didn't want to think about Liv's village, Dragekall. Is it even considered a village anymore? More like a camp of survivors if Liv didn't kill those that remained. How did Liv even get away? Can she breathe fire like the lindwurm? He laughed at the thought. Dragons of all kinds seem fierce breathing fire, but a petite girl… young lady… seems kind of odd. Perhaps controlling fire with her mind? Now that was a chilling thought.

Halfdan got a spark that caught his tinder on fire. Excited, Halfdan put the flint down and lightly blew the spark to get it to light. It didn't catch and went out. He sighed from frustration as he put the stone and tinder down to stand up and stretch. Reaching his hands into the air Halfdan felt a gentle breeze touch his body. There have been times before where he had to camp without a fire. Not always due to weather but always resulted in an unrestful night's sleep. He tried again and again but the spark wouldn't take. Dusk was upon them and Halfdan could hear the rest of his companions making their way to him. He sighed, not wanting them to see he failed to produce a fire.

Ulv ran up to Halfdan happily holding a large brown trout to show off. His hair and pants were still wet from jumping into the lake.

"Well, how were you able to catch that? I heard you splashing in the water?" Halfdan said still upset about the fire he wasn't able to produce.

"I found it! It was dead floating in the water. But Liv said that since its gills are still pink that we can still eat it." Ulv said with a big grin.

"I don't think we will be able to eat soon." Halfdan said gloomily looking at the fire pit with cold twigs and sticks. "I want to try and use magic, but I'm worried about Magnus being able to find us if I do. He told me that it's like sending out a signal every time I use any of my *new found powers*." He said, emphasizing new found powers in an ironic tone.

"I actually wanted to do a little experiment." Elora said, running out from behind Liv. "When Magnus tried to cast on you it reflected back onto Magnus himself. The aura you gave off when I first met you is different, or near nonexistent now. I've never seen anything like it. It's almost like you're a mirror."

"You do seem different, Halfdan." Liv said quietly. "You're eyes aren't blue anymore. Since we found you they look... different. I almost didn't recognize you when you looked at us."

"What?" Halfdan asked as he made his way to the water's edge to look upon his reflection. "I can't see my reflection the sun is going away. What's wrong with my eyes?"

"They look fine." Liv said with a weak smile.

"That doesn't make me feel better." Halfdan said, still trying to see his reflection.

"Your eyes were blue before. They're grey now. Like all the color was dulled out." Liv said quietly as if she wasn't sure if what she was saying was correct.

"Your nose is less crooked too. I think getting punched fixed it." Ulv said loudly without care of offense.

"Thanks, Ulv." Halfdan said, sarcastically. Giving up on trying to see his reflection.

"It could be the stress or getting punched in the face?" Elora said. "Ugh! You fools are getting me off track! Halfdan, I want you to try and do a simple fire spell. I'll be on the other side of the lake trying to sense your intent. I'm not as skilled as Magnus, but it is worth a try. If Magnus does sense it we will be gone by morning. Also, I have a feeling that the villagers are going to keep him occupied from looking for us right now. So it is a good time to try my theory."

"I've never done a fire spell." Halfdan said, nervously. "And I'm worried about us being found again."

"Tell me, if you wanted to do a fire spell, what would you do?" Elora asked more kindly than usual. "There is no wrong answer."

Taken back by Elora's pleasant tone Halfdan had to think for a moment. Rubbing the back of his head as he pondered. "Uh... I'll hold my hands out at the sticks and say 'fire'?"

"I see you got your poetry prowess from the back end of the All Father." Elora scuffed at Halfdan.

"You said there was no wrong answer!" Halfdan retaliated.

"Magic works best with old languages. Think of magic as a living breathing entity. It responds best with Latin, Greek, Hebrew or any languages of the ancients. Something it's used to hearing. Ignis means fire in Latin, try saying that. Focus on your intent, feel the energy around you and act." Elora turned around and began to run off. "Don't burn the forest down!"

Halfdan let out an irritated sigh as he watched Elora scamper off in her cat form.

"You sigh a lot." Ulv told Halfdan.

"I'm just breathing." Halfdan said, louder than he intended.

"It's alright Halfdan." Liv said, placing her hand on his shoulder. "I can give it a try if you can't."

"Ok." Halfdan turned towards the fire pit. He closed his eyes and steadied his breathing. Thinking the word *ignis* over and over again in his head. When the time felt right he opened his eyes and threw his palms forward. "Ignis!"

All that the group saw was a gentle breeze of nature tumbling some leaves over the sticks.

"I don't get it!" Halfdan said with anger and disappointment. "I can do so much but can't do the simplest things."

"Simple is relative and different for everyone. Wouldn't Frode snap his fingers?" Liv snapped her fingers in response.

Halfdan made a smug face to mock the situation and snapped his fingers.

Ka-boom!

The sticks ablaze went flying in every direction. Halfdan and Liv turned and ducked as burning sticks bounced off them. Ulv went running and jumped in the lake in terror as he screamed. Halfdan started patting his body down as he checked to see if he was on fire.

Liv did the same before stepping on some burning leaves, extinguishing them.

"Are you ok?" Liv yelled to Ulv as she extinguished the last rogue flame.

Ulv lifted his head out of the water and shook it like a dog trying to get their fur dry. "Yeah!"

Elora came running as fast as her little cat paws could go. "What happened?"

"The fire was a little more excessive than I thought it would be." Halfdan said watching Liv pick up burning logs with her bare hands, unafflicted by the flames' temper as she tossed them back into fire pit. Elora seemed too irritated to notice what Liv was doing.

"It's like your pure destruction!" Elora scolded Halfdan.

"No one got hurt." Halfdan said, gesturing to Liv and Ulv.

"Ulv, come here." Elora said, looking blankly at Halfdan. Ulv scampered out of the water and stood next to her, dripping lake water. "Ok, now turn around."

"Is there something wrong?" He turned around briefly. Not noticing the back of his hair was burned, browned and frizzed.

"We'll get him a hat, problem solved." Halfdan said without a care.

"Oh Ulv," Liv said, making her way to him. "Your hair must have caught on fire." She said while stroking his hair, accessing the damage.

"I don't look as bad as Halfdan, right?" Ulv asked Liv.

"What's wrong with the way I look?" Halfdan said, sternly.

Elora giggled before she spoke. "You just need a bath and trim. You do look completely mad."

"More like a cave troll." Liv added with a smirk, looking at Halfdan to let him know she was just teasing him.

"Is that supposed to make me feel better?" Halfdan said as he huffed and picked up the fish that Ulv dropped. "I'll gut this fish." He shook the fish jokingly at Liv and Elora. "And as it cooks I'll go take a lake bath."

"Your odor might kill more fish for us to eat, so maybe take a bath first." Elora snickered.

"Careful cat, or I'll snap my fingers and burn your fur off." Halfdan said followed by a malevolent laugh as he gestured his free hand like he was going to snap his fingers again.

Elora hissed and climbed up the nearest tree. Leaves rustled as she disappeared with only a few tree seeds falling from her movements.

Liv didn't want to listen to the bickering anymore and spoke sternly. "Enough, we don't have much sun left. I'll gut the fish. Halfdan, how about you clean up in the morning. If you get wet now you might be cold all night. How about you tell us a story? Old guys like telling stories."

"I'm thirty two, that's not old." Halfdan said angrily as he tossed the floppy fish to Liv.

"I'm surprised you have all your teeth." Elora yelled down from the tree.

"Thank you. I take good care of them." Halfdan said with a smile to show off his teeth, not letting Elora get to him.

"I'm seventeen. How old are you, Elora? It's hard to tell with you looking like a cat." Liv spoke loudly up the tree.

"Rude." Elora jumped down from the tree. "I think I'm twenty two? I don't even know what year or season I was born."

"How old am I?" Ulv asked happily, wanting to join the conversation.

"I'm sorry I don't know. I don't even know who your mom is. You just showed up and I started feeding you." Liv told Ulv as kindly as she could.

Ulv huffed and crossed his arms. "I don't care. Time is dumb anyway."

"Do you remember anything from being a dog?" Elora asked Ulv.

Ulv thought for a moment. "I don't really think about the past that much. But now that you ask it's all fuzzy and jumbled together, like a dream. I remember turning into a human and everything after

71

that." Ulv again was deep in thought when a concerned look crossed his face. "What If I forget how to be a dog?"

"You've been a dog most of your life. I'm sure it will come back to you when you turn back." Halfdan said as confidently as he could to reassure Ulv.

Elora had a big cat grin on her face as she spoke. "I can have Halfdan try to turn you back right now if you want? No promise you won't burst into flames."

Ulv widened his eyes and tensed up at the thought. "I can wait."

Halfdan chuckled and started to tend to the fire. Elora found a safe spot and attempted to take a cat nap as birds chirped angrily at her. Ulv watched as Liv gutted and cleaned the fish by the water. With Halfdan's axe she cut the fins off the fish. Then with a smooth motions she used the axe's tip to cut the belly of the fish working from back to front. With her fingers she scooped the fish's innards out onto a large leaf to dispose of later away from camp. With a few quick motions Liv rinsed the inside of the fish with water. With a clean stick Liv put the fish on mouth first and let the rest of the fish's body balance. By now the sun was almost set and Liv held the stick over the fire to cook the fish. Ulv sat close to Liv and intently watched the fish as Halfdan sat on the log.

"I do have a story to tell." Halfdan said, breaking the silence. "If we keep watching the fish cook it will seem like forever. I want to tell you how Liv's mother, Linna, and I met. It was when the landscape was inhabited with clans rather than villages and war with rival clans were the norm. The clan we belonged to was Snjár and we sustained our lifestyle with raids across the ocean towards the west and south. No one died from old age but searched to die with honor in battle. Unmarried women would often fight with us and were called shield maidens. Linna was a shield maiden, she could fight better than I. She could use a bow, throw an axe and cut down any foe with a sword. When we were alone she would show me how to fight. Your mother had a difficult beginning and it made her stronger than I. Soon we were considered old enough to aid in a raid if we wished to go. I was socially obligated to go and Linna wanted to go with me to keep me safe. I was seventeen and she was sixteen, we were only allowed to scout out good locations to raid before then. I was so excited, we were finally able to make our own raiding stories and sit in the great hall with the rest of our clan. So, we went on a raid together with a few other clan members and our *Hersir. We rode together in our longship for weeks, relying on the stars to guide us before hitting land. The both of us were scared but acted brave. The tales of raids were grand and soon we would be in them. But soon we saw what a raid was really like. We were killing farmers and religious men who didn't know how to defend themselves. We were wolves in a sheep pen. Linna saw how bothered I was and agreed to flee with me as soon as we got back. We left our family behind and together went inland. It wasn't easy, we were both young and spent most nights hungry and cold. We thought we had enough skills to sustain ourselves but soon we were traveling from clan to clan begging for food. But we had each other, and that was enough for us. As we were traveling we heard tales of the villages across the ocean moving their silver inland and away from the shores. That they began to build walls and better defenses. Clans began to panic. Their lands were infertile and couldn't rely on farming alone to sustain all. With this change came a new age. Rather than raiding innocents and fighting for honor clans began expand their craftsmanship and trade. This made it easier for Linna and I to find work and blood relations were no longer needed to be a member of a clan. The people we used to raid brought not only their goods but requested us to follow their religion in order to continue trading. Soon many people accepted this god and raids finally came to an end. Clans soon turned into villages and some chieftains became jarls and expanded their village. As these changes were happening we were staying in a barn in Dragekall. That is when Linna met Liv's father and we went our separate ways."

"Why did my mom never tell me?" Liv was amazed and confused. Finding it difficult to imagine her mother fighting and killing. Now that Halfdan said something, Linna punching her neighbor was starting to make sense.

"I think she was scared. I don't think she even told your father." Halfdan said, realizing he might have made things worse. "Your mother was a warrior out of fear."

"Do you miss Snjár?" Ulv asked. "Because I miss Dragekall."

"I'm homesick. But for a home I never had. Snjár wasn't a home." Halfdan looked down to keep from making eye contact.

There was an uncomfortable silence before Ulv broke it. "I think the fish is ready."

Everyone made happy sounds of gluttony as they ate. The portions were small, but they felt like they were eating the best fish that anyone has ever eaten before. Picking fish bones out of their mouths and flicking them into the woods. After drinking from the lake and feeling content, everyone laid down to sleep. The moon slowly began its dance across the sky as Liv gave up on sleeping. She sat on the log next to the fire looking up at the stars without a cloud in the sky to conceal their beauty. Thinking about home, being hurt by her neighbors, never seeing her parents and brother again kept Liv awake. It's easy to ignore the pain when you're busy but now there was nothing to distract her.

She watched as Ulv rolled onto his back and began snoring. Liv smiled to herself. There was a time where snoring made her livid, but now it brings back memories of spending the night with her family. Right as Liv began to feel her eyes getting heavy she heard a rustling near by. Unsure what to do Liv sat still with her eyes closed and listened. More rustling but even closer. Was it an animal? People looking to hurt them? Was there a more sinister reason why the doors to Rivinnsjo were closed? Liv's thundering heartbeat, along with Ulv's snoring, was making it difficult for her to hear. She didn't want to wake everyone up for a silly reason like an animal stirring in the dark. Perhaps deep down she was too afraid to yell out.

Liv calmed her nerves, telling herself it was most likely an animal looking for food or curious as to what they were doing. She opened her eyes to look around and instantly spotted two yellow eyes staring back at her. The figure was concealed in the forest as the eyes blinked and disappeared. Liv laid awake the rest of the night feeling watched the entire time.

CHAPTER 4

HULDUFOLK

Halfdan looked around the familiar room of the inn they were in the night before. The beds were made and tight. He walked and looked at his disfigured hands as he opened the door. Walking down the steps, avoiding of the sounds of the squeaking wood. The inn was empty and quiet with only a small mouse scurrying about on the counter. Halfdan's ears picked up a familiar sound, but it was muffled. He made his way to the main door, swiveled the simple block of wood keeping it locked. As Halfdan opened the door he heard distant screaming.

Fear rushed over Halfdan like warm water. He felt a pull, like he was falling down and suddenly woke up with a gasp. He never had such a vivid dream before. It seemed so real, he felt his surroundings with all of his senses. An overwhelming experience, similar to the dream he had back in Dragekall. Halfdan looked to see Liv staring at him, she looked just as worried.

When dawn was upon them Liv woke Ulv and Elora. She told them about Halfdan's vision and what she saw in the woods. Now that everyone was unsettled, the group promptly started to head back to Rivinnsjo. The brisk morning making them walk faster and squint their eyes. As they were approaching the door they could see a guard opening it to let some of the villagers out. Two well-dressed men with long bows and arrows out for a morning hunt. They didn't seem interested in talking to anyone so Halfdan walked up to the guard who was still standing by the door. The guard was wearing light leather armor and had dark circles under his eyes.

"We tried to come in yesterday, but the door was closed. Is everything alright?" Halfdan asked as friendly as he could.

"Ah." The guard said, sleepily. "A girl is missing. We decided to do a lockdown to see if anyone took her. Couldn't find her."

"What does she look like?" Liv asked, concerned for the stranger.

"Tall for her age and long dirty blond hair. Wearing a green dress and has a wooden bead necklace. If you see her, let us know." The guard said scripted as if he has been repeating himself for some time now as he rubbed his tired eyes.

"Do you think someone took her?" Liv asked again, wanting to know more.

The guard looked around to see if anyone was listening before speaking to Liv quietly. "Her step mother wants her to marry some merchant. He has money but is older than her. We locked the door to keep her in. But we can't keep the doors locked forever. I hope she ran away with some lover. I couldn't imagine selling my daughter off. But you didn't hear this from me. I'd do your business and take off soon if I were you, strangers."

Liv nodded her head to the guard and the group went inside. Liv never saw houses with so many decorative details and all of them had second levels. But she was no longer interested. She couldn't help but think about that girl. The whole group was thinking about her.

"I'm a dog and even I know that's not ok." Ulv said to the group disgusted.

"Unfortunately, people make life complicated for others. Love is something special that not everyone can afford. That's what makes people want it so bad." Halfdan paused for a moment to look around. "I know where the bakery is so we can get some bread. Then we can get out of here." He said, leading the group through the village that was slowly waking up.

Soon enough the group was out of Rivinnsjo and on their way to Kibera. Their bodies still sore from their travels the day before, but they kept up a good pace to try and make it to their next destination before nightfall. The sun was high in the sky when they heard some commotion ahead of them. Halfdan was going to tell his companions that they should be cautious but Liv, Ulv and Elora began running ahead to see what was going on. Halfdan got his axe ready and ran behind them.

They stopped to see a girl in a green dress, her skin complexion was similar to warm gold and fair. Her amber eyes burned with anger as she stood defensively as four men dressed in black clothing surrounded her. They cut down a tree to block the road. Trying to stop a merchant's wagon with goods, but thieves weren't picky. Oddly, rather than the girl being scared the men were. They pointed their swords at her but the tips were visibly shaking. The girl had her hair tucked behind her ears revealing that they were pointed.

"Get any closer and I'll curse you!" The girl yelled, with her hands up in a defensive pose constantly turning to keep her eyes on the thieves.

"Let her go!" Halfdan yelled, stepping closer to the group of men circling her. "The guards are on their way to collect the girl! Go now and I'll tell them you did no harm."

One man turned and ran into the woods, breaking formation, setting off the other men to run in different directions. The girl untucked her hair to cover her ears as Liv approached her.

"Are you ok?" Liv asked the young girl as she looked her over.

"You're not going to let the guards take me, are you?" The girl asked, sheepishly.

Liv winked at the girl with a smile. "We're heading to Kibera if you want to come with us? It's safer to stick together."

Halfdan walked up to the girl and handed her what they had left of the hearty brown and grainy bread. "Let's get out of here before they realize no guards are coming." He whispered.

The girl smiled and followed the group as they rolled their bodies over the fallen tree to continue on their path.

"My name is Ulv, what is your name?" Ulv said with glee, getting up close to the girl.

"Freyja." The girl said, leaning away from Ulv.

"Give her some space you menace." Elora scolded Ulv as she jumped on Liv's shoulders to rest. "My name is Elora. I possessed a cat. It's a long story."

"Honestly, after everything we've been through I'm not surprised the Hidden People are real." Halfdan told Freyja.

"I'm not supposed to tell anyone." Freyja said, ashamed of herself. "I'm only half *Huldufolk. My stepmother doesn't like my dad telling me about my mother. But my mother saved my father from starving in the woods when he got lost, he said that she was the most beautiful women he has ever laid eyes upon. Nine months later I was found on my father and step mother's doorstep. I was wrapped in elk skin and had this necklace." Freyja instinctively played with the necklace as she spoke. "It's the same necklace my father saw my mother wearing. That's all I have from my mother. I was hoping to get the Hidden People to take me to my mother, but none of them will talk to me. Humans don't like me much either, including my half siblings. They say I'm ugly and dirty."

Halfdan shook his head and spoke. "People are afraid of what they don't understand. I can't promise you that we can find your mother. But you can stay with us as long as you like."

"I think your siblings were just jealous. My brother used to say anything to get me upset when we were younger." Liv showed a faint smile. "Your secret is safe with us."

"Thank you." Freyja smiled back, less ashamed of herself. "What are you going to Kibera for? Do you live there?"

"We are looking for work." Halfdan stopped, turned and kneeled to be at face level with Freyja. "I want to be honest with you. The work we are going to do is going to be dangerous. We have enemies following us. At any time you want to go home all you have to do is tell us."

"I know." Freyja said, confidently. "We all have similar problems."

Halfdan nodded in agreeance as he stood up to continue leading the group to Kibera.

"You're a dog too?" Ulv asked Freyja as she took a bite of bread.

Freyja looked at Ulv surprised. "I think you're the only one with that problem."

Ulv crossed his arms and scowled.

"So we have a dog turned into a man and a woman trapped in a cat." Freyja spoke with some food still in her mouth.

"Halfdan has horrible powers to curse dogs into people and Liv has a dragon spirit." Ulv blurted out.

"Wow!" Freyja looked at Liv with big eyes. "Can you breathe fire?"

Liv wore a nervous smile and blushed. "It's really not that interesting."

"I can see in the dark!" Freyja said with contained energy. "But I can't see colors very well."

"Lucky." Ulv said with distaste. "I miss seeing in the dark. I feel so vulnerable."

"Perhaps someone in Kibera will be able to turn you back into a dog." Freyja said with her eyes still fixed onto Liv.

The group heard some rustling in the forest near them. Frightened it might be the thieves again they quickened their pace. The closer they got to Kibera the more they could smell it. The sun was getting ready to set when they laid their eyes on Kibera. Liv was impressed and if it wasn't for the smell she would have been jumping with joy.

Liv never saw so many people packed into one place. Since Kibera was built on a hill Liv could see an old wall that was once used to protect the people that resided, but now houses overflowed and went beyond the wall. A wide and rapid river cut through the city and fed into the ocean, where boats, large and small, moved about. In the middle of the city was a large fortress where the Jarl lived. The land once had more enthralled than free, exporting slaves was the reason why Kibera once did so well. Kibera, formally called

Bekkr in front of the Jarl and his Karls, got its unformal name due to its poor state. In this new age raids for slaves are in the works of being abolished.

As the group looked upon Kibera, Halfdan thought about Freyja. "Freyja, I think we will have to change your clothes."

Freyja looked at Halfdan confused.

"Your dress looks expensive. It will draw unwanted attention." Halfdan explained.

"Maybe we can rough it up a bit." Elora suggested.

Liv saw the sad look Freyja's face made at Elora's suggestion. "How about you wear this cloak? If we find a dress you like we can buy it. When we make some money that is. Elora, can you ride on Freya's shoulders then. Without the cloak your nails are sharp."

Elora knew it was really to keep an eye on Freyja. She jumped off and stretched her feline body lazily. Liv took off the cloak and put it around Freyja. Without the cloak's fuzzy wolf pelt collar, Liv's bob cut hair that was forced upon her was more noticeable. The cuts were uneven, but her blond wavy hair concealed it well. Freyja was shorter than Liv so the cloak dragged on the ground slightly, but it would have to do.

Halfdan stared at everyone to make sure they were paying attention before he spoke. "When we get in, keep your eyes from meeting others. Don't let anyone pressure you into buying anything. If someone is asking for help, assume it's a trap. If you get lost, only ask a guard where Norvick's Inn is. If the guard wants you to follow them in a direction where you are out of sight, don't. It's not easy living in Kibera, it brings the worst in people. We need to stick together."

Elora rolled her yellow eyes and jumped onto Freyja's shoulders. As they made their way closer to Kibera the city began to look bigger and bigger. The houses on the outskirts look new compared to the ones deeper within the city. People trying to sell goods made the streets even more crowded. Horses pulling wagons pushed through the crowds of people and would relieve themselves in the street. Along with people tossing dirty water out onto the dirt roads, making the dirt roads muddy. Freyja did her best to lift the cloak to keep it from dragging on the ground.

All around them was a flair of emotions. People having good days. People having bad days, yelling or getting beaten by guards for stealing food. Voices speaking strange languages and dressed in foreign clothing. Stands and stores were selling things that they have never seen before. Herbs with odd smells, artwork with different mediums, cloth with intricate patterns, animals that you could only have dreamed of before. Liv was busy looking around when she caught sight of a man selling his thrall to someone else in exchange for a fine cloak. She met eyes with the thrall who looked back at Liv. Her heart sank and the thrall was tugged along with his new master.

Liv felt someone reach for her hand, it was Freyja. Liv looked at her with a sad smile. Freyja smiled back and led Liv to Halfdan who was still pressing forward. They soon came upon an old building. A sign hung out and swayed in the wind. There were no words on the sign, just a carved picture of a drinking horn overflowing with mead.

Halfdan opened up the door to let Liv, Elora and Freyja in. It took him a moment to realize someone was missing. "Where is Ulv?"

"I thought he was behind us." Liv looked back into the busy street.

Halfdan let out an irritated sigh. "Of course there are no guards when you need them. It will be best if we wait here for him."

"Are you sure that's a good plan?" Liv asked, not reassured that Ulv will find them.

"What do you want me to do? Put up missing dog posters?" Halfdan took a moment to calm himself. "He is smarter than you think. We will wait here for a while, if he doesn't show up then we will go looking for him."

"Halfdan! What are you waiting for? Come on in!" Yelled the inn keep across the inn and behind the counter. His inn was decorated with items from Constantinople and Islamic markets along with posters on the wall. Mercenaries were looking at the posters while drinking their mead and ale out of wood mugs with metal handles. Pulling down posters for work that they wanted to claim.

"Hello Norvick!" Halfdan walked up to the bar. Freyja and Liv followed.

A young lady came running out from the back, she had a heart shaped face with long curly hair. Wearing a blue apron dress she gave Halfdan a hug and spoke with a British Isles accent. "I recognize that voice! I told Norvick that you would come back. I need to keep stirring the mead, but I'll come back out to talk." The young lady waved before she disappeared again.

"She's right, you know. I was thinking about going through that chest you left here." Norvick let out a hearty laugh. His bald head gleaming and his thick beard moved with the laugh. "Now who are these beautiful young ladies you have here?"

"This is Liv, Linna's daughter." Halfdan put his hand on Liv's shoulder. "And this is Freyja, and the cat is Elora."

"Linna's daughter, huh. Halfdan used to talk about your mother a lot!" Norvick let out another jolly laugh.

"I need to know if there is any work for a runaway." Halfdan said, trying to change the topic.

"I assume it's for a runaway freeborn, not a thrall. Either way, if they are your friend I'll make sure to not give out the job." Norvick smiled at Halfdan before picking up a mug, dipping it into a kettle filled with mead and handing it to Halfdan. "Are you looking for any other work?" Norvick asked while getting another mug ready for Liv. "How long will you be in Kibera?"

"Depends on the kind of work I pick up. Something... simple?" Halfdan asked.

"Simple doesn't pay well. Since when do you ask for *simple* work?" Norvick asked, handing Liv a drink. Getting another one ready for Freyja.

"Ugh, I think Freyja would like a water. Do you have any food?" Halfdan asked Norvick.

Norvick shrugged and put the mug back and went into the kitchen.

"Sorry, I just don't think kids should drink." Halfdan apologized to Freyja.

"I'm thirteen." Freyja said, disappointed.

"Yeah, a kid. I'm already helping you find a home. Not run away and party." Halfdan whispered.

"But I am old enough to be married?" Freyja replied, pushing Halfdan's buttons.

Halfdan let out a big sigh and pushed his mead across the counter towards Freyja. "Ok, take a sip without making a face. Then you can have as many mugs of mead and ale as you want."

Elora sneered and Liv leaned over to watch Freyja take a big sip. As soon as the thick fermented hops and honey hit her tongue she let out a full body expression of revulsion.

"Why would you drink this?" Freyja said with total disgust.

Halfdan smiled as he pulled back his mead, basking in Liv and Elora's laughter.

Norvick came out of the kitchen holding a tray with four wooden bowls. Three of them heaping with beef stew with carrots and potatoes and one with milk. Placing the stew down with broth running over the edge.

"And milk for the kitty cat." Norvick gently placed the bowl down in front of Elora and went to pet her.

"Don't." Elora said sternly, batting Norick's hand.

Norvick retracted his hand and looked wide eyed at Halfdan.

"Yeah, that cat isn't really a cat." Halfdan looked around to make sure no one was looking at them. "I'll tell you later."

"I've seen a lot, but never-" Norvick was interrupted by a man slamming open the door.

Everyone in the inn stopped to see a city guard, distinguished with leather arm cuffs with the city seal on it, escorting Ulv. The guard had Ulv by the triceps and looked angry. Old scarred cuts on the guard's face made him look menacing, and his large muscles made Ulv look like a small boy.

"I'm looking for this man's keeper." The guard said with a deep demanding voice. "I caught him trying to make a dog his wife."

The inn was silent for a moment before the patrons erupted in laughter. Halfdan turned around and chugged his mead.

"What should we do?" Liv whispered to Halfdan.

"Don't tell me you are associated with this man?" Norvick leaned on the counter as he asked Halfdan.

"Take care of my freaks if the guard kills me, will you?" Halfdan jokingly asked Norvick, slammed his empty mug down before turning around and making his way to the guard.

"Hi Halfdan!" Ulv yelled happily over the laughter.

"Shush, would you?" Halfdan said sternly not wanting other patrons to hear his name being affiliated with a man courting a dog.

"Outside." The guard said, glaring at Halfdan as he tightened his grip on Ulv.

Halfdan gulped. "Whatever you say."

"I kind of want to watch." Elora said, quietly.

"You're not going to want to watch. Not from here anyway, we can watch from upstairs." Norvick said before heading upstairs.

Liv and Elora looked at one another before running after Norvick. Freyja shoved some food in her mouth and followed.

CHAPTER 10

DRAGON FEVER

Halfdan walked back into the inn with Ulv beside him. Patrons snickering at them and making comments. Liv, Elora and Freyja came running down the steps; quickly sitting down, trying to act like nothing happened. Norvick was walking slowly behind them.

"I saw you all poking your heads out the window to watch." Halfdan hissed through his teeth.

"You were always good at getting out of situations." Norvick commented, getting Halfdan another mug of mead.

"I got lucky." Halfdan said, taking the mug from Norvick. "I told the guard that Ulv ate too many panther cap mushrooms as a kid and was never the same. Apparently his father did the same but with black henbane."

"Ah… I think we should talk." Norvick said before turning his head to call out. "Beatrice!"

The young lady that spoke with the British Isles accent came out. Her hands on her hips showing her irritation.

"Can you keep an eye on the inn for a moment?" Norvick asked confidently but wore a nervous crooked smile.

"Don't take too long. The mead isn't done yet and I still have the ale to make." Beatrice told Norvick, watching him walk upstairs with Halfdan. She then looked at Ulv who was eating Halfdan's stew. "So… did you?"

"No! I was being a gentleman and asked her first." Ulv said, disheartened as he looked at the stew. "She wasn't interested."

"Ok, I was wondering the same thing." Elora blurted.

Beatrice looked shocked at the cat and then back at Ulv. "Perhaps I should not be the one to brew mead anymore."

"No, no there is a simple explanation. The cat is a person and Ulv here was a dog." Liv told Beatrice as if it was common knowledge.

There was an awkward pause before Freyja spoke. "It's easier not to think about it."

"We shouldn't talk about it much where others can listen. I'm sure Halfdan is explaining everything to Norvick and he is making scenes of it." Liv told Beatrice between bites of stew.

Upstairs in his office Norvick shook his head at Halfdan. "None of this makes sense."

"I know it's hard to believe." Halfdan pleaded.

"So..." Norvick deepened his brow in thought. "You betrayed Frode. Blackhare's men shot you full of arrows. After all of that, Frode still chose to save you. With your new found powers you decide to use it to take a baby lindwurm's soul and give it to Liv, in the process burning your hands. Since the lindwurm's baby is dead it takes its anger out on Dragekall. In turn the villagers decide to take their anger out on Liv and sell you to this Magnus guy, who is being manipulated by Blackhare. That's where you meet Elora, but she was a mouse then. You end up finding Liv again. In your travels you find a girl who is running away from an arranged marriage with an older guy. After all of this, you decide the best place to go is my inn."

Halfdan was stunned with a lack of words. The word betrayed still stung, but it was the correct word to use. "Uh... Yeah." Was all he was able to murmur.

Norvick leaned against the wall and crossed his arms. "Honestly... If my Beatrice was dying and you were holding out on me, I could have done the same." Norvick looked at Halfdan like a mad dog and talked sternly. "Promise me, if Blackhare's men start to sniff their ugly noses around here you need to disappear."

"Understood." Halfdan said, still stung by Norvick's sum up of his life thus far.

"If this Blackhare business blows over, I need you to come back here in the spring." Norvick demanded.

Halfdan looked at Norvick confused.

Norvick spoke with a big grin that lit up his face. "I'm taking her back home."

Back downstairs Beatrice kept a skeptical eye on Elora, praying under her breath. She felt that ever since coming to this foreign land that it was inhabited by heathens, sure the cat was a demon. Elora could tell that she made Beatrice uneasy and that brought her mischievous joy.

Liv could tell that Beatrice was uneasy as she moved about. "How do you know Halfdan?" Liv asked, knowing that getting someone to talk about themselves usually makes them feel more comfortable.

Beatrice got a shy look at her face. She wasn't used to people asking about her. "It's a long story."

"It's ok, we got time." Liv said, intrigued.

Beatrice began to nervously clean the counter as she talked. "I was taken with my mother when I was very young. I was fortunate enough to stay with her when we were brought here. We worked as farm hands in the town over. My mother protected me from the advances of our master and his friends. She stood up for me and they beat her to death. They left her where she fell. When you're in thralled there is no respect when you are alive and less when you die. I stayed with my mother, fighting off dogs and vultures with a stick. Norivck was looking for his wife and daughter who disappeared and Halfdan accompanied him, helping him the best he could. They ran out of leads of his wife and daughter's whereabouts and were making their way back. That's when they found me. They helped me bury my mother's body and Norvick bought me with the last of his money. I don't remember everything, but I do remember Norvick asking me what my name was. He never referred to me as his thrall. I am blessed." Beatrice leaned in to whisper. "He even lets me keep my tips."

Liv was shocked, almost regretting that she asked. She looked down at her bowl. It was empty, she didn't even remember eating all of it.

"Oh, do you want more?" Beatrice asked with a smile.

"Yes, please." Ulv asked, holding out his bowl.

Beatrice took everyone's bowls and went in back.

"And I thought my life was rough." Elora blurted.

"I feel horrible for her." Freyja added, thinking about the thralls that her father owns.

"I can't believe that Halfdan didn't tell me. If I would have known I wouldn't have pressured her." Liv said upset at herself.

"If she didn't want to talk about it she would have said so." Elora said in a not so comforting tone. "She said that she is blessed, that means she is fine."

Liv looked at Freyja, who looked deep in thought. Before Liv could ask Freyja if she was ok Beatrice walked back in. With three bowls in hand she distributed them but deliberately didn't get Elora more milk. All Elora did was scowl at Beatrice, who in return ignored her. Beatrice worked hard helping other patrons. Refilling their drinks or reading the posters on the wall to those who were illiterate.

Liv decided to save her second serving of stew for Halfdan. Watching Freyja and Ulv scarf down their food. She then began to look at the posters on the wall. Looking at the odd symbols. How the lines and shapes put together had meaning.

Elora walked across the counter to Liv and laid down. "You don't know how to read, do you?"

Liv looked at Elora with anger and vulnerability. "Of course I know how to read."

"Then read for me. What do those posters say?" Elora said with glee.

"I thought you weren't supposed to be talking." Liv said with the tips of her ears turning red.

Beatrice walked over, dipping her fingers in a water bucket and flicked her fingers at Elora. Sending water droplets flying at her, wetting her fur. "Bad demon cat." Beatrice murmured under her breath.

Liv and Freyja both snickered as Ulv wore a faint smile. Elora looked around and saw people staring so she bit her tongue.

"Being unletterd is not uncommon. I can read some of the better ones to you." Beatrice offered to Liv with a smile.

"I would appreciate that, thank you. Ulv, can you save this for Halfdan?" Liv pushed her bowl of stew towards Ulv.

Ulv nodded and watched Liv follow Beatrice. Freyja quickly finished the last bit of her stew and joined them.

Elora got up and plopped herself in front of Ulv. "You're quiet."

"I'm just sick of being confused." Ulv sighed. "When do you stop feeling embarrassed?"

"You don't. You have to learn to stop caring. It actually took me some time to learn how to transform properly. Once I was transforming into a beautiful woman. Imagining her face, long beautiful hair, slim long arms and legs. I imagined everything but her backside. I walked into town with a horse tail sticking out from under my skirt. Before, when I would remember that day it would sting. But it's funny now, because I am sharing it with you."

Ulv ran his fingers through his hair and pulled out a feather. "Even as a dog I loved watching the birds. Now as a man I watch them and feel envy. To be as free as a bird and go anywhere you wish." He twirled the feather in his fingers. "Have you ever transformed into a bird before?"

"No. I've actually never heard of a shapeshifter transforming into a bird. Just tales of the old gods turning into birds." Elora told Ulv, watching him play with the feather.

Ulv smelled the feather and continued to examine it. "I think it's an owl feather. I found it while we were traveling. Do you think you could use it and tell me what it's like to fly?" Ulv put the feather down for Elora to look at.

Elora batted the feather like a cat. "I can try. It's going to take me a while to transform. The detail of each feather might take longer than fur."

Ulv heard steps squeaking and looked to see Halfdan and Norvick coming back downstairs. Norvick went back into the kitchen and Halfdan sat down next to Ulv.

Ulv pushed the bowl of stew to Halfdan. "Liv saved you some."

"Thanks." Halfdan said as he took a big scoop and finally ate with content.

Liv ran up and sat next to Halfdan. "I found some work for us! We will be looking for a horse thief!"

Halfdan shook his head and talked with his mouth full. "Nope, I already talked to Norvick and selected something better."

"Oh?" Liv said and tilted her head, curious.

"We will be keeping an eye on a pond. The young men of a village keep mysteriously drowning. Everyone else is busy with the fall harvest, they have a place for us to sleep and modest pay." Halfdan said as he took another spoonful of food.

"That sounds boring, what is the honor in that? Also, we have a young man with us." Liv gestured to Ulv.

Halfdan smiled imagining Ulv drowning. He shook his head back into reality. "It's safe and easy. Going out and hunting people is dangerous. You are fighting people who have nothing to lose. When people have nothing it makes them unpredictable. Making sure I keep everyone alive until we all have proper weapons and experience is my priority."

Liv grumbled in dissatisfaction and walked back to Beatrice and Freyja.

Halfdan caught Ulv looking at him with big sad eyes. "I won't let you drown." Halfdan said angrily.

"What? No, I just wanted to know if you are going to finish your food?" Ulv asked, looking hopeful.

Halfdan slid his bowl back to Ulv and watched Beatrice lead Liv and Freyja into the kitchen. Too tired to care he watched Ulv eat the stew, barely chewing.

Norvick came back out from the kitchen with his own bowl of stew. "Every year I have less and less honey for mead. I'm going to have to learn how to make whiskey or wine to get me by."

"That dirt water the *gauls like to drink?" Halfdan asked, disappointed.

"I have to adapt or else I'll get stuck in the past. You know that better than anyone." Norvick smiled again as he spoke. "Beatrice seems happy, not a lot of women come in here for her to talk too."

"It doesn't help that when young men try to talk to her, you strong arm them. What are you going to do when she is gone?" Halfdan asked, watching Norvick's grin go away.

"I hope that if someone has my daughter that they would bring her home. I have done a lot of bad in the world. When I exported thralls across the oceans I treated them like livestock. Like they were less than human. It made it easier to deal with. I can still hear them crying, making me wonder about them." Norvick shook his head. "We have talked about this before."

"I hate to do this to you, but together we only have twelve silver." Halfdan said with hurt pride.

Norvick let out a hearty laugh. "I still owe you money for helping me rent this place. You and your friends will always have a room ready for you here."

"Be careful with what you're offering. With the willingness of people to join I'll have a village following me around soon." Halfdan said with little amusement, taking a big chug of his mead and placing it on the counter empty.

Outside Beatrice led Liv and Freyja through the city, pushing their way through the crowds until they were standing outside a trade shop. Beatrice nodded to a man who made eye contact with her out the window. He nodded back and without a word Beatrice walked through a thin alleyway and waited by the back door. The young man who nodded earlier came out and slowly closed the door. Liv could tell he was enslaved. He was thin and clothes were old, but he looked happy to see Beatrice. He eyed Liv and quickly glanced at Freyja.

"Do you have a shield or any weapon you can part with?" Beatrice asked, quietly.

"What do you have to trade?" The young man asked, not as equally secretive.

Beatrice saw Liv move her hand to grab some silver and grabbed her arm, stopping her. "Can we do a trade like we did before?"

The man grinned and nodded.

"Do you have any clothing you can part with?" Beatrice whispered to Liv.

Liv felt her face warm and became flustered. Unsure on what to make of the situation. "Um, I guess I don't need my apron." Liv took off the brown apron and handed it to the man. With the apron in hand the man promptly turned around and opened the door. Before he could slip in Liv saw the man hold the apron to his face and take a big inhale.

"He was ok with an apron? I had to give him some of my undergarments for a dagger." Beatrice said, disappointed.

Liv was at a loss for words. Feeling violated in a way.

"What? Would you have rather given him your silver? Your coin bag looks empty, I was only trying to help. You aren't even working in a kitchen, you look odd trying to get mercenary work wearing an apron." Beatrice said to defend herself.

Liv relived her memories of making the apron with her mother. Then she thought about those thieves who surrounded Freyja before. An apron doesn't do much good to defend a person. Liv let out a deep sigh. "You're right."

The door opened again and out came the man handing Liv an old battle worn shield and spear. Caked with dust from sitting around and dirt from heavy use. The man jumped a little when he heard someone yelling for him in the shop. He promptly closed the door without a word. Beatrice and Freyja got close to look at the shield and spear with Liv. The leather straps for the shield were old and dry and the spear head was beginning to rust.

"Let's go back, I can help you clean up your spear and shield." Beatrice said as she turned to head back.

"Do you have any paint?" Freyja asked. "I've seen artwork of shield maidens. Their shields always had beautiful designs on them."

"I'll have to look." Beatrice thought for a moment before looking at Liv. "I'm sorry if that interaction made you uncomfortable. That man we talked to use to play lead roles dressed as a women back home. He still does shows in secret once in a while, to remind us of home."

"Why don't they use a real woman in your acts back home?" Freyja asked, confused at Beatrice's homeland customs.

"The *nobby thought it was indecent for women to do public performances for money." Beatrice said with a shrug.

Liv began to feel out of place again. She didn't know how to read, what public performances they were talking about and what nobby meant. Liv looked at Freyja who seemed to understand, making her feel more embarrassed.

The three young women began to make their way back. Watching their step as the sun began to set, the buildings casting large shadows in the street.

"I'd rather not have Norvick find out I traded my undergarments once for a knife." Beatrice said and chuckled.

"Why did you do that anyway?" Freyja asked, innocently.

"If my mother had a blade perhaps she wouldn't have been taken. Fighting back is better than to surrendering, that's what I have learned. I didn't understand that Norvick was buying my freedom at the time. Now I have my own silver and could have bought it. Never-the-less, I still keep the blade on me." Beatrice pulled out a blade that was hidden under her apron. "I'll never let anyone take me again."

"What was your homeland like?" Liv asked Beatrice as they walked inside the inn.

"Last that I remember it was on fire. Norvick was going to take me back in the spring and help me look for family, if I have any left. But I'm worried that I won't fit in anymore, that I've been here for too long." Beatrice said with a sad but focused expression.

Liv looked at Freyja, both unsure on what to say. They weren't kidnapped and in thralled. It was difficult to relate to Beatrice.

"I'm sure you are ready to go home and never look back. I wish I could see your home land. It sounds interesting." Liv said, trying to lighten the mood.

"When I get back I want to stay up all night and wait for the first light. I want to see if the morning air smells different." Beatrice made sure her knife was tucked away as she held the door open to the inn.

Before Liv took three steps in Halfdan turned around to greet them.

"Where did you find that antique?" Halfdan slurred as his body rocked back and forth on his seat.

Liv stared at Halfdan for a while until she realized what he was talking about. "My shield and spear aren't that old. Not much of a relic as your axe." Liv said with a smirk

Norvick laughed, causing patrons to look to see what they were laughing at.

Halfdan grabbed his axe and jokingly tried to console it as if Liv hurt the object's feelings. Not a moment later Halfdan snapped his head to look at Norvick. "Get me my chest."

Norvick rolled his eyes and walked upstairs. After some commotion Norvick came back downstairs with a large chest and slammed it on the counter in front of Halfdan. Norvick left to attend to other patrons as Halfdan dusted off the chest. It was old and had many nicks and the lock was missing as if someone used force to get it off. The chest creaked as it was opened and let out a musty odor, reminding Halfdan of when he was imprisoned and left in the dark at Rossvatnet. Halfdan pushed the memory away, sobering him up a bit.

Liv, Ulv, Elora, Freyja and Beatrice leaned in close to see what was inside the chest. First Halfdan pulled out an old deer pelt and then a blanket that had some deer fur on it. Under the blanket were two old daggers, simple in design but sharp.

Halfdan could see Freyja staring intensely at one of the daggers and handed it to her. "People would pay me in what they had, I don't need a dagger anyway."

Freyja accepted the dagger with a smile and unsheathed the dagger to look at it more intently.

Halfdan looked around to see if anyone else was looking before removing a false bottom. In the secret compartment were three cloth covered items. Halfdan unwrapped one of them revealing a whetstone and handed it to Liv. Before Liv could thank Halfdan he began to unwrap the second item revealing five unmarked gold coins.

"You've had gold this whole time and you wanted us to sleep outside hungry?" Liv whispered to Halfdan.

"This is my emergency *bribe the guard to let me out of the dungeon* money. Not *live like a Jarl for one night* money." Halfdan whispered as quietly as an intoxicated person could.

"How can you bribe a guard if the gold is here?" Beatrice whispered.

"Norvick knows it's here, he would come looking for me eventually. Now all of you know if something happens to me. Only in an emergency." Halfdan said as he pointed his finger at all of them.

"What's that?" Liv asked, pointing to the third covered item.

"Nothing." He quickly as he began to put the false bottom back to cover it up. "Just a backup whetstone, it doesn't work very well."

"I would sharpen weapons for extra money, so I have some experience. I can help you if you want?" Beatrice offered Liv.

"You were going to look for paint too?" Freyja asked, eager to decorate Liv's shield.

Liv could hear Beatrice say something, but she wasn't listening. Instead, Liv looked at Halfdan. She would wake up to Halfdan tossing and turning, murmuring in his sleep every night since he came back from being captured by Magnus. His inability to get decent sleep and travel lead to Halfdan being more susceptible to the mead.

"Why don't you go to bed?" Liv suggested to Halfdan, grabbing the chest to bring back upstairs.

"Ok." Halfdan said disappointed as if he was a child being scolded.

"I'll be back." Liv said to the rest of the group who were busy talking amongst themselves.

Standing up and doing her best to carry the large awkward chest as she followed Halfdan. Nervously watching him stumble up the stairs, knowing that if Halfdan fell back he would take her out. Halfdan walked down the hall and opened a door to a room that he had stayed in before. The room was small but enough to sleep in. Halfdan walked up to the bed, looked at it for a moment then flopped his body onto it. The small bed squeaked with the force of Halfdan's body.

Liv quickly put the chest down in the corner of the room and stretched her arms. She turned to tell Halfdan goodnight but she could hear him snoring face down in the bed.

"That was quick." Liv said quietly to herself.

Liv looked at the chest again then back at Halfdan. "Are you awake?" Liv asked a little louder with no response.

Liv quietly moved the chest away from the wall and slowly opened it. Taking out the deer skin and laying it on the floor to quietly place the fake bottom on it. Liv took all five of the gold pieces and replaced them with five silver. She was ready to put the false bottom back when she noticed the supposed second whetstone. Deep down Liv knew it couldn't have been another whetstone, if it was no good then why hide it?

Slowly, Liv unwrapped the mystery item to find a small wooden box. Liv took the lid off the box to find a simple wooden horse that looked like it was carved by hand. As Liv picked up the wooden horse to examine it she saw an old hammered ring under it. The ring was small and thin, meant more for a woman than a man. Halfdan rolled over in his sleep, making Liv jump a little and made the ring rattle in the box.

Liv quietly but quickly put the chest back together and tip-toed out of the room. After slowly closing the door to the room Liv let out a sigh of relief and made her way downstairs. She saw Freyja painting the shield with a put together paintbrush, tuft of fur tied to a stick, and black ink. Ulv and Elora watched Freyja paint as Beatrice sharpened her spear. Next to Beatrice were other patron's weapons. After seeing her use the whetstone the patrons paid Beatrice to sharpen their arms as they drank.

CHAPTER 11

THE WOLF AND THE DOG DO NOT PLAY TOGETHER. HÁVAMÁL ~ NORSE PROVERB

Halfdan woke with a sudden throbbing in his head. He slowly opened his eyes to look around the room to get his bearings, daybreak slowly lighting the room. Norvick enjoyed overserving Halfdan, causing him to wake up with head pains every time he stayed at his inn. The urge to hydrate motivated Halfdan to get out of bed, making his head pound harder. Halfdan shuffled down the hall and down the steps onto the main floor. On the counter Halfdan saw that Liv's shield had a dragon painted on it in a circular motion, so it looked like the dragon was biting its tail.

Halfdan shuffled into the kitchen and found a bucket of water. Dipping a ladle in the water and taking a slow sip, letting the water invigorate his body. Shuffling out of the kitchen and into the drinking hall, Halfdan looked at the small fireplace. He grabbed a poker and looked for embers but the ashes were cold. Halfdan grabbed some logs that were next to the fireplace and placed them within before taking a few steps back.

"Ignis." Halfdan whispered as he snapped his fingers as quietly as he could.

A burst of flames reached out and up from the fireplace. Halfdan fell back and instinctively shielded his face from the heat. When Halfdan looked back at the fireplace he saw that a tapestry above it caught on fire. Halfdan sprung up and grabbed the tapestry, ripped it off the wall and tossed it in the fireplace in a panic. The heat of the flames aggravated Halfdan's hands, as if his skin remembers the feeling of being burned. Halfdan rubbed his hands as he watched the tapestry burn and smoke up the room.

"No playing with magic indoors." Halfdan whispered to himself as he listened to footsteps upstairs making their way down the steps.

The first one down the stairs was Norvick. Halfdan could tell that Norvick noticed that the tapestry was gone almost instantly.

"It was a bad idea to hang that over the fireplace anyway." Norvick told Halfdan as he patted him on the shoulder and joined in watching the tapestry burn. "I packed you a bag with some soap and a comb. You should care about how you look."

"Subtle, thank you Norvick." Halfdan said with a neutral tone.

"You're not a lone wolf anymore. It can make things more complicated at times, but you will get used to it faster than you think." Norvick stretched his back and began to walk towards the kitchen as he spoke. "Let me start some breakfast so you and your companions are well fed and ready to travel."

Halfdan tried his best to help Norvick cook but was promptly kicked out of the kitchen. The smell of breakfast brought Ulv and Elora downstairs. It took Halfdan a moment to recognize Elora who now was in the form of an eagle owl, large with her feather mottled with brown specks and barred wings and tail. Feathery ears and large orange eyes gave Elora an unusually friendly appearance. Ulv carried her and placed her on the counter, her talons clinking on the wood as she tried to steady herself.

Liv, Freyja and Beatrice came running down the stairs and looked at Elora in amazement. None of them saw an owl up close before. They asked Elora to fly but unlike a true graceful owl she fluttered about like a drunk butterfly and hit the floor with a thud.

Norvick prepared everyone a breakfast of smoked salmon, eggs and sliced tomatoes. Everyone ate and talked about their nights. Liv, Freyja and Beatrice talked late into the night and watched a play that was cut short by the city guards. Elora made up a story of her and Ulv catching an owl. In reality Ulv found an empty room upstairs and protected Elora as she transformed.

Norvick talked about a rude customer who thought Norvick was reading the posters incorrectly to other patrons. Norvick asked the accuser to read the posts then, but it turns out the customer was illiterate.

Soon it was time to go. Halfdan, Liv, Freyja and Ulv gave heartfelt goodbyes with hopes of seeing Norvick and Beatrice again in the spring. Halfdan carried his axe and a simple leather bag packed by Norvick, Liv armed herself with her new shield and spear, Ulv carried Elora and Freyja hid her knife under the cloak as they walked outside. Starting off on a new journey full and well rested, they headed out of Kibera and continued north to follow along the ocean's edge before making their way inland to the village of Thorpe.

Their skin still tacky from the salty air the group made their way to Thorpe well before sundown. Walking into a small village it was obvious that all who resided here were farmers, relying on Kibera for protection and nothing else. Villagers looked at Halfdan and his companions, obviously judging them for being outsiders and weary to approach them. The group awkwardly made their way to the middle of the village square and stood there, unsure on where to go.

Ulv noticed a man stepping out of his house and making his way toward them with a young boy following behind him. Three small children tried their best to look out the windows, one jumping up and down to try to get a better look. The man was covered in dust and dark circles around his eyes making him look older than he really was. Despite being overworked the man had a friendly grin and extended his hand to Halfdan. Halfdan took the stranger's hand and could feel calluses and dirt on it.

The man talked as he squeezed Halfdan's hand while he shook it. "You must be here answering the job posting we put out in Kibera. You cannot understand how grateful we are that you are here. My name is Sindri."

"I am Halfdan," Then using his free hand to point to his companions as he introduced them to Sindri. "This here is Liv, Ulv,

Freyja and the owl is Elora. Tell me about this pond we are supposed to look over."

Sindri let go of Halfdan's hand and looked around a moment before he spoke, his grin disappearing. "If the other villagers seem distant it is because of this pond. We keep telling the boys to stay away from it, but…" Sindri looked down at the young boy who followed him out and was hiding behind him, gripping his father's pant leg. Sindri put his hand on the boy's head. "We need you to keep our boys from going to that pond. I've been neglecting my fields to watch over it. Ever since my father died I had to pick up responsibility as leader of Thorpe. Let me tell you, being a leader is fun until people start to die."

Halfdan was going to try to get Sindri back on track before Liv spoke up.

"I'm sorry about your father. What did he die of, if you don't mind me asking?"

"Old age, fortunate enough. Passed away in his sleep three months ago. Before all the drownings started." Sindri spoke with a heavy heart. Obviously missing his father's guidance.

"How many boys have drowned in this pond? Any similarities?" Halfdan asked, curious.

"Four. The first was Tyr, he was about twelve. Then Ivar, the baby of his family, he was nine. Gunnar was sixteen and was a strong swimmer, I know that. Birger, Dustin's only son, was fifteen. No one knows why they were at the pond alone or why they went into the pond." Sindri turned his head to speak to his son and spoke to him softly as if not to frighten him. "Oakley, can you go back by mother. Let her know I'm taking these fine folk to the pond."

The boy sheepishly nodded his head and ran off towards the house. Halfdan could hear the other children yelling to Oakley as he opened the door.

Sindri grinned as he watched his son step inside and closed the door. "I have nightmares of finding him in the pond next. As soon as I stop the drownings I'll find a new leader for my people."

Sindri spoke as if he was reassuring himself. There was a moment of silence before Sindri spoke again. "Follow me, the pond is close."

Sindri led the way as villagers looked and whispered to one another. Liv, Ulv, and Freyja huddled close to Halfdan as he followed Sindri.

"Any leads on the cause of the drownings?" Halfdan asked, trying to feel out the situation.

Sindri waved his hand in the air as if to dismiss Halfdan's question. "If I knew you wouldn't be here. If I had more evidence I could have city guards here to help. I talked to everyone in Thorpe and all I get are more questions. People are pointing fingers or growing more superstitious. Perhaps it is something more innocent, boys trying to prove their strength or courage. All I ask is that you guard the pond, it is off limits to everyone. We have a well and a river for water so don't let anyone guilt you. I'll be out in the fields helping with the fall harvest. My wife will come out and bring you food, but I'll be honest, I wasn't expecting four of you."

"We will manage." Halfdan said with confidence. Certain that they will have plenty of time to look for food as long as one person is guarding the pond.

Soon the pond was in view. Like Sindri said, it was close to the village. The pond was surrounded by trees so it was somewhat hidden and secluded. The sun was hitting the pond so it was shimmering, making it hard to think of it taking the lives of four boys. Little fish swam by the water's edge and bugs made the pond hum with life. The water was clear and inviting, as if it was beckoning to be swam in.

Sindri showed the group the structure he built, it had three walls and a roof. Enough to protect from the rain and keep an eye on the pond. It would be a tight squeeze for all of them and Sindri offered his house if there was ever a storm. There was some fire wood and a fire pit for the night. Sindri left to get some more blankets and food for the evening. Halfdan, Liv, Ulv, Elora and Freyja watched as Sindri walked away. As soon as Sindri was out of earshot the group began examining the shelter with more scrutiny.

"This is not what I imagined when I read that we would have a place to stay." Halfdan said with a sour look.

"I miss Norvick's inn already." Freyja said sadly as she sat under the structure disappointed.

"It's starting to get too cold to sleep outside. How long until these people finish their harvest? Their fields looked hardly worked on, it could take weeks." Liv said irritably as she placed her shield and spear down before rubbing her arms.

"Probably busy mourning the loss of those boys. The pond is so close to the village I'm surprised that no one could hear them drown?" Freyja said and began picking grass for entertainment.

"You'll be surprised, people just go under and don't come back up. Anyway, this is easy work. There are five of us. As long as one of us is here to guard the pond the rest can go out and enjoy this weather before winter. Tomorrow I am going out and talk to some of the villagers. If we figure out the cause of the drownings we can leave this depressing village. Perhaps Sindri missed something." Halfdan looked deep in thought after he spoke, looking at the pond.

Ulv placed Elora on top of the roof and smelled the woodwork. "It smells like chickens."

"The wood might have been repurposed from a chicken coop." Liv said as she gave the structure a gentle push, testing its sturdiness. "Do we have to stay away from the pond?"

"We?" Halfdan asked, harshly.

"The only one who needs to stay away from the pond is Ulv." Elora said as she stretched her wings. "Unless the pond grows hungry for young women."

"What about me?" Halfdan asked, pointing to himself.

"You're old." Freyja said, innocently.

"I am not that old." Halfdan said disappointed and kicked the structure and as jolt of pain promptly made him regret it. "This thing is sturdy."

"If it only had a door." Elora said, flapping her wings like a fledgling.

"You're an owl, you can sleep in a tree." Halfdan spoke as he collected some sticks that fell from the trees and tossed them into the fire pit.

"Don't start the structure on fire." Elora mocked Halfdan, turned around to fly away, only to glide a short distance and hit the ground.

Ulv went and picked up Elora and placed her back onto the structure. Halfdan wanted to poke fun at Elora's flying skills but noticed that Sindri was coming back with an armful of animal pelts and blankets. Beside him was a woman carrying a basket and a small pot.

"This here is my wife, Abia." Sindri spoke with a big grin, pleased to show off his wife.

Abia carried herself confidently and had long straight brown hair. Her beauty complemented her strength, not thin and frail like the women in the city.

"This here is Halfdan, Ulv, Liv and the little lady here is Freyja." Sindri did his best to use his eyes to point out to Abia who he was naming.

Before the group could exchange greetings Sindri began to lay the animal pelts and blankets under the structure, still running on instincts of taking care of his children. Freyja got out from under the shelter and did her best to help as Halfdan, Ulv and Elora awkwardly watched. Liv caught Abia looking at her, beckoning Liv to talk to her.

"Sindri is deathly afraid of birds, but he will never admit it." Abia whispered to Liv with a sly smile. "I've seen that man fight a bear, but it is the birds that do him in. Please don't mind him ignoring your pet owl, but my kids have been talking about that bird since you arrived. Would you mind if they saw it sometime, away from the pond of course." Before Liv could say yes. Abia began talking again. "I noticed you all were traveling light." Abia handed the basket and old pot.

"Thank you." Liv accepted the gifts and was relieved. She could tell Abia was being polite and giving them food. Cooking pots weren't cheap and would make their travels more tolerable. Liv noticed that Abia was staring at her husband. Liv turned and noticed that Sindri was doing his best to avoid Elora's gaze, perched at the end of the structure and intently staring at him as he worked.

Abia gently put her hand on Liv's shoulder. Making Liv turn back to her. "Thank you for being here."

Liv stiffened up, uncomfortable that this woman was staring into her eyes and was standing so close to her. "Of course, as soon as I heard what was happening I wanted to come and help. We all did."

"Alright!" Sindri clapped his hands in completion of making the beds. "If you need anything you know where I will be."

"It was nice meeting all of you!" Abia smiled and waved as she joined her husband to leave. The two quickly headed home and they disappeared into the village, eager to return to their children.

"That was normal. Not odd at all." Elora finished her comment with a hoot.

Liv put the pot down and removed a cloth that was covering the basket to see a bowl with several venison steaks and some fresh wild horseradish in a smaller bowl. Just like that, the group's night turned into a good one. The group used the flint and stone to start a fire, since they did not trust Halfdan to start a controlled fire with magic. Cutting the venison into strips and skewered, everyone held their steaks over the fire as Ulv cooked Elora's strip for her. Halfdan, Liv and Ulv put some horseradish on their venison.

With some sunlight left Ulv collected some branches and sticks and Liv and Freyja used them to make a smoker. With three large branches around the fire pit and leaning together to stand up in a tepee formation. When smaller sticks were placed, resting on natural bump outs from the branches, making a simple smoker. Leftover venison was cut into thin slices and were draped over the sticks. The heat of the smoke was used to cook and dry out the meat, preserving it for later.

Before the sun disappeared to rest, Halfdan left and found a well in the middle of the village, using the pot to transport the water back to camp for everyone to drink out of. No one talked to one another as they passed the pot to one another to take sips. Weary from travel, one by one they began to fall asleep as the stars above began to shimmer above them.

Early morning air and a dying fire was enough to wake everyone up, along with the familiar rooster call in the distance. The venison was dry and not pleasing to look at, but the group was hungry again and decided to finish it off. Halfdan, Liv and Ulv used the horseradish again to try and cover up the gamey taste of the venison. Elora's beak and talons made easy work of the dried venison as everyone else's jaws hurt from chewing. Peer pressure got to Freyja, and stuck her pinky in the horseradish to try it before putting any on her dried venison. As soon as Freyja tasted the horseradish her face turned red, everyone laughed as she contorted her face in disgust. She covered her mouth and got up and ran towards the village to search for water.

"Wait for me!" Liv called to Freyja, running after her.

"Wait!" Halfdan yelled after them, holding up the empty pot. "Could at least fill this with water for the rest of us." Halfdan gave up on getting Liv's attention and got up. "I'll be back. Keep an eye on the pond."

Ulv watched as Halfdan walked away with sad eyes, not wanting to be the only one able to watch the pond. Elora kept flapping her wings and hopping around on the ground.

"You're getting better." Ulv told Elora.

"Don't watch me. It makes me nervous." Elora scolded Ulv with some attitude. Knowing that Ulv was just saying that, for she was not making any progress.

"Ok." Ulv replied sadly, turning to look at the pond.

Curiosity got the best of Ulv and he walked up to the pond to examine it. He saw a small silver fish swim away as his shadow casted over the water. Ulv sighed and kneeled down and stuck his hand in the water, the cold sent a shiver through his body. Suddenly, Ulv was bothered by the sudden silence and turned to look for Elora. She was gone. Ulv got up and looked around again.

Nervous, he walked up to the structure and looked behind it. Elora wasn't there either, but there was a stick. Ulv picked up the stick and examined it, noticing that there were familiar teeth markings on the stick. Ulv turned back to look at the pond and was startled to see a large white dog looking back at him. The dog barked at Ulv as it wagged its tail, its mouth open in a doggy smile as it looked at the sick and back at Ulv again.

"You want the sick?" Ulv asked the dog as he walked up to it.

The dog barked again and pranced a little closer to the pond. Ulv could tell that the dog wanted him to throw the sick into the pond. With the stick in one hand, Ulv tossed the stick into the water. The dog barked again as it leaped into the pond making a big splash as it swam to fetch the sick. With the stick in its mouth the dog swam back to Ulv. As soon as the dog's feet could reach the ground that was under the water it ran out of the pond to give Ulv the stick, dropping it by his feet. Ulv picked up the stick and tossed it into the pond once more.

Again, the dog jumped into the water and swam to the stick. Before the dog could retrieve the stick it let out a yelp and went under the water, splashing around as it did. Ulv stood there and watched without a look of fear or worry. He stood still and watched as the dog failed to surface. Ulv heard some rustling in the woods, it was Elora hopping out of some bushes she fell into earlier as she was trying to fly. Ulv looked at Elora and then back to the pond.

"Is that a dog?" Elora asked in a panic as she hopped to Ulv's side as fast as her little legs could go. "Are you not going to do anything?"

Ulv continued to watch the splashing as he spoke, not breaking his glance to look at Elora. "That is not a dog."

CHAPTER 12

WHERE WOLF'S EARS ARE, WOLF'S TEETH ARE NEAR.
VOLSUNGA SAGA ~ NORSE PROVERB

Before Elora could say anything Ulv picked her up and ran towards the village. Ulv ran past some villagers before running into Halfdan, Liv and Freyja who were making their way back.

"What is wrong?" Liv asked, visibly concerned as she looked at Ulv and Elora.

Ulv tried talking but he was trying to catch his breath. Elora spoke for him. "There is a dog drowning in the pond, well it looked like a dog."

"What do you mean, it looked like a dog?" Halfdan asked, sternly.

"It was pretending to be a dog, I can tell. It wasn't acting like a real dog. It was different, I could feel it." Ulv said with a dry voice. "It wanted me to toss a stick into the pond, I did. Its fur didn't retain water. The water would just roll off. Never smelled like a wet dog, not once. Then it was acting like it was drowning to try and trick me to go into the water. It wanted to drown me, I think it's how it tricked those boys."

"All of you, go get Sindri and meet me by the pond." Halfdan ordered before handing Freyja the pot, spilling some water and then reaching out and grabbing Elora. "You're coming with me."

"Hey!" Elora protested, not enjoying being manhandled and grabbed.

Halfdan turned and ran back to the pond. He didn't want Sindri to see that all of them abandoned the pond that they were supposed to be guarding. Plus, if he got back soon enough he might be able to catch a glimpse of this creature.

When Halfdan reached the pond he could see some ripples in the water, showing that there once was movement. There in the middle of the pond floated the stick Ulv tossed for the dog. The muck in the bottom of the pond was stirred up, making the pond cloudy. The water was still, but Halfdan could feel the monsters presence. A dark aura now filled the water. Bugs that once hovered above the water's surface were now gone and the birds who resided in the surrounding trees stopping their singing.

Halfdan bent over to place Elora on the ground, but kept an eye on the pond. There was a thought itching the back of Halfdan's brain. Deep down he had a feeling that he knew what was in the pond, but he couldn't recall what it was.

Halfdan walked up to the pond and cautiously scooped some water with his hands, taking a sip and spitting it out. Despite the water's earthy taste there was a hint of *lemmikki flower.

Halfdan stood up and thought for a moment. "I know that nymphs, water spirits, like perfume and flowers. Would that mean that other water entities like flowers?"

"What are you talking about?" Elora asked, still salty about being grabbed at.

"What color was the dog?" Halfdan asked, ignoring Elora's heated question.

"It looked white, but it went under the water before I could get a good look at it." Elora answered, looking at Halfdan as he rubbed his head trying to think. Elora's large eyes caught sight of Sindri, behind him was Liv, Ulv and Freyja who were making their way to the pond. "They're coming."

"Good, I want to talk to them here. Keep an eye on the pond as we talk." Halfdan commanded rather than ask.

Elora didn't appreciate being talked to in such a manner, her feathers puffed out a bit and kept her eyes lazily on the pond.

Halfdan waved Sindri over and Liv, Ulv and Freyja followed him. Sindri looked a bit uncomfortable, perhaps even a little nervous, but he did his best not to show it. "What is going on, Halfdan?"

"Your pond has a nökken." Halfdan told Sindri.

Sindri's face went from worried to straight up irritated. "You are lying. Those are tales told to entertain children."

"Ulv wouldn't lie. He saw a dog trying to trick him into swimming into the pond. Ulv, what color was that dog?" Halfdan asked Ulv but kept his eyes on Sindri.

"White." Ulv answered timidly.

Sindri shook his head in discontent. "Nökken are water spirits that look like handsome men who trick women into jumping into water to drown them. Those are stories to scare children, they aren't real."

"Nökken are shape shifters. They can be men, silver fish, a white dog or even a white horse. All of whom use different tactics to drown their victims." Halfdan informed Sindri.

"And all are stories to keep kids from going into water." Sindri added, angrily.

"Elora, what do nökken like and dislike?" Halfdan asked Elora as he picked her up and held her up to face Sindri.

"Nökken like riddles, music and water lilies, just as much as they like to drown humans. They dislike steel and you can toss a steel needle in the pond. Also said to dislike steel crosses but I think that is just religious propaganda to make you buy an expensive cross." Elora spoke confidently, enjoying Sindri's jaw drop as she spoke.

Sindri took a step back and watched as Halfdan put Elora back down. There was a moment of silence before Sindri spoke again. "How do we get rid of this monster, this nökken?"

Halfdan wore a slight smile. "Surround the pond with steel needles and drain the pond. You have enough people, if everyone helped the pond will be gone and so will the nökken. Just make sure not to pail the water into a different body of water. We don't want it to escape into a different waterway, pour it on dry ground."

"I can't make everyone in Thorpe come to drain the pond." Sindri said, nervously.

"Sure you can, you are their leader." Halfdan said in a matter of fact tone.

Sindri broke eye contact with Halfdan and looked upon the pond. "Let me talk to my wife. I will be back."

The group watched Sindri as he left. As soon as Sindri was out of sight Halfdan gestured to Freyja to hand over the pot, she obliged. Halfdan immediately dumped the water out and walked up to the pond's edge.

"You hear that you *Argr! Come up here and we can talk or you can stay there and watch your pond dry up!" Halfdan yelled across the pond.

Halfdan watched the pond and soon some bubbles reached the surface and soon two deep dark eyes came up just above the water. The nökken watched as Halfdan stepped into the pond and lowered the pot into the water, the open end facing the creature.

"Now, you can get into this pot. I get you out of here and everyone is happy. Or you can decline my offer and you can become a fish out of water." Halfdan said calmly, not showing the nökken any fear. However, deep down Halfdan was nervous. His consciousness was yelling at him to get out of the water. Halfdan didn't know what he was doing, he was guessing. The nökken didn't move, hesitant about Halfdan's offer.

"Your death, your choice." Halfdan said, lifting the pot out of the water.

"Wait!" The nökken yelled in a wet and deep panicked voice as it dipped back into the water.

Halfdan lowered the pot back into the water and watched as a little silver fish swam into the pot. Careful not to pour the fish out, Halfdan lifted the pot out of the pond and walked to the shelter and placed the pot inside. Liv, Ulv, Elora and Freyja watched on in bewilderment as Halfdan took a few steps back and snapped his fingers. Instantly and violently the shelter and blankets inside combusted in flames, a plum of black smoke filled the air.

Halfdan turned to look at his friends, who watched the fire with wide eyes. "We need more wood." Halfdan told them.

"How much?" Liv asked, troubled at how Halfdan's face showed no emotion.

"As much as you can find." Halfdan answered. "Hurry!"

Everyone, excluding Elora who watched the fire with demonic glee, spread out and began collecting and adding wood to the fire. When Halfdan was satisfied with the size of the fire he picked up his axe that was leaning against a tree.

Halfdan looked at Freyja. "Have your knife ready."

Freyja nodded nervously and unsheathed her knife from the cloak.

Halfdan then looked at Liv. "Where is your shield and spear?"

Liv looked back at Halfdan disappointed and pointed to the fire. "It was leaning against the shelter."

Halfdan looked and noticed burned wood that looked circular like her shield. He was so caught up in the moment he didn't notice. "Sorry." Halfdan said and handed her his axe.

Soon villagers began to show up and see what was going on. Too nervous to approach the strangers, they stood at a distance and were talking amongst themselves when suddenly Sindri came barreling through. Before Sindri could yell at Halfdan a dog came running out of the shelter, its white fur darkened by fire. The dog cried as it tried to dash past Halfdan and Liv to the pond.

By instinct Liv kicked the ignited dog, knocking it off its paws. With a thud the dog landed three paces away from the pond. The dog wiggled its body to try to get back onto its feet. Before the dog could get its footing Liv raised the axe above her head with both hands and swung it down.

Villagers screamed, some began to run back to their houses as others followed behind Sindri. Halfdan, Liv, Ulv, Elora, Freyja, Sindri and a handful of villagers looked upon the dog. Some gasped and covered their mouth as the dog began to change into its original form, the nökken. Short and stocky, whatever parts weren't burnt

113

were scaly and a dark mossy green color. The nökken's feet and hands were oddly human looking but its nails were more like talons. Its large black eyes looked out and slowly began to turn milky in color. Its mouth was wide open and was filled with little dirty teeth, similar to a wolf fish.

The air was still with silence before Sindri broke it by slapping Liv in the back. "Our hero!" Sindri exclaimed and the villagers began to cheer.

Sindri politely asked for Liv's axe and used it to chop off the nökken's head and hands, handing them off to villagers who held them high like trophies. Villagers grabbed Liv and dragged her away as Halfdan and Freyja did their best to keep up with her.

Ulv sat down next to Elora as she watched everyone run back into the heart of the village.

"Aren't you worried that you'll lose them?" Elora asked Ulv.

"No, I can smell them out. Especially Halfdan." Ulv said as he rubbed his nose. "I wanted to ask you, did it bother you? Watching that nökken get killed?"

"Do you consider myself a murderess?" Elora asked, skeptical.

"Not at all. You're not like that." Ulv said with an uncomfortable smile.

"It might be able to shapeshift, but a nökken is more like a water troll. It would have been nice to ask it why it was killing. But it is a little late now. Humans like to kill and then ask questions later. Makes it difficult to learn about different creatures." Elora let out a big sigh. "Let's get out of here, this thing's viscera smells like rotting fish."

Elora fluffed her feathers and braced herself for Ulv to pick her up. Ulv carefully held Elora as they walked back to the village to look for their friends, leaving the burning shelter and nökken corps behind them.

CHAPTER 13

DEATH'S MARK

Halfdan woke up in a daze. He had an ache in his back and a throbbing head. Once his eyes were able the focus he noticed Elora was asleep, roosted and cozy in the rafters above him. Looking around Halfdan remembered that they were celebrating with the villagers in their longhouse. Halfdan sat up, realizing that he fell asleep on the table. Looking at the ground. some other villagers fell asleep on the hard dirt floor. Halfdan moved empty cups out of his way and rolled off the table brushing off crumbs that stuck to him. Stepping over people, Halfdan looked around for the rest of his companions but couldn't find them. He figured that since he couldn't find Sindri that they were with him at his house.

Halfdan stepped out of the longhouse and the bright sun assaulted his eyes. With a groan Halfdan looked around to see if he could recognize Sindri's house. After wandering around to get his bearings Halfdan found Sindri's house. His children were playing outside, fighting one another with sticks. Halfdan could hear Sindri's booming voice through the door before he knocked.

Abia opened the door with a smile. "Halfdan, come on in. How are you feeling? You fell asleep and we couldn't wake you up so we let you be."

Halfdan walked in and saw the rest of his companions sitting at a table with Sindri. Abia closed the door and offered Halfdan a seat and handed him a cup of water. Halfdan accepted the water with great enthusiasm.

"It was quite a celebration, it went on until late at night. I anticipate not many people working their fields today to recover." Sindri said with a laugh. "I've got something to show you."

Sindri got up and walked to the fire mantle and grabbed what looked like a stone formation. It wasn't until it was placed in front of Halfdan that he realize it was the nökken's hand. Two of its fingers were missing and when Halfdan picked it up it felt like crumbly sandstone, little bits of grey fragments flaking off onto the table.

Sindri shook his head in disappointment. "Someone already dropped the head and the other hand got wet and turned into mush. That's all that is left for a trophy."

"Ah, well we like to travel light. You can keep it." Halfdan said with a weak smile, putting the hand back down on the table.

"Liv said the same thing, just wanted to make sure." Sindri took the hand back and placed it back on the mantle.

"That thing is bad luck." Abia said, placing a plate of bread and white fish in front of Halfdan. "We already ate, so eat up."

"Thank you." Halfdan said slowly picking at the food, his stomach turning at the sight of the fish.

"Was Elora still in the rafters? She flew up there after some kids petted her. She refused to come down." Ulv asked Halfdan.

"Yeah, it seemed like she was still asleep." Halfdan replied, eating a bit of bread.

Sindri sat back down with a box and opened it. Halfdan could recognize the sound of items clinking and sliding about, silver coins were in the box.

"All the villagers pitched in what they could, just keep in mind that last year the rain washed away most of the crops so we didn't have much saved." Sindri spoke with a shameful look on his face, avoiding eye contact as he pushed the box towards Halfdan.

Halfdan grabbed the box and looked inside. Without moving any of the coins he could count twenty two silver. Halfdan grabbed ten and pushed the box back to Sindri. "Distribute the rest to the families who lost their boys, they will need it."

Sindri took back the box, surprised. "Well, this is a first. Is there anything else we can do for you?"

"Do you have a tub to bathe in?" Halfdan asked bluntly as he handed Liv the ten silver to put into her leather pouch.

Halfdan noticed Sindri looking at his wife for approval.

"As long as you don't mind that the tub is small. If you help me collect water I can heat it up for you." Abia spoke for Sindri.

Sindri stood up and pushed the chair back under the table. "As you do that; I'd like to talk to the bereaved, make sure they are ok. I'll make sure they get their share of the silver as well. After that I should tend to my fields, I'll take the children with. If I don't see you folks before you leave just know that you always have a place to stay. Can't thank you enough." He said before shaking everyone's hand and kissing his wife goodbye. Sindri walked out the door and called to his children before closing it behind him.

"Let me look for the water buckets." Abia said before walking into a different room.

Halfdan took the opportunity to slide the plate to Ulv, who began to scarf down the food without a word.

"So," Halfdan cleared his throat. "What happened last night?"

"You don't remember?" Freyja asked, raising her eyebrows.

Liv laughed. "As soon as they brought the mead out you started drinking like a fish out of water. What do you remember?"

Halfdan thought for a moment, rubbing his eyes as he did. "Um, I remember talking to people."

"Yeah, you did. You also told the black smith that he could take us to Rokeby. Its two villages over. Guess the black smith has an uncle that lives there and told him about a wolf problem. You got excited and told him you could kill the wolf and that you could convince the Jarl to pay us to do so. Guess everyone in Rokeby is calling it a spirit wolf, determined to devour all the livestock and torment the people who dare speak its name." Liv leaned back in the chair and put her hands behind her head. "By the look on your face Halfdan I can tell you never killed a wolf before."

"Like it matters." Halfdan said without a care before taking another sip of water.

117

"You were telling people we are expert monster killers. That a wolf stands no chance with us. I've never killed anything in my life." Freyja said, raising her voice at Halfdan.

"Look at that, Halfdan. You made Freyja so upset that she is yelling." Liv said with a smirk.

"I'm not yelling!" Freyja said even louder.

"When is this blacksmith even taking us to Rokeby?" Halfdan asked, concerned that he won't have enough time to take a much needed bath.

"He said not until later. So I am not sure. He is making me a new shield right now." Liv said with a playful glare at Halfdan.

"I said I was sorry about starting your shield on fire. I felt bad, Freyja did a good job painting it." Halfdan said, sincerely.

"It's ok," Liv said "I can paint the new one." Freyja almost jumped out of her chair in excitement, pulling out a broken nökken fingers from her sleeve. "I'm going to use the fingers as pigment." She exclaimed.

Halfdan almost began choking on the water he was sipping as Abia walked back into the room. Freyja quickly stuck the finger back up her sleeve as if she wasn't supposed to have them.

Abia put down seven buckets of different sizes onto the table. "Do you know where the river is?"

"Yeah, we passed it when we first came here." Freyja answered confidently.

"There is a shortcut. If you walk out this door and keep going straight you will find a path, it cuts through some folk's property, but they don't mind." Abia said, picking up the empty plate that was in front of Ulv.

"Thank you." Freyja said, taking one of the larger buckets.

"Yes, thank you." Liv said to Abia, handing out two buckets to Halfdan and two buckets to Ulv.

"Thank you." Halfdan joined.

Ulv grumbled and followed behind Halfdan, Liv and Freyja as they walked out the door. Abia was correct about the shortcut and the group made their way back to the house with buckets full of water. When they opened the door they could see that Abia had a fire going and a large cauldron over it. She took the water and added two buckets of water into the cauldron, filling it a little over half way. Halfdan watched as Abia tossed a handful of dried herbs and flowers into the cauldron. The rest of the buckets Abia took to a side room where the tub was.

"Ladies first." Abia said, cueing Halfdan and Ulv to go outside.

"I'm going to look for Elora." Ulv said, taking off back towards the longhouse.

Deep down Halfdan knew that Ulv wasn't going to come back until it was time to go. Halfdan decided to take this opportunity to go back to the pond. Walking slowly and taking in the fresh air Halfdan reached the pond. He admired the pond for a moment then looked at the remains of the nökken. There wasn't much left, just a pile of ash. Sometime after the creature died its body turned to stone. Halfdan could see some small shoe prints in the ash, some kids must have come over and kicked the nökken's body causing it to crumble apart. Like a stone thrown off a cliff, little bits and some large chunks were scattered about.

Halfdan then began sifting through the burnt shelter. All the embers were grey and cold, but the deeper he sifted he could feel some residual heat. Soon Halfdan found what he was looking for, the pot. Covered in burnt wood it was still warm to the touch, but not hot enough to prevent Halfdan from picking it up and taking it to the pond. As soon as the pot touched the water it began dispersing its filth, making a grey and black cloud around it. After cleaning off the pot Halfdan examined it. Other than the wire handle being warped the rest of the pot was fine.

Being bent over made Halfdan's stomach turn, causing bouts of *emesis to escape him. After feeling his stomach settle, Halfdan scooped some water out of the pond to rinse his mouth and spat it out in the tall grass. Cautiously, Halfdan got up and staggered to a tree to lean against. Letting the cool earth and gentle breeze sooth him.

Stiffness awoke Halfdan, not realizing that he fell asleep. Halfdan opened his eyes and jumped in fright by the sight of a huge buck looming over him. Candles on all thirty points of his rack burned angrily, popping and flickering about wildly as wax dripped down and around Halfdan. He instinctively tried to scoot back but only rubbed closer against the tree he was resting on.

"Jovi." Halfdan spoke the buck's name under his breath as he looked upon the great beast with bulging eyes.

"Disappointing." Was all that Jovi spoke to Halfdan as his lips parted to show a slight smile.

Jovi began to lean in towards Halfdan and his smile grew as he did. Halfdan began to notice that Jovi's teeth weren't that of a herbivore but rather large, white and pointed like that of a wolf. Jovi's hot breath dried out Halfdan's eyes, causing him to blink. When Halfdan opened his eyes again he noticed that it was Liv who was leaning over him.

Halfdan could hear that Liv was trying to talk to him, but he wasn't listening. Instead he looked around, panicked. He could feel his body shaking, unsure if it was fear or the cold. By the pond Halfdan noticed Freyja picking up the pot that he cleaned up earlier.

"I think you had a nightmare." Halfdan heard Liv speak this time. He met her eyes, looking upon him with concern. Liv kneeled down to be closer to Halfdan and she put her hand on his shoulder.

"Are you ok?" Liv asked.

Halfdan just looked at Liv for a moment. He thought about how much she reminded him of Linna at that moment. Halfdan's hand twitched, deep down he wanted to grab Liv's hand but he decided against it.

"Yeah, I'm ok." Halfdan murmured.

"Freyja and I already collected fresh water for you. Abia is warming it up now." Liv stood up showing off a black dress with white accents and sharp designs sewn onto it. "Abia said I could have it. She washed my other dress so it is drying now."

"It looks good on you." Halfdan said before getting up with a groan. "You should look for Ulv, he is trying to skip out on bath time."

"We will in a moment. Freyja wants to see the nökken remains." Liv said as she and Halfdan turned to watch as Freyja rummaging around the nökken rubble.

"Ok, have fun with that." Halfdan said before making his way back to Sindri and Abia's house.

In the distance Halfdan could see able bodied villagers working in their fields. Halfdan squinted his eyes searching out Sindri and his kids, but everyone was too far away to distinguish. It didn't take long for Halfdan to reach the house, noticing it was the only house with smoke billowing out of the chimney. Halfdan knocked on the door before entering, expecting Abia to be there when he entered but she was gone. He looked around, he could see Liv's dress hung up by the fire to dry along with the cloak that Freyja was borrowing. The bottom of the cloak was beginning to look warn from Freyja dragging it on the ground, but he didn't mind. Halfdan noticed his axe laying on the table. Liv most likely left it there for him. However, at that moment Halfdan decided Liv should keep it. As Halfdan was looking at the drying flowers and herbs hanging from the ceiling he heard Abia come out from the bedroom.

Abia stopped moving and looked at Halfdan making him feel uncomfortable. It felt as if she was looking right through him.

"You look like shit. What happened?" Abia asked brashly.

Halfdan couldn't help but let out a nervous chuckle. "I have a recurring nightmare, that's all."

"Tell me." Abia said genuinely concerned. "The water is still heating up. We have time. Sit down."

Halfdan did as he was told and sat down. He watched as Abia grabbed another wooden cup and ladled water into it. She then sat down by Halfdan and handed him the water.

"Thank you." Halfdan said as he gingerly took a sip of water, afraid to get sick again. He could feel Abia looking at him, waiting for him to tell her about his nightmare. As much as Halfdan didn't want to share, he knew that Abia wasn't going to let him leave until he told her. "Alright, so... This buck appeared to me once in a dream. I was imprisoned and the beast came to me and demanded that I stop this woman in exchange for power. This women wasn't only responsible for killing innocent people but also for me being imprisoned, she wanted me dead as well. I escaped and figured I was safe. Then today, in another dream, the beast was displeased that I am not keeping my end of the bargain." Halfdan kept his eyes fixed on the cup, not wanting to see Abia's face and her reaction to his story. "Talking out loud about it makes it all seem unreal. I am apprehensive about confronting this woman. For once in my life I have other people I need to worry about."

"If this woman, who may be living in your dream or reality, is willing to kill you. If she is willing to do that then she is willing to kill those you love. Have you told them what is happening?" Abia asked, knowing that Halfdan's dream might be more than he is leading on.

Halfdan caught Abia looking at his scarred hands for a moment. "No, not completely." Halfdan said tapping the water cup with his fingers, watching the water ripple in the cup. Then ashamed of his hands' appearance, he hid them under the table.

"You should, I can tell they care about you." Abia got up and started sifting through the dried flowers that were hanging from the ceiling, stopping to pick dry little purple flowers from a long stock that has little green leaves and adding them to the cauldron.

"Was that hyssop?" Halfdan asked.

"You know your plants. I'm impressed." Abia said as she tossed in a chunk of white oak bark and a small branch of pine needles.

"My mother taught me to identify plants and an old friend of mine taught me how to use them." Halfdan took another sip of water, gently put the cup down and hid his hands under the table yet again.

Abia then opened a little wooden container and put in a pinch of salt. "This should hopefully help with the nightmares. Plants can be used to heal not just the body but the spirit as well. Bathing in this should make it difficult for that buck to harass you in your dreams, I hope anyway.

Halfdan rubbed his hands together under the table nervously as he spoke. "This has been on my mind, but the pond tasted like lemmikki. Lemmikki flowers are used as a remembrance to someone you lost, correct?"

"It's known that nökken tend to water lilies, so I wouldn't be surprised if they also enjoy flowers from land. My husband told me that you said the nökken enjoyed riddles and music. Sindri's father liked to go to the pond and come up with riddles and love poems about his late wife. When Sindri's father passed away that's when the nökken began to attack. The creature might have enjoyed Sindri's father and could have missed him, thus why the lemmikki. No one probably told you, but the rest of the villagers began to think Sindri or his father's spirit was the cause of all the drownings, until you came. It hurt Sindri, his father did so much for his neighbors. Putting them before himself, even going hungry. He only ate if he knew everyone else had food. How easy it is to forget someone's kindness once they are dead." Abia shook her head as she checked the clothing that was drying. "That is my opinion anyway."

"Is your husband still going to lead the people of Thorpe?" Halfdan asked, remembering Sindri talking about finding a replacement.

"I think so." Abia said, grabbing some cloth to protect her hands.

Halfdan smiled after hearing that Sindri will still be guiding his people. Individuals who don't want to be leaders are often the best to be in charge.

"The water is hot and ready. Smells good too." Abia stirred the cauldron then used the large wooden spoon to scoop out the chunk of bark and pine branch. Protecting her hands with cloth

123

scraps Abia lifted the cauldron by the handle and away from the fireplace.

Abia awkwardly made her way around the table and opened up a door that led to a small room. Halfdan couldn't see much but he could hear Abia dumping the hot water into a tub, mixing with cold water that was fresh from the river.

"There is a fresh towel and the girls left some soap and a comb in there." Abia told Halfdan as she made her way around the table and placed the cauldron back on its hook over the fireplace, unbothered by the weight. "I'll go get fresh water to clean your clothes."

"Thank you." Halfdan said getting up, excited to clean off.

"No need to thank me. Raising kids, that's all I do is clean." Abia said, grabbing two buckets off the floor and walking out the door.

Halfdan walked over to look into the small windowless room. In it was a small-oval shape tub and the water was steaming up the room. The floor was still wet from Liv and Freyja. There were juvenile deer antlers mounted on the wall with a thin towel hanging from it. There was a small stool and a long table, about the same height as the tub, on it was a large candle, bowl with a bar of soap that Norvick gave them and a comb. There was also a razor, tweezers and a simple blown glass mirror in a rough hexagon shape.

Halfdan began to take off his clothing when he realized that there were white specks on his pants. With his nails, Halfdan scratched at one of the specks and rolled the tacky substance with his index finger and thumb. Halfdan froze when he recognized what it was, wax. He immediately wiped the wax off and struggled out of his pants like they were on fire. Halfdan folded the dirty clothing and placed them on a chair next to the fireplace. He ran back into the bathing room and slammed the door behind him, engulfing the room in darkness with only a candle to light the room. For a moment the candle flickered about from the door being slammed, casting wild shadows in the room.

Halfdan stood still for a moment, he thought about how much he disliked being in a room with no windows. However, he asked if they had a tub and from experience Halfdan knew that it could be weeks before he could bathe again. Halfdan let out a deep sigh and quickly got into the tub and felt the warm water relax him, not realizing how sore he was. Afraid to close his eyes, Halfdan watched the botanicals float around him.

Soon Halfdan heard Abia come back and began washing his clothes and shuffling about. Abia moved about with haste and it wasn't long until she yelled that she was going out to the field to talk to her husband. Halfdan could feel the water slowly cool and so he began to shave and pluck out some nose hairs, using the mirror to help guide him.

Halfdan carefully put the mirror down and thought a moment before picking it back up. He wanted to look at his eyes, remembering his companions telling him they weren't blue anymore. When he mustered up the courage and looked at them he sighed in relief. Worried that his eyes were similar to the dead cloudy grey that Magnus' undead slaves had. Halfdan's eyes were a cold grey now that resembled steel more than anything. He couldn't help but feel disheartened. Loose women at the inn always complemented his blue eyes and so he got a blue tunic to match them. Now he'll have to get a grey tunic.

After cleaning up Halfdan quickly dried off and went out to grab his clothes that were drying by the fireplace. They were still damp but he didn't want to sit around in a towel. Halfdan checked his pants and was happy to see that the wax was taken off. He noticed that Abia placed a pair of black leather gloves next to his leather pouch. Liv must have left it here, wanting Halfdan to take it back. Looking in the leather pouch Halfdan grabbed two silver coins and hid them in Abia's salt container for her to find later.

Halfdan decided to sit by the fire so his wet clothes didn't give him a chill. Outside Halfdan could hear people talking, but he was content watching the fire. Soon Freyja came running in and began collecting Liv's old yellow dress.

125

"The black smith is outside, he is ready to go when we are!" Freya said with excitement, grabbing the axe off the table and ran back outside.

"Ok." Halfdan yelled after Freyja as he began to put his boots back on and tucking his pants in them. He grabbed the cloak and put it on, enjoying its familiarity and warmth. Before reaching the door Halfdan turned back and grabbed the gloves off the table trying them on. They were a perfect fit. When Halfdan walked outside he saw people crowded around the back of the black smith's cart. People were talking to Liv, Ulv and Freyja and handing them items.

"Time to go!" yelled Abia to the group. "If Birger doesn't leave soon he'll get stuck in the dark!" Abia then walked up to Halfdan. "You all set?"

"As set as I'll ever be. I'm not used to such a big goodbye." Halfdan said looking upon the group of people.

"This will most likely be the last visitors they see till spring. Plus, your Liv is very popular." Abia said with a smile. "I hope the gloves fit well. I made them for Sindri but they were too small for him. Now I stick to making mittens." Abia handed Halfdan an unadorned drawstring pouch. Halfdan could smell the pine, salt and hyssop contained in the bag. "Just in case those nightmares come back. When you're done you should dump the water out towards the rising sun. I'm not sure why, but that's what my mother always did. You take care now. If you need anything, we will be here."

Abia gave Halfdan a hug, catching him off guard for a moment. He couldn't help but think about the last time someone hugged him. Halfdan could hear Liv and Freyja calling him so he left to join them in the back of the cart. Birger the blacksmith laid down blankets for them to sit on. In the cart were three boxes containing nails along with the little pot and Liv's new shield. The cart began to roll and Halfdan waved goodbye to Abia.

Halfdan then looked at Liv, Ulv and Freyja to see what they were given. "What did you all get?"

126

Freyja put on a hat with a fuzzy fox fur base and a black pointed top that flopped over to one side. "I got a fun hat! I like it because it hides my ears."

"I got this jacket." Ulv tugged at the fabric, already wearing it but leaving it unbuttoned to expose his bare chest. The jacket was as red as Ulv's hair and was lined with a brown weave design. Ulv took a quick whiff of it and wrinkled his nose. "It smells like dirty water."

"Maybe one of the boys was wearing it when they…" Halfdan stopped before finishing his sentence. Realizing that Liv and Freyja were looking at him in horror. "Never mind. Um. What about you, Liv? What did you get?"

Liv opened up an old travel pack and dug around in it. "Dried goods, water bladder and some apples. That was very nice of them. This pack will come in handy. What about you, Halfdan?"

Halfdan lifted his gloved hands to show companions.

"Look good. The gloves make you look intimidating." Liv complemented Halfdan.

Halfdan couldn't help but notice the sad disappointed look on Freyja's face. "What's wrong?"

"I liked looking at the insignia on your hand, but maybe it's good to cover it up." Freyja told Halfdan.

Halfdan took his gloves off and looked at his hands. Liv and Ulv leaned over to see if they could notice the insignia as well.

"I don't see anything." Halfdan said, confused.

"Me neither." Liv added.

"I see it." Ulv said as Halfdan and Liv looked at him skeptical.

"Where?" Halfdan asked with annoyance.

"Your left palm." Freyja told Halfdan.

Halfdan looked at his left palm more intently and used fingers to try and feel anything. "What does it look like?"

"It's a weird design." Freyja said, grabbing Halfdan's hand and using her index finger to trace the design. "I thought it was a tattoo at first, but it glows red sometimes before we go to bed."

"I don't see a design, it looks like a death mark to me." Ulv said, confidently.

Halfdan just glared at Ulv then continued to watch Freyja draw out a circular design with some other marks. It was difficult to decipher. He would need Freyja to draw it out on parchment to get a good idea on what it looks like. When Freyja stopped tracing with her finger Halfdan could still feel a tingling sensation to where he clenched his hand in a fist then extended his fingers before putting his gloves back on. Seeing Freyja's young undamaged hands compared to his, defined by fire, made him happy that he had gloves. Halfdan would catch people looking at his hands often and it made him self-conscious.

"They're waving to us." Birger spoke rough and loudly.

Halfdan, Liv, Ulv and Freyja looked and noticed people in their fields stopping their work to wave. The group waved obnoxiously back at them, Freyja laughing as they did. Halfdan looked back at Birger, feeling odd that he didn't introduce himself. But then again, he might not remember meeting him after drinking. Birger was covered in black soot, making Halfdan think that maybe Birger's grey hair and shirt might actually be white. The rough blacksmith seemed like a man that prefers to communicate in grunts rather than words.

Halfdan then noticed that the horse pulling the cart had a foal walking freely beside it. It wasn't long until the foal was growing weary and Birger stopped to put the foal in the cart. Everyone in back adjusted so the foal could lay on the blanket with them. It wasn't long until Liv pulled out apples and began cutting them for Freyja and Ulv to feed the foal. Liv had to teach Ulv and Freyja that the best way to feed a horse is to place the food in the palm of your hand so they don't accidently bite your fingers.

Freyja kept looking at Halfdan, trying to see if he noticed anything different. She couldn't take it any longer. "Do you think we're missing anything?"

"I wasn't going to say anything. I thought you all forgot about her." Halfdan said with a smirk.

Freyja frowned at Halfdan as Ulv waved his hand into the air.

"We were expecting more of a reaction." Liv said disappointed as she looked out into the sky.

Without a sound Elora glided down from the sky and perched herself on the side of the cart. Halfdan could tell that Elora wanted to make a rude comment but she was interrupted by the foal thrashing about in fear as it began breathing heavily through its nose. The foal was unable to get enough footing to stand up but it was able to accomplish kicking Ulv out of the cart. Ulv fell onto the dirt road with a thud as mother horse stopped the cart on her own, turning her head and looking to see what was going on. Birger turned too and began laughing as he watched Halfdan, Liv and Freyja stumble out of the cart to get away from the foal.

The foal's hooves scratched the wooden cart as it moved about, stumbling off the cart behind them and galloping to its mother's side. Birger kept laughing as he snapped the reins, beckoning his horse to continue moving. Halfdan lifted Ulv off the ground as Liv and Freyja hopped back on the moving cart. Halfdan and Ulv moved quickly to get back on the cart, not wanting to be left behind as the horse began to pick up speed. Ulv got back onto the cart without a problem. Halfdan scowled and damned Ulv's youth under his breath as he ran behind the cart a bit to catch up. Liv and Freyja playfully beckoned him to hurry. With some effort Halfdan threw himself into the cart. As he was catching his breath he looked up to see Elora, still perched on the rail, bobbing up and down playfully as her feathery ears pointed straight up.

"Stupid bird." Halfdan said between breaths as he gently pushed Elora, causing her to flap her wings to regain balance. "Why don't you fly ahead and look for thieves?"

"There won't be any thieves where we are going." Birger said, keeping his eyes forward. "The lone wolf, spirit wolf, Hati, a nightmare, whatever you want to call it. It's out there, waiting."

Everyone in the back of the cart shot looks at one another. This was the first time Birger said more than four words to them.

129

"What makes this wolf so different?" Halfdan asked, doubtful.

"It's nimble, fast and deadly. Just like any other wolf. But this one thinks like a man. It can undo traps, unlock gates and memorize a man's routine. Worse, it's not afraid of fire." Birger said, spitting after he spoke. "That's what I'm told anyway."

Halfdan began to feel in over his head. Facing Blackhare was starting to sound safer.

"Do any of those things sound familiar?" Halfdan asked Elora.

Elora shrugged her wings. "I'll need more information and to see things with my own eyes."

"How would you know that a wolf isn't afraid of fire?" Freyja asked, a look of puzzlement on her face.

"Campfires can protect you from wolves. That is most likely why the thieves are scared." Liv informed Freyja. Liv then looked at Halfdan with sad eyes, obviously something had been on her mind. "Halfdan, I'm sorry that everyone was giving me credit for killing the nökken. You were able to trick it out of the water, I just got lucky and dealt the final blow."

"No need to be sorry. I don't like all the attention anyway. It was fun watching you kill that thing, you didn't even hesitate. I wanted to tell you that I talked to Abia about the nökken before we left, Sindri's father used to go to the pond and practice poetry and riddles. We think that is why the nökken started attacking right after Sindri's father passed." Halfdan told the group.

"Sindri also talked about excessive rain last year. Perhaps the nökken got swept into the pond when that happened." Liv added.

"I believe it." Freyja said with enthusiasm.

Halfdan looked over at Ulv, who wasn't paying attention to anything they had been talking about. Instead, he was busy gazing at the scenery. Glancing up at the occasional bird flying overhead and smelling the air whenever there was a breeze. The bliss of being like a dog is living in the moment. Ulv wasn't worried about the future like Halfdan, or much of mankind for that matter.

Rather than getting angry at Ulv's beautiful ignorance Halfdan decided to close his eyes and inhale the air. He noted the smell of moisture and looked up into the sky and noticed dark rain clouds in the distance ahead of them. Halfdan began to worry again, hoping that there would be a place for them to stay if it rains.

The scenery would change as the cart moved on. They would travel through woods and hills and eventually come out to a manmade clearing for animals and crops. They passed through villages without stopping for it was a race with time, only stopping once because the horse demanded it. Stopping by a river, the mare looked back at her master to be let free to drink and Birger obliged.

Halfdan was second to get off the cart, the rest of his companions followed his lead. Stretching and groaning as they made their way to the river to drink as well. Liv brought her water bladder and filled it up at the river, knowing that if a horse is willing to drink from a river that it must be safe.

The stop was brief and the horse was hitched up again and everyone got back on the cart. Birger carried the foal up front and sat it next to him. The foal took up most of the room but Birger didn't seem to be bothered. With a snap of the reins the cart was moving again toward Rokeby.

Everyone other than Ulv was beginning to grow weary of looking at trees and their own feet dangling off the edge of the cart. There was one more village to travel through before reaching their destination. The cart rocked their bodies back and forth as it rolled on, the sensation started as soothing but was growing nauseating with each rock they hit.

"How about I teach you guys some magic?" Elora asked with uncertainty that she tried to mask with a lackadaisical tone. It was obvious that she missed learning and wanted to pass on what she knew.

Halfdan saw a sparkle in Liv and Freyja's eyes as they agreed. Ulv shook his head no and growled a little when he was ignored.

"There are five elements to practice. Fire, water, earth, air, and most of all spirit. I want you to cup some water in your hands and try to freeze it. Think about the cold and channel it through your body. Like I've said before, the older the language the better magic can respond. I would recommend saying sicut cor hyemis durabis. It means like the heart of winter you shall freeze. Sicut cor hyemis durabis." as Elora spoke she made sure to make eye contact with Halfdan, Liv and Freyja. Letting them try their tongue in Latin and praising them for their efforts.

Liv held the water bladder and poured a little water into Freya's cupped hand. Halfdan took off his gloves and cupped his hands to accept some water as well. Liv awkwardly tried to pour water for herself before Ulv helped her. Halfdan sat there and watched the water slowly drip out of his hands and onto his pants, listening to Liv and Freyja beckoning the water to freeze.

Halfdan closed his eyes and blocked out his surroundings. Forcing himself to focus on the sensation of the water in his hands before letting the ancient word durabis echo through his body, opening his eyes as he did. Halfdan watched as the water froze and cracked with anger in his hands. Just as quickly as the water froze it exploded, sending little frozen spikes to bite into Halfdan's skin. In Halfdan's peripheral vision he saw everyone else in the back of the cart flinch in pain. The foal whinnied in surprise but Birger was quick to begin petting the foal, calming it.

"Sorry." Halfdan told them as he looked at everyone, making sure they were ok. He saw little red dots on exposed skin where they were hit with ice. Liv and Freyja must have spilled their handful of water on themselves because parts of their dresses were wet. Halfdan avoided making eye contact with Ulv, sure that his eyes were like daggers.

Liv grabbed the water bladder from Ulv and gave it a little squeeze so some water came squirting out of it onto Halfdan's tunic.

"Hey!" Halfdan protested.

"Now we're even." Liv said with a playful smile as Freyja laughed.

"This is why it's not recommended to transfer your powers to someone. It's not safe. It is best for someone to learn from scratch, it is slow but it's better than accidently hurting innocent people. From now on it might be best for you to practice away from your friends." Elora told Halfdan before telling Liv and Freyja to try again.

Halfdan watched Liv and Freyja try to freeze the water. Focusing their intent at the water that was slowly escaping their grasp. The first one to give up was Freyja and joined in with watching and encouraging Liv. Liv kept trying, telling Ulv to give her more water. Even taking sips of the water she was cupping in her hands to try and feel more connected with it. Liv gave up and flicked the water away onto the dirt road when Birger told the group that Rokeby was insight.

Liv, Ulv and Freyja began bouncing around in the back of the cart to get a better look. Twilight was fast approaching and the houses within Rokeby began to light up one by one as the cart got closer. Birger stopped the cart in front of a blacksmiths house and workshop that resided right outside of Rokeby. Without a word Birger scooped up the foal and got off the cart and gently put the foal down next to its mother before walking inside the house.

Halfdan and his companions watched on, unsure on what to do. Soon Birger came out of the house with yet another box of nails and a man walking behind him who was also carrying a box of nails. Everyone but Elora, who continued to stay perched on the rail of the cart, got out of the cart to get out of the way for Birger and the stranger to add the extra cargo.

Halfdan looked at the new blacksmith, who resembled Birger except for being stout of stature and walked around with a crooked smile. Unlike Birger who was big, balding and angry looking.

"Birger told me you all are here to slay the big bad wolf." The man said with a big grin and his hands placed upon his hips.

"And you must be Birger's uncle?" Halfdan asked with uncertainty.

"Bah!" The man barked and turned to Birger who was already walking back to the house. "Birger! Why must you tell people I'm your uncle? I'm not that old. We're only a year apart."

Birger let out a happy grunt, the corners of his mouth showing a faint smile, before he walked back into the house to grab another box.

"I'm sure my brother talked your ear off the whole way here. I am Balder, and you all are?"

"I am Halfdan, this here is Liv, Freyja, Ulv and the owl is Elora." Halfdan said introducing everyone.

Birger came out and put the last large box of nails on the cart. "All set?"

"That's all of them." Balder told his brother.

Birger looked at Liv and Freyja. "Ladies can ride in the cart." He then looked at Halfdan and Ulv. "You two can walk behind."

Balder let out a nervous chuckle. "Sorry all the nails can overburden the horse. It's really not that long of a walk to the Jarl." Balder turned and quickly got into the front seat of the cart where Birger was already sitting and waiting.

Freyja got onto the back of the cart and Liv squeezed in next to her, boxes taking up a space where Halfdan and Ulv were once sitting.

"I could use a stretch of my legs anyway." Halfdan told Ulv as he briskly walked behind the cart.

Ulv glared back at Halfdan with malice and spoke with a wicked tone. "You know, I am starting to think I'm not going to be turned back into a dog anytime soon. After watching you burst things with hellfire and make water explode, I do not want you trying to turn me back. I'll end up all over the place, just a red

134

smear on the earth. No offense to Liv and Freyja, but with how slow they are learning I'll be thirty by the time they can turn me back into a dog."

"Thirty isn't that bad. What's wrong with being human anyway? You can sleep in a house, eat decent meals, plus you get to live longer." Halfdan said trying to deescalate Ulv's anger.

Ulv stopped walking and stared at Halfdan with big sad puppy eyes. "What?"

Halfdan stopped walking and turned to look at Ulv. Ulv's sad eyes pulling on Halfdan's heart strings as he realized he said something that would ruin more of Ulv's innocents. "I'm sorry Ulv, but dogs don't live as long as humans do. It's just how the world is."

Ulv broke eye contact and looked down as he walked. Halfdan watched him for a moment, unsure on how to comfort him.

"Way to go!" Elora yelled at Halfdan from the cart, her owl ears eavesdropping on their conversation.

Ulv looked up at Elora then Liv and Freyja. "Everyone knew that dogs don't live for long? How long do dogs live for then?" Ulv lifted his arms and then slapped them back down again dramatically as he spoke.

"Uh, like eight. Maybe older than that if they are lucky." Halfdan told him, not wanting to lie.

"What!" Ulv yelled in disbelief rather than asking Halfdan to repeat himself.

Some people began to look out their windows to see what was going on. Ulv's eyes darted around as if he was looking for a thought that escaped him.

"I don't mind being human for a bit." Ulv finally answered, his tone friendly again.

Halfdan leaned his head back to look up into the sky to thank the gods that the dog topic was over with. As they traveled closer to the Jarl's fortress the sound of construction filled the air along with the smell of fresh cut timbers. Soon the Jarl's large fortress was in view. The already standing section was made of

135

stone as was circular in shape, while the new addition was being built with wood and came out of the fortress side. The fortress was surrounded by a large cast iron fence and protected by two guards in matching leather armor that was primarily black with yellow details. The guards looked at the content in the cart before they opened a tall arched gate to let the cart in.

People were working hard but were nowhere near completion. The reason why Balder and Birger made so many nails was so they could continue adding wood siding. Before the cart could stop people came running over to grab the cargo to get it under some tents, talking about rain. Ulv ran over to pick up Elora to get her out of the way while Liv and Freyja got out of the cart and stood awkwardly out of the way.

Halfdan looked around and noticed a man sitting in a lavished chair with a chalice in hand and two guards by his side. The man's chin was tilted upward with a smug look on his face as he looked upon the people working. No one needed to tell Halfdan that the man was the Jarl. In that moment Halfdan missed working for Sindri and knew that the Jarl was going to be the complete opposite. There was only a gate and guards by the Jarl's house and nowhere else in the Rokeby. He wasn't worried about the people living in his town, only himself. It was obvious that the Jarl was looking down at the people who were working on the addition, and most likely everyone else.

"Let's get this over with." Halfdan told him and began walking over to the Jarl.

"Stop right there." Demanded a young man behind Halfdan.

Halfdan jumped a little, startled. When he turned around he saw it was a guard.

"The Jarl will not be listening to anyone's concerns until next month. Come back then. I'm going to have to ask you to leave." The guard said sternly.

Halfdan did his best not to laugh. Young guards were always testy and trying to prove themselves and Halfdan found it amusing every time. "I wish to speak to the Jarl, it is regarding the spirit wolf or whatever you want to call it."

"You will have to come back here tomorrow and make a request to speak to the Jarl." The guard said while taking a step closer to Halfdan in an attempt to intimidate him.

"Make a request? I traveled all day to get here. I see the Jarl right over there, he looks like he has some free time to talk to me." Halfdan stopped a moment and watched the guard grab the hilt of his sword. "Look, if anyone can stop this beast it's me and my companions. I'm just here to help."

The guard looked Halfdan over once more before letting go of his sword. "Wait here." Keeping his eyes on Halfdan the guard walked up to the Jarl, then kneeled in a show of respect before speaking.

Halfdan watched as the two spoke, getting a better look at the Jarl. His face was long and had sharp features. Long straight black hair would fall in front of the Jarl's face as he moved his head, but the man made no effort to brush the hair away. The Jarl glanced at Halfdan for a moment. In response Halfdan raised his hand but rather than return a friendly gesture the Jarl just looked away. Little droplets of water began to fall, not enough to say it was raining but the Jarl stood up and retreated indoors and his two personal guards followed behind him. Two servants came running out and began to move the Jarl's chair elsewhere as the young guard made his way back to Halfdan.

"The Jarl Ellingboe said you should go to Deacon Hallvard. Morrow the Jarl will send someone to collect you." The young guard told Halfdan with an earnest tone of annoyance.

"Where is Deacon Hallvard?" Halfdan asked in equal annoyance.

"Out the way you came." The guard turned and walked away.

Halfdan rolled his eyes and made his way back to the cart. His companions, Balder and Birger were watching Halfdan's encounter with the guard. Halfdan walked up and asked the two brothers if they could take him to Deacon Hallvard. They agreed and everyone piled into the empty cart and headed off. Two guards opened up the gate to let them out and quickly closed it behind them.

Birger drove the cart down the main road then headed west. Houses became few and far between and the rain let up a moment but thunder rumbled in the distance. Soon, they arrived at Deacon Hallvard's residence; a simple chapel that looked like it was built in a hurry. As soon as Halfdan, Liv, Ulv and Freyja got of the cart Birger snapped the reins for the horse to move again before anyone could thank him. Balder turned around to wave goodbye and wished them luck on killing the wolf.

Halfdan looked at Liv and Freyja then at Ulv who was holding Elora under his jacket, they all looked miserable. "Let's hope this Deacon guy opens the door."

As Halfdan began to walk towards the chapel he could hear his friends shuffle close behind him as he firmly knocked on the door. Halfdan turned a little to face his companions and tried his best to speak in a low voice. "Have any of you been in a chapel before?" Halfdan watched as all of them shook their heads no. "You might see artwork of a guy nailed to some wood, don't worry they won't do that to you." Halfdan then thought for a moment. "They might hang you though if you piss them off. I've seen that."

Just then the door to the chapel began to open and out came a young man. His face was long with sharp features. He was clean shaven with short black hair and wore a white nightgown. "The door wasn't locked, you are free to seek shelter here whenever you need it. Come in and know that we don't like to hang people here, if I can help it anyway." The man winked at them and held the door open.

Halfdan walked inside and everyone followed behind him. Inside was enough pews to seat about twenty four people and the only décor was a cross in the front where the priest would share his message. Liv, Ulv and Freyja walked past Halfdan and began to look around.

"I am Deacon Hallvard and currently taking care of services until we get a new priest. May I ask what brings you to Rokeby?"

"The Jarl told us to come here." Halfdan told him.

In an instant the smile disappeared from Deacon Hallvard's face and the kindness in his eyes turned cold and calculating. Then the face became familiar to Halfdan, Deacon Hallvard was Jarl Ellingboe's son.

CHAPTER 14

WOLF IN SHEEP'S CLOTHING

Deacon Hallvard could tell that Halfdan noticed the resemblance to the Jarl. Hallvard's eyes went from cold and calculating like his father's, to sorrowful with a strained smile. "I'm afraid that if my father sent you here then you aren't a priority."

Halfdan raised an eyebrow. "Your father said that he would send someone to collect us tomorrow."

"I will be impressed if he does. He can get... distracted. Also, for your sake, don't call him my father when he is accompanied by anyone else." Deacon Hallvard informed Halfdan, his smile becoming difficult to fake.

Halfdan frowned for a moment as he put everything together. "Did he build this chapel to keep you here?"

Deacon Hallvard let out a short sad chuckle. "Is it that obvious? It's not much of a secret. My father lost the respect of Olav the Peaceful when my mother asked my father to take me. It was difficult for him to disprove our relation." Hallvard smirked and gestured to his face. "My father was given Rokeby to get him out of the king's court. The king and his bishops felt that if my father couldn't stay loyal to his wife, then he wouldn't be loyal to the kingdom. Then my father had the idea of building a chapel and having me assist a priest from overseas, thinking it would win back favor with the king. The real reason was to get me out of his hair and away from his wife and my half siblings."

Halfdan felt odd but honored that Deacon Hallvard was willing to share such private facts of his life. But the awkward feeling compelled Halfdan to try and change the topic. "What happened to the priest?"

"Oh, well he was attacked by a wolf. He survived, but left the next day to go back to his homeland. That was a few weeks ago, I'm starting to think my father isn't looking for a replacement. Deacons aren't even supposed to do services. Don't tell anyone, but I was just given the title. I can't even read the *codices that the priest left behind, it's written in a different language." Hallvard confided in Halfdan, making it apparent he hasn't been able to talk openly to someone in some time now.

"We are actually here to slay the wolf." Halfdan told Deacon Hallvard expecting a happy response.

Instead Deacon Hallvard became nervous, perspiring a little and eyeing the back door in the chapel. "I don't think you want to stay here and sleep on the pews. How about I take you to my friend's place? He disappeared a few weeks ago so it would be nice to see some life at his house again. Let me just run in back quick to grab a lantern."

Halfdan watched with concern as Hallvard moved hurriedly through the chapel and opened up the door to in back. Thinking that Deacon was hiding something, Halfdan tried to get a good look in the room but Hallvard quickly closed the door behind him. Halfdan then walked over to his companions who were rifling through some codices that were left in the front pew, Elora reading the Greek written scripture to them for entertainment. Halfdan explained than Deacon Hallvard will be taking them to a missing person's house to sleep. Liv, Elora and Freyja were growing more incredulous about the situation and didn't know if staying in a stranger's house was any better than sleeping on pews that were too hard for comfort. Ulv remained indifferent and seemed happy simply to be along.

Hallvard came out wearing a brown cloak and had a pair of worn boots on. In one hand, he had a lit lantern and in the other he had a brown jacket that was sewn with mismatched thread and gave it to Freyja. Telling her that townsfolk give him extra fabric to make jackets, hats and mittens for children in his free time. Freyja thanked Hallvard and took the jacket with enthusiasm. She spun

141

around for Liv and Elora to look, who complimented it saying it was beautiful on her. This made Hallvard smile and Halfdan could tell it was genuine. Hallvard then beckoned everyone to follow him, despite acting a little odd Halfdan felt confident that Hallvard wouldn't take them anywhere that would put them in danger.

Out the front door and around back was a trail that led into the woods and up a hill. With only a dim lantern to light the way, the shadows of the forest came to life in everyone's imagination creating monstrous shapes that formed and loomed about.

Thunder in the distance rumbled through the air as Hallvard spoke. "The house used to belong to a man called Oberon. He was a bit of a hermit. Oberon's existence was discovered when farm houses began to encroach on him until finally the chapel was built below the hill he called home." Hallvard put on a sad smile again. "When Oberon stopped visiting me I assembled a search party, but he was never found."

Halfdan tried to get a good look of Hallvard's face as he spoke. His sadness seemed genuine but Halfdan could see a hint of anger in his eyes. As open as Hallvard was he could be difficult to read at times.

"I'm sorry you couldn't find your friend." Freyja told Hallvard in a comforting tone. "Are you sure it's ok that we stay in his house?"

"Of course!" Hallvard said in a weak voice and gave an almost nervous smile. "My father found out about the house and wanted to claim it and rent out the property. But I begged my father to wait a little longer in hopes that Oberon would come back. In the meantime, I've been taking care of the property."

When they finally reached their destination, Halfdan was disheartened to see that the house was actually a modest cabin with a grass roof. It would be a tight fit for all of them.

"The grass on the roof is a little long since the goats went missing after Oberon. You can help yourself to the chickens that are left. The chicken coop was ripped apart so the chickens can be difficult to find at times." Hallvard said, trying to fill in the awkward silence that was left as Halfdan and his companions looked at the cabin. When Hallvard opened up the door to the cabin a chicken that was hiding in a bush nearby ran inside and squatted by a box near the door. Hallvard laughed and lifted the chicken and placed it in the box. "This here is Peapod. She's at the bottom of the pecking order and gets bullied by the other chickens, so at night Oberon would let her come inside. Now, even in Oberon's absence, Peapod expects to come inside at night when I check on the place. Well, you know where I'll be if you need anything." Hallvard put the lantern down on the table and quickly departed into the darkness. Unbothered by the lack of visibility, trusting his feet to know where to go on the familiar path.

Halfdan looked at his companions, hoping to share in the odd situation. Instead, Freyja began petting Peapod who let out little clucks of joy as Liv, Ulv and Elora began to look around. Inside the cabin were the bare necessities to survive. Ulv noticed that there were two chairs, one looked old and one looked new as if it was recently made. Both slightly turned towards one another. Liv put down her axe and shield to pick up a cup and frowned at the dust circle it left behind.

With a sigh, Halfdan took off his gloves and attempted to light the fireplace, transferring some of the flame from the lantern onto a stick and back to the fireplace. Once Halfdan was able to get the fireplace going he grabbed the axe that Liv put down and eyed Peapod. The chicken had hopped out of the box and was now sitting in Freyja's lap. The chicken was beginning to close its eyes, taking in all of Freyja's affection. Halfdan relaxed his shoulders as he let out a defeated sigh and grabbed the lantern and went outside with the axe still in hand.

The rain was coming down harder than before, making it difficult for Halfdan to scan the trees and bushes for any chickens that might be about. Halfdan then decided to check around in the shrubbery that Peapod was in. To his delight there were six eggs laying together hidden within the plants.

Halfdan put down the axe and lantern and rolled the eggs closer to him. One by one Halfdan began washing the eggs off in the puddles that were forming around him before placing them in the crook of his arm as he carried the axe and lantern back to the cabin. When he opened up the door he saw that Peapod was back in her box and that the rest of his companions were busy going through Oberon's belongings in his bedroom.

"You guys shouldn't be going through someone else's stuff." Halfdan scolded them as he awkwardly put the lantern and axe down before putting eggs on the table, careful they didn't roll away.

"He has a romance story in here! It's called *The Forbidden Love*." Elora yelled from the room.

Halfdan was at a loss for a moment before walking into the room to look at the *runes for himself. As Halfdan walked away one of the eggs rolled off the table and cracked open on the floor. Peapod jumped out of her box and ran over and began pecking at the orange yolk. Hearing one of the eggs break caused everyone to come out of the room to look at Peapod as she indulged in eating her own egg.

After a long moment of audible disgust, Halfdan decided to put some pots and cups outside to collect rainwater. As they waited, Halfdan decided to read the romance story that was carved on a wood plank out loud for everyone, changing some words and skipping parts for Freyja's sake, and only stopping to check on the water collecting.

When there was sufficient water in the pot Halfdan added it to the fire and continued reading until the water began to boil. Halfdan added the eggs and read a few more runes until taking the eggs out and adding them to a new bowl with cold rain water. Everyone watched the eggs as they cooled, growing more hungry in anticipation.

Ulv was the first to grab an egg out of the cold water, unable to control himself. Liv had to stop him from taking a bite and told him to peel the shell off first. For a moment everyone was tapping their eggs on the table and began peeling them. Everyone stopped

144

peeling their own eggs when they noticed that Ulv's egg had a developed chick in it. Ulv kept peeling and popped the whole chick in his mouth, chewed a little bit and swallowed.

"What?" Ulv asked, noticing that everyone was looking at him. "Did I not get all the shell off?"

"Just wondering how you liked it." Halfdan asked, still in shock.

Ulv shrugged his shoulders and licked his lips. "Not as chewy as the venison."

"Nice." Halfdan said, giving his peeled egg to Elora who was trying to peel her egg with her beak. "I'm going to get the cups outside."

When everyone was done eating Halfdan finished reading the story. The actual ending was a bit too risqué so Halfdan made up an ending, to which everyone complained saying it was unrealistic and vague. After the complaints were finished they decided it was time for bed. Halfdan and Ulv tried their best to sleep in the chairs as Liv, Elora and Freyja went into the bedroom.

It didn't take long for Ulv to give up and decided to sleep on the floor. Halfdan stayed up and watched the fire, too nervous to fall asleep. Between the sounds of thunder Halfdan couldn't help but think he heard a wolf howl in the distance.

Halfdan was woken up by the sound of someone knocking on the door. Morning light was peeking through holes in the cabin, highlighting dust floating about. Ulv grumbled and got up off the floor and opened the door for Hallvard. The smell of late night *petrichor filling the musty cabin as Hallvard walked in.

"Sorry for waking you." Hallvard said to Ulv and Halfdan.

"It's ok." Halfdan said getting up and stretching his sore muscles.

Hallvard held a letter in his hand and extended it to Halfdan. "It's a letter from my father for you."

Halfdan took it and noticed that the wax seal was broken, with a raised eyebrow Halfdan looked back at Hallvard.

Hallvard's face turned red in embracement. "I'm sorry, I just wanted to see if my father was going to treat you well. By the looks of it, he isn't."

Halfdan looked at the letter quickly, skimming it, then folded it back up and tossed it on the table with disgust.

"If there is anything I can do, let me know. I'm going to head out and help out some parish members. If my father is going to force them to share their food with me I might as well help them when I can. I will be back to check on you all before nightfall. God bless and bring you peace." Hallvard left, gently closing the door behind him.

"Uh, yeah you too." Halfdan said back awkwardly to the door. He was still unsure of the new religion that has grown in popularity. Although it's been introduced to his land for over two hundred years, Halfdan's home village was not accepting. Refusing any notion of blessing their ships with the new singular god. Uncomfortable memories of raids long ago filled Halfdan's mind and he promptly pushed them away.

"What's going on?" Liv asked as she opened up the door to the bedroom and walked out with Freyja behind her.

Elora flew out of the bedroom and landed clumsily on the table. "Is that the Jarl's insignia?" Elora asked as she examined the red seal on the letter. The design on it had the world tree and the roots make out the letter's J.E. "This Jarl *bacraut really thinks he's the center of the world."

"Yeah." Halfdan agreed. "The Jarl isn't going to support us. But he granted us permission to hunt the wolf. If we slay it before next *Sun's Day we can negotiate payment with him. Until we have the wolf in hand we cannot approach the Jarl or his guards." Halfdan informed everyone with obvious anger in his tone, not realizing that he was clenching his fists.

Liv stretched quick before speaking. "Let's think. Wolves are more active at dawn and dusk. Let's go out and talk to some locals and get an idea of where this wolf is seen the most. We can ask for supplies and we can come back here, make some traps and get them out and set before dusk." She suggested with confidence.

"But they said that the wolf can undo traps." Freyja added nervously.

"You can't trust everything people tell you." Elora told Freyja then looked at Halfdan with her big eyes. "Especially that Hallvard guy, I don't trust him."

"He did seem eager to get us out of the chapel." Halfdan admitted.

"Let's go through his stuff." Elora blurted.

"Elora!" Liv exclaimed in a disgusted tone before giving a mischievous smile. "I was thinking the same thing."

Halfdan began rubbing his temples in disbelief. "You two can't be serious?"

"I think we should go through his room too." Ulv said, shamefully. "When Hallvard opened the door to his room I could have sworn I smelled something."

"What do you mean by *something*?" Elora asked, concerned.

Ulv looked at the ground for a moment before speaking. "I don't know for sure, but I know it wasn't human."

"Let's go." Halfdan said, making sure his friends were looking at him. "We make this quick. No taking anything. Hallvard is still the Jarl's son, so we have to be careful if we don't want our heads freed from our bodies."

Halfdan watched and Liv picked up her axe and Elora jumped onto Ulv's shoulder. When everyone was ready Halfdan opened up the door and watched as Peapod ran out the door first. Halfdan jumped a little, forgetting that the chicken was still in the house. Peeved, Halfdan walked out the door and led his companions down the hill to the chapel. The morning air was crisp and the wet ground squished beneath their feet. Birds chirped happily, splashing about in the shallow puddles that had formed during the nights rain.

Soon the chapel was in sight. Halfdan kept looking around as he got closer to make sure no one was outside before opening the chapel door. Like Hallvard said, he never locked it. Halfdan went inside and gestured to everyone to quickly come in before closing the door. Everyone stood in silence before Halfdan called out for Hallvard. There was another silence and everyone stood still and listened. When there was no response Halfdan moved quickly down the aisle to the bedroom door. Everyone watched Halfdan as he jiggled the door handle.

"Locked." Halfdan whispered.

"Maybe we can crawl through a window." Liv whispered as she turned to leave.

Everyone followed behind Liv as she quickly moved through the chapel and peaked out the main doors, making sure the coast was clear. Satisfied that it was safe, Liv walked out and began to make her way around the building as everyone followed her.

To everyone's surprise a window that would have led into Hallvard's bedroom was boarded up from the inside. Freyja kept walking alongside the building and noticed a door in back and ran to get everyone to show them the scratch marks on it. Some scratch marks were old and some were fresh, layered over one another. Some scratches started from the top of the door but most accumulated at the bottom, as if the beast who made them was trying to dig its way in.

"Hallvard's holding back information." Elora commented as she stayed perched on Ulv's shoulder.

Halfdan walked up to the door and felt the groves of the scratch marks before trying the handle. It was locked. "We will set up traps around here." Halfdan said sternly as he looked around the tree line before making eye contact with Ulv. "Smell the door."

Ulv nodded his head and approached the door and began to sniff it, moving up and down the door before letting out a quick snort out his nose. "The rain washed most of it away." Ulv commented before getting on his hands and knees to try and smell under the door, causing Elora to lose her balance and hop off Ulv's shoulder.

Ulv smashed the side his face against the ground as he tried his best to get his nose under the door before taking a few sniffs. "Smells like a wolf but different." Ulv said his voice muffled by the door.

"What do you mean by different?" Liv asked, unsure on what to make of Ulv's comments.

Ulv got up and looked at Liv, the side of his face was covered in wet dirt. "Smells are starting to blend together, it's difficult for me to tell. He could just have a wolf pelt in there." Ulv then bent over to pick up Elora.

"Is Hallvard a wolf monster?" Freyja asked nervously as she looked around.

"He seems like such a nice guy." Liv added, shaking her head in disappointment.

"We have to keep treating him like we don't suspect anything. After we put some traps out we will catch him in no time and then we can collect our money and leave." Halfdan said as he checked the ground, making sure they didn't leave any tracks. "Let's go and talk to some locals."

Halfdan led the way as they walked away from the chapel and made their way to rural farm houses. Residents were more than eager to talk to Halfdan and his companions about the wolf that has been terrorizing them. One man went as far as putting his livestock in his house to keep them safe. Soon all their stories began to sound the same. The wolf would kill livestock but would rarely consume what it killed. The only time the wolf is spotted is when it is leaving carnage in its wake and often seen heading in the direction of the chapel, causing people to stop going to hear the word of their new god.

When Halfdan would ask if they had any materials to spare he would be told yes, but that their efforts were in vain. Many people tried putting traps out but they would be destroyed. Dogs that were once protecting their livestock now cower in their shelters. People were starting to give up and contemplating moving away, worried that they would end up a victim of the wolf

149

themselves. Stories spread about the priest being attacked and that the wolf must have killed the hermit, Oberon.

With the materials that Halfdan and his companions collected they continued to set snares on animal trails that they found near the chapel. Making sure the loop of the snare was large enough for a wolf and hidden where trails got narrow. With a wood shovel they found in the cabin they began to dig simple pits and would make spikes out of wood and secure them at the bottom of the pit. When they were satisfied they would cover the pit with branches and leaves.

When they returned to the cabin there was Hallvard, standing outside the door with food in hand. He asked how they were doing and everyone tried to do their best to act friendly. Soon Hallvard headed back to the chapel and everyone ate and went to sleep, tired from a long day of setting up traps.

In the morning, everyone ran out of the cabin to check the traps only to find them all dismantled. The rope for the snare would be chewed up into small bits and the pits would be uncovered and the spikes dug up and scattered about. The group looked at one another in disbelief.

CHAPTER 15

THE MADMAN OFTEN TELLS THE TRUTH.
NORSE PROVERB - UNKNOWN

Days began to repeat themselves. They were spent collecting materials to make new traps. Traps were made and set. Peapod would be let back inside for the night and Liv and Freyja would either practice reading or be practicing magic with Elora. The only difference was that Hallvard began showing up less frequently. Giving Halfdan and Ulv time to hide in the trees and watch the back door of the chapel, but nothing would ever happen.

Now it was the night before Sun's Day, the last day the Jarl gave Halfdan to complete his task. Halfdan was sitting in the chair and was watching the fire as Ulv laid on the floor snoring. Already irritated that the wolf was evading all their taps and that tomorrow was their last day, Halfdan decided to step outside. Halfdan stood outside and stared into the darkness, soaking it all in. He then looked at the full moon and the occasional clouds that would obstruct the moon's light, casting a richer darkness into the night.

Halfdan pulled his cloak closer to his body as the night air began to chill his body. He watched the moon a little longer before walking down a short trail that Freyja found earlier, leading to a natural spring. There were stones placed in a crescent shape to help the spring pool up and then the overflow would spill over and run toward a small river not that far away. Halfdan knelt down and watched the water that would bubble out of the ground, gently kicking up the sandy bottom.

After taking his gloves off Halfdan put his scarred hands in the pool of water, feeling how cold it was before cupping the water and splashing his face. Halfdan began to drink the water, trying to suppress his hunger. With Hallvard visiting less they were scarce for food and Halfdan would rather see everyone else eat than himself. The crisp earthy water sent a shiver through his body as he used his cloak to dry his face and hands.

The nippy night air was beginning to chill Halfdan's body more, prompting him to head back to the cabin. The closer Halfdan got to the cabin the more sickly he felt, unsure if it was hunger or nerves. As soon as Halfdan saw the cabin his heart sank as his stomach turned, the door was wide open. The warm welcoming light from the fireplace became more menacing looking through the open door as it casted light upon the lone wolf. The great wolf looked at Halfdan with its yellow eyes, one of its ears was cropped and its fur was black as the abyss. In its mouth was Freyja's jacket collar with Freyja still in it. Freyja looked back at Halfdan with wide eyes, utter fear rendering her immobile.

The wolf and Halfdan looked at one another for what felt like eternity until the wolf began sprinting away, dragging Freyja with it. Halfdan yelled incoherent words at the wolf and ran after it. The wolf was running down the path towards the chapel making it easier for Halfdan to follow. The wolf was able to get ahead. Unbothered by the extra weight of Freyja in its jaws. Halfdan pushed through the running pains and kept sprinting after the wolf, trying his best to keep it in sight.

Soon the chapel was in sight and the wolf made its way to the back door. Halfdan cursed as some of the trees concealed the wolf. When Halfdan ran around the trees he stopped when he saw the wolf wagging its tail as it scratched at the door with Freyja still hanging limply from its jaws. Halfdan watched as Hallvard opened the door. Hallvard gasped in surprise and immediately scolded the wolf to drop Freyja. The wolf obliged and Hallvard immediately checked Freyja, making sure she was ok.

Halfdan was relieved to see Freyja sit up, but buried the feeling and put on a face of anger as he approached Hallvard. Hallvard straightened up when he saw Halfdan and took a step back.

"Tell me the truth!" Halfdan demanded, trying his best to be intimidating.

Hallvard's complexion turned pale as he looked at Halfdan but he didn't respond. Halfdan could feel his face turn red in anger and was quickly growing impatient. Slowly Halfdan moved his right hand behind his back and snapped his fingers, sending the trees behind him bursting into flames.

Hallvard dropped to his knees and wrapped his arms around the great wolf's neck. The wolf whimpered nervously as Hallvard buried his face into its fur and began to cry. Confusion washed over Halfdan and he could feel the heat of the flames behind him begin to die down.

"Just don't kill him, please." Hallvard said quietly between tears, lifting his face to look at Halfdan. "He's not a bad person."

"Person?" Halfdan asked, looking at the wolf's eyes. The wolf looked back at Halfdan with its intelligent eyes and began whimpering again like a puppy.

"My dad. I don't know why but my dad did this to Oberon." Hallvard said and began crying again, wiping his tears away with the sleeve of his nightgown before taking a deep breath.

Halfdan averted his eyes from Hallvard's tears and walked over to Freyja and helped her up. "Are you ok?"

Freyja nodded her head as her eyes began to swell with tears. "Yeah. I'm sorry I just froze up, I don't know why."

Halfdan gave Freyja a long hug, something he had never done to her but it felt like the right thing to do. Halfdan could feel Freyja shaking as she hugged him back even harder. Once Freyja let go to wipe away her tears Halfdan instructed her to go back to the cabin. Freyja nodded and ran off into the darkness.

Halfdan watched as Freyja left and waited until she was out of sight to approach Hallvard. Halfdan loomed over Hallvard and pulled him up by his nightgown so they were face to face. The wolf growled but Halfdan ignored the wolf as he pulled Hallvard close to him. Hallvard made nervous sounds as he was pulled about and lifted off his feet.

"Tell me everything." Halfdan said as he let go of Hallvard, dropping him to the ground.

Hallvard cleared his throat before he began telling Halfdan the truth. "Pastor Kólos told my father about Oberon. I was visiting Oberon at his house one night when the guards came. They beat us and then took us to my father. The guards put us in separate rooms but I could hear them, my f-father and siblings, did something to Oberon. Made him this monster. They did this strange chant. I couldn't make out any words. Then, they took me back to the chapel and they brought in this cage that had Oberon in it. The guards opened the cage and left. I could hear them block the doors." Hallvard stopped talking and hugged himself before speaking again. "They thought Oberon would kill me. Then in the morning for prayer everyone would find me dead and eventually the townspeople would capture Oberon and kill him too. That was the idea anyway. I wrote my father a letter, telling him that if he wanted to kill me that he needs to do it himself. I haven't heard anything from him since. Not until you came. I'm sorry that I lied to you, but I did it to protect Oberon. He's my only friend."

"You told me Oberon attacked the priest, that's why he left." Halfdan asked, trying to understand the situation better.

Hallvard rubbed the back of his head nervously. "It was me, I beat him up for telling my father about Oberon. I just put a wolf pelt over myself and attacked him at night."

"That's not very Deacon like." Halfdan commented with a devilish grin.

"I had a moment of weakness. Also, I've told you I'm not a Deacon. I'm sure I can't be one now after all of this. Pastor Kólos knew that my father wouldn't let Oberon stay anyway." Hallvard said, replacing his tears with anger.

"Because he hasn't been paying his taxes?" Halfdan asked.

"That, and he's part of the hidden people. Like Freyja. Oberon has been watching her. He's nervous for her, probably why he brought her here." Hallvard pat Oberon on the head. "I try to keep him in my room, but he is good at getting out."

154

"You knew?" Halfdan asked, referring to Hallvard knowing that Freyja was only half human. If Freyja didn't show her ears it was impossible to tell she was part Huldufolk.

Hallvard looked up at Halfdan, surprised. "Well, yes. After meeting Oberon It's easy to spot the difference. Don't worry, I didn't tell anyone. I can keep a secret."

"Does your father or siblings know how to use magic?" Halfdan asked, trying to figure out how they transformed Oberon into a wolf.

"Heaven, no. Rumors say that a man by the name of Magnus came and gave my father a shadow codex in exchange for anyone who could use magic. If you could go and get that codex away from my father, maybe we can change Oberon back." Hallvard looked at Halfdan with hope in his eyes.

Halfdan rubbed the stubble on his face as the thought of Magnus' name rang in his head. Magnus was trouble and getting his codex could give some insight on what he is up to. Thoughts of revenge for Magnus beating him and locking him up came to mind, but Halfdan pushed those thoughts away. "Figure you can't go because the guards know you. Do you know how I can get past them?"

"Guards are money hungry; I have some donations I can give you. Just avoid my father's personal guards as they are by his side at all times. Servants at the house pray with me. If you can get to them and tell them that you are there on my behalf they will be more than happy to help." Hallvard turned and went into his room to get some silver coins.

Oberon the wolf followed behind Hallvard, giving Halfdan an opportunity to look inside. Hallvard's modest room and furniture was all scratched up from Oberon. Hallvard came back and handed Halfdan seven silver coins. Halfdan couldn't help but grimace at the amount. Seven silver coins, some cut in half, wasn't worth it for a guard to possibly lose their job over, but it will have to do.

Hallvard saw Halfdan's visible displeasure. "Sorry, father raised the tax and people don't have much to give."

"Go to my friends and let them know where I am going. Tell them everything you told me." Halfdan told Hallvard as he put the coins in his leather pouch. "If I am not back by daylight they need to go back to Norivck."

"Norvick, right. Will do. Thank you. I am sorry I cannot do much in return." Hallvard said with a weak smile.

"Just let me keep Magnus' codex. It's dangerous in the wrong hands." Halfdan then promptly left, ready to get the job over with. Hearing Hallvard yell good luck and thanking him as he slipped into the darkness.

Halfdan wasn't looking forward to the long walk to the Jarl's house and with each step he grew increasingly nervous. Breaking into houses wasn't difficult, but there are going to be guards at the ready. Halfdan also couldn't help but feel disappointed in Liv and Ulv for sleeping through a wolf breaking in and taking Freyja. But it shows how easy it is for people to sleep through a break in.

By the position of the moon Halfdan figured it was midnight by the time he reached the Jarl's fortress. Halfdan kept his distance and found a good shadow to sit under and watched the guards for a while. Unlike before there was only one guard at the gate and he was busy flirting with his intoxicated girlfriend who showed up to keep him company. Satisfied that the guard was busy he walked around the fence, making sure he stayed in the shadows as he looked for an easy place to enter.

As he moved along the fence he came upon a tree whose branches overgrew the fence. Satisfied, Halfdan climbed up the tree and shimmied across the branches. Hesitating a moment to look around before dropping from the branches. Halfdan already knew where he wanted to enter, the new addition to the large building. For the old addition was more of a fortress. No windows are good protection from wars and thieves. However, Jarl Ellingboe's addition had plenty of windows. Halfdan wasn't sure if it was the

Jarl's vanity or ignorance that caused him to destroy the buildings defenses, but it will make a good break in point. Halfdan waited till cloud's covered the moon's gleam to run across the yard towards the new addition.

Peeking in through the window, he didn't notice any movement and attempted to open windows. The first two were locked but the third one opened without a fuss. The builders were still finishing the interior so he didn't have to worry about bumping into any furnishings as he slid through the window. Halfdan closed the window behind him as he began to move about, pausing every so often to listen for any movement. Content that there was nothing of interest in the new addition, just hammers and nails lying about. Halfdan made his way towards the temporary white curtain that divided the new addition from the old.

As Halfdan moved the dusty curtain out of his way he felt the blood drain from his face when he saw the Jarl and his two personal guards before him. They were standing there waiting for Halfdan. Halfdan stood frozen as he watched the Jarl cross his arm and give Halfdan a smug look.

"Looks like we have a rat problem." Jarl Ellingboe said as he lifted a hand and lamely waved it in Halfdan's direction. "Seize him."

Halfdan's heart skipped a beat at the Jarl's words and watched as the guards took a step towards him. The guard's movement caused Halfdan to turn and try to run, but the guards were faster. One guard grabbed Halfdan and put him in a headlock as the other took the opportunity to punch Halfdan in the head repeatedly until Halfdan went limp.

CHAPTER 16

FEAR NOT YOUR DEATH, FOR THE HOUR OF YOUR DOOM IS SET, AND NO ONE CAN ESCAPE IT.
VÖLSUNGA SAGA ~ NORSE PROVERB

Halfdan awoke feeling old hay beneath him. When he slowly opened his eyes he saw that he was in a small metal cage and pillar candles in the four corners of the room he was held in. He saw the Jarl's mouth move as he talked to two other people in the room, but Halfdan could only hear the ringing in his ears. Halfdan continued to look around trying to remember what happened. He could feel his tongue move around a gap in his teeth where a molar should be. The iron taste of blood reminded Halfdan that he had been in a fight.

As Halfdan continued to watch the people talking he noticed that Jarl Ellingboe was grasping a purple codex. Halfdan's eyes widened as his memory came back to him. He was there looking for Magnus' codex. The codex that the Jarl used to transform Oberon into a wolf. Hallvard said that they had Oberon in a cage when he was transformed into a wolf.

Panic ran though Halfdan as he began to look around more frantically trying to think of any spells he could use to escape. The only spells Halfdan knew could result in killing everyone, including himself. He could cast fire and burn them or perhaps even try to summon ice to freeze the Jarl and his companions, but he would still be locked in a cage. Halfdan couldn't help but feel regret for not learning different spells that could help him in this situation.

The ringing in Halfdan's ears began to fade away as he could hear the Jarl call his name. Halfdan stopped looking around to make eye contact with the Jarl and his two companions, a young man and woman. The young man looked well fed and had a round face and neckbeard. The young woman had a round face but looked sickly thin. They both looked to be around the same age as Hallvard. Halfdan figured that the two must be Hallvard's half siblings. Halfdan couldn't help but think it was funny how Hallvard looked more like his father than his siblings, who must resemble their mother. The amusing thought went away when Halfdan saw the young man grab a bucket of water and fling it at him.

Halfdan flinched as the cold water drenched him. "Seriously? You already took my dignity by putting me in a cage."

The Jarl laughed and his children joined in. Then the Jarl gave Halfdan a wolfish grin. "I thought thieves had no dignity. Couldn't kill the wolf so you came to rob me instead?"

Halfdan laughed, causing the Jarl's grin to turn into a scowl. "I'm here to turn Oberon back into a human. Just need Magnus' codex and I'll be on my way."

Jarl's shoulders tensed up before he spoke with scorn in his voice. "Oberon isn't human, he's an unholy half elf mongrel. I assume his people's *connection to nature* kept him from losing control." The Jarl said condescendingly.

"Hallvard is your son. Why transform his friend into a wolf? To kill your own son?" Halfdan asked, trying to pull at their hearts.

The young man spat on the ground, as if the question left a bad taste in his mouth. "We lost our place in the king's court because of him! Now we get to listen to these peasants complain about food and rent. How pathetic."

The Jarl put his hand up, causing the young man to stop talking and put his head down. "Taking care of two problems at once, really. We want Hallvard punished and I can't let the hidden people taint my land. Now that you are here, we have a chance to get this curse right. We will transform you into a wolf and you will go mad with bloodlust, killing Hallvard and your little friends. Then, just like a real wolf, you won't be able to stand a stranger wolf in your territory and kill Oberon for us. I will raise the rent and taxes again and put a reward for killing you, Halfdan the wolf, and the townsmen will be so desperate and put all their effort into killing you. After that it will just be a matter of time before one of the townsmen traps and kills you."

Just then the Jarl held up his hand to show Halfdan an object between his thumb and index finger. At first Halfdan thought it was a small rock, then his mouth dropped open when he realized it was his missing tooth. The Jarl lifted his chin and gave a crooked smile at Halfdan's recognition and promptly turned and walked to a table at the far side of the room. Halfdan watched as the Jarl dropped the tooth in a rock mortar bowl and began crushing the tooth with the pestle. The sound of the tooth being crushed into powder made Halfdan cringe and cover his ears.

Halfdan forced himself to watch as the young woman combine a red pigment into linseed oil to make a paint. As the young woman was mixing the paint the Jarl added the tooth powder into it. The young man grabbed a dried white wolf paw off the table and walked towards Halfdan. Halfdan continued to watch as the young woman walked next to her sibling and held the bowl for him to dip the paw into the paint. In a circular motion around the cage the young man used the paw to trace cryptic symbols.

When the circle was complete the two siblings placed the bowl and the paw back on the table and joined their father, who had the codex open on the table. They all looked over the codex one last time before turning and walking towards Halfdan. The Jarl stopped in front of Halfdan just before the circle and his children stood behind him, bowing their heads.

In unison all three began to chant twisted words as all the candles in the room dimmed on their own. Halfdan couldn't help but feel conflicted, it seemed like he should be afraid but deep down he wasn't. He watched on helplessly and anticipated the worst, shivering as his wet clothes clinging to his body and the smell of paint and damp straw filled the air. Halfdan couldn't help but think about Oberon, did he yell for help or did he just sit and wait to become a beast like he was doing.

160

Soon the little specks of tooth in the paint began to glow and vibrate as the air became thick with magic. Halfdan looked down at his gloved hands, waiting for them to turn into paws. Just then the air seemed to clear and the candles lit up again. Confused, Halfdan looked up at his captures to see the Jarl grabbing at his sides as he leaned forward. The Jarl clenched his teeth as he let out a sickly moan as his son moved to help steady him. The young woman took a step back and nervously bit her lip.

Louder, the Jarl's moan turned into a growl as wiry brown fur busted through his skin as if it was thin parchment. The young man jumped back as his father's body grew larger. Fingers growing longer and curled, revealing long nails. His neck became thicker as his ears became tall and pointy. When the Jarl opened his eyes they were bright yellow and filled with a deep hunger. The Jarl twisted his body to look at his son, making his now snouty face more noticeable to Halfdan.

In a blink of an eye the beast jumped on the young man and began to maul his face. The young man could barely let out a scream before the beast broke his neck. The young woman let out a scream loud enough for the both of them as she ran past Halfdan and out the door. Halfdan sat still and watched as the beast lifted its head to watch its daughter run. The beast's entire body seemed fidgety in anticipation as it rose up and ran after her, leaving Halfdan alone in a room with the bloody carnage. Halfdan turned his body to look out the now open door. He could hear the woman's scream abruptly stop as two guards ran past the door in pursuit of the beast.

Halfdan laid on his back and began frantically kicking the door to the cage in an attempt to break it open. The beast let out a booming howl that rumbled through the fortress causing Halfdan's heart to beat rapidly like a rabbit's. He scooted as far back as he could in the cage and summoned fire from his hands, focusing it at the door and making it hot as he could muster. The harder Halfdan focused the more blue and white the flames became. The flames became so bright that Halfdan had to close his eyes, breaking his concentration and extinguishing the flames.

When Halfdan opened his eyes he saw that the door and its frame to the cage was now glowing liquid metal. Feeling triumphant, Halfdan then inhaled deeply and slowly let out a gust of air as if he was blowing out a candle, focusing his intent to freeze the metal. Halfdan watched as his breath froze, causing the metal to pop and crack in contact.

Some of the straw was still smoldering as Halfdan crawled out, causing his eyes to burn while he looked at the dead body before him. The young man's throat was ripped open and his body was raked open from the beast's claws. The man's eyes were open wide and unfocused, still wearing a shocked expression. Halfdan couldn't help but feel disrespectful by accidently mutilating the body more. The deceased legs were close to the fire he summoned, causing some of the pant legs to burn away and the shoes to char. Halfdan could see some of the visible skin that split open from the heat. After satisfying his morbid curiosity, Halfdan swiftly moved to the table and grabbed Magnus' codex before running out of the room and down the hall in the opposite direction of the beast.

Halfdan moved quickly as he prayed to no one in particular, hoping that he wouldn't run into the beast again as he looked for the exit. After wandering around disoriented, Halfdan began following frightened servants attempting to run out of the building; just as the beast came bursting through a door knocking down one of the servants. He turned and ran the other way, listening to the screams behind him. Halfdan ran through the hall and had to jump over the young woman from before, mauled in a similar manner as her brother.

Out of breath Halfdan began thanking the gods when he saw the familiar white curtain that divided the old and new addition, allowing him to exit the same way he came in. It was still night time as the full moon almost completed its journey across the sky. Halfdan kept running across the lawn before coming up to the fence. Halfdan threw the codex over the fence then scaled over the fence and fell down the other side. After picking up the codex, Halfdan continued to run until the Jarl's house was out of view. Halfdan only stopped to catch his breath and listen to see if he could hear anything. When all he could hear was his own heavy breathing he continued to move at a jog, fear motivating him to keep traveling.

Halfdan was halfway back when he heard the familiar harsh hiss of an eagle owl. Halfdan stopped jogging and looked up to see Elora circling him overhead. He held out his arm for Elora to perch. Elora flew down and did just that, her talons dug into Halfdan's arm causing him to swear. Despite the pain Halfdan was still happy to see Elora. Halfdan explained to Elora what happened between heavy breaths then asked her to fly back to the Jarl's house and see what was going on. Elora obliged, flapped her wings and took off silently into the night and disappeared into the dark like a ghost.

After watching Elora fly away Halfdan began jogging again. When the chapel was in sight he saw the glow of candles through the windows. Halfdan smiled when he saw silhouettes begin to move when he was in view. Soon Liv opened the door to the chapel and Ulv and Freyja came pouring out to greet him. Halfdan informed them that Elora found him and that she will be back soon.

When Halfdan walked into the chapel he stopped to look at Hallvard standing next to an unfamiliar man. The stranger had pale skin similar to a sun bleached okoume timber, green eyes and brown hair. The man smiled, amused that Halfdan didn't recognize him and tucked his hair behind his ear to show off that the right ear was cropped and the other pointed. It was Oberon.

"You're not a wolf anymore." Halfdan said, somewhat disappointed that he risked his life to get a codex to turn Oberon back in the first place.

"I'm not sure what happened. I was hoping you could shed some light on the situation." Oberon said softly. "But first let's get you some water."

Halfdan nodded, water has been on his mind ever since he began making his way back. Halfdan walked over to the pews and

163

sat down with a huff. Hallvard went and got Halfdan a cup of water before getting Oberon to turn a pew around so they could sit across from Halfdan. Liv, Ulv and Freyja sat next to Halfdan and looked at him, eager for him to tell them what happened. Halfdan took a sip of water and looked at the wood cup, unsure on how to tell Hallvard that his half siblings were dead.

Halfdan started from the beginning, telling all of them how he broke into the fortress. About how he was captured and beaten. Explained that he woke up in a cage and how they tried to cast a curse on him, but something must have gone wrong. Halfdan explained how the Jarl turned into a monster and killed his own children. Halfdan watched as Hallvard began to grieve. Despite not being close to his half siblings he was still hurt by the loss. All of Hallvard's thoughts of someday getting to know them were gone. Then Halfdan finished the story by telling them how he escaped and ran into Elora, sending her to investigate more.

Oberon nodded to agree with Halfdan's story. "They performed the same ritual on me, rather than a tooth they… they used my ear." Oberon stopped talking to feel his cropped ear. A stern look grew on his otherwise cheerful face. "Obviously they were successful in transforming me into a wolf. Not that monster you described. When they turned they filled my head with thoughts. Tormented me with thoughts of killing Hallvard and other villagers, but I was able to suppress my hunger by killing livestock." Oberon shivered, not from the cold but the uncomfortable thought of his mind being manipulated so.

Uncomfortably, Oberon went on to tell them that he would watch them during the day and would follow behind them to destroy the traps they set. Waiting for a moment where he could try and take Freyja away from them, explaining that was trying to protect her from the Jarl.

The talking stopped when there was a tapping noise on the glass window. Elora was perched on the windows ledge. Innocently trying to get attention to get let in she almost looked like a demon outside the window with her big yellow eyes. After a quick fright Liv got up and opened the chapel doors.

Elora flew in and perched on top of a pew next to Hallvard, taking a moment to adjust her wings before speaking. "The Jarl is dead. When the guards killed him he must have transformed back because the guards are scared, worried that they will be executed for killing the Jarl. With the Jarl and his children dead it most likely ended Oberon's curse. But it doesn't explain how Halfdan wasn't affected by the curse and the Jarl was. Hard to believe they messed up the second time when they got the curse correct the first time."

Oberon put a hand on Hallvard's shoulder. "You should go. It's your birthright and burden to bear. The King knows you're next in line."

Hallvard lifted his sad eyes to look at Oberon. "Can you come with me? I have no idea what I'm doing."

Oberon smiled and gently patted Hallvard on the back. "I was already planning on it." Oberon then looked at Halfdan. "I need to check on Peapod first. Halfdan, could you come with?"

Halfdan moved about awkwardly in his seat, unsure what Oberon wanted. "Uh… Sure."

Everyone watched as Oberon led Halfdan away. Halfdan could hear his companions talking to Hallvard by the time the chapel door closed. The sun's rays were already lighting up the morning and the birds began to sing their songs. Halfdan's feet were sore and it took some motivation to catch up with Oberon.

Oberon waited for Halfdan to be close before speaking to him, continuing to look forward as he did. "I'm sorry I took Freyja in the middle of the night."

"Its fine, I understand."

"That's not really the reason why I wanted to talk to you alone." Oberon said, more seriously with a blank expression.

Halfdan looked at Oberon confused and nervous. "What is it then?"

"I want to look at the mark on your hand. When you were setting traps I would see something. I want to look at it."

165

Halfdan took off his left glove and held his hand out. Oberon stopped walking and grabbed Halfdan's hand and brought it close to his eyes to get a better look. Halfdan didn't know Oberon for long but he was doing a good job of making him uncomfortable. Oberon stood looking at Halfdan's hand for some time before letting go and recoiling as if the invisible marking offended him.

"What is it?" Halfdan asked, concerned.

"Who is Jovi? Your demon master, warlock?" Oberon said as he took a step back away from Halfdan.

"I don't understand?"

"Don't act. You won't fool me." Oberon said angrily, hands up defensively and close to becoming fists.

"I don't see anything. Believe me, please. I need to know what he did to me."

Oberon looked at Halfdan with a frown and relaxed some. He could see fear and desperation in Halfdan's eyes. Oberon let out an exaggerated breath before speaking again. "It's written in *Alfheim, old elvish. It's a mark on your soul. It lets Jovi find you no matter where you go. It is also a protection insignia. It will send any spell or curse set out to you back to the owner."

Halfdan looked at his hand, amazed yet feeling violated that his body had been tampered with. "That's why the Jarl turned into a monster but not me?"

Oberon nodded. "It only works once, then it needs true darkness to recharge."

"True darkness?" Halfdan asked Oberon again as he made his way to his cabin.

"I'm not sure. I don't know magic or spells or curses. I just teach other hidden people how to speak human and how to act like one."

"Why do they want to do that?" Halfdan asked, surprised.

"Generations ago elves and darkelves could travel between the nine realms. Suddenly the doorways between the realms were closed off. Trapped here the two elf races tried to work together to get it open again, but it ended in conflict. The elves blamed the

166

darkelves for not getting the door to work and the darkelves complained that they needed more time. So horrible was the fighting that the darkelves no longer consider themselves part of the elf race, now calling themselves dwarves. Honestly the fighting has been going on before the doorway was closed." Oberon stopped talking to open up the door to the cabin. Peapod jumped out of her box and began pecking at Oberon's bare feet. With a gentle smile Oberon picked Peapod up and held her close to him. "My adoptive mother was a midwife and lived here, alone in this cabin. The hidden people's maternal morbidity is higher than a human's and they often went to my adoptive mother for help. When she helped deliver me my birth mother refused to take me. I guess half breeds like me and Freyja are a liability. We are more human and can't hide and move through the forest like they can. Being more human isn't a bad thing though. It's easier to blend in. Elves need a little more help learning how to act human. With their numbers dwindling some would rather live on a farm than continue with their nomadic lifestyle." Oberon put Peapod back down and watched as she ran to her familiar bush before closing the cabin door. "Sorry, I forget I talk a lot. Makes people uncomfortable."

Halfdan shook his head. "It's ok, I enjoy hearing about your people."

Oberon gave Halfdan a genuine smile, happy that he didn't mind. As Oberon led the way back to the chapel he continued to tell Halfdan about the hidden people. He talked about how they enjoyed sweets, cream and bread because their nomadic lifestyle made it difficult for them to farm. In contrast the Elves' diet was more protein based. They found human art and buildings interesting and could spend days looking at them. To pass time the hidden people enjoyed singing and dancing, even though it looked different compared to human singing and dancing. Oberon couldn't find the words to describe how unique the Elves' dancing was, other than it was fluid like water. Back at the chapel Hallvard was waiting outside, dressed in his modest deacon clothing and ready to go.

Before Oberon left with Hallvard he turned to Halfdan with an inscrutable expression. "I can tell there is more you aren't telling me. That is ok, but you should confide in your friends."

Oberon then extended his hand Halfdan. Halfdan took it and both shook hands.

"Also, thank you. For everything. You could have easily killed Peapod and eaten her. But you didn't. You even risked your life to try and save me. Most people would have given up. I hope in the future I can repay you." Oberon smiled and turned to join Hallvard.

Hallvard and Oberon waved to Halfdan as they made their way down the road to the fortress. By now the sun was up and the people of Rokeby were beginning to start their morning. Halfdan stood outside to watch Hallvard and Oberon until they were out of sight.

When Halfdan was done and entered the chapel he saw Liv holding the purple shadow codex up to Elora. Trying to focus her vision Elora bobbed her head in a circular motion as owls often do. Ulv sat in front of Freyja who was braiding his red hair.

Halfdan walked over and sat down by his companions and decompressed. After groaning about how sore his feet were he noticed everyone looking at him. "What?"

"What did Oberon want to talk to you about?" Asked Freyja as she finished decorating Ulv's hair.

Halfdan felt his stomach do a quick jump for some unknown reason. He knew that Abia and Oberon told him that he needed to tell his friends what was going on. "Just wanted to thank me." He blurted without thinking.

"With the Jarl dead, who is going to pay us?" Elora asked without looking up from the codex.

"Maybe Hallvard will. I wouldn't count on it though. Can't win every time. We can head back to Norvick's inn and regroup." Halfdan said with his eyes closed leaning back in the pew.

"Can we at least ask Hallvard for more food?" Ulv asked with sad puppy eyes.

"I'm sure Hallvard and Oberon will be coming back. I'll wait here for them. How about you guys go back to the cabin and clean it up for him. We left it worse than how we found it. I just need to sit here for a bit." Halfdan said, beginning to nod off. He could hear everyone groan as they got up and exited the chapel, closing the door behind them.

Halfdan couldn't remember falling asleep when he was startled awake by a constricting sensation. At first he thought that there was rope tied around his midsection to keep his arms down and around his legs to keep him from standing up. When he looked down he noticed that they were two large black snakes with glowing green eyes. When he struggled to get free the snakes hissed and constricted more. Halfdan winced in pain and struggled to breath.

Suddenly the sun outside disappeared and darkness filled the chapel. There was just enough light for Halfdan to see a shadow creep up behind him. Two disfigured clawed hands gently reached out and rested on Halfdan's shoulders. Halfdan felt his breath escape him and felt his body tremble as he slowly looked up.

Jovi loomed over Halfdan. When their eyes met Jovi gave a wide grin that showed off his pointed teeth. The longer Halfdan stared at Jovi the bigger the grin grew until it was unnaturally wide.

"Did you really think that your pretty flowers could keep me away?" Jovi said calmly as he made his way around the long pew to stand in front of Halfdan.

Halfdan looked upon Jovi, who reassembled more of a monster than a buck now. Jovi stood on two hooved feet and was up right like a man. His fur was no longer brown and white but grey and black but still had a face and antlers that resembled a buck's. The candles on each point were now replaced with bird skulls and ivy looped and dangled off the rack.

Without thinking Halfdan began to struggle against the snakes who constricted even harder. Halfdan felt a rib crack and would have screamed but there was no air in his lungs to do so. Jovi reached out with his left claw and grabbed Halfdan's jaw to keep his head still.

"Disappointing. I will forgive you this time. But your insubordination can not be ignored. I will take one eye, for now. You have until the next full moon to kill Blackhare." Jovi stopped talking and purred a little. "Please hold still, I don't want to damage your eye as I pull it out of your skull. Now, what eye should I take first?" Jovi lifted his right claw and tapped his nose playfully as he thought. Watching Halfdan's body as it struggled for air. Slowly Jovi lifted his right claw at Halfdan's right eye. "This one."

Halfdan had no choice but to watch as Jovi reached out for his eye. He felt the claws carefully slide under his eyelids and around his eyeball. Without a word Jovi pulled and the ripping sensation of the eye being removed echoed through Halfdan's body.

The pain was so great that Halfdan couldn't see out of the one eye he still had. Halfdan could taste iron as blood ran from his empty socket and down his face.

The sound of Jovi's hooves clicking on the floor as he walked away filled the silent chapel. The snakes released and slithered away towards their master. Halfdan sucked in air and covered his eye socket with his hands. He wanted to scream. Not a scream from pain or fear but a scream for help and comfort. But Halfdan didn't want to give Jovi that satisfaction. Instead Halfdan sat there and took deep painful breaths and pushed the pain away. Coldness like a winter storm seeped in and all Halfdan could feel was his heart race.

CHAPTER 17

ANGER MEANS YOU CARE

Halfdan woke up and slowly opened his eye. He was laying on a bed and was covered with layers of fine fluffy blankets. The bed was so soft he never felt anything like it before. He imagined it was similar to laying on a cloud. Halfdan opened his eye more and looked around. He saw all of his companions including Hallvard and Oberon sitting in chairs around the bed, looking at him. He felt his face blush in embarrassment, uncomfortable that he was being watched but also grateful that he wasn't alone. The room filled with sighs of relief.

"Good, you're awake." Liv said with a gentle smile.

"Need me to fetch the healer?" Hallvard asked softly.

Halfdan smiled and closed his eye. "If you keep treating me this well you'll never get rid of me."

Everyone gave weak chuckles before the room fell silent again.

"We will leave you with your friends. If you need us you know where we will be." Oberon said as he stood up and quietly moved his chair to the wall.

Hallvard did the same and followed Oberon out of the room. Halfdan noticed that Hallvard was wearing exquisite green robes and furs, similar to what his father wore.

"So, is he a Jarl now?" Halfdan asked, looking at Liv.

Liv nodded. "Ceremony is tomorrow. Strangely enough, Hallvard was listed in the family tree. With his half siblings being dead no one else has birth rights. Everyone is buzzing with excitement. The first thing he is going to do is lower the tax. The new addition to the castle is going to be redone and used for extra food storage for the town in case of a famine." Liv looked at Halfdan with a more serious look in her eyes. "You're lucky that Hallvard sent a carriage to collect us for the ceremony tomorrow. We were able to get you here for help."

"Can you tell us what happened already? We've been waiting for over a day now." Elora asked with her usual lack of compassion.

"He just woke up, give him some time." Freyja scolded Elora.

"You're right. There are a lot of things I have been keeping from all of you." Halfdan preemptively looked at the stone ceiling and metal chandelier that hung above. Chairs creaked in the silent stone room as his companions leaned closer. Halfdan wanted to avoid Liv's expressions toward what he was about to tell her. "When I was locked away by Magnus I had a dream. A buck with candles on his rack told me he went by the name Jovi. Jovi said that he is responsible for keeping the gods and goddesses away. Then he told me that he would help me escape if I agreed to kill Hilda, but we know her as Blackhare. I agreed and that is what the mark on my hand is. Jovi left it on me and Oberon was able to decipher it, he said it is written in old elvish. It is used to track me so I cannot escape from Jovi. However, I am able to reflect magical attacks back to the original sender. When I was imprisoned, Magnus was going to use magic to send me flying across the room for his amusement. Instead, Magnus was the one pinned against the wall. That's how Elora and I were able to escape. That also explains why the Jarl's curse betrayed him, turning him into a monster rather than me. Ever since I met Jovi I've been running in the opposite direction of Blackhare. Because I worked with Blackhare before and I know she is a formidable foe. Jovi warned me that if I disobeyed, that he would take my eyes." Halfdan grimaced, feeling phantom sensations of his eye being removed. "He took one and told me if I don't kill Blackhare before the next full moon that... he will take the other."

"You worked with Blackhare before?" Elora asked, genuinely confused and hurt. Blackhare was the one who corrupted Magnus and destroyed the school she attended.

"She was going to reward me if I led Frode into a trap. Things…" Halfdan paused to take a deep breath." Things didn't go as planned, I thought Blackhare was going to keep him alive but she lied. Her henchmen were going to kill both of us. I got shot with three arrows and Frode used his powers to make trees fall, killing those sent to kill us. Rather than leaving me for dead, Frode gave me his life instead. I think about it every day and wish I never let Blackhare tempt me. I'm haunted at night by his memories, Frode's memories." Halfdan let out another deep breath before continuing. "However, with Frode's life I am able to use magic but I have no idea what I'm doing so I usually end up hurting people. Like I usually do."

"Why would you betray Frode?" Liv asked.

Halfdan couldn't tell if Liv was sad or angry by her tone. He turned his head to look at Liv expecting to see tears. She sat there looking back stoically. That made Halfdan worry. "I couldn't let you die."

"Why not? You barely knew me then. It doesn't make sense, Halfdan. When things don't make sense that means something is being left out." Liv said with a mild tone but her face was flush, trying to keep her emotions in.

"Linna asked me to come and help." Halfdan said, not directly answering Liv's question.

Liv stood up from her chair, her hands were in tight fists and visible heat was coming off of her. Freyja nervously scooted her chair away as Ulv stood up with Liv. Ulv tried to reach his hands out to Liv to console her but his hands jerked back, hurt from heat. Liv just stood there glaring at Halfdan as she got hotter and hotter.

"Maybe you should go outside." Ulv commented nervously, remembering what happened last time Liv got like this.

Liv turned to grab her chair, rather than quietly moving it to the wall she threw it, causing it to smash into pieces. Without hesitation Liv stomped out of the room and slammed the door behind her. Ulv and Freyja ran after Liv, leaving Elora and Halfdan alone in the awkward silence. It didn't take long for a guard to come in and see what the commotion was about. Halfdan lied and said a chair broke under Ulv's weight. The guard apologized and informed Halfdan that the chairs were old.

Elora stood in her chair and waited for the guard to close the door before speaking. "Way to go, Halfdan. You said you were going to open up and then you clam up again."

"She scared me." Halfdan said, pulling the covers a little closer to himself. "Are you mad at me as well?"

"For working with Blackhare? No. It just means that we are closer now. We have a common enemy. If anything you hurt yourself. We have a lot of ground to cover before the next full moon." Elora thought a moment before making happy owl sounds. "If we don't kill Blackhare in time, can I take your eye out for you? It would be so funny for Jovi to come and see it's already gone."

"If Liv doesn't get to it first, sure." Halfdan said, looking blankly at the chandelier above him.

"I overheard Hallvard talking to the blacksmith about making an eye for you." Elora informed Halfdan before jumping on the bed next to him. "That way you don't have to wear an eye patch."

"Nah, I'm just going to walk around without one and make you all look at my empty eye socket." Halfdan said cheerfully with a faint smile as he heard Elora's displeasure. "Read anything good in Magnus' shadow codex?"

"It's difficult to decipher. The first few pages are just silly stuff like charms to attract money or love. Then it just gets darker from there. Revenge and transformation spells. Some pages are missing. It's not good."

Halfdan sat up, wanting to ask Elora if there were any transformation spells in there that Magnus might have used on his students. Before he could say anything Halfdan looked at the clothes he was wearing. Halfdan pulled at the white nightgown and looked at Elora. "Tell me you guys weren't in here for this."

Elora laughed. "Nah, the handmaids are washing your bloodied clothes and wanted to put you in a clean bed. We waited outside. It was hilarious. They were freaking out thinking something was wrong with your hands."

Before Halfdan could disagree he got an uneasy feeling. He could feel his heart pulling him to go outside. Elora noticed the change in Halfdan's aura, he was worried. She didn't complain when Halfdan picked her up and ran out of the room. Elora told Halfdan how to get out of the fortress and soon they were standing outside.

There were screams in the distance, not of fear but surprise. Beyond the nearest tree line a circle of fire appeared. It wasn't like a normal fire. It smelled of brimstone. It went up and inhaled all the trees around it and quickly disappeared. All it left was a black bloom of smoke that was dissipating in the air.

"Check on Freyja and Ulv, I'll be right there." Halfdan told Elora and tossed her into the sky before she could reply.

Rather than watching Elora fly away Halfdan ran into town to look for a horse to steal. He would bring it back, but saying that isn't enough to prevent some limbs being broken by the guards. Halfdan doubted that anyone would stop a grown man running around in a nightgown with bandages wrapped around his head. It worked, people would look away and pretend that he wasn't there. Something about the unpredictability of a crazy man makes people nervous.

It did take long for Halfdan to find a trade shop with some horses tied up outside. Halfdan ran up and untied one of the horses and quickly hopped on. As he beckoned the horse to run he could hear the owner running outside and yell at him. Deep down Halfdan didn't want to get labeled a horse thief, but the owner will have to cope. Liv was in danger and Halfdan needed to get there before the guards.

There was still smoke wafting up and into the air for Halfdan to follow. The horse was swift and agile as it ran through the busy streets. A simple manure cart was in the middle of the street, blocking the path. Rather than stopping, the horse jumped over it. For a moment Halfdan was lifted into the air and had to hang on to prevent falling off the horse. When the horse landed on the ground Halfdan landed back down into the saddle. As the horse continued running Halfdan swore to himself to fight off the pain. Before Halfdan knew it, the horse was running through a wheat field and soon plunged into the forest. The trees obstructed the smoke so Halfdan had to hope that the horse continued to run toward the fire. The horse was tall so Halfdan had to keep his head down to prevent getting smacked in the face by a tree branch.

Suddenly the horse skitted to a stop, its instincts kicked in and it refused to go farther. Halfdan got off and calmed the horse, pulling its head close and talking to it. He thanked the horse and promised to bring him back to his owner. Right when Halfdan was about to tie the horse up to a tree Ulv came stumbling out. He was out of breath and sweaty with some leaves stuck in his red curly hair.

"Is she close?" Halfdan asked.

Ulv nodded and pointed deeper into the forest.

"Hang on to the horse. If guards come, tell them you found it and want to give the horse back to its master." Halfdan told Ulv as he handed him the reins.

Halfdan followed the path of broken branches that Ulv created. After fighting his way through a bush Halfdan came upon Elora perched on a branch near Freyja. Both stood before a large circle, all the plants and life that was once in that circle were gone, leaving behind black ash. Elora and Freyja looked back at Halfdan nervously before turning to look back at a mound in the middle of the clearing. Dirt was being flung about followed by deep grumbling.

"We just got here, I don't know what to do." Freyja said as she nervously played with her necklace.

"Guards will be here soon, I need you to stall them for me." Halfdan said, keeping his eye forward, watching dirt being flung about.

Halfdan took a deep breath before taking a step into the clearing. The hot ash was warm under his bare feet. Before Halfdan reached the mound the digging stopped and was replaced with growling. This didn't stop Halfdan, he kept moving closer. He walked up the mound and looked down into a large hole that was dug in the earth. A bright light came from within followed by heat.

Halfdan squatted down and looked into the hole. "Liv, I'm sorry. I didn't want you to think about your mother differently. The truth is, your mother left me because I didn't have a house or any money. At the time it didn't matter, but when she was pregnant with you things changed." Halfdan watched as the light within the cave dimed and little red and yellow embers came wafting out like fireflies and lazily hung in the air before gradually dying out. After taking another deep breath Halfdan continued. "I'm not sure if she ever told your… father. He knew the both of us had been together, but he wouldn't turn your mother away. I was never angry at Linna, but I thought about the both of you every day. When I received the letter saying you were sick, I was devastated. I told Frode everything and he told me that he would come with to help you. Before we arrived the cunning and even the healers gave up on the people of Dragekall. There was no cure. That's when Blackhare came, she gave me false hope. But I was willing to do anything to save my daughter. Even if that meant betraying my best friend and taking an innocent baby lindwurm's life. I'm not a good person, but seeing you makes me want to be."

There was a long silence until Liv came crawling out of the hole. She sat down and looked at Halfdan for a moment before she spoke. "So… you said that you have Frode's memories? What are they like?"

Halfdan smiled and huffed some air out of his nose. He couldn't help but find it amusing that Liv, after everything he told her, would want to know that. "It's almost like my dreams are now just his memories, besides the regular nightmares. They are somewhat fuzzy and bounce around from his childhood. My favorite is when he is playing with his pet cat, Bjørn. Once he went outside and saw a fox attacking Bjørn. He wished ill will upon the fox and it turned inside out in front of his eyes. That's when he knew what his calling was, but he didn't want to use it to hurt people. He found a mentor but I don't remember anything after that."

"Bjørn, that's a fun name for a cat." Liv said with a smile that faded as she looked around before making eye contact with Halfdan again. "If you have any more dreams, would you tell me?" Liv asked, intrigued about Frode's memories.

"Of course." Halfdan said, feeling like he should reach out to hug Liv. Instead he stood up and extended his hand to Liv.

Liv took Halfdan's hand and stood up. She wanted to ask him about the wooden horse and ring that she found, but that would reveal to Halfdan that she went through his chest. Instead she smiled, feeling less alone in the world.

CHAPTER 18

FIGHT YOUR FOES IN THE FIELD, NOR BE BURNT IN YOUR HOUSE. VÖLSUNGA SAGA ~ NORSE PROVERB

Once Halfdan and Liv met up with the rest of their companions they saw a group of angry villagers talking to Freyja. Freyja was using sweet words on one of the villager's whose voice Halfdan recognized. It was the man who was yelling after Halfdan for stealing his horse. Freyja was able to convince the man to let Halfdan go without public justice, telling the man that Halfdan's actions were due to a war related nightmare. After Halfdan gave a sincere apology the villagers then began to ask about the fire. Freyja and Ulv played dumb but explained that the fire extinguished itself and no harm was done.

After the villagers were satisfied they dispersed. Halfdan and his companions made their way back to the Jarl's fortress, all relieved that Freyja was able to deescalate the angry mob. Freyja went on to explain that she watched her father negotiate numerous times. He taught her that as long as you told people that you understood what they were saying, no matter how intense and absurd it was, and asked for a compromise with a smile; that was the key to calm down almost anyone. It was just listening to their relentless rambling in the beginning of a divergence that was the hard part.

Back at the fortress Halfdan could see a group of guards at the far end of the property. As he got closer he could hear Hallvard speaking loudly, close to yelling and reprimanding the guards for not going to see what the fire was about. Hallvard went on saying that his person and property weren't the only thing worth protecting, that they had a responsibility to protect everyone who resided in Rokeby.

Once the guards were dismissed Halfdan could see Hallvard writing on old parchment with a piece of charcoal that was wrapped in fabric to keep his hands clean. When you're going to be Jarl you have to think about those things, and must be presentable at all times. Hallvard shook his head as he added on his never ending to-do list. Oberon stood behind him holding Peapod, looking over Hallvard's shoulder to see what he was writing. Behind both Hallvard and Oberon were a group of men digging four graves.

Hallvard stopped writing to look at Halfdan with a scowl before returning to his notes, not looking up as he spoke. "Shouldn't you be resting?"

"Shouldn't you have a steward taking notes for you?" Halfdan said, hearing his companions move about nervously behind him. He couldn't help but smile when he heard Elora snickering.

Hallvard looked up from his notes and smiled at Halfdan, enjoying the playful banter. "My new advisor and steward is occupied at the moment."

Oberon smiled and lifted Peapod up briefly for everyone to see before putting her down. Peapod didn't seem to mind and began to peck at the ground looking for bugs.

"New advisor?" Freyja asked, cheerfully.

"Yes." Hallvard said as he finished his notes before looking up again. "When I first arrived my father's advisors lied to me. Saying that an assassin came in and killed my father and half siblings. They were twisting things to make me afraid to live here. After I requested the advisors to collect the parchment I needed to claim my birthright I relieved them of their duties. Informing the guards and advisors that I knew what happened, but we don't need the people of Rokeby knowing that my father's own guards killed him. Furthermore, I don't need old men following me about and praising my every movement, I need people who I can trust. Oberon is who I trust."

Hallvard then stopped talking, put his right hand over his heart and took a deep bow to Halfdan and his companions. Halfdan felt out of place, he never had someone bow to him before. Unsure what to do, Halfdan bowed the same way and he could hear his friends following his lead and bowed as well.

After the respectful bowing, Hallvard spoke again. "My home is welcome to you all, whenever you are in need. However, I have a feeling that you would not be staying long. I was told that you could use some horses to get to your next destination, wherever that may be."

Halfdan couldn't help but tilt his head in confusion. Even Oberon looked at Hallvard, unsure of what he was talking about.

Hallvard smiled at everyone and pointed up towards the sky. Halfdan nodded in recognition as to who Hallvard was talking about. Despite Oberon accusing Halfdan of being a warlock, Hallvard still believed that his God was willing to help Halfdan.

"Now if you excuse me, I have to coordinate with the cemetery in Bjørgvin. I'm going to exhume my mother and bring her here. It's going to be a hassle, I can tell already." Hallvard said begrudgingly and quickly made his way back to the fortress with Oberon right behind him.

Halfdan walked up to the group of eight men who were digging the graves. He could feel head pains coming on and his eye socket was throbbing, but he needed to get some curiosity out of the way first. "I'm surprised Hallvard is going to lay his mother next to his father."

The men stopped shoveling and looked at the older man that was digging with them. The man shook his head sadly. "No, we already dug a spot for his mother by the flower garden. This one here is for Lady Ellingboe. Hallvard refused to use the people's money to support her mushroom indulgement. She got all huffy and went out into the woods to get her own. From what I heard she was eating all kinds of mushrooms. She couldn't tell them apart. Handmaids found her dead this morning."

The men started digging at the four graves again, done with the conversation. Halfdan took a few steps away from the diggers to have a private conversation with his companions.

"And here I thought wealthy people had their shit together." Elora said, still perched on Ulv's shoulder.

"I'm just happy Hallvard has this shit together." Freyja said with a smile, happy to join in with the swearing. "I think the people of Rokeby are going to be better taken care of now that Hallvard is taking over."

"I actually forgot that Jarl Ellingboe had a wife." Halfdan added, backtracking a little. "Anyway, do any of you know what the celebration is going to be like tomorrow? Never witnessed a Jarl, well… be declared a Jarl the same day as a burial."

Liv shrugged her shoulders. "As far as I know, there is a burial ceremony for the deceased. Still think it's weird that Hallvard's God wants bodies put in the ground. The King might be here, Hallvard is still waiting for a carrier with the news. After the burial Oberon will announce the new Jarl to the people and then." Liv stopped to do a little dance. "We celebrate."

"Well, I better get my beauty sleep." Halfdan said, before he could turn to walk away Liv stopped him.

"Before you go, I just wanted to tell everyone that I am sorry. I don't want to be an angry person. Looking back at what I did, I feel silly." Liv said with hurt pride.

"Liv, it's ok. It's the dragon soul." Freyja told Liv trying to comfort her.

"I don't want to use that as an excuse. My father… uh." Liv's cheeks blushed as she looked at Halfdan awkwardly for a moment before looking away. "Well, my step-father used getting drunk as an excuse to yell at times. I don't want to be like that."

"What was that?" Elora asked with her feathery ears pointing up in amusement.

"Um… Uh…." Liv became flustered, unsure of what to say.

"Do you want me to tell them?" Halfdan asked Liv and watched her as she nodded yes.

"Linna didn't tell Liv that I am her father." Halfdan said, purposely leaving out some of the embarrassing details.

"Oh! That's right, because you and Linna ran away together!" Freyja added.

Everyone turned their head to look at Freyja as she covered her mouth.

"You weren't there for that story." Liv said, squinting her eyes at Freyja.

"I'm sorry." Freyja peeped between her fingers. "I was spying on all of you in the Rivinnsjo forest. I saw everything. Even Ulv's hair catching on fire. I was just waiting for all of you to fall asleep so I could steal some food. I was scared and I didn't know if I could trust you. When Liv spotted me I left, I promise."

"If you would have just came out and said something I would have been less scared!" Liv laughed in amusement as she ran her fingers through her blond hair. "I was up all night. I thought you were a monster or a bear. What a relief."

"Anyone else got secrets they want to tell?" Halfdan asked, intrigued but his words came out in a tone of annoyance.

"I still find dogs attractive." Ulv added, unashamed.

Halfdan closed his eye and lifted his hands in the air for Ulv to stop. "Anyone else other than Ulv."

Elora straightened up and fluffed her feathers before speaking. "This might come as a shock to you. But I am actually… a shapeshifter."

Elora looked around and was disappointed to see no one was surprised. It took a moment for Halfdan and Liv to pretend to be shocked. Freyja grimaced as Ulv looked around nervously.

"Seriously?" Elora said as she glared at Ulv with her big yellow eyes. Ulv purposely looked in the opposite direction to avoid Elora despite her being on his shoulder.

"Agh! I am sorry! I can't keep words in my mouth. It just slipped when I was talking to Freyja." Ulv said, disappointed in himself.

Freyja began to play with her necklace. "I'm sorry, I told Liv because I thought she knew."

Liv crossed her arms. "I can keep a secret, I don't know how Halfdan knew."

Halfdan blushed. "I was peeing behind a tree when I overheard Freyja and Liv talking. I don't think you knew I was there. Sorry."

"I don't know why you didn't just tell us? You don't have to be ashamed." Liv added.

Elora looked around before talking again. "You don't care? None of you? Not worried I'm going to murder you and take your place?"

"The only thing that bothers us is your attitude." Halfdan said before Liv elbowed him in the gut, causing Halfdan to let out a quick huff of air.

"No Elora, we care about you. We know you wouldn't do that. You helped Halfdan escape from Magnus and you taught me how to read. I don't think you realize how important that is. Now I can read all the sexy stories that Norvegr has to offer." Liv said with a smile and a wink.

Halfdan rubbed his head. "Ok, no more talking about secrets. I'm going to go lay down if you need me."

As Halfdan turned to leave he heard the rest of his companions laughing as they continued talking with the gravediggers behind them flinging dirt. Back inside the fortress Halfdan took three steps in before servants came out and scolded him for tracking in dirt. Halfdan kept apologizing, but he knew he was fighting a losing battle, no matter what he said. The same handmaids from before came to Halfdan's rescue and took him to the bathing room. They filled a large circular wooden tub with hot water and asked if he needed any help. Halfdan politely declined and only washed and dried his feet before running out of the bathing room and down the hallway to his bedroom. There he saw his clothes laid out on a made bed. The leather bag Norvick gave him was sitting on the nightstand.

Halfdan was relieved to see the fabric pouch that Abia gave him was still in the bag. Halfdan picked the small pouch and smelled it taking in the salt, dried hyssop, pine and oak bark. Back in the bathing room Halfdan put the whole pouch in the hot water, rather than dumping its contents out for the servants to clean out later. The last thing Halfdan wanted was to be scolded again by Hallvard's headstrong servants.

In front of a mirror Halfdan slowly took the bandages off his head. The bandage that covered his eye was crusted with blood and had to slowly be peeled off. Halfdan stood there looking at himself. The skin around his eye socket was purple and sore. He sighed, repulsed by his own reflection.

"He had to take my good eye, too." Halfdan whispered to himself before getting in the tub.

Halfdan couldn't help but feel relieved that he was soaking in the mixture that Abia gave him. It already felt like it's been multiple seasons since he talked to Abia and Sindri. Despite Jovi telling Halfdan that the plants didn't protect him, it still gave a false sense of protection. Rather than sprawling out in the large tub Halfdan hugged his knees and fought off tears. He was tired but afraid to sleep, nightmares would haunt him and Jovi could come back to harass Halfdan further.

The distant sound of a door opening vibrated through the fortress and Halfdan could hear Liv talking and laughing. Halfdan couldn't help but ponder about leaving Liv here in Hallvard's care as he went out to face Blackhare. Clenching his fist Halfdan shook his head, he couldn't leave her again.

Halfdan washed his hair, cautious not to let any of the dirty water run in to his eye socket. After shaving his beard Halfdan got out of the tub, dried off and headed back to his bedroom. The stone floor was cold, causing Halfdan to quickly scamper through the winding hallway. He thought how Jarl Ellingboe was viciously attacking those who called the fortress home only a few nights ago in these same halls. Now the stone floors were cleaned of blood and doors replaced, hiding any evidence of the beast and its path of destruction.

Back in the bedroom Halfdan closed the door and draped his towel over a chair before sliding into the bed, careful not to kick off any of his clean clothes off onto the floor. Halfdan smiled as he felt the soft textures surrounding his body.

Halfdan woke up with a frown when he heard knocking on his door. "Hang on!" He called out as he reluctantly got out of bed and quickly dressed.

When he opened the door he was surprised to see Liv standing there waiting for him.

Liv looked in the room briefly before looking back at Halfdan. "Oh, I thought maybe you had someone in here with you."

"And why would you think that?" Halfdan asked, unsure what Liv was getting at.

Liv put her hands behind her back and swayed about. "Oh, I don't know. You were in your bedroom for a long time. I overheard the handmaids talking fondly of you."

Halfdan thought for a moment and felt like an idiot for not picking up the hint when the handmaids asked if he needed help bathing. There was definitely plenty of room in the tub. Halfdan blinked his eye a few times before snapping back into reality.

Liv giggled at Halfdan's reaction. "Let me fetch some warm water. I can clean up your eye for you. The burial is going to start soon."

"What?" Halfdan asked, surprised as he looked around. The old part of the fortress didn't have any windows and it was disorienting to figure the time of day. "I was asleep for that long?"

Liv looked Halfdan over with a frown. "Are you sure you're ok? Do you have a fever?" Liv reached out to feel Halfdan's forehead and cheek. "Hmmm, you seem ok. If you need to rest I can let Hallvard know you can't make it."

"No, no, I'll be fine. How is Hallvard doing?" Halfdan asked, trying to change the topic away from himself.

"Stressed. Very stressed. He wanted more time before the burial but the bodies are already starting to… well, turn. Oberon hired a team of carpenters to make these wooden boxes to bury them in. They look nice, too bad they are going in the ground. I can tell you more later after I get some warm water."

Halfdan watched as Liv began to walk away. "Hey! Could you bring me something to eat?"

Liv kept walking away as she yelled back. "He took your eye not your hands!"

Halfdan smiled, even when Linna was with him she couldn't banter like Liv could. He retreated back into his room and waited for Liv to return, occupying himself by coaxing the coals in the fireplace back to life.

Sometime later Liv came back with a tray, one half had a cup of water and a plate with some crackers and cheese and the other half had a bowl of warm water and a fresh cloth in it. Behind her was Ulv, who styled a new haircut. The sides and back of his hair were shaved off leaving only hair on the top of his head. The hair was braided and tied back. Freyja was wearing a crown that she made with vines and decorated with oak leaves and acorns. In her arms was a basket with materials to make another crown for Liv and Elora. Elora made her grand entrance by flying into the room, circled around a bit before she landed on the bed.

Before Liv could put the tray down, Halfdan grabbed the cup of water and took a sip. Liv wrung out the wet towel and handed it to Halfdan. Halfdan took it and thanked Liv as he pressed the warm cloth to his eye. Liv, Ulv and Elora talked amongst themselves as Freyja started work on another crown. After watching Freyja intertwine the vines together Halfdan looked back at the tray and took a slice of cheese.

As he put the cheese in his mouth he saw a strip of leather on the tray behind the bowl. When he picked it up he noticed that it was an eye patch. With a shallow breath, Halfdan removed the cloth that he held over his eye and looked at the dry crusty blood on it.

Slowly, Halfdan took his gloves off and walked over to a mirror that was hanging on the wall and tied the eye patch on. Everyone stopped talking and watched Halfdan look back at his own reflection.

Halfdan let out a quivering sigh before speaking. "It hasn't even been a year, and I can barely recognize myself."

CHAPTER 19

FORGIVE US OUR SINS, FOR WE OURSELVES FORGIVE EVERYONE WHO IS ENDEBTED TO US. COLOSSIANS 2:14

Halfdan and his companions were invited to the burial ceremony before the locals were allowed entry. Usually held for immediate family, but Hallvard had none. Instead, Hallvard invited his new servants, guards and close friends to give their respects to the late Ellingboe family. This also gave everyone time to talk amongst one another and coordinate before the gates opened to the public.

The Ellingboe family rested peacefully outside in their wood burial boxes for the wind to cast away any foul odors. Their burial boxes were laid in front of the fortress, head end towards the fortress and feet end towards Rokeby. As if the family was to look upon its subjects that they cared for so recklessly one last time. A line was already formed and there was enough room between each deceased for people to look at the family from both sides.

The first person Halfdan and his companions saw was Jarl Ellingboe. He had been dressed in new clothes and a fur pelt covered his feet all the way up to his midsection, possibly to cover the wounds he sustained when the guards killed him. The Jarl's hands reached over the pelt and limply grasped a hilt of a sword that rested on his body. Halfdan looked intently at Jarl Ellingboe's face, almost expecting it to look beastly. It didn't, instead the Jarl's face was pale and wet looking. His lips already beginning to dry out and misshapen.

Next was Lady Ellingboe, who wore a white dress with a decorative white veil covering her hair and face. The veil did little to cover the purple and red coloration on the Lady's face, but that did little to deter people from touching her in mournful affection. Lady Ellingboe's hands rested over her heart with the left hand on top to show off her beautiful yet gaudy wedding ring, metal manipulated to look like an open rose with a red stone in its center.

The two deceased heirs went in order of their birth, the young man then the young woman. Halfdan and his companions never got their names and now it was too late to ask. This didn't stop them from quietly giving their respects. The young man's face was pale and stitched back together. Halfdan noticed that a furred collar on his tunic was used to cover his throat that was once ripped open. Like his father the young man's hands reached out and limply held the hilt of a sword that rested upon him.

The young woman was also pale and matched her mother's white dress and a veil to cover her fatal wounds. Some brown blood was beginning to seep through her white dress and Halfdan asked a servant for a white blanket they could use.

Halfdan and Liv lifted the young woman's arms for the servant to carefully place the blanket around her. While holding the young woman's cold arm Halfdan couldn't help but hear three older men talking to Hallvard, who was standing at the end of the line with Oberon next to him. The old men were telling Hallvard that the burial boxes needed to be closed. Halfdan looked up into the sky, not wanting to be caught eavesdropping. Hallvard stood there and listened to the men complain before telling them that the people of Rokeby have a right to see Jarl Ellingboe and his family one last time.

Halfdan watched as the old men stomped away and the servant asked Halfdan to put the arm down. He apologized and looked at the young woman one last time. Everyone watched as Freyja took off her crown of vines and oak leaves and put it in the young woman's hands.

"She doesn't have anything to take with her." Freyja said mournfully as she carefully put the crown in the young woman's stiff fingers.

After giving their respects, Halfdan and his companions walked over to Hallvard who had witnessed Freyja give his deceased half-sister a crown. He wore a smile on his face but his eyes were sad and tired.

"Thank you for being here." Hallvard said with a subtle bow of his head.

"You're looking better, Halfdan." Oberon said with a slight smile as he shuffled about, uncomfortable in his new clothes. The fine burgundy tunic, boots and gold pendant made him match his title better than the hermit rags he wore before.

"Thanks to the both of you. Your hospitality is greatly appreciated." Halfdan said before speaking quietly to Hallvard for no one to overhear. "How are you holding up?"

"The speech I have to give is keeping me occupied. First impressions are important and not everyone in Rokeby went to hear God's message." Hallvard said as he grabbed his hands to stop them from shaking.

"I'll be right behind you." Oberon whispered to Hallvard. "You practiced your speech all last night and this morning. After you get a few words out everything will fall into place."

"Everything is just happening so fast." Hallvard said as his face suddenly began to turn green. "I'm going to freshen up." Hallvard added before promptly turning and briskly walking back inside the fortress.

Oberon watched as Hallvard disappeared in to the fortress and let out a gentile exhale. "You should have heard him praying last night. I just need to get him through today." Oberon turned and put on a smile that could not conceal the worry and sadness. "We will be opening the doors to the public soon, if there is anything else you need before then?"

"I'm sorry." Liv spoke up softly. "I just wanted to know if the King is attending."

Oberon shook his head no. "He gave his regards but it was late notice for him to arrive and has prior engagements. However, the King informed Hallvard that a date would be made for him to travel to the Bjørgvin. No offense, but the King's absence has made things easier for Hallvard." Oberon stopped talking and noticed that Halfdan and his companions were looking back at him like fawns, unsure what to do. "So," Oberon explained. "Hallvard will most likely be waiting in the study as the villagers give their respects. After that Hallvard will come out and lead the way to the new family cemetery in back. He will give a service. After service we will come back here for Hallvard to be declared Jarl. Then he will give a speech. After that we will celebrate. If you get confused just follow the hoard of people. Now if you excuse me, I need to get things ready before we open the gate."

Halfdan and his friends stepped aside and watched as Oberon collected guards and instructed them on how he wanted them to stand. There was one guard standing at the head of each casket with their sword in front of them with the tip in the ground and using both hands to hold the hilt of the sword. Oberon got two more guards to hold an old war banner with the family crest on it. It was obvious they were for decoration, for they were too pristine to have ever been used in battle. Then Oberon collected servants and instructed them to keep villagers in a line and gently guide them through the deceased as quickly as they could. If they let everyone take their time it would be midnight before the ceremony actually began.

There was already a group of villagers forming outside the gate, eager to see the deceased Jarl. Once the gate was open Halfdan and his companions stood back and took note that more townspeople seemed pleased than distraught over the Jarl death. Some people brought items that they placed in the burial boxes, some prayed over the deceased and others whispered to one another about the state that the bodies were in.

Overhearing the rumors was of great amusement to Halfdan and Elora. Rumors about assassins were the most prevalent. There were some who thought a family had feud gone deadly, while others were convinced a bear got into the fortress and killed the trio.

The rumor that was the closest to the truth, that the Jarl turned into a monster, was the one that people disregarded.

The servants kept the line moving but soon it was difficult to move around without bumping into anyone. The crowd went silent as Hallvard stepped out of the fortress and watched as he silently said goodbye to his father, step-mother and half siblings before carpenters came and nailed the lids to the burial boxes. The sound of the hammers nailing the lids was eerie and echoed through the still crowd, reminding everyone that one day death will come for them as well. Once the lids were secure guards came and lifted the burial boxes up onto their shoulders, turned and followed slowly behind Hallvard who led the way towards the new family cemetery.

Before each designated plot the boxes were placed in front of the holes dug for them. Hallvard provided prayers for the deceased, but the crowed was so large that the people in back couldn't hear a word that was said. As Hallvard was giving rites Halfdan looked at the wood burial boxes, each one decorated with flowers and wildlife with a cross carved out on the lid.

When Hallvard was done with service a group of eight men came and laid out four sturdy and long pieces of rope in front of the young woman's box. The men then lifted the box and placed it on the rope before lifting the box again by the rope. It was painful to watch as the men shuffled over the hole and slowly gave the rope slack for the box to be lowered into the earth. As the burial box slowly disappeared Halfdan read the name on the headstone. *Revna Ellingboe.*

When the burial box was lowered the men shimmied the rope out and began the process again for the young man. His headstone read *Raul Ellingboe.*

As they were lowering Lady Ellingboe to her final resting place, Halfdan couldn't help but think about Frode. He didn't have a headstone, a gathering of people to say goodbye or prayers of any kind. Despite Hallvard's father wanting him dead, Hallvard still gave his family the burial that he imagined they would have wanted. Even if it was just for the public.

Halfdan and his companions watched as Jarl Rainer Ellingboe was lifted and slowly lowered into his grave. One of the men's arms began to shake, strained from all the heavy lifting. His hands gave out and with a loud thud the foot end of the box hit the bottom as the headend pointed straight up towards the sky. The crowd gasped and a wave of murmurs fell upon the people. Everyone watched Hallvard for his reaction. He covered his mouth to hide a smile and shook his head at himself as he guested the men to continue laying his father to rest.

When the men were done correcting their mistake, Hallvard walked up to the man who let go of the rope. The crowd began to stir, expecting Hallvard to strike the man down. Instead Hallvard put his hand on the man's shoulder who was looking at the ground, ashamed. Halfdan could hear Hallvard tell the man that he was forgiven and that accidents happen.

Hallvard then turned and began to make his way back with Oberon a few steps behind him and the guards marching in tow. The crowd split silently allowing Hallvard to make his way through. After the guards passed the crowd began to walk behind them, creating a sad and silent parade.

Back in front of the fortress Halfdan and his companions were surprised to see a small platform was put together while they were away. The wood looked old as if it was tucked away for some time and recently put together for Hallvard's speech. In the front of the platform was a green tapestry with the family crest colored in gold.

Hallvard walked up the steps to the platform with Oberon behind him and two guards. The rest of the guards surrounded the base of the platform as the crowd began to move in close.

Halfdan could tell Hallvard was nervous, it was in his eyes. Hallvard put his hands on the railing to stop them from shaking as he looked at his subjects, who looked back at him in anticipation.

Hallvard closed his eyes for a moment and when he opened them again his eyes looked beyond the crowd of people as he spoke. "I wanted to thank you all for being here today to share our sorrow with one another. The loss of my family was of great surprise to us all. There are rumors that I will not confirm or deny, but know that the culprit responsible for this heinous crime has been dealt with."

There was some disappointed murmuring from the crowd, but Hallvard kept moving forward with his speech. "Some of you know me as your deacon from church, and stories of not being able to feed your family and affording rent and taxes have not fallen on deaf ears. From this day forward rent and tax will be reduced, past debt to my father will be forgiven and the Jarl's private hunting lands will be open to all who call Rokeby their home."

With those few words the crowd erupted with a frenzy of excitement. Hallvard smiled as people began jumping and yelling with joy as some hugged and kissed. Halfdan noticed a mother holding two young boys begin crying tears of relief. Oberon opened up a wood box that was hidden up on the platform and pulled out a simple gold coronet and placed it on Hallvard's head. Hallvard looked surprised and gently touched the coronet that was placed upon him.

With a big grin Oberon extended his hands towards Hallvard and yelled over the cheering crowd. "I present to your new Jarl; Maikel Hallvard- Ellingboe!"

Halfdan joined his companions in cheering, it felt good to belong in a group of people yelling with happiness rather than rallying for battle. The cheering went on as doors to the fortress opened and servants rolled out five large barrels of mead and ale. Halfdan could feel his mouth watering as the barrels were placed onto their stands. Halfdan closed his eyes and basked in the hoppy mist that escaped from the barrels as the taps were hammered in.

CHAPTER 20

DON'T MESS WITH ALE IF YOU ARE WEAK. A CLEAR
HEAD IS GOOD COMPANY. DRINK IS
A DANGEROUS FRIEND.
HÁVAMÁL ~ NORSE PROVERB

The smell of barn animals woke Halfdan. He looked around to see three highland calves sleeping next to him. Halfdan reached out and petted one whose head was resting on his chest.

"I've heard stories, but I never thought they were literal. *Heh-heh*." Halfdan laughed unenthusiastically to his own joke.

The calves' ears twitched towards Halfdan's voice, but they didn't open their eyes. Halfdan laid there for a moment longer until he couldn't bare the uncomfortable hay any longer. He apologized to the calves and got up. Mother highland cows watched intently as he left the barn.

It was barely morning by the time Halfdan got back to the fortress. The guards and servants were still sleeping and wood mugs laid on the muddy ground around barrels. He checked all five of the barrels and they were bone dry. Disappointed, Halfdan walked around the fortress to check on the Ellingboe family cemetery. Birds were beginning their morning calls as Halfdan looked at the four graves. They were filled in with dirt and the top of each headstone was decorated with red cedar branch arrangements.

Halfdan continued to walk around the fortress when he came upon Hallvard, who was standing in the flower garden. All the blooms are gone for the season, but with the array of plants Halfdan could only imagine what the garden looked like in the spring. Halfdan stopped in his tracks when he realized that

Hallvard was standing next to a burial box. It was recently carved and similar to the ones for the Ellingboe family, but the sides were carved with cats playing with butterflies.

Halfdan turned to walk away when he heard Hallvard talking to him.

"She just arrived a little before you got here." Hallvard said keeping his back turned to Halfdan.

"Did she like cats?" Halfdan asked, trying to keep the conversation pleasant.

"Yes, especially the yellow ones. She also liked flowers and butterflies." Hallvard stopped and snuffled a little. "It's nice being called Jarl rather than *oskilgetinn. When my mother gave me up she said it was for the best. That I would be better off. I would have a warm place to sleep and three meals a day. That's all she asked for from my father. He couldn't even do that. The second she left my father told me that my mother would bed anyone for money. The only reason why she gave me up was so I wouldn't catch on. It might be true, but she was the kindest woman I knew. She would feed stray cats and let them come inside during bad weather. I think that's why I enjoy Oberon's company so much, just like the cats he didn't judge me." Hallvard then put his hand on the box and felt the carved cross on top of it. "They aren't sure if this is my mother. She was buried without a headstone. But I like to think this is her."

"What was your mother's name?" Halfdan asked, sincerely.

"Sigyn Hallvard. Hallvard isn't really a last name. I remember her telling me how she got it, but I don't remember the details." With one last sniffle Hallvard rubbed his eyes and turned to face Halfdan. "I'm sorry. I guess I feel comfortable telling you all of these things because I might never see you again."

"Thanks, that's comforting." Halfdan said, jokingly in a sad attempt to lighten the mood.

The corners of Hallvard's lips lifted a little as he shrugged. Halfdan noticed dark circles around Hallvard's eyes, making him look older than he really was.

"Did you get any sleep?" Halfdan asked and watched as Hallvard shrugged again. "I can watch over her if you want to get some sleep?"

"No, I want to be here." Hallvard said sternly before relaxing a bit. "I don't wish to wake up the diggers yet. They had a busy day yesterday, along with the guards and servants."

"Do you want to be alone or do you want me to get Oberon for you?" Halfdan asked, unsure if he was interrupting.

"He will find me when he wakes up. I'm surprised you are up actually. The handmaids informed me that the barrels held the strongest mead and ale they could make. Most people stopped at one." Hallvard said in a tone that was either impressed or disappointed.

"I could tell, first time I woke up in a barn in a long time." Halfdan said, amused with himself.

Hallvard let out a little laugh. "You are quite the intriguing man, Halfdan. Tell me more about yourself."

"I'm just a mercenary and a babysitter."

Hallvard eyed Halfdan before sitting on the ground and leaning his back against the wooden burial box that contained his mother. "I see, but I find it difficult to believe that a boring man drinks themselves stupid and falls asleep with animals in a barn. Especially when there is a bed in a fortress for him." Hallvard then patted the ground next to him to get Halfdan to sit next to him.

"Bad habits." Halfdan said with a sigh as he sat his sore body down next to Hallvard.

"Where are you from?" Hallvard asked.

"I'm afraid to say, it's close to here and I don't know if people are looking for me."

"Ah, so you aren't so boring." Hallvard said with a strained smile.

Halfdan smiled too and gave in. "I ran away with the love of my life. I left behind all my obligations. We would sleep in barns often, until she left me for another man. But that's all in the past now. I have my daughter with me. But I made some bad choices for that to happen. I have blood on my hands and made bad agreements. I gave them my word but I didn't follow through. It cost my eye and now my daughter and her friends are mixed in with my bad business."

Hallvard thought and rubbed his chin before speaking. "Does it have to do with that Magnus fellow and that codex?"

"In a way. We crossed paths before. He locked me in a room for three days. I have to deal with the lady he is working for." Halfdan said starting to feel sick to his stomach, unsure if it is from nerves or drinking.

"I see... I didn't like it when he took our two witches or what you might call staff-carriers away. They never hurt anyone. Who is he working for?"

"Blackhare." Halfdan said as if the name hurt his tongue. "We have reason to believe that she is controlling Magnus to do her dirty work."

Hallvard straightened up after hearing what Halfdan told him. "Blackhare? She is in the King's court and one of his trusted advisors."

Halfdan's stomach turned. Things just got more complicated.

"I don't understand. Why would a powerful Seidr dispose of simple witches that weren't bothering any one?" Hallvard said in disbelief.

Halfdan was silent for a moment until a thought crossed his mind. "It's like asking why a King would kill a Jarl."

Hallvard closed his eyes and briefly shook his head. "Power. She is eliminating the competition for something big. Smart of her to get Magnus to do the dirty work so word doesn't get back to the King."

"Unless the King gave her the go ahead." Halfdan leaned his head against the burial box. "When things don't make sense that means I'm missing something. I don't know if I should go against Blackhare or Magnus first."

"Magnus could be anywhere. We know where Blackhare is. Take off the leader and the plan will crumble."

"Wait…" Halfdan turned to look at Hallvard. "You know where Blackhare is?"

"Yes, I thought you did as well. I apologize, I thought you knew more than I did. There are maps and I can show you where her castle is. Weather permitting it's about a three week ride south of the Bjørgvin. Castle was called Edge Keep, it was abandoned for a long time before Blackhare moved in. Before my father was given the title of Jarl he was humiliated by the King to be a personal currier for a few months, which often ended with me delivering letters. Edge Keep is larger than my fortress and she has many servants. They were… sickly. Their eyes were pale and skin pulled tight which was uncomfortable to look at. Whenever I tried to talk to to the servants they would just stare at me, as if waiting to be told what to do next." Hallvard looked out into the distance at nothing in particular, reminiscing of Edge Keep. "Blackhare would meet me outside, but there was a lot of noise coming from within the castle. When I first heard the place being called Edge Keep I figured it was by a cliff or ocean, but it wasn't. Most likely called Edge Keep because it's on the edge of nowhere. You know a place is bad when you leave feeling drained."

Halfdan picked up a pebble and tossed it over the garden as he thought. "Will you get in trouble, telling me all of this?"

Hallvard picked up a pebble and tossed it farther away. "Does it matter? After all, I am bound to make some people angry at me. If so I would like it to be for a good reason. When you do make sense of it all I know you will make the correct decision."

Halfdan picked up another pebble and tried to toss it farther away but it just landed short. "So… Maikel?"

Hallvard groaned. "Yes, Maikel. I had to change my name to be able to work with the church. The priests gave me the name."

"Hmm, ok. Can I ask what your birth name was? I am unsure if it is rude to ask."

200

Hallvard hung his head to hide a smile. "You are going to laugh."

"I can keep a secret." Halfdan said, intrigued.

"Fine." Hallvard said followed by a deep inhale before speaking again. "My birth name was Thor."

Halfdan grimaced to try and cover up a smile.

"You can laugh, Oberon did when I told him. My mother must have thought I would be strong as I grew. Instead I was frail, just arms and legs. Never liked violence. The priests said my name was heathenistic and pagan. When I was baptized they changed my name. I didn't mind until I learned that Maikel was the church's guardian. Just like how Thor was the protector of Asgard. Both names aren't a good fit for me, in my opinion. If there was an angel that was known for pushing parchment I would change it." Hallvard chuckled to himself. "Oberon told me that the people are calling me Hallvard the Kind after what transpired yesterday."

"It was kind of you to forgive your people's debts."

"I had no choice." Hallvard rubbed his head. "I was going through the tax records, trying to figure out how so many people owed so much and yet had so little. The farther back I went I soon realized none of the math made sense. It was clear that the people who couldn't read had extra numbers added to what they owed. Information was wrong or missing, making it impossible to figure out what each individual person truly owed. I was so frustrated that I tossed the records into the fire place… Please don't tell anyone."

Halfdan let out a sympathetic laugh. "I would have liked to see that. It's difficult to imagine *you* getting mad and throwing parchment into a fire. It's for the best. There is no war, famine or sickness going around. People will be able to use this time to recover and make their lives better. Everyone gets a fresh start. Especially the farmers, after losing most of their livestock to Oberon."

"I hope you're right, that the people will be able to prosper." Hallvard said as he stood up.

Halfdan looked to see Oberon walking over to them. He got up and greeted Oberon before taking his leave, sure that Hallvard needed to talk to Oberon alone. Back inside the fortress Halfdan could hear people beginning to stir out of bed as he retreated back into his bedroom.

When he opened the door Halfdan frowned when he saw Ulv sleeping, sprawled out in his bed. Halfdan grumbled as he walked over to the side of the bed and nudged Ulv awake. Ulv sat up and practically squealed when he saw Halfdan. Before Halfdan could step back Ulv scooted his knees to the edge of the bed and gave Halfdan a hug.

"I lost you! Where were you?" Ulv yelped out happily as he continued to hug Halfdan. Then Ulv began to sniff Halfdan's tunic as the one sided hug continued. "You smell like cows."

Halfdan grimaced at Ulv before looking through the open doorway to see the three handmaids standing still in the hallway, returning his gaze. Their mouths hung open as they looked upon Ulv's hip level embrace of Halfdan.

Halfdan could feel his face turn red as he tried to push Ulv off of him. "Would you let go. I know, I know. I smell like cows." Halfdan looked back at the doorway to see the handmaids were gone, giggles trailing behind them as they ran down the hall.

Ulv let go, too happy to be bothered. "Where did you go? We were all so worried. You weren't there to see Liv fight a guard. It was so funny. Then people brought food! It was roasted goat. You missed it. Will we be coming back here after we kill Blackhare?"

"Hold up." Halfdan said trying to wrap his head around everything Ulv was saying. "Liv got into a fight with a guard?"

"Yeah. He touched her hair and tried to kiss her. Liv told him to back off. He called her some mean words and she punched him. Broke his jaw. The other guards saw and thought it was funny. So they made a ring." Ulv made a circle shape in the air as if Halfdan didn't know what a ring was. "People were placing bets. Liv beat up four guards before Oberon broke it up."

Halfdan sat on the bed as he rubbed his forehead. "I should have been there." He said in a sad tone, disappointed that he wasn't there for his daughter. "I'm surprised Oberon didn't say anything to me. I saw him earlier this morning."

"I think Oberon wanted Liv to tell you. Oberon was more upset at the guards if anything." Ulv said, still sitting on the bed and looking at Halfdan.

"Well that's good. Don't want our hosts to be mad at us. If Liv is well enough I'd like to leave today. Hallvard knows where Blackhare is. The sooner we get this done the sooner we can go on with our lives."

"Do you want me to get everyone?" Ulv asked.

"Nah, let them sleep. We have a lot of traveling ahead of us." Halfdan said, despite being eager to leave.

"Ok!" Ulv said as he crawled back onto the bed and slid under the covers.

Halfdan looked at Ulv with annoyance. "Don't you have your own bed?"

"Well… yeah. But I got this one warmed up already." Ulv said before rolling over so his back was facing Halfdan.

Halfdan pressed his lips into a hard line as he fought off his anger. Rather than sleeping in bed with Ulv he left the bedroom. Halfdan wandered around the fortress for a while in hopes of finding a map. Instead Halfdan found the kitchen and it was filled with servants preparing breakfast for everyone, leftovers from yesterday made into a stew. The food wasn't ready yet and Halfdan was promptly kicked out of the kitchen and back into the cold stone hallway.

As Halfdan wandered on he found the great hall that encompassed the majority of the space of the first floor of the fortress. He passed the great hall a few times previously to get to his room, but this was the first time Halfdan looked around in it. There were two long tables that had benches on each side and at the end of the hall was the Jarl's throne. Halfdan walked down the hall and looked at the throne, tempted to sit in it but decided against it.

Instead Halfdan walked around the edge of the hall and looked at the artwork that decorated it. Tapestries with the family crest on it, animals mounted on the wall and an outdated map of Rokeby.

Halfdan then looked at an old wooden carving of the previous Jarl before Ellingboe. It was an older man with a short beard wearing fine chainmail and *lamellar armor. The man had a stern look on his face as he held a large steel battle axe. Underneath would have been the previous Jarl's name, but it was hacked away with possibly a small knife and no longer legible.

Next to the sketch was a large tapestry of the Ellingboe family. In it was Jarl Ellingboe sitting in his throne with his son, Raul, to his right and his wife and daughter, Revna, to the left. Hallvard was not amongst them. Raul and Revna looked younger, leading Halfdan to believe that the artwork must have been made when they first got to Rokeby.

Wandering on Halfdan found a recently made door that led to an old spiral staircase. Intrigued, Halfdan walked all the way up and lifted a hatch that led to the roof of the fortress. Two guards stood up and sat back down when they realized it was just Halfdan. The guards continued on with their conversation as Halfdan looked over the town. Halfdan found great pleasure looking down at the people as they walked through the busy streets. Then Halfdan walked to the other side of the roof to look at the garden. Hallvard and Oberon were still there watching as two men were shoveling dirt off of a cart, filling in Sigyn Hallvard's grave.

Halfdan felt bad for looking at such an emotional moment and retreated back down the staircase and opened the door to the second level. Unlike the first floor this one was silent. There were six doors and Halfdan figured one had to lead to a room with a map. The first two doors Halfdan tried to open were locked. The third door opened to an office. There was a large desk with a stack of parchment, letters and a quill with ink. The wall was lined with shelves that held many scrolls, old blocks of wood with runes, loose parchment and a few codices. Halfdan walked to the fireplace and noticed the fire was about to go out. By habit Halfdan added a few

204

logs and noticed some burnt parchment in the far corners. Halfdan smiled when he remembered that Hallvard destroyed the tax records.

Unsure if the scrolls were organized Halfdan decided to look at the codices. Most of the codices looked as if they were never opened. There were sagas, poems, ledgers, war tactics, and tales of far-away lands but no maps. Halfdan picked up a worn codex that was titled *Civil Unrest Amongst Kin*. As Halfdan looked in the book he realized it was hollowed out to hide loose parchment. As Halfdan looked through the book's contents, travel sized drawings, it took his hungover brain a moment to realize what he was looking at. They were of people in the act.

"Why can't I find a normal codex for once?" He whispered to himself.

Just then Halfdan heard the door to the second floor of the fortress open. Halfdan stood still until he heard two sets of steps getting closer to the door of the room he was in. Flustered, Halfdan put the drawings back into the codex and closed it. As he went to put the codex back on the shelf his depth perception failed him and the codex fell to the floor, sending sexual sketches scatter across the floor.

Halfdan dropped to his knees and franticly began picking pictures up, crumbling them into a ball and tossing them by the fire. Some landed in the heart of the fire, others bounced close and rolled away. The door opened by the time Halfdan had his arms going in different directions trying to collect the rest, but the effort was in vain. Halfdan looked up to see Hallvard and Oberon looking back at him. Halfdan stood up and looked at the pictures that were sprawled out around him.

With one hand Halfdan rubbed the back of his head and brought the hand around to rest under his chin. "I don't know. I don't have anything to say."

"I see the servants told you where to find my father's private library." Hallvard said unamused as Oberon picked a picture off the floor with a foxy grin.

CHAPTER 21

GOLDEN EYE

It was close to high noon by the time Halfdan, Liv, Ulv, Elora and Freyja were standing outside of the fortress saying goodbye to Jarl Hallvard and Oberon. Not only did Hallvard promise the group his swiftest horses he also gave Halfdan a leather travel bag and informed Halfdan not to open it until nightfall. Unsure of what to make of the gift Halfdan agreed.

Soon the stable attendant who cared for the Jarl's horses came walking out with only three horses. "The other horse refused to be saddled." The stable attendant said irritated, not at the horse but that he had to admit that something was wrong.

"Odd." Oberon said, thoughtfully. "She seemed fine yesterday. We could give them the black one, but she has an abscess in her mouth."

"Perhaps it's a sign." Hallvard said softly to Oberon.

"It's ok, Liv and Freyja can share a horse. We will manage." Halfdan said, still grateful for the horses.

"No." Freyja said, almost in a whisper.

"No? What do you mean?" Liv asked Freyja, concerned.

Freyja straightened her back, clenched her fists and stood her ground as if she was ready for a fight. "It is a sign. I want to stay." Suddenly Freyja's eyes grew big and watery. "Oberon said the Huldufolk sometimes travel through here in the spring. I might be able to find my mother if I wait here." Tears began to run down Freyja's face as her voice wavered. "I was just afraid to leave you guys."

Without a word Liv knelt down to give Freyja a hug. Ulv did the same with Elora on his shoulder who wrapped her wings around Freyja's head, causing a giggle escape from Freyja. After they were done Halfdan went over and gave Freyja a long hug.

"You take care of yourself. We will see you again soon, I promise." Halfdan told Freyja as he wiped her tears away. Then Halfdan looked at Hallvard and Oberon who both smiled and nodded to let him know that they would watch over Freyja. Halfdan gave Hallvard and Oberon a sad smile and nodded back, knowing that they both would care for Freyja with all their heart.

Liv dug in her bag and pulled out the oak crown Freyja made her yesterday. "I'll be wearing this when I see you again. You better make yourself another one so we match." Liv said as she put the crown on her head before whispering something into Freyja's ear.

Halfdan watched as Freyja covered her mouth to hide a giggle to whatever Liv was telling her. Deep down Halfdan felt relieved that Freyja was going to stay safe with Hallvard and Oberon. Still, it hurt to be leaving her behind.

"Still got your dagger?" Halfdan asked Freyja who pulled the dagger out from her coat, surprising Hallvard and Oberon. Halfdan then looked to see Ulv crying in an unmanly fashion. "Ulv, it's going to be ok. If you don't stop crying you're going to make me cry. I have a mean demeanor I have to uphold when we leave."

Ulv used the sleeve of his red coat to dry off his tears and snot as Halfdan patted him on the back. Halfdan then walked over to the stable attendant and asked him if the horses had names. The man was more than happy to tell Halfdan that the yellow one with the brown mane was Hulda, white one was Molka, and the one with the brown head and white body was Embla. These horses were traditional Icelandic horses and Halfdan knew they weren't the fastest but reliable and sturdy. The stable attendant apologized that the horses were all mares, as if it would hurt Halfdan's pride to ride anything other than a stallion. Halfdan could care less but let the man explain that the stallions were trained for battle and not suitable for traveling. Halfdan knew this, traveling with war horses was a battle itself. Difficult to keep them reined in and war horses tend to bite.

Hulda looked older and so Halfdan gave her to Liv. Liv would be lighter for Hulda's back and Halfdan figured the mature mare would be less likely to spook and throw Liv off. With her leather travel pack from Thorpe on, Liv mounted the yellow horse without a problem. Halfdan held the reins as the farmhand adjusted the stirrup for Liv's feet. Once Liv was all set Halfdan gave Liv the reins and handed her his battle axe. Liv confidently put the old axe in the leather holster belt that she purchased in the market sometime after Halfdan fell asleep. Halfdan couldn't help but notice some of the skin on Liv's knuckles were scabbed over and swollen. Before he handed Liv her shield, that was now painted black and adorned with a white wolf crouching on its hind legs as if preparing to smite a lindworm, Halfdan flicked Liv's knuckle.

"Ouch!" Liv yelped as she rubbed her knuckle.

"The guards you beat up, do they look worse?" Halfdan asked Liv with a stern face.

"It was all in good fun." Liv replied with a lax tone. "Made one ninety, would have been two hundred if Oberon didn't take the Jarl tax." Liv then looked up and took her crown off and waved it in the air at the guards who were on the flat roof of the fortress.

Halfdan had to squint his eye to get a better look. The guards were waving and yelling back at Liv, some of them had black eyes and one had a broken nose. When the guards noticed Hallvard looking at them they went silent and stepped back out of sight.

"You basically robbed them." Halfdan said, fighting off a smile as he handed Liv her shield.

Liv took the circular shield and put it on her arm as if it was light as a feather. "They were drunk and hesitated because I'm a woman. That was their mistake. Just had to push them off center and land a punch before they regained their balance."

"How did it feel?" Halfdan asked.

Liv gave Halfdan a crooked smile. "Felt good."

"Don't let it get to your head." Halfdan said as he playfully slapped Liv on the leg.

Halfdan had Ulv get on the mare Embla because she seemed skittish of Elora. It was going to be a long ride and Halfdan figured it would be entertaining. Halfdan had Elora perch on his arm while everyone watched as Ulv mounted the horse with the gracefulness of a cow walking a narrow plank. Ulv didn't put his foot in the stirrup to throw his leg over, instead he just threw his whole body and slid off the other side of Embla. Everyone was disappointed when the stable attendant stopped Ulv who was going to try and get a running start for his second attempt. After patiently explaining how to get on, the stable attendant was successful at getting Ulv on the horse. Everyone clapped their hands at Ulv's accomplishment, but rather than replying Ulv sat on the horse not moving a muscle, his eyes wide with fear.

"Ulv, breathe! You're going to be fine. It's just a horse." Liv said upon her horse, but her words had no effect on Ulv.

"You got this!" Freyja yelled to Ulv for encouragement.

Halfdan and Elora both noticed Ulv's hands trembling in fear as his knuckles turned white from gripping the reins.

"This isn't going to work." Elora said to Halfdan who sighed in agreement.

It took some effort to get Ulv off his horse and the compromise was to tie Embla to the white mare, Molka, and have Ulv sit behind Halfdan. Halfdan grimaced as he heard people snickering but Ulv sat happily behind Halfdan. Elora perched onto Liv's shield and the group was ready to go after one more goodbye to Freyja.

The group would periodically turn to wave goodbye until the fortress was out of sight. Halfdan frowned as the townspeople pointed and laughed but Ulv was unfazed by the taunting. It wasn't until they were out of Rockeby that Liv began to voice her grievance about leaving Freyja behind.

"I just wish she would have said something sooner. This feels so sudden." Liv said with a heavy heart. "She's safe there but what if she doesn't find her mother? What will happen then?"

"Hallvard might adopt her and she'll be the next Jarl. Next time we see her she might be mad with power." Elora said, theatrically.

Liv shook her shield, causing Elora to flap her wings as she hung on with her talons. "You're not helping!"

"I have a feeling that she will be ok." Halfdan said as he petted Molka.

"I dislike vague optimism, I'm not a child." Liv said as she glared at Halfdan.

Halfdan continued to pet Molka as he spoke. "After getting my eye pulled out I had a dream. I flew in the air like a sparrow and watched below as Freyja ran through the woods with other Hidden People. She seemed happy. We just have to believe that she knows what she needs to do to be happy."

"What, so you can see the future now?" Liv asked, skeptically.

Halfdan shrugged. "Little bits and pieces. Not enough to make a full picture. Usually have visions like that after something traumatic happens."

"Any visions on us defeating Blackhare?" Elora asked.

"No, unfortunately." Halfdan replied, disappointed.

"Ulv, beat Halfdan up so we can get a vison." Elora said, her feathers puffing out in excitement.

"What?" Halfdan said with concern as he looked at Liv for support, but all she did was purse her lip out as she contemplated the idea.

"Can we wait till we get off the horse?" Ulv said in a nervous tone.

"Hold up, we're not going to start beating me up to maybe see the future. I could end up seeing something unrelated." Halfdan said unimpressed with everyone's eagerness to give him more trauma.

"We could end up just laming him more." Liv said with a sly smirk.

"What's the point in seeing the future anyway? It's not like you can change anything." Ulv asked, hugging onto Halfdan more as Molka staggered on a rock.

"I think people just want reassurance that they are doing the correct thing." Liv said in a way that sounded more like a question than an answer.

"Also along the lines of being less afraid of the unknown. If people have an idea of what's going to happen it's less scary." Elora said as her feathers began to smooth down.

"Guess I'm used to the unknown. Never knowing what the next job will be. I think it's fun." Halfdan said with a smile as he turned to look at Liv. "Especially more fun now that I'm not doing everything by myself."

"So, what's our plan?" Liv asked with a big smile back at Halfdan.

"Going back to Norvick's Inn. After spending the night there we continue south. We're going to be spending a lot of nights outside, should take us three weeks to get to Edge Keep. Once we find it I'd like to spend a night watching it, get an idea of what we're up against. Then we make a game plan from there. Figure out her routine and if there are any weak points to get into the castle. Hallvard said that Blackhare has numerous servants and described them to be servants. However, they sound similar to the thralls that Magnus had." Halfdan thought for a moment before saying something that has been on his mind for sometime now. "If any of you want to sit this one out and stay with Norvick I understand. I don't want any of you to feel obligated to join me. This is my problem."

"You're not getting rid of us that easy." Liv said in a playful way but there was a hint of irritation in her words.

"That *baulufotr *tik has it coming." Elora exclaimed as her feathery ears pointing up into the sky and her round yellow eyes grew angry.

Everyone stared at Elora for a silent second, surprised by her words. Liv was impressed with Elora's combination of swear words and memorized it for the future.

"Uh, yeah what she said." Ulv added, uncertain what Elora actually meant but appreciated her enthusiasm.

It was well after dark by the time the group reached the outskirts of Kibera. They went to a stable just outside the city and knocked at the keeper's door. It took a long moment before the stable master opened the door, irritated that Halfdan and his companions were interrupting his dinner. When the man was given fifteen silver by Liv his demeanor changed and happily accepted to care for the horses until morning.

Everyone but Elora was sore, traveling by horse was faster than walking but the leather saddles weren't the most comfortable. The walk to Norvick's Inn was slow but they eventually reached their destination. Norvick's Inn was quieter than usual and Norvick spotted Halfdan as soon as he opened the door.

"It's not spring yet!" Norvick bellowed over the counter to Halfdan, amused with himself before going pale. "What happened to you?"

Beatrice came running out of the kitchen as if she was going to give everyone a hug before she stopped in her tracks. "Where is Freyja?" She asked concerned, expecting the worst.

"She's fine. Let's talk in the kitchen." Halfdan suggested, not wanting anyone to overhear their conversation. The people in the inn were mercenaries and willing to do anything for money, including selling information.

Norvick checked on his customers before stepping in the kitchen with everyone. Halfdan informed Norvick and Beatrice in great detail about the Nökken in Thorpe and the wolf beasts in Rokeby. He then told them that Freyja was staying with the Jarl and Oberon and that their new task was to kill Blackhare. Halfdan explained what happened with his eye, it wasn't easy for him and it almost hurt to say but he felt like he owed it to Norvick to tell him the truth. Halfdan explained the snakes and how they constricted

212

him and took his breath away. Without thinking Halfdan grabbed at his chest where his rib cracked from the pressure.

Just then Halfdan looked at his companions, realizing he made a mistake. He had been purposely withholding details for reasons unknown. Halfdan could see hurt in Liv's eyes that he didn't tell her his tragic story sooner. It was too late now and Halfdan continued with his story. He talked about how Jovi taunted him and that he could feel the monster's claws wrap around his eye before pulling it out.

After Halfdan finished telling his story there was a long awkward silence. Then Halfdan remembered why he kept out details, it was the looks of pity he was getting from everyone as Beatrice clasped her hands and prayed. Halfdan would rather the situation be laughed at than being looked upon as if he was deserving of sympathy.

"This isn't good." Beatrice said after her silent prayer, her eyes distant. "If this demon wants you to kill Blackhare, aren't you benefiting it? You can't be doing that. What does it have to gain from this?"

"Blackhare isn't a saint either. Figured Jovi just wants to cut out the competition. Said something about her becoming so strong that she would be considered a goddess." Halfdan leaned his tired body against the wall before continuing. "Whatever Jovi has in mind I just want him to leave me and my last eye alone, as shallow as that may be. I gave that monster my word anyway. That and there is no saying that Blackhare won't come after all of you. She already got her puppet, Magnus, to capture me once."

"The next full moon is still some time away, sure you don't want to stay longer than just a night?" Norvick said as he looked at his weary friend.

"You know me, Norvick. Something will most likely happen along the way that will slow me down." Halfdan then gave Norvick a weary smile. "Thank you, I do appreciate it."

Norvick let out a quick breath. "Alright, why don't you have a seat? Fill your bellies before going to bed."

"Thank you!" Ulv exclaimed as he rushed out of the kitchen to sit down.

Halfdan and Liv with Elora sill perched on her shield followed behind Ulv and sat at the counter. Liv sat on the stool that Freyja sat on the first time they arrived at Norvick's Inn. After getting Elora on the counter Liv put her shield down and let her shoulders slouch.

As Halfdan looked at his daughter he couldn't help but feel for her. She was close to Freyja and Halfdan knew the feeling of leaving a friend behind. To try and keep her occupied Halfdan gave Liv his travel pack.

"Hallvard told me I should open it after nigh fall." Halfdan said with a tired smile, his eyes getting heavy.

Liv straightened up and opened the leather pack. The first thing she pulled out was a small box, wrapped with parchment and string. Liv untied the string and carefully unfolded the parchment. "It's a note." Liv said before she tried to read it. "We hope… this eye… is a good… replacement… for the one you lost… It is made… from… my late family's… jewelry… Take care… and… God Bless… you and… bring you peace." Liv then handed the note and box to Halfdan.

Halfdan skimmed the note, Liv read it correctly. He then opened the box and he could feel his eye grow big in surprise. It was a solid gold eye. Halfdan examined it, once expecting a fake eye to be round but this one was flatter. Halfdan put his index finger on his lips, communicating to his companions that he didn't want them to talk loudly about what he was going to show them. Liv and Ulv leaned in and Elora hopped closer.

"Now that is a fake eye." Elora whispered.

"Hallvard and Oberon know style." Liv whispered as she touched the cold golden eye.

"What do you think Norvick is making for dinner?" Ulv whispered to Halfdan who replied with squinting his eye.

"The only words I can make out is unrest and kin." Liv said.

Halfdan looked, not noticing that Liv pulled out the warn codex *Civil Unrest Amongst Kin* from his bag. Without thinking Halfdan grabbed the codex from Liv's hands. Liv's hands stayed in the air, no longer holding anything as she looked at Halfdan with raised eyebrows.

"Sorry, it's just... uh, a dumb codex." Halfdan said, not convincing anyone.

Halfdan then felt the codex being ripped out of his hands and watched as Ulv opening the codex. Halfdan covered his face as he hear Ulv say "It's just men and women wrestling... naked."

Halfdan kept his face covered as he heard other patrons walk over to Ulv's words. The inn was shaken into an eruption of laughing and amusement as people, including Liv, began to help themselves to drawings.

"Those aren't mine." Halfdan said to no one in particular, wishing there was a hole for him to crawl into as he kept his face covered.

"That's what they all say." Elora said with fiendish delight.

CHAPTER 22

THERE IS MORE HONOR IN ACCUMULATING LITTLE BY LITTLE THAN IN REACHING FOR THE SKY AND ENDING UP FLAT ON YOUR FACE.
VANTSDÆLA SAGA ~ NORSE PROVERB

Halfdan was eager to leave in the morning, worried the longer he stayed at Norvick's Inn the more he would yearn to spend another night. He knew the days ahead were going to test his new companions. Not only was it a race against the stars but also against the seasons, as there is no way of knowing if there will be an early snowfall. If it happened to snow, Halfdan would have to get accustomed to being blind.

The map that Jarl Hallvard gave them was old, written on leather and only identified cities and towns with martial power. Hallvard thoughtfully included the locations of two villages Halfdan will pass through before reaching Edge Keep.

The first village was Geiranger and known for its bog iron. Halfdan was pleased that it took them only five days to travel to Geiranger from Kibera. By now they had a good rhythm for traveling. They would leave early in the morning to make most of the daylight. Elora would fly ahead and report anything odd or potentially dangerous that was ahead of them. At high noon they would rest the horses and stretch their legs. When the sun was eight fingers away from the horizon the group would look for a place to rest either in a barn or tavern floor.

After passing the farming village of Njardarheimr their luck ran out and they were forced to begin camping outside. The road soon turned into a game trail and the group found a camp of three fur trappers. The weathered looking men were hidden in a small clearing under tall birch trees. There was a standstill where everyone was looking at one another, unsure if one group was friendly or not. Then an older trapper with a long white beard and a balding head waved them over. Halfdan got off his horse and Liv did the same. Ulv was on his own horse but Embla still had to be tied to Molka for Ulv was still too nervous to guide her on his own.

"Have a seat, travelers. We would appreciate your company. There is plenty of food and drink." Said the older man, his smile showing how accustomed his face was to the sun.

Next to the seasoned trapper was another man who was short but made up for it in strength. On the other side was a young, lengthy man that had three white and tan *Norrbottenspritz dogs by his side. All of them sat on pelts laying on the hard ground around a campfire with a kettle hanging over the fire. The three trappers scooted closer together to make room for everyone to sit by the fire. As soon as Liv sat down the three men silently fought with one another to give her a bowl of rabbit soup and a cup of ale from a large travel bladder. At first it seemed the trappers were excited to have company and then Halfdan realized they were aiming their hospitality towards Liv.

"You found our randevu point." Said the older man, glowing after Liv accepted his bowl and watched as the other men dolefully handed their bowls to Halfdan and Ulv. "After tonight we will go our separate ways and meet up again before winter. From here we travel together to Bekkr and ship our furs overseas to Brittan. My name is Ketil. This is Audun and Orm with his dogs. Still naming the dogs. Usually wait to see if they survive their first bear or wolf attack before their names are given."

"My name is Halfdan. This here is Liv and Ulv. The owl's name is Elora, she came with a name."

"Was your owl out before? We saw it flying around. Never saw an owl flying around in daylight before." Said Orm, pleasantly surprised.

"Yes, we let her fly on ahead sometimes." Liv said between sips of soup.

"Not much out here past Njardarheimr. Don't seem like trappers to me." Audun said with a rough stern voice as he eyed Halfdan and Ulv.

Halfdan looked at the trappers before responding, contemplating on telling them the truth. "We're traveling to Edge Keep. Have a message for Blackhare. Ever been there before?"

"Ah." Said Ketil, leaning back a bit. "Stayed in the building once when it was abandoned, during a bad storm. I was happy to hear someone moved in, thought they would bring it back to glory. Instead it's more ghostly than before."

"What was it before it was abandoned?" Halfdan asked, trying to get Ketil to give up some more information.

"Despair has tainted that palace. How old tales go, it was once a watch tower. After all the clans were combined it was forgotten, turned into a hideout for bandits. Then someone with money was exiled for smearing dirt on a chieftain. Halfdan figured the spot would be perfect for a new town and built a castle off the old tower. Was so focused on the castle that he didn't think about the land it was on. It's mostly rocks. Not enough dirt to plant anything and not enough vegetation for livestock. Starved to death in his castle, along with most of the people who followed him to build the new town. The exiled man promised those workers land he didn't even own. Best assumption is that he figured if he built on the land and took care of it then it would belong to him." Ketil took a small sip of ale before continuing. "Went back last spring, just to look. Seems like the young woman who lives there has a lot of help, no clue how she feeds them all."

Halfdan gulped and looked at Liv and Elora who was perched on her shield. They both looked back at Halfdan, all three knew that Blackhare didn't need to feed her reanimated slaves.

"So, what is it like spending most of your lives in the woods?" Liv asked, genuinely curious.

Ketil let out a laugh that turned into a cough. "Its fine, make decent money and you don't have to deal with neighbors. It's peaceful, except the one time I was chased by a pack of wolves.

Climbed up a tree. Stuck there for three nights until the wolves finally gave up."

"That's nothing." Audun said before clearing his throat, not used to talking after spending years on end alone in the woods. "I was stalked by a bear for eight days. Didn't sleep or eat, just kept moving. Two times the bear got close and I could feet its foul breath on the back of my neck. The whole time I kept thinking about how no one would know I was gone. That's why I'm friends with these fine men."

The wiry man named Orm, meaning serpent, who sat close to Liv and surrounded by three sleeping dogs let out a demeaning laugh at Audun. "Every time you tell that story you add an extra day. We all know the most dangerous beast is man itself." Orm then turned his whole body to face Liv as if he was just telling her his story. "I was caught hunting on private lands. I knew what I was doing but I was a kid, figured I could slip in and out without anyone noticing. I was wrong and was caught in short time. In my opinion, not one man should own so much land. Anyway, I was captured but escaped before they could toss me behind iron bars. That's why I got the name, Orm. That, and I can do this." The man then began to bend his arms and hands in the opposite direction of their intended purpose.

Liv let out a loud gasp before she began laughing, amused at Orm's feats. Ulv began gagging, causing the dogs around Orm to lift their heads to look at him.

Halfdan could see now how Orm escaped, if his joints could bend in such a way he could easily slip out of restraints. Orm dressed, acted and even sounded like a Norsemen but the more Orm talked the more his accent would slip. His rich harsh tones identified himself as *Ostmen and Halfdan figured Orm ran here to avoid further justice for his crime. Most people would be offended having a nickname meaning serpent, but Orm seemed almost delighted by the given name.

"What about you, travelers, have any stories to share?" Ketil asked as he poured more ale into his cup and handed it to Halfdan.

219

"Oh, well-" Halfdan started before being cut off by Ulv, who had already finished his rabbit soup.

"I was a dog once! Then Halfdan turned me into a human. Used to make me angry but I don't mind being human anymore. I'm allowed indoors, eat decent meals and I get to live longer now. I just don't like the constant thinking. Can I have some more soup? It's good soup."

Ketil, Audun and Orm looked at Ulv with blank expressions before turning their gaze to Halfdan. Halfdan gave a strained smile and tapped his finger on his head. The trappers gave Halfdan a slight lift of their heads to show understanding before Audun took Ulv's bowl and filled it up with more soup. Ulv took back his bowl and dug into the soup with great enthusiasm.

"I'm pleased you like the soup." Ketil said with a faint smile. "I used to be a cook at a tavern. Could make a meal out of anything you gave me." Keitl then lifted his left hand and showed the group that he was missing his pinky finger. "Made a small cut in my finger and it got infected. Infection grew and they had to cut my finger off to prevent it from spreading. Got me thinking. Realized that I didn't enjoy cooking, spending my days over a warm fire in a small room. Quit my job, sold my house and bought hunting and trapping gear."

"I bet it's nice being out in the woods. No religious zealots or drama." Liv said while she rubbed her hands together. "Can I ask if you ever saw anything unusual in the woods?"

Orm shook his head no. "Only see weird stuff when I head into town to sell my pelts."

"Saw a fallow buck eat a dead doe once." Audun said, followed by a shocked expression as if he didn't mean to speak out loud. He turned to look at his fellow trappers, worried about being criticized. "Figured I ate something bad and was just seeing things."

"I believe you. If people can go mad so can animals." Said Ketil as he offered to refill Audun's mug with ale. "Maybe even forest spirits trying to scare you off."

"Saw a reindeer carrying around another reindeer's head entangled in its antlers." Halfdan said as he scrapped up the last of his soup. "Didn't know what to make of it. Seemed so unreal and the fact that I could smell it made me realize I wasn't imagining anything."

"That is gross." Liv said distastefully, she would have put her soup down in disgust but was so hungry she finished the soup anyway.

The talking, storytelling and singing of songs went on late into the calm chilly night. Once everyone ate their fill the small kettle of soup was put on the ground and everyone watched as the dogs pushed one another away to get a good lick of the savory leftovers. Ketil and Audun were first to get up and retreated into their makeshift tents made of branches and animal skins. Halfdan added logs to the fire and retrieved blankets that were placed under their horse's saddles. Ulv took a blanket and fell asleep before his head laid on the animal pelt beneath him, preventing the cold earth from absorbing his heat. Halfdan put a blanket next to Liv and watched as Elora flew up into the darkness and perched in a tree.

As Halfdan laid down he could hear Liv and Orm whispering and stifling laughter to each other on the other side of the fire. Halfdan felt conflicted, he was happy that Liv was talking to another man but deep down he wanted to shake Orm up and tell him to leave his daughter alone. He laid awake for a while, listening to Liv whisper her life story to Orm before his tired body fell asleep.

Halfdan woke up with a shiver and sat up to look around in the foggy morning air, the only sound of a woodpecker in the distance. Liv was asleep curled up under a blanket with a dying fire between them. The tents that held the three trappers were gone. It was early morning but the men were already packed up and deep in the forest. Halfdan was relieved to see that their horses were still by the campsite, nibbling on the long grass around them. The hairs on Halfdan's neck prickled and turned to see Elora perched in a tree staring silently back at him with her big unblinking eyes.

"Why?" Halfdan grumbled quietly at Elora. "Why are you like this?"

"I didn't even do anything?" Elora said innocently, but deep down she was pleased to have frightened Halfdan.

"I didn't even hear them." Halfdan said, referring to the three trappers.

"Neither did I, just woke up a little before you did. Perhaps they were ghosts. I didn't even notice them when I was flying ahead."

Halfdan shivered a little and convinced himself that it was the damp morning air. "Oh? I figured you did it on purpose, thinking it would be funny for us to run into them. Anyway, lots of people dislike saying goodbye. They probably figured it was better to leave before we woke up. Just surprised they left the furs that we were sleeping on behind." Halfdan looked at the sleeping Liv and Ulv for a moment before talking to Elora again. "Wake them up."

Elora fluffed up and braced herself before leaping high into the air. She flew up, circled around and swooped down and hissed. Most people would imagine that all owls made cute little hoots, but eagle owls did not. Their call was far from pleasant and Halfdan smiled as he watched Liv and Ulv scrabble to their feet in fright.

"Why?" Liv yelled as she shook her fist at Elora before glaring at her father. "Just you wait!"

"This is the second time." Ulv said defeated as he wrapped the blanket around him and shuffled closer to Liv for comfort.

"You're wide awake now. It's all in good fun. Come on, let's get going." Halfdan said as he walked over and picked up his blanket and began to fold it.

"Where did they go?" Liv asked as she looked around as if the trappers were just misplaced.

"Left before I woke up, we should take these pelts with us." Halfdan told Liv as he examined the pelts that were left behind.

A sad look grew heavy on Liv's face while she rubbed Ulv's back. "Didn't even get to say goodbye to Orm."

Ulv looked sleepily as he leaned his head on Liv's shoulder as she continued to rub his back, watching as Halfdan tried to fold and shove the pelts into his travel bag.

"Trappers are like that, they live in the woods for a long time and they can act a little awkward. All three of them agreed that they will come back here before winter. Maybe write a message in the dirt or with rocks. If he doesn't get it I'm sure we will run into him again." Halfdan said and watched Liv's face for an expression. Her face lit up a little as she stopped comforting Ulv to collect rocks to leave a message. Ulv watched on for a moment before helping Liv collect rocks with the blanket still wrapped around him.

Halfdan put his and Liv's blankets on Hulda and Molka and saddled them before watching Liv finish up her message. Halfdan wanted to ask what Liv was writing but figured she would tell him if she wanted him to know. As he watched Liv finish putting rocks together Halfdan couldn't help but feel mixed emotions. Liv was happy to talk to Orm and was hurt that he was gone, but a man named after serpents couldn't be good news. However, he was gone now and they had to press forward. Halfdan felt bad for telling Liv that they might run into him again, but the truth is he doubted it. Trappers often went missing or traveled to new locations for better hunts.

The group estimated seven days of travel left and made sure they were going in the correct direction by checking the *fishermen constellation at night. When the stars were hidden behind clouds at night was when Halfdan got nervous, worried that they would end up going in the wrong direction. When the clouds didn't obstruct their view Halfdan would find himself looking up at the moon. It was once comforting but now the moon acted like an hourglass, showing Halfdan how little time he had left until his other eye was removed.

Each night the moon would grow brighter and brighter, a beacon of despair. When the group was on their forth night camping outside a bear attacked the nervous horse, Embla. Hulda and Molka ran away snorting as the bear used its massive weight to sit on Embla. Halfdan, Liv and Ulv woke up in a frenzy and saw the bear biting at Embla's legs. Liv picked up her shield and axe, ready to fight off the bear but Halfdan yelled at her to run. Without thinking Halfdan grabbed the two packs before running behind Liv and Ulv. The bear was too content to run after them and soon Halfdan, Liv and Ulv stopped running. They stood by a babbling brook and looked around nervously and listened to the forest to see if they could hear the bear but all they could hear was Embla, not braying but screaming similar to a freighted pig but louder. When the pitiful sounds form Embla stopped Ulv shuddered and hugged himself. Liv closed her eyes tight and hung her head, distracting her thought with the sound of the brook running carelessly over the rocks.

"Guess we're walking." Halfdan said without thinking. Liv looked at her father dumbfounded and shook her head at him as she fought off a smile.

"You're messed up." Ulv said quietly as he bent down by the river and splashed water on his face.

"We would be wasting our time looking for Hulda and Molka on foot. They got us this far." Halfdan then looked at the discomforted faces of Liv and Ulv who looked back at him with despair. "Look, I feel bad for Embla. But think of it this way, the bear was obviously hungry and needed to fatten up for winter."

"Do you think Elora is ok?" Ulv asked while rubbing his arms.

Halfdan looked at Ulv and pointed at his legs. "We got legs, she's got wings. She's fine. If anything she is safer in a tree than standing on the ground like we are."

Halfdan's comment caused Ulv and Liv to look around more nervously and Halfdan noticed that he was doing the same.

"Let's climb up a tree." Liv said calmly but there was a nervous tone in her voice.

"Agreed." Ulv said and walked up to an old oak tree that was by the creek.

Liv put her axe in her leather holster and leaned her shield against the tree. With ease Liv climbed the tree and sat on a sturdy branch. Halfdan had to give Ulv a boost and watched as he scampered up the tree, half expecting him to fall down. After watching Ulv pick a spot up high in the branches Halfdan then grunted as he hoisted himself up into the tree and made his way up. He wasn't sure if he was high enough to be safely away from a bear, but Liv and Ulv were higher up and that comforted Halfdan.

The leaves in the old oak tree were beginning to turn yellow and most had already fallen to the ground. Everyone sat quietly in the tree and looked around trying to spot Elora. Halfdan was beginning to grow sore and contemplated climbing down when he heard rustling on the other side of the brook. Another bear that was larger than the first came lumbering out and walked across the brook, splashing water with each step. Halfdan sat still and could hear Liv and Ulv holding their breath. Without thinking Halfdan held his breath as well, his heart beat thrumming in his ears. The bear lazily walked over to the tree and sniffed Liv's shield, as water and drool dripped from its mouth covering the decorated wood. Curiously the bear used its long claws to push the shield. The shield fell over and the bear jumped back startling itself. After a few more cautious sniffs of the shield the bear lumbered on, occasionally lifting its head to take in deep snorts of air.

Halfdan figured the bear heard their horse crying out in agony and is following smell of death and an easy meal. Shortly after the bear walked away they could hear the bears fighting over the horse, their roars cutting through the forest.

Halfdan snapped out of thought when he heard Ulv whimpering and looked up to see Liv scanning the area, desperate to see Elora. As Halfdan sat in the tree he thought about what he should do. Should they stay in the tree or make a run for it? What if there are more predators out there?

Suddenly Liv let out a sigh of relief. "There she is." Liv said in a hushed tone as if the bears would hear her and come running over at any moment.

Elora landed on the branch by Ulv and hopped over closer to him. Ulv raised an eyebrow at the fit of brown fuzz Elora held in her beak. He held out his hand and Elora happily obliged. Slowly, Ulv examined the fuzzy mystery item before smelling it.

"It's bear fur!" Ulv said loudly in disbelief before covering his mouth with his free hand.

"I snatched it off of one of them while they were fighting." Elora said loudly, unaware of how uneasy the rest of her companions were. "So busy fighting that they didn't even notice me."

"That's neat and all, but can you look around to see if there are any more bears ahead of us? Before we get down." Liv said in a high-pitched voice as she hugged one of the branches that was in front of her. "It's only a matter of time before one of the bears loses the fight and comes looking for another meal."

"Fine." Elora said in an exasperated tone before flying off.

The rest of her companions watched helplessly as Elora disappeared into the tree line. The sound of bears fighting for a second time back at camp pierced their ears.

CHAPTER 23

WHO CAN SAY WHAT SORROW SEEMINGLY CAREFREE FOLK BARE TO THEIR LIFE'S END. VOLSUNGA SAGA ~ NORSE PROVERB

Halfdan stepped out into a small clearing holding handfuls of the blankets and pelts they left behind at their previous camp site. Sitting by a large fire was Liv butchering her horse, Hulda, who was found with a broken leg. Elora spotted her while she was looking for bears and saw her hoof stuck in a burrow, most likely caused by her frantically fleeing. Molka was not found and everyone figured she was long gone. Liv's back was facing a cave entrance where Ulv was keeping an eye on Elora who was now taking the form of a bear. Elora demanded a large meal be prepared for her, explaining that she would need to eat a large amount after she was done.

"I can't believe you went back." Liv said without looking up from her work. Her hands were covered in blood and her face was blank, but Halfdan knew that she wasn't happy about him going back to the bear ridden camp site. She was also hurt by the fate of her horse but happy to have something to eat.

"There were tracks but the bears were gone. I was careful." Halfdan said as he put the blankets and pelts on the ground before sitting down next to Liv. "How are things going here?"

Liv put the axe and chunk of thigh meat down to stretch her fingers. "There was some screaming. When she said that it was going to be painful, transforming from a small beast to a large one, I didn't think much of it. But it sounds horrible. Not sure if it was all in my head, but I swear I could hear her bones breaking."

Halfdan let out a *hmm* in thought and understanding. "She's been in there for a long time, it's close to night fall. I was hoping she would be done by the time I got back."

A long howling cry escaped from the cave. Halfdan watched as Liv closed her eyes and grimaced. He knew that look well for he used to do the same thing. When someone let out a scream, that agonizing scream of pain, it sends out a wave of needles over your body. You begin to feel sick because you want to help that person, but there is nothing you can do to help. All one can do is sit there while listening to the screams as they make you stir crazy.

Liv opened her eyes and saw her father studying her. "It's difficult to listen too."

"When her screams stop bothering you, that's when you have to worry. Want me to finish cutting up the horse?" Halfdan asked already picking up the axe.

"Normally I'd say that a blind man can do better, but have at it." Liv said standing up and headed over to a pond of stagnate water to wash her hands.

"I'm not that bad! People used to pay me for my wood carvings you know." Halfdan said to Liv's back as he took off his gloves.

The bloody meat was slippery in Halfdan's grasp and the lack of sensation in his burned hands caused him to rely on his vision over touch. Before he could cut the meat away from the bone Halfdan heard a commotion in the dark cave. It started off as a feminine scream that slowly turned into a deep roar that shook the ground Halfdan was sitting on.

"Stop! Slow down!" Ulv yelled out, his voice echoing in utter fear for his friend from within the cave.

Halfdan turned to look and squinted his eye to focus on what was happening within the belly of the cave. There were grunting sounds that grew louder and louder and soon a bear, larger than any bear Halfdan as ever seen, came barreling out of the cave. The bear sprinted to the pile of meat stacked by the fire, grunting with each lunge until it was close enough to throw its whole body on the raw horse flesh. Horrible smacking sounds escaped from the bear's mouth as it began to gorge.

It took a moment for Halfdan to realize he dropped the axe and meat and scooted away. When terror was replaced with irritation Halfdan stood up and grabbed the meat and threw it at Elora's furry shoulder.

"I hope you get worms!" He yelled at her with a scowl.

Elora only turned her beady eyes at Halfdan and let out a low growl between bits of food, crunching bones with her teeth, before looking back at her meal.

Taken back by this Halfdan looked up to see Liv still standing by the pond and noticed her taking a step back, distancing herself from them. Halfdan frowned and noticed Liv's eyes were focused on something else. Following her gaze Halfdan looked to see Ulv standing at the mouth of the cave. His face was pale and sweaty and he was grabbing at his left arm just below the elbow. Halfdan's mouth turn dry when he noticed blood running over Ulv's fingers. Looking back Halfdan recalled, even as an owl, Elora never ate any raw meat. His whole body and spirit went cold when he finally put everything together, Elora went feral.

The first step back toward Ulv was forced, the second one came easier and Halfdan had to fight the urge to run. Slowly he made his way to Ulv, never turning his back to Elora.

"You going to be ok?" Halfdan whispered to Ulv.

The corners of Ulv's mouth twitched for a moment before he could murmur "Yeah."

"Slowly make your way to Liv, don't run or turn your back to Elora." Halfdan informed Ulv, slowly leading the long way around to Liv.

"How do you know about dealing with bears?" Ulv asked Halfdan in a whisper that was near impossible to understand.

"Man in my home village, used to talk to him all the time before he was killed. He would go out in the woods and feed bears." Halfdan replied quietly as he took side steps to keep facing Elora.

"What happened to him?" Ulv asked mimicking Halfdan's movements.

"He was eaten by a bear, but that's not important." Halfdan said and looked to see Ulv staring at him the same way a dog looks at their master after they pretended to throw a stick, a mix of dissatisfaction and treachery.

As Halfdan and Ulv slowly made their way Elora continued to stuff herself, stopped to throw up, then continued eating as if nothing happened. Ulv stopped moving and covered his mouth. Halfdan's ear twitched when he heard a faint gag escape from Ulv's mouth. A childish joy rose up in Halfdan, he couldn't help but make a gagging sound and to his delight Ulv involuntarily gagged a little louder. Halfdan gagged again and laughed when Ulv retched even louder, bending his body forward as if he was on the verge of sympathetically throwing up.

Something snapped in Halfdan's brain, he could feel it. The stress of everything they went through caused him to laugh harder than any sane person would have. It felt like he was one step closer to insanity, but it felt good to laugh. It took a nervous shove from Ulv to get him to stop and Halfdan looked up to see Elora staring at them with her head tilted. The little head tilt of confusion would normally have been cute to see, but the blood on Elora's snout made it unsettling.

No one moved as Elora moved her gaze to the trees and then the cave. Halfdan was contemplating calling out to Elora before he heard Liv confidently yell out first.

"How are you feeling?" Liv yelled to Elora in a voice you reserve for crazy people.

Halfdan and Ulv couldn't see Liv at first but soon noticed that she was halfway up a tree. Rather than scolding Halfdan and Ulv for acting like fools Liv used the distraction to climb out of harm's way, and Halfdan admired that.

Elora opened her mouth as if she was going to say something. Instead, she looked down at the raw meat she was once so feverishly partaking in and her stomach contents escaped her.

This time she sounded more exaggerated and human. This pushed Ulv over the edge and pitched his contents as well. Some spattered on Halfdan's boot but he figured he deserved it.

After some panting Elora finally spoke "I'll be back" before slowly disappearing into the woods. Ulv wanted to go running after Elora but Halfdan stopped him by putting his hand on Ulv's shoulder.

"Let her be." Halfdan told Ulv in a somber tone. Ulv turned and the deep sadness in his eyes stung Halfdan's heart. He didn't want to leave Elora alone but Ulv listened to Halfdan and sat down with a huff.

Halfdan sat next to Ulv and examined his arm. "Good thing your coat is red. The bleeding is good it will get the dirt out of the wound. Can you move your hand?"

Ulv wiggled his fingers and stretched his arm. "I feel fine, just got scared is all."

By now Liv finished climbing out of the tree and came running over. "You well, Ulv?"

"He'll be fine." Halfdan answered for Ulv.

"What happened?" Liv asked standing in front of Ulv, not looking at Halfdan but intently staring at Ulv's face.

"I'm not sure." Ulv said avoiding making eye contact with Liv and blinking often. "It was just an accident."

"You're a bad liar." Liv said sternly before softening her tone. "Ulv, you can tell us. We won't get mad at Elora."

Ulv looked at Liv with those same hurt sad eyes. "I gave her my word. I already told one of her secrets. I don't want to do it again."

Liv knelt down to be at eye level with Ulv. "I can respect that. Can you just let us know if we need to worry about this happening again? Perhaps there is something we can do to help?"

After nervously drumming his fingers on his knee Ulv looked at Liv again, some hope glimmering in his eyes. "Do you think you can help?"

"We will try and keep it discreet if we can." Liv said with a smile, hoping to get Ulv to return one as well but he didn't.

Ulv shifted his jaw from side to side as if he needed to get it working again in order to speak. He was quiet for a moment before he finally said anything. "Elora told me that there once was a shapeshifter who worked with a group of thieves. The thieves would kill a merchant and the shapeshifter would take the form of the merchant. At night the shapeshifter would unlock the shop and let his fellow thieves in. In the morning the shapeshifter would report his shop had been robbed and give a description of different thieves or groups of bandits in order to take out the competition. The thieves decided to do one last grand robbery before going their separate ways. They made plans to rob a Jarl. This Jarl never left his home but the Jarl's son would often go out to hunt. When the thieves killed the Jarl's son the shapeshifter took his form, but this time the shapeshifter actually believed he *was* the Jarl's son. The shapeshifter went to the Jarl and told him about the thieves in the woods and the Jarl sent his guards to kill them all. It wasn't until the shapeshifter died in battle that everyone found out that the Jarl's son was fake. Elora explained was that every time a shapeshifter takes a different form they forget about their original form, little by little. The more you can't remember the easier it is to get lost as someone else."

Liv looked at Halfdan with a frown before looking at Ulv again. "Elora told us that she doesn't remember her original form since she was a child."

"Elora doesn't have you sit in there with her to keep her safe, does she?" Halfdan asked in a more serious voice than he intended.

"I couldn't do it." Ulv said as he swayed back and forth, tears beginning to run down his face. "Something was wrong and I knew it but I couldn't do it."

Liv leaned in and gave Ulv a hug and didn't let go. Ulv rubbed his face on Liv's shoulder and let out a sniffle. Halfdan

232

couldn't help but feel awkward just standing there, unsure what to do.

"I put the rock down. If I would have hit her in the head before she was done it would have killed her. But I couldn't. I figured that if I talked to Elora she would snap out of it. Instead… she swiped at me. When Elora turned into a cat and an owl nothing like this ever happened." Ulv said then let go of Liv to rub his eyes with the palm of his hands.

"That was brave of you, what you did." Halfdan said and stood up, offering his hand to Ulv.

"I don't feel very brave." Ulv said and took Halfdan's hand to be pulled up.

"That's because bravery and idiocy go hand in hand." Halfdan said with a smile and brushed some dirt off of Ulv's coat. "Trust me, you were brave."

Liv lifted her black dress and ripped the end of her smock. She then put the fabric in the small pot and filled it with water before placing it over the fire. As they waited for the water to warm Halfdan helped Ulv take his jacket off. Liv twisted the water out of the fabric before using it to wipe the blood off Ulv's wounds. Ulv grimaced as Liv examined his wounds but not once did he complain. The scratch wasn't to the bone and there was no debris to be found. Liv washed off the stained fabric and wrung it out even more before using it to tie off the open skin that started bleeding again.

Halfdan tried to wash off the coat. The rip could be mended but there would forever be a brown stain where the blood seeped into the wool. It was growing dark by the time Halfdan hung Ulv's coat in a tree to dry and decided to start cooking and drying some of the meat that was left.

Elora promptly came back to camp when she smelled horse cooking over an open fire. Liv was happy to see her again but not as much as Ulv who was practically jumping for joy. Both Liv and Ulv acted like nothing happened. Halfdan wanted to say something but wasn't sure what specifically, then figured he should let it go and just be happy that everyone was alive and accounted for.

CHAPTER 24

EDGE KEEP

Grudgingly, Halfdan suggested that they not leave in the morning but rather spend an additional night so that everyone could rest. Everyone was weary after the long travel and incidents with more than one bear. No one argued so to prepare for a more comfortable stay Liv went into the cave and chased out the spiders and swept out old leaves before laying down pelts and blankets. In the middle of the cave Liv left a clearing where they would add hot rocks from the fire outside to warm up the stony shelter.

The hot rock idea didn't last long and Elora woke up to find everyone sleeping next to her for warmth. In the morning everyone ate and dried out some more horse as they spent the day laying around.

Late into the night the group woke up to something stirring about outside the cave. The fire outside was dying out, preventing them from seeing. Elora mustered up the courage to take a look but noticed it was only a lynx sniffing around the camp sight, its spotted feline body already hightailing away by the time it was sighted.

When Elora explained that it was only a lynx Halfdan let out a sigh of relief while unknowingly clenching his chest. Halfdan's face turned red when his companions looked at him studying his reaction. "I thought it was another bear." Halfdan explained but in reality he thought it was Jovi, coming to punish him for taking a day of rest.

No one wanted to leave the next morning. Their aching bodies protesting that one day of rest was not nearly enough. Despite the pain the group packed up and back tracked to their previous camp site. What was left of Embla was scattered about the old camp site with griffon vultures so occupied with fighting over her innards that they didn't notice Halfdan, Liv and Ulv watching them. When Elora stepped out into the clearing, the vultures lifted their bloody heads to look at her bearish form before flying off. This gave the agile song birds a chance to swoop down and peck at the horse's fat before flying off again.

Nature was making quick work of the horse's remains. If Embla's skull wasn't missing it would have taken a stranger a moment to identify the corps. As Halfdan looked at Embla's exposed rib bones reaching out towards the sky he couldn't help but be thankful that the bear chose her instead of them.

Continuing down the trail, Elora let Ulv and Liv take turns riding on her back. Ulv was more enthusiastic about riding a bear than a horse and actually managed to fall asleep for a moment. Liv was giddy and couldn't help but play with Elora's round fuzzy bear ears Elora tolerated the unwelcomed affection with muffled growls.

The trail took them up and down lush hills, winded around lakes and past some of the largest trees that they have ever encountered. After two days of travel the trees that once surrounded them soon became sparse and were replaced with boulders and weak vegetation. The trail was now open and had a gradual incline. There wasn't much wildlife; an occasional bird or rodent would cross the path but more often it was just the wind that would keep them company. The trail was more gravel than dirt and quickly grew uncomfortable to travel on.

When it was time for their high noon rest Halfdan asked if they could walk a little further up the trail, insisting that he could hear something and that the hill was blocking the sound. Encouraging everyone to at least walk up the hill to reach the two stacked stone pillars, each on one side of the rocky trail. Everyone grumbled but agreed and followed behind Halfdan as they walked up the steep incline. If you lost your footing you could have easily rolled back down the hill, it wouldn't kill you but would have left you bloodied.

Soon everyone in the group could hear odd sounds and looked at one another unable to recognize the source. Perhaps frogs but it was getting late in the season for them to sing their songs. Liv suggested it was deer grunting and Elora thought it was the wind hitting the rocks creating distorted sounds. Just before Halfdan reached the top of the hill he froze for a split second, ducked then quickly scurried to the left pillar. Liv and Ulv did the same and followed behind Halfdan and Elora did her best to hide behind the pillar on the right. No one spoke as they peeked around the pillars at their destination, Edge Keep.

Edge Keep was as large enough to keep an English noble but not much more. It was tall and rectangular in shape with a nine sided stone wall around it for protection. The castle was built behind a *moraine so the naturally formed hills could be used to hide it. Behind Edge Keep was a white capped mountain, protecting the castle's rear.

The sound was coming from the large amount of reanimated thralls that wandered about aimlessly. Occasional guttural sounds would escape from the thralls as they bumped into one another or when they tripped on what was left of a house's foundation; remnants of of the people who first built this place and failed to tame the land.

Almost like unwanted dogs that were kicked out of the house the thralls were dirty and unkempt. Constantly looking at the door waiting to be let in again or perhaps waiting for orders from their master, Blackhare. Most of the reanimated slaves wore typical everyday clothes but some donned robes that were either black, brown or red. Halfdan recognized the red robes, they were worn by the Rossvatnet students. As he wondered why Magnus' students would be here he glanced at Elora who looked back at Halfdan with fire in her eyes.

"Do you think Magnus is here with Blackhare?" Halfdan whispered to Elora.

Elora peeked around the pillar again and stared at the thralls for a while until answering Halfdan. "Magnus uses his students as

237

protection, only sending out three at a time to do his bidding. By the looks of it most of my fellow students are here. There is no way we can take on Blackhare and Magnus at the same time. We need to wait for one of them to leave."

"We will take turns watching the keep, using the hill as cover. As we wait for either Blackhare or Magnus to leave we need to try and learn any routines or weakness in the castle to get in." Halfdan paused for a moment to look at the light blue sky, picturing the moon in his mind as he noticed an overcast coming in their direction. "If I remember correctly the moon isn't going to be full for about another six days. Better to take this time to rest up and devise a good plan of attack."

"The plan to come here to kill Blackhare was easier to imagine before, well… actually before seeing the place." Ulv said leaning over Liv who was kneeling, both looking around the pillar to stare at Edge Keep and its thralls.

"What if we can't get in? Starting to feel like we're attempting the impossible." Liv whispered, keeping her eyes on the closest group of wandering undead.

"Doesn't matter if a plan is executed properly, as long as everyone makes it out alive. If we can't kill her it wouldn't be the end of all good things if I lose another eye, especially if you help me out." Halfdan said, followed by a lame smile to Liv.

"Is it the responsibility of a woman to care for a man she just recently learned was her father?" Liv said in a neutral, matter of fact tone.

The pillar didn't hide all of Ulv's face and Halfdan watched as his companion curled his lips and grimaced with big eyes that darted to the ground. Elora did not attempt to contain a chuckle. Liv turned and smirked at Halfdan, letting him relax a little but still unsure if she meant what she said.

However, Halfdan knew his daughter was right. Just because he fathered her it didn't mean Liv owed him anything. Even in his effort to save Liv's life he ultimately made his daughter's life more difficult, forcing her to travel from one village to another without a place to call home. Halfdan figured he should just be grateful that she has tolerated everything so far without any complaints.

As Halfdan looked at the moss growing on the stone pillar he promised himself that in the spring he would get a house. Even if that meant putting pride aside and asking for help from Norvick or Jarl Hallvard. If the house was small he could make it work. Halfdan wasn't confident in his skills to build a home but he would try if it came down to that.

"Halfdan? Did you hear me?" Liv whispered, slight irritation in her voice.

"Hmm?" Halfdan murmured, thoughts laboring over a house disappeared as he came back to reality of murderous intent to please a malevolent entity. "Sorry, what was that?"

"What should we do now?" Ulv repeated for Liv, who was skeptically looking at her father.

"Right." Halfdan said and looked around and gestured towards the east at a grand boulder protruding out of the hill about fifty paces away. "We can hide behind the rock. If we all take turns watching the keep, using the hill as cover, the group resting can also keep an eye on the north for any newcomers. Might get lucky and catch a supply cart, wouldn't be surprised if she gets everything she needs delivered."

"You can't be serious." Elora said, annoyed.

"What?" Halfdan said and shrugged at Elora as he gestured to the vast emptiness around them. "Sorry there are no inns or taverns. Would you rather sleep with Blackhare? I'm sure she has a spare room."

Elora huffed at Halfdan and her tone grew more cross. "Every night I wake up with all three of you single formed wimps sleeping on me. So now I get to sleep on a pile of rocks while you all get a cozy bear bed."

"Technically, I've had two different bodies." Ulv chimed in happily, ignorant of Elora's fury. "I told you I was a dog before."

"Shut it, puppy breath. You're lucky I didn't catch you eating the last of the dried horse strips." Elora said her voice no longer a whisper. Liv shushed her as politely as she could but it only made Elora's anger grow. "Don't tell me to be quiet." Elora hissed and stomped her big bear foot. Unaware that she was standing on an oval rock that slipped out from under her. The world slowed down for everyone to watch as Elora tumbled forward and smack her head into the pillar before her.

Elora staggered back and watched as the stony pillar swayed back and forth before five rocks off the top tumbled down. The sound of rocks colliding with one another echoed across the land.

Halfdan closed his eye and clenched his fists and waited for the last rock to finish rolling down the hill before breaking the silence again. "I'm contemplating asking *Freyr to stop my anger and strengthen our friendship. But most of me want's to ask Thor for the power to smite you down, Elora."

Elora rubbed her forehead with her large brown paw before looking sympathetically at her companions. "I had that coming."

Ulv peered around the pillar before warning everyone in a shrilled voice. "They're coming."

Halfdan didn't waste time looking to see how far away the reanimated slaves were, he scurried down and jumped from rock to rock towards the large boulder for cover. He could hear his companions close behind him, their breaths heavy as each step loosened rocks that were sent rolling down the incline. Liv's dress became entangled on a dead twig and slowed her down. The rest of her companions were watching from behind the boulder, silently whispering for her to hurry. She got her dress free and ran, Halfdan held his hand out and when she grabbed it he pulled Liv in.

As the group fought to steady their breath they could hear sturdy footsteps followed by animalistic groaning. Everyone watched as Ulv slowly peeked around the boulder, his body started shaking as he looked at his companions. Ulv pointed outward and his mouth moved but he couldn't get any words out.

"They're coming?" Liv whispered, nervously.

Ulv shook his head yes and cowered behind the boulder. "Seven of them."

Halfdan opened his mouth, he was going to say some encouraging words to Ulv. Something about staying confident and fighting with your head was the key to success for battle. But all that slipped away when a hail of rocks came down upon them and one rogue rock struck Halfdan in the head.

CHAPTER 25

VALKYRJA

Halfdan opened his eye and took in the trees and grass surrounding him. When he stood up it took him a minute to realize that the rock he was leaning against was once a familiar large boulder. Now only half of it was sticking out, the rest underground, and it was discolored with different types of moss. Halfdan rubbed his head and looked around, puzzled and unsure on what to do. He couldn't shake off the feeling that he forgot something.

The sound of people talking reached Halfdan's ears and he followed the sound up the hill. Slowly he reached a clearing and saw people wearing tight fitted clothing that exposed the skin of their arms and legs. There were white tents, shiny closed in carts and thin string was tied up to form square shapes on the ground. In the distance was a mountain and at the base was a pile of rocks, but a few remained stacked together allowing the imagination to picture what the ruins once looked like.

Halfdan stared at the rubble, feeling that the rocks made something of great importance but its meaning was now lost. Losing interest Halfdan walked over and looked in one of the tents. A man with grey slicked back hair and odd circle wires around his eyes talked heatedly into a glowing black slab. Although some of the words the man was saying were familiar to Halfdan most of them were intangible and foreign. All Halfdan could understand was that the man wanted more time to dig.

Figuring the man was crazy Halfdan carried on and walked over to see two women digging. Halfdan felt cold and wondered how the two women could wear such thin clothing. One of the women had brown hair that was tied back and another had the shortest hair he had ever seen on a woman. Both the women talked in the square hole they made. Amused that these people enjoyed looking in the dirt Halfdan took note of how slowly and meticulously the two women dug, cautiously removing unwanted earth.

Suddenly the two women buzzed with excitement when they found something. Halfdan leaned over to get a better look. Hidden within the rocky soil appeared to be a hand grasping something. The woman with the tied back hair went to grab whatever the hand was holding. The short haired woman quickly slapped the other's hand and seemed to be scolding her, but she didn't listen. Eager to find out what it was the woman with the tied back hair slowly lifted the hand and grabbed the item. With a soft brush the woman carefully brushed the dirt away. Halfdan leaned in closer and so did the short haired woman.

It was a golden eye. Halfdan frowned and then realized it was *his* golden eye.

As quick as lightning the once limp hand sprang to life and grabbed the woman's wrist, eager to take back its treasure. The two woman screamed. Halfdan jumped back, startled and when he opened his eye again his vision was fuzzy and it felt like his head was split open.

There was commotion all around him. Halfdan blinked again and could see silhouettes looming over him. But he looked past them and squinted his eye as he looked at a fair maiden with stunning armor and a gold spear in hand riding a flying boar that was large and fearsome. Like a moth to flame Halfdan was mesmerized by her. The fair maiden looked back at him, blew him a kiss and disappeared behind the clouds.

When Halfdan blinked again his companions came into focus. He watched as their mouth's moved but all he could hear was ringing. "I'm fine." Halfdan tried to say but wasn't able to hear if he said it coherently. He knew what the eternally enthralled that Blackhare had damned needed, but he didn't have enough time to

243

express that to his friends. Without waiting Halfdan sat forward and pulled out his bag and began digging in it.

"I never get to keep anything nice." Halfdan murmured to himself as he pulled out the box holding his eye and opened it.

"What?" Liv asked him and Halfdan was finally able to hear.

"What's going on?" Ulv said nervously while trembling.

"Did you think of something?" Elora asked unfazed by the situation.

"Those aren't just thralls, they're draugrs. Blackhare killed all those people and cursed them to become these monsters that can only rest when guarding treasure. The school was a perfect first target because the students didn't have anything of value." Halfdan then handed his golden eye to Liv. "Throw it at them."

Rocks began to rain down on them again. Liv didn't question Halfdan's reasons, she confidently stood up and stepped out into the open and threw the fake eye as hard as she could. One of the draugr swiped the eye out of the air with one dry hand. This quickly evaporated Liv's confidence as she felt her courage drain away. These draugrs were strong with their unblinking cloudy grey eyes constantly open and alert. Slowly the draugr pulled in his hand and looked at what it caught. The draugr let out a happy gurgling sound and showed its treasure the others who let out a similar pleased sound. To Liv's surprise the group of draugr turned and went back up the hill and disappeared.

"Did it work?" Halfdan asked weakly and went to wipe sweat off his brow and realized it was blood. Halfdan felt the top of his head and winced before wiping the blood off his hand on Ulv's jacket. Ulv only frowned back at Halfdan, no longer trembling in fear.

"Yeah." Liv said, puzzled. "Honestly surprised it worked."

"Let's see what they are up to." Elora said and started making her way up the rocky hill with Ulv and Liv behind her.

"Ok, I'll wait right here." Halfdan said disappointed that his companions easily left him behind.

Before reaching the top of the hill Elora, Liv and Ulv laid on their bellies and crawled the rest of the way. When their eyes peeked over they saw the group of draugr that attacked them eagerly make their way through the aimless crowd of thralls that slowly began to move as one like a group of bees, all eager to understand what the small group had.

Slowly the draugr made a small clearing, leaving only one draugr in the middle. At first it seemed like that draugr was laying down but it was actually using its hands to drag its body across the ground. Either in life or in its new agonizing existence the draugr's legs were broken. The one draugr who caught the golden eye approached the paraplegic draugr and showed it the eye. At first the draugr seemed confused then reached up and accepted the gift then began letting out a dry and throaty barking sound. Like a wave all the other draugr began barking, each one unique and grotesque.

Ulv covered his ears and frowned. "I think they are trying to sing."

"That's them singing?" Liv said her voice muffled out by the noise.

Just as quickly as the singing started it stopped and the draugr that gifted the gold eye began moving rocks. With one hand the paraplegic drauger began moving rocks as well. Three more draugrs staggered over and helped move rocks with amazing speed creating an oppression in the ground. Then slowly the thralls made way for the paraplegic draugr to scoot and drop itself into the opening. Then the draugr straightened out its legs then laid down out of sight. One by one the other thralls came and placed one rock into the opening, some more carefully than others.

"What just happened?" Liv asked looking at her friends with disbelief.

"Halfdan was right, they're draugrs. Blackhare and Magnus must have done this to them. I was a fool. Should have figured that out on my own. Just hoping there was a way to bring them back." Elora said and slowly shook her wide head in disapproval. "There is no coming back from this."

"I don't get it. If we kill Blackhare and Magnus won't they turn back? Just like when Jarl Ellingboe and his kids died Oberon turned back." Ulv said, hopeful.

"You can't bring draugrs back to their original life, Ulv." Elora said, solemnly.

"I don't understand." Liv said looking back at the draugrs taking turns placing rocks over one of their own. "I thought people who were greedy in life turned into draugrs. Never resting to forever lay awake to protect their treasure."

"Tales also say that they will enter the dreams of people who wronged them in life, driving them mad. Yet Blackhare and Magnus seem unaffected. All I know is-" Elora stopped and looked at one of the draugrs pointing in their direction. "We have to go."

Halfdan watched as his companions practically came sliding down the hill to him with fear in their eyes. He knew they were spotted and it was time to make a break for it. Halfdan quickly stood up and instantly regretted it. His head began to pound and he could feel himself swaying before he gave up and leaned against the boulder for support. Halfdan gritted his teeth and swore under his breath.

"Dad, get on Elora's back. We need to get out of here." Liv said running to her father to try and support him.

Halfdan rubbed at his temples and squinted his eye to avoid the sunlight. "We can't outrun them. They are too fast. Will the draugrs accept silver coins? That counts as treasure, right?"

"I'm not sure." Elora said, rare anxiety in her voice.

Liv swung her bag forward and pulled out a large leather pouch that jingled with the familiar sound of her winnings. "Guess we will have to find out. What's the worst that could happen?"

"They could tear us apart." Elora said soberly and took a moment to look at her companions. "In case we all die a horrible death... I just wanted to take a moment to thank you, for allowing me to call you my friends. It is an honor to die with you."

"May we all drink and be merry again, together, in Valhalla." Halfdan said and gave a strained and sad smile to his friends. The words *I'm sorry for getting you all into this* was on the tip of Halfdan's tongue, but he figured now wasn't the time for pity. For the first time Halfdan gave Liv a hug that didn't feel provoked and awkward and he didn't want to let go.

"What happens when you die?" Ulv asked, the last of his innocence breaking apart as the sound of the draugrs approaching them vibrated the smaller rocks loose and down the hill.

"All you can do is hope." Liv said, breaking from her father's embrace to squeeze Ulv's hand. Then as one the group stepped forward, ready to face whatever fate was laid before them.

Liv expected the draugrs to come down on them like a horrible flood. Instead the undead thralls stopped at the crest of the hill and looked down at them. Liv began contemplating tossing the silver to them when they all slowly made their way down and surrounded her and her companions. The draugr that caught the golden eye Liv threw before stepped forward and studied Liv.

Holding her breath Liv held out the bag and watched as the draugr stepped closer. She could see the monster was once a man close to her age. Now his skin was tight with mold growing on it. However the muscle underneath looked firm and hard as stone. He had nothing protecting his feet and his clothes were holding together by threads.

Liv continued to hold her breath as the draugr reached out and took the bag. His dead cold fingers ran over Liv's causing her to get goose bumps. She was certain her face had a look of revulsion but she tried her best to keep eye contact with the monster before her.

The draugr opened the bag, took a quick glance and looked back up at Liv with his sunken grey eyes. The skin on the draugr's face was tight, pulled back and expressionless but Liv couldn't help but feel that the monster knew she had more. She could feel herself losing the stare down. For a moment Liv contemplated lying but sympathetically figured they deserved what she has been hoarding for herself. Liv let out a defeated sigh. She knew this day was coming, just didn't want it to be today.

247

"Fine." Liv said to the monster and grabbed her travel bag and dug deeper.

Reluctantly Liv began handing the draugr handfuls of golden bracelets, rings, pendants, hair clips and chains. Along with some golden trinkets and then lastly Halfdan's five unmarked gold coins.

Liv had to push down the anger inside of her. She didn't want to give up her gold and wasn't ready to have a conversation about it with her companions, especially her father. Right now she could feel them staring at her. She could only wonder what they were thinking. But all that melted away when she saw the monster before her hold up the mound of gold he was given in the air for the rest of the draugr to see.

In a rush of excitement the draugrs began their barking again and rushed in. Liv knew she wasn't the only one who let out a scream when they began touching her arms, hair and face. She quickly recognized it as sign of affection but Liv stood frozen as if a bucket of poisonous spiders were dumped on her. Liv wanted to brush them away but didn't want to trigger any negative reaction. So, Liv stood still while the draugrs touch her with their cold smelly hands with their long dirty finger nails.

Liv heard Elora greet someone and slowly turned around to see draugrs dressed in muddy red and black robes touching her bearish form. They got in so close they were practically standing on top of one another in an attempt and touch Elora's face. One put its hand in Elora's mouth as she tried to speak, causing Elora to try and spit out the taste.

"That was my mouth! Take it easy. Yes-yes I'm happy to see you all. Surprised you all could recognize me." Elora stood up on her hind legs to get her head out of reach and caught a glance of someone. She blinked, almost in disbelief. "Magnus?"

Magnus, behind the rest of the red robed draugrs let out a long wailing moan at the sound of his name. His white robes weren't as dirty as the rest and he only had a sprinkling of mold growing on him. But his skin was tight, long grey beard a mess and had those grey milky eyes like the rest of them. His wailing didn't stop and with Magnus' mouth wide open Elora could see his tongue was cut out. Draugrs turned and began putting their hands on Magnus, trying to console him.

"She got you too, huh." Elora said, the anger that was once constantly burning behind her eye's died as she watched her classmates console the teacher that betrayed them. "I forgive you too."

Magnus' horrid crying stopped at those words and he looked back blankly at Elora, all of them looked with a sense of eagerness.

Elora stood taller and sucked in a breath before speaking out amongst the crowd. "Blackhare has affected us all. Her silver tongue has tricked the best of us, even King Olav. You no longer have to do your captors bidding in hopes of release. Thanks to Liv's generous gift..." Elora used her large paw to gesture at Liv who only pressed her lips into a hard line at the comment, still displeased about giving away her hoard. "You can now rest. All that I ask is that you help get us into that keep so we can avenge you."

The draugrs began letting out throaty sharp huffs like a chant as they rushed in and grabbed Elora and lifted her up. She couldn't help but let out a sound of surprise and heard the rest of her companions do the same as their feet left the ground. The draugrs were strong, inhumanly strong and continued their chant as they began running back up the hill.

Halfdan couldn't help but feel like a child being picked up and tossed about. Then Halfdan's body was high in the air, dozens of dead clammy hands supporting his back and legs. Halfdan couldn't help but smile; if it wasn't for the odor this would have been more fun being carried around like a hero. Ahead of him he watched as Liv yelled triumphantly and laughed as she waved her hands in the air. Ulv flailed his arms and legs while wiggling about, trying to get away from the sea of hands but not getting very far. Behind him Elora acted more like a bug tipped over on its back, her paws bounced around limply as she looked around in disbelief to what was happening.

The group watched as the draugrs carried them to the keep, wondering how they were going to get them inside. Were they going to break down the door? Throw them over the stone wall? Perhaps make a bridge by stacking draugrs on top of another. Wonder turned into fear of treachery as the group watched the draugrs carry them past the keep. The group turning their head in unison as Edge Keep was nearly behind them before sharing glances with one another.

Without warning the draugrs stopped running and stood still. Halfdan watched in horror as Liv was dropped and disappeared into the undead crowd. Before Halfdan could scream after his daughter Ulv let out a yell as he went out of sight. As Halfdan was turning to try and ask Elora what was going on the hands that once supported him gave way letting his body fall onto the rocks below, knocking the breath out of him.

CHAPTER 26

WEALTH DIES. FRIENDS DIE. ONE DAY YOU TOO WILL DIE. BUT, THE THING THAT NEVER DIES IS THE JUDGEMENT ON HOW YOU HAVE SPENT YOUR LIFE.
HÁVAMÁL ~ NORSE PROVERB

Laying on the ground Halfdan's body was reeling from the dead weight drop to the ground. All he could do was open his mouth and wait for air to enter his lungs as he watched the draugrs step over him. Some of the thralls with treasure already began making their own holes in the ground to lay in. Others worked feverishly to disperse the gold and silver, making sure everyone received their fair share. Finally able to take shallow breaths, Halfdan sat up and noticed Liv on her feet, unharmed. The draugr that she handed her stolen gold to was next to her, brushing away pebbles on the ground and then lifting a trap door. With its bony fingers the undead thrall pointed into the mouth of the trap door and then moved his finger towards Edge Keep.

Slowly standing Halfdan noticed Elora helping Ulv up. Relieved that everyone was alive Halfdan made his way to Liv who was still standing next to the draugr that revealed the trap door.

"You alright there, you took your sweet time getting up." Liv said to Halfdan with a mischievous smile, poking at Halfdan's age.

"Try getting thrown around in a boat for most of your youth. Don't think I forgot about all that gold." Halfdan said giving back a mocking smile at Liv and watched as her smile turned into a frown as she defensively crossed her arm.

"What was that all about?" Elora said with impish glee as she joined the group with Ulv beside her. "Didn't know you were a thief."

"I'm not a thief!" Liv said throwing her hands into the air and then resting her hands on her hips.

"So people just gave you all that gold?" Ulv asked not believing Liv.

Liv stumbled on her words for a moment before letting out a defeated sigh. "Fine! It all started when I took the gold out of Halfdan's chest. I had good intentions. Figured it was best to have the gold on us, in case of an emergency. Then... It just got out of hand."

"You have no idea what I had to do to get that gold." Halfdan said, more upset that his life savings was gone than Liv stealing it.

"Oh?" Elora said, growing more amused. "Looking at you, I figured you had to pay not the other way around."

Halfdan didn't return a comment to Elora and settled with glaring at her.

"I don't understand." Ulv said with a confused look. "Why steal gold and not something important... like food?"

Liv looked out into the distance, reflecting on the gold that she lost. "I felt like a crow with a shiny stone. Gold is just mesmerizing and I couldn't leave it behind."

"Carful Liv." Elora said with true apprehension in her voice. "Gold and gems are a slippery slope for you. Tell me, has any story of a dragon hoarding treasure end well for the dragon?"

Liv let out another sigh and leaned her head back, no longer wanting to be in this conversation. "No."

The draugr that was with them pointed harshly into the darkness of the trap door and grunted as it looked blankly at the group.

"Guess it's time to go." Liv said with a smile as she tied up the corner of her dress, making it easier for her to walk down the dusty steps.

Her companions followed behind her. Elora tried her best to squeeze her large bearish form through the narrow passage. Halfdan turned back to see if the draugr was going with them and watched as the cursed being slammed the trap door closed, engulfing them into darkness.

"Nice." Elora commented as she let out a loud sneeze as dust tickled her nose.

Halfdan took off his left glove and shook his hand vigorously before the once invisible seal on his hand began to glow a bright light, illuminating the tunnel in a sickly green hue. Halfdan let out a hiss between his teeth as a sharp pain ran through the top of his head. It quickly vanished and Halfdan took a moment to study the seal, it was intricate but none of it made sense to him.

"That's neat." Liv said as she looked around the lighted tunnel and all the spider webs that hung in the corners.

"Death's mark." Ulv said in a quiet voice.

"Whatever." Halfdan said not amused before looking at the integrity of the tunnel. "This tunnel doesn't look very promising. Crumbly and I can smell a good amount of moisture. Let's hurry and see where it goes. Be careful and try to be quiet; our voices could carry elsewhere and alert Blackhare."

Liv led the way down the tunnel, her axe and shield at the ready. Halfdan followed behind her lifting his left hand to light the way with Ulv and Elora close behind him. The tunnel echoed with their footsteps as the occasional flake of stone would drop down from the ceiling. Spiders and bugs scurried about, spooked by unwanted guests.

At the end of the long tunnel was a wooden spiral staircase that led up to another trap door. Slowly the group went up and everyone watched nervously as Liv opened the trap door enough to get a peek of the surroundings.

"The staircase continues up." Liv whispered. "Seems to be the old part of the watch tower. I believe there is a door to the rest of the keep in front of us."

Everyone stood still, when there wasn't any commotion Liv opened the trap door more. After looking around Liv crawled out of the trap door and held it open for the rest of her companions. Once Halfdan got out he quietly walked to the door Liv believed led to the rest of the keep. He rested his ear against the door and he could feel a cold hum vibrating the door.

She's on the other side of the door came to Halfdan's mind in Jovi's voice.

Stepping back Halfdan looked at his companions. Liv was still holding the trap door as Ulv pulled on Elora until she completely cleared the trap door, than began brushing the cobwebs off of her coat. Lifting his index finger to his lips Halfdan signaled to his companions to be quiet. Then with the same finger Halfdan pointed to his companions and then pointed up the stairs before signaling that he was going through the door, alone.

Concern grew on their faces, but they nodded in understanding to Halfdan. Ulv and Elora started heading up the stairs. Liv slowly closed the trap door and before she could walk past Halfdan squeezed her shoulder and smiled. Somewhat tense, Liv smiled back before following behind Ulv. Halfdan watched the rest of his friends as they disappeared up the spiral staircase as he put his left glove back on.

As Halfdan opened the door he could feel his heart beat racing. To his surprise the addition to the tower that made up most of Edge Keep was vast and wide, practically one large hall. In the center of it was a pool of water with three large pillars that acted like a cage around a crude sphere made of glass with metal seams. The sphere rotated and without the door to protect Halfdan he could feel the hum and cold energy that escaped from the object. Blue and white light whirled around like a storm, contained in the sphere. Stepping farther into the hall Halfdan noticed a large arched doorway to his left and in a corner by the door was a pile of staffs and wands. Each one made with care and decorated to match each creator's personality, but now discarded without a care.

Halfdan jumped when he heard the door behind him slam close. When he turned he noticed Blackhare hiding behind the door and used one hand to close it as she lazily leaned against the stone wall that once made the tower.

Blackhare was wearing a flowing sapphire dress with black accents. The bottom layer of her long white hair was braided into two long strands and wrapped in black ribbon. She was a small woman but her confidence made her seem bigger than she was. Halfdan grimaced in disgust as Blackhare gave him a feline like smile.

"Did you honestly think you could sneak up on me?" Blackhare purred. "My, Halfdan, you sure do look different since last time our paths crossed... what is it called? The Squealing Pig?"

"It *was* called the Singing Boar." Halfdan said with anger and irritation.

"I see you noticed my invention." Blackhare said, carrying on without a care about the Inn that once resided in Dragekall. She walked past Halfdan to get closer to the sphere and chuckled when Halfdan took a step away from her. "Magnificent, isn't it? I never get bored talking about it. I enjoy explaining what it does every chance I get. Even though everyone who has seen it ends up dead. I noticed that my little pets betrayed me and let you in here."

"What did you do to them?" Halfdan asked, not taking his eye off of Blackhare.

"Think about the bigger picture here. A seidmadr could never compare to the insight of a seidr. Honestly, the audacity of men at times. But that is all irrelevant to the energy they all can give me. No more bits and pieces of the future. With my orb I can see the future in great detail. I can also shape it with ease, but that draws energy from the orb. So I have to refill it from time to time. Such a drag; I'm starting to run out of people. I'll have to start gathering my little energy sources from different parts of the world. Not all of them are as dumb as you and walk right where I need them, seidmadr." Blackhare walked closer to the orb and stopped at the pools edge and knelt down and looked at her reflection. "Now tell me, when did you learn the gift? You seemed rather dull before."

"I thought you could see everything?" Halfdan said, scornfully. Trying to keep Blackhare talking as he thought on how to kill her. He lost the element of surprise and now he needed to outsmart or overpower her. Halfdan made the mistake of underestimating her before and didn't want to make the same mistake again.

Blackhare let out a laugh and put the tips of her fingers in the water and slowly swayed the ice cold water around. "I have better things to do than constantly keeping tabs on you. Kings can be rather demanding. He is funding my passion so I have to tolerate it, for now. You are not that important, Halfdan. Sooner or later I knew we would cross paths again. However, I was hoping the next time I saw you your head would be on a silver platter." Waiting for a response Blackhare kept moving her hand in the water sending out ripples. Growing bored she spoke again. "I can sense Frode in you. You cannot control his power. Honestly, he was destined for better. That's why I wanted him dead. Couldn't have any competition you know. There is something else you're not telling me."

Blackhare stood up and swiftly turned and flicked water droplets from her hand onto Halfdan's boots. Instantly the water froze into sharp spikes all around his feet, preventing Halfdan from moving. Letting out a cry of pain Halfdan tried to break free but couldn't.

"Tell me." Blackhare said as she slowly stepped closer, looking directly into Halfdan's eye.

"Jovi, he told me I needed to stop you. I was just going to let things go but he wouldn't let me." Halfdan said between pants of pain as the cold bit into his skin.

Blackhare scoffed. "Jovi, that poor thing. Honestly you'd be surprised the entities that try to talk to you. If you had proper guidance you would have known how easy it is to keep them at bay. Once you start talking to them it's impossible to get them to

256

stop. It's like getting sand in your boots; can't be rid of them. They will wear you down to the bone… or eye, in your case I assume."

"If you can shape the future why didn't you use your orb to stop the plague in Dragekall?" Halfdan growled. "Don't you work for the King? Shouldn't you care about his people?"

"Ha! You can't be serious. This is why I never take a seidmadr seriously. Too short sighted and can never understand the complexity of situations. Kings and Queens can be manipulated into doing anything I wish after I earn their trust. Then, if things fall apart it's their head, not mine. After creating the orb I looked into my future to see how I would die. Why not, it's my orb. I'm wise enough to prevent my own death. That's when I saw that a girl from Dragekall would lead to my death. So I used the orb's power to besiege the village with a plague. Unfortunately it didn't work as well as I wanted. There was a learning curve with the orb. It is a bit finicky. Turns out that the orb requires double the energy sacrifices for some of the deaths I caused. Apparently not every soul is as strong as others. Before I could finish my curse I heard Dragekall burned to the ground. How odd." Blackhare pondered for a moment before looking at the tower door. Puzzled as a man and bear came running out and headed to the main door.

Halfdan turned as far as his frozen feet would let him and watched in disappointment as Ulv opened and closed the door after Elora. A wave of heat hit Halfdan and he turned to see Liv standing there, visible fire flaring erratically all around her like a star.

"You." Liv said trembling in anger. "You are responsible for the plague. Should I put Blackhare on your urn, or would you prefer Hilda?"

"Don't call me that!" Blackhare yelled in fury as she pulled a boney wand out from her sleeve.

Halfdan braced himself as Liv exploded into a ball of fire, sure this was going to be the death of him. Blackhare, desperate to save her orb, moved her wands about with her eyes closed while murmuring ancient words from her people. Water from the pool came rushing out and collected itself in front of Blackhare. With her free hand and wand Blackhare gestured to the water before her and quickly lifted her hands up. The water spread out and grew up like an ancient tree before freezing, making an ice wall deflecting the fire. The heat caused the ice wall to crack, creating white veins through the thick ice. Halfdan was surprised that the ice wall saved him and considered himself lucky to be close to the orb, but it was quickly melting.

Before Blackhare could collect herself and plan her next move Liv, now in the form of a lindwurm engulfed in flames, came slithering over the remaining wall causing the ice to steam. Unpassed, Liv opened her mouth wide and bit down on the surprised Blackhare. Blackhare screamed as Liv shook her about like a dog trying to kill a small rodent.

Destroy the orb! Jovi yelled in Halfdan's mind.

Now that Blackhare was distracted Halfdan summoned fire from his hands to melt the ice around his feet. The fear in Halfdan's heart caused the fire to come forth with such intensity, setting his legs and boots aflame. The ice was gone but the pain from the burns was so great Halfdan couldn't move. Discomfort drove Halfdan to peel off his boots, exposing horrible blisters that popped and oozed. He withered on the ground and watched hopelessly as a rock from the keep came loose from the wall and flew across the room striking Liv in the head. Letting out a roar Liv dropped Blackhare before staggering back and falling to the ground, shaking the building.

Pushing back the pain Halfdan got up and staggered to the orb. Stepping into the now shallow pool, Halfdan lifted his hands to the orb as it began to lower to meet him. Halfdan could feel the life that was trapped within the orb, its hum was becoming more like a scream of agony and despair.

"Stop!" Blackhare yelled, crawling her way to him and the orb. She was bloodied and burned. Her long white hair was gone with only little burnt tuffs upon a mostly bald head. "You do not have enough control to use it!"

"I don't need to control it! Just need to use it!" Halfdan yelled back with a smile as he watched Blackhare's mouth drop open as he touched the orb.

Halfdan didn't put any thought in his intent as his fingertips touched the cold glass of the orb. Once his skin made contact the orb burst, sending out a wave of energy knocking Halfdan onto his back into the pool.

When Halfdan opened his eye again he noticed the hall was darker now that the orb was gone. He sat up and felt a shock of pain in his abdomen and saw a large glass shard protruding out of him.

CHAPTER 27

OLD FRIENDS ARE LAST TO BREAK AWAY. SAGA OF GRETTIR ~ NORSE PROVERB

Halfdan felt cold as he watched his blood run out of him and disburse into the pool. His mind was numb and unsure on what to do. Turning his head in search of Liv, his gaze fell upon Blackhare laying where he saw her last but with her own shard of glass protruding from her head.

Relief washed over Halfdan when he saw Liv stand up. A dark bruise was forming on the side of her face, but she was fine. Halfdan could feel himself reaching his hand out to her but it fell short as his world turned black.

Tired, weak and out of breath Halfdan fought to open his eye. He looked around with his blurry vision and saw a man with bound hands being led to a chopping block secluded in the deep darkness of the woods with only lit torches to light the way. Young Frode ran past Halfdan not noticing he was there and ran towards the bound man. The bound man was Frode's mentor and looked up at Frode with a brave smile.

The mentor kneeled down and tried his best to fix Frode's hair with his bound hands. "I told you not to come here."

Frode tried to speak between his sobs that only grew louder.

Frode's mentor tried to wipe away the tears. "Look at me... Remember what I told you. You're a seidmadr, you help people who are in need of guidance. The world is like looking into a reflection, you are not responsible for what happens to it. Focus on yourself and ignore the cruel people of the world. No matter what you do, there will always be evil eager to replace one another. The stars might have told us that you would be a merciless wizard out for blood that would kill thousands, but the second I looked into your eyes I knew that couldn't be true. I've said this before, if you find yourself hating a group of people or even just one individual you need to learn more about them. The more you know the more difficult it becomes to hate."

"Don't go." Was all Frode was able to muster, tears not subsiding.

"I have to. The guild asked if I believed in you enough to take your place. I said yes. But know that I will always be with you, guiding you." The mentor said and threw his bound hands over Frode and pulled him in close. Frode hugged his mentor and cried harder into his robes not wanting to let go.

A group of five men and women dressed in different elaborate robes holding staffs walked up to Frode and his mentor, causing them to stop their embrace. Horror caused Frode to stop crying and look up at the leader of the group who signaled to one of the men escorting his mentor to hand him an axe. To Frode's surprise the leader dropped the oversized axe into his hands.

A wolfish grin grew on the leader's face as he looked down at Frode. "Prove to us your loyalty."

Frode looked down at the axe then looked up at his mentor who was about to say something before he was punched in the gut and pushed back down onto his knees by his escorts.

Looking back at the leader Frode maintained eye contact as he let the axe roll out of his hands and onto the ground. "I do not need to prove my loyalty to you. I am not a killer."

The leader gave Frode a warm smile. "Perhaps your master is right, you are not a killer. Still, I would like to do one more test."

Frode watched as the leader bent down to pick up the axe off the ground. Without warning the leader swiftly turned and brought down the axe on to the mentor's skull, splitting his head open. Blood sprayed onto Frode's face as his mentor's body went limp and dropped to the ground with the axe still lodged in his head. Frode covered his mouth with both hands and trembled as his mind raced on what to do. Halfdan could feel every emotion and how hatred and revenge overwhelmed Frode's body.

Closing his eyes Frode pushed the feelings away. Thinking *I need to prove them wrong* over and over again in his head despite how easily it would have been for him to curse them and make their insides out, just like the fox that attacked his beloved cat. It would have been so easy. Frode wanted them to suffer for what they did, but he couldn't. He promised his mentor, his best friend and father figure, he wouldn't.

The leader of the guild studied Frode and let out a triumphant huff. "I still think it's just a matter of time. We will be watching."

Halfdan watched as the members of the guild walked into the shadows and vanished. Leaving Frode behind with his dead mentor. Halfdan reached out wanting to console the child before his surroundings began to melt and reform into a village with dead bodies scattered about. A younger Linna stood outside in front of one of the houses that wasn't engulfed in flames, in her hands was a bow and a flaming arrow. Halfdan almost didn't recognize his younger self as he came out of the house with a bag of stolen goods thrown over his shoulder.

"Think I got it all." Young Halfdan said as he stepped over bodies to stand by Linna's side as she shot the arrow into the grass roof of the farm house.

"Wish there were more houses to burn, this is fun." Linna said with a smile. "Let's head back and see what everyone else found in the chapel."

Young Halfdan groaned as he walked. "I don't want to get back into that boat. The earth finally feels steady under my feet."

"Tell me about it. We always get stuck in the boat with all the thralls too. Remember when your father had to stop Gunnar from throwing the thralls over the side of the boat because he grew sick of their crying." Linna said and mocked the way they cried and even pretended to rub her eyes.

Halfdan walked behind them and watched as his younger self playfully shoved Linna who gave a hard push back causing young Halfdan to fall over. Linna laughed as she helped young Halfdan up who was laughing now as well.

The joy stopped when Halfdan recognized a man approaching them. He was broad with arms swollen with muscle and covered in blood. Two bearded axes resting in holsters, one on each side of his hip. Never had Halfdan seen the man use a shield in battle and would often pull arrows out of his own body with a laugh, unaffected by the pain.

Young Halfdan straightened up trying to mask the fear on his face. "Hello father."

"Where is your sword?" His father asked, sternly.

Halfdan grimaced as he watched his younger self search his body then remembering that he must have dropped it during the beginning of the raid.

"Why are you not covered in blood from battle?" His father asked again but louder. When the young Halfdan didn't reply he grabbed him by the ear and pulled him forward. "Answer me!"

"He used my bow!" Linna lied for Halfdan. "He is better with a bow."

"We will see about that." Halfdan's father said and pulled him by the ear, leading them to the rest of the raiding party.

Halfdan watched as his younger self looked at Linna, utter fear in his eyes unsure on what was about to happen. But Halfdan knew, he wanted to turn and walk away but he was compelled to follow his former self. Halfdan watched as his father threw his only son on to the ground, getting everyone's attention as they formed a circle around them. Linna stood in formation, looking at young Halfdan with pity for the humiliation.

"Has any of my kin witness my son kill?" His father asked as he slowly walked around his son who staggered to his feet. "No one will vouch for my son?"

Young Halfdan looked around and noticed his raiding party, his family and neighbors, avoiding making eye contact with him.

"Not one!" His father exclaimed stopping in his tracks, taking one of his axes and dropping it in front of his son. The same axe Halfdan would carry for years and one day, unbeknownst to him, gift to his daughter. "Well, that is about to change. We are not taking back any slaves today."

Both young and old Halfdan's turned and looked at the bound group, huddled together by the boats. The group was made up of young children, women and frail men too old to fight back. Halfdan's father picked a boy out of the group who looked to be a few years younger than Halfdan. The would be thrall was given the other axe and pushed into the ring. The young boy held the axe awkwardly in his hands. Tears ran down the young boy's face as he muttered something in a foreign tongue. Young Halfdan didn't need to understand, he knew the boy was pleading for his life.

"Hurry up!" Yelled Halfdan's father amongst the other shouting from the rest of the raiding party.

"I'll make this quick." Young Halfdan told the boy as he felt his own tears run down his face, feeling himself lifting the heavy axe in the air. "I'm sorry."

Halfdan turned and closed his eye, not wanting to see what his former self did. He covered his ears and dropped down to his knees. "Make it stop!" He cried out and suddenly the noise around him stopped. When Halfdan opened his eye again he noticed that he was in a white void.

"Hello, Halfdan."

The familiar voice startled Halfdan causing him to turn around. It was Jovi. Wearing all black he had a body of a man, a head of a wolf and the familiar buck rack without any decorations. One eye was yellow like a wolf and the other was grey and human and Halfdan recognized it as his own eye. The mismatched beast smiled at Halfdan as if they were old friends.

"What do you want from me?" Halfdan asked hoping that Jovi would leave him alone after killing Blackhare.

"Just taking back what is mine. You can't move on after you die with my seal. Now tell me, do you think Frode will be waiting for you on the other side? What about your father?" Jovi gasped and spoke in a gleeful tone. "What about Linna?"

"I'm not giving it back." Halfdan said with a glare.

Jovi's smile went flat. "That's not how this works."

"I can't die yet. There are things I still need to do. I can't leave my daughter behind." Halfdan pleaded.

"What makes you think you are deserving of my sympathy?" Jovi asked in a tone that was already accusing Halfdan of being unworthy.

"I don't." Halfdan blurted.

"What?" Jovi said, taken by surprise.

"I don't deserve your sympathy. Please. There has to be something I can do for you. You seem like someone who has a lot of enemies. No offense." Halfdan said knowing that Jovi could send him off doing something far worse than killing power mad women. Desperate for more time Halfdan was ready to make any deal if Jovi was willing.

Jovi contemplated for a long moment, taking slow steps around Halfdan as if he was studying livestock. Halfdan could feel himself growing more eager for a response unsure if Jovi was just toying with him.

Jovi stopped pacing and looked Halfdan directly in the eye. "I'll be honest, not because I like you I just know what kind of person you are. You aren't going to like this deal. Your daughter is most likely better off without you anyway. She'll probably go off and get married and forget all about you."

"So what?" Halfdan said growing more irritated feeling that the conversation isn't going anywhere. "As long as I see, in person, that she is ok."

"Alright. Spare me your sorrows." Jovi said then grabbed hold the base of his antlers and broke them off his head.

Halfdan grimaced at the sound of the antlers breaking free from Jovi's skull. Jovi looked back at Halfdan with a face that showed no expression of pain or discomfort. Blood began running down Jovi's canine face as he stepped closer to Halfdan.

"Your spirit is already gone to *Valhalla… or *Hel, wherever it deserved. To keep you from wandering around aimlessly like your dragur friends I will have to give you a sliver of my spirit. Your body with either accept it or not, we will see." Jovi said stepping closer to Halfdan to loom over him. "Now, hold still while I put your crown on."

Halfdan's mind raced with a million questions making it impossible to grab just one and make it a complete thought. Unsure if he was making a grand mistake Halfdan watched as Jovi lifted the antlers and slowly brought them down upon his head. The base of the antlers bit into Halfdan's skull causing him to let out a sharp gasp.

Opening his eye again Halfdan looked around to notice he was leaned up against a stone wall. He was within a small shed like structure that was once used to hold animals. The door was gone allowing snow to drift in. Halfdan felt like he should be cold but the bitter air was somehow welcoming. Feeling as if he was being watched Halfdan turned his head and to his surprise Frode was sitting next to him.

"You're finally awake." Frode said with a sad smile.

"Frode!" Halfdan exclaimed and quickly sat up before groaning in pain and grabbing his abdomen.

"Take it easy." Frode said as he put a reassuring hand on Halfdan shoulder.

"I'm sorry, for everything. You are-"

"I know, Halfdan. You don't have to tell me. I've been with you this whole time. Our friendship was important to me as well." Frode paused to look at the entry way.

Halfdan followed Frode's glance and noticed his mentor standing in the doorway patently waiting and smiling back at them, a large brown cat brushed up against the man's leg and also started at Frode.

Halfdan looked back at Frode, letting in a quick uneasy breath. "You have to leave me again, don't you?"

Frode nodded his head. "You're going down a path I cannot follow."

Remembering his interaction with Jovi Halfdan quickly lifted his hand and felt the top of his head. The crown of antlers was not there. Putting his hand back down Halfdan couldn't help but draw a blank on what to say. For days Halfdan had wished to speak to Frode again and now he didn't know what to say. "When will I see you again?"

"Hopefully not anytime soon." Frode said with a warm chuckle. "Before I go, I wanted to tell you how proud I am of you. You have told me the things you have done. But I never told you that I admired that you never made up excuses to justify your actions. You accepted them and carried that burden. But you need to let that weight go, you've tortured your mind enough. You have malevolent energy keeping you alive and if you don't keep a strong mind it can fester. I don't want you to become like Jovi. Try to do something kind once a day, even if it's something small like feeding a stray dog or putting a bug outside rather than killing it. It won't cure the unsteadiness but it will keep you on track."

Frode patted Halfdan on the shoulder, got up and headed to the door and walked out with his mentor and cat into the snowy weather. Once Halfdan lost sight of Frode he felt a deep emptiness within himself that made him uneasy. Within the void Halfdan could feel a sliver of anger and despair that Jovi had left within him.

CHAPTER 28

ENJOY THE GOOD YOU ARE GIVEN.
HÁVAMÁL ~ NORSE PROVERB

Sitting in the dilapidated shed a little longer Halfdan collected his thoughts. Blackhare was dead. He owed Jovi another favor, but what that was is unclear. Frode has moved on.

Looking at his clothes they were frozen stiff from being in the pool then dragged outside into the frozen temperatures. His tunic had blood and a long cut where the shard of glass killed him. The wound was still red and irritated, but not as deep anymore. Halfdan's pants were burned and his feet still had blisters.

As Halfdan's thoughts began to wonder of his daughter and the rest of his companions he gathered the strength to stand up. Stepping into the snow Halfdan imagined the cold would anger the burns, but it was oddly soothing. Looking up into the sky the clouds that were dropping down the occasional snowflake didn't extend over the keep, but instead created a circle clearing in the sky where Halfdan could see *bifrost.

The green and yellow light kicking and slithering in the calm night without a care in the world. Halfdan could hear Liv upon the roof whistling to the bifrost causing it to dance with her song. He ran through the snow to the castle's door. The large arching doors weren't barricaded and Halfdan let himself inside. The hall of the keep had been cleaned up. No glass remnants laid on the ground, however the pool was frozen. The pile of staffs and wands were organized along the wall with great care. The stone that was used to strike Liv remained where it fell. The hole where the stone once resided in the wall now let the occasional snowflake blow in.

As Halfdan made his way to the old tower he now noticed how the stones that were used to build it looked more weathered than the new addition. Once inside the tower Halfdan felt a welcoming warmth from the glow of the candles illuminating the spiral staircase. As he walked up the steps he passed the first landing with a door when he heard another door up ahead open and close. Wanting to surprise Liv, Halfdan quietly moved up the steps and saw an unfamiliar figure. It was a youthful man of average height and build with long brown hair. Wearing a dark robe the man started to make his way up the stairs.

Swiftly, Halfdan caught up with the man and grabbed him by the back of the robe and pulled him back. Jumping out of the way Halfdan watched as the man rolled down the wooden steps and quickly ran down to meet him at the landing. The man groaned in pain and was surprised when Halfdan sat on his chest, using his knees to pin the stranger's arms to the ground.

Before Halfdan could land a punch on the man he yelled out.

"Halfdan! You fool! It's me!"

Astounded, Halfdan got off the man but didn't offer to help him up.

"We thought you were dead. Starting to wish you would stay that way." The man said with a glare as he rubbed his sore muscles.

Halfdan wrinkled his nose as he thought, then it hit him. "Elora?"

"Yeah, no shit." Elora said still glaring at Halfdan. "You happy? This is my original form."

"I don't understand." Halfdan said, now feeling horrible for what he did to Elora.

"Lot has happened since you, well… we thought you died. Since you destroyed the orb, magic is damaged. I don't know if it's just here or everywhere, but you can feel it. Magic doesn't flow regularly anymore. But Liv seems unaffected since she was close to the orb, so I'm sure you still have your powers." Elora gestured to herself and looked at Halfdan with a smile. "Could you do me a favor and make me more, well, womanly? You did throw me down the stairs after all?"

Halfdan frowned. "Why would you want to be a women? I don't care, I'm just curious."

Elora shrugged. "Why not? If you flirt with guys you can manipulate them and they give you things. That, and people are more likely to help a women than a man. Also, women are sexy and nicer on the eyes. Overall I just feel more comfortable looking feminine than like this. Wouldn't you want to be a women if you could?"

"No, not really." Halfdan said bluntly before letting out a nervous breath. "I can try my best. It was easy enough to transform Ulv."

"Don't make me ugly." Elora said brashly before readying herself.

Halfdan took off his gloves, cracked his fingers and relaxed. Murmuring under his breath Halfdan closed his eyes and pictured a fair maiden in his mind as he placed his hands on Elora's broad shoulders. As soon as Halfdan felt Elora's shoulders begin to slim down a piercing pain jolted from the top of his head and down his spine.

Stumbling back Halfdan watched as Elora's sharp features softened as he leaned against the stone wall. Halfdan's world was spinning as Elora examined her new self.

"Not bad." Elora said, not realizing Halfdan made her look like Liv but with long brown hair. Unaware that Halfdan was struggling, Elora took off the drab robes to reveal a flowing crimson dress that she stole from Blackhare's wardrobe. "Little tight, but not bad."

Halfdan felt the top of his head and could feel two sharp bumps under his scalp. Shaking, Halfdan noticed that the seal on his left hand was glowing. Realizing that he was no longer using Frode's magic but Jovi's. Elora noticed that Halfdan was losing his balance and ran to his side to support him.

"What's wrong?" Elora asked Halfdan, her voice now recognizable.

"I'm fine." Halfdan said weakly. "Take me to Liv, I need to see her... What's that smell?"

"Blackhare's room is filled with rabbits." Elora said guiding Halfdan up the tower. "Hope you like rabbit stew because we are going to be eating that a lot until this weather subsides."

"Could give me moldy bread right now and I'd be happy." Halfdan said with a painful smile.

"I'll make you something to eat after I drop you off with Liv." Elora said with a slight grin.

On the rooftop Liv continued to whistle with Ulv turned back into a dog sitting next to her, occasionally howling at the bifrost to sing with Liv. As Liv petted Ulv she remembered the last time she petted him like this she was watching her father and brother burn in a pyr.

"What are we going to do now?" Liv asked Ulv who could only look back at her. His tail was wagging as he looked at her with emotional eyes, trying to express that he felt the same way. Lost.

Liv and Ulv turned when they heard the trap door open. Ulv barked and whined before running to the door. At first Liv expected him to greet Elora, but to her surprise he was jumping at Halfdan who was being supported by Elora. Liv's breath was taken away, unsure if what she was seeing was true.

"Dad?" Liv asked.

Halfdan stepped out onto the roof and opened his arm and Liv came running to him and gave him a tight hug that squeezed the air out of his lungs.

"Come on Ulv, let's get something to eat." Elora said quietly and closed the door behind them. Leaving Halfdan and Liv alone on the roof of Edge Keep.

With Liv still in his arms Halfdan looked up and gazed upon the bifrost. Despite feeling empty and wondering where his soul could be Halfdan was grateful to be here, right now, holding his daughter.

271

"Why does Elora look like me?" Liv asked leaning back to look into her father's eye.

"You were on my mind when I transformed her." Halfdan admitted bashfully. "I was eager to see you, I wanted to make sure this wasn't a dream. That I'm really here. That I didn't lose you."

"I thought I lost you too." Liv said fighting back tears.

"I will never leave you. No matter what, I will always be by your side." Halfdan said, releasing Liv from his embrace and grasping her hand as they both looked up into the sky and whistled together.

ACKNOWLEDGMENTS

My Father, Joseph, for editing my book and always encouraging my writing, even when it was at its worse. Without your support this book would not be here today.

Hannah, for pushing me to my full potential. Your kind criticism and encouragement made me a better writer.

Brandon, for your contagious optimism and encouragement. Most of all your patience and assistance while publishing this book.

APPENDIX

Alfheim: World or domain of elves in Norse mythology.

Argr: Viking swearword that is not taken lightly. Means unmanly and coward.

Asgard: World or domain of the Norse gods.

Ashmen: What German Viking tribes or Ascomanni identified themselves as Ashmen.

Bacraut: Norse for asshole

Baulufotr: Viking insult meaning cow foot

Bifrost: Northern lights or aurora borealis. Considered the rainbow bridge that connects the Norse Gods to earth.

Bjørgvin or Bergen: Royal city / capital that King Olav III would reside in along with Oslo and Nidaros/Nidaróss. King Olav is said to be the founder of Bjørgvin.

Cairn: Mound of rocks. Could be used to bury a body under or used as a marker.

Codex: Predecessor of the book. Pages were made of papyrus or parchment rather than paper.

Eir: Norse Goddess or Valkyrie of help, medical skills, mercy and protection.

Emesis: vomit

Fisherman Constellation: More popularly known and Orion's belt and points to the north star.

Freyr: Norse God of kinship, peace, good weather and harvest. He had a golden boar named Gullinbursti who was the God of storms and summer.

Gauls: Viking slang for foreigners.

Hersir: Started at a word for a farmer who owned land and status of leader. Then became a title for someone who organized and led raids.

Huldufolk / Hidden People: Icelandic for Elves

Jarl: In a social class a Jarl is just below a King. They were wealthy and owned land.

Lamellar: Type of armor made from thin plates.

Lindwurm: Part of the dragon family but has no wings or hind legs.

Moraine: Topographical accumulations, hills, left by glaciers. Indentation created into the earth by glaciers are called kettles.

Nobby: Old English slang for noble

Norrbottensprits: Breed of dog from Norway that was used for hunting. Very cute. Look them up, you won't regret it.

Norvegr: Old Norse meaning "North Way" later becoming Norway.

Olav III or Olaf III: King of Norway from 1067-1093 also called Olav the Peaceful or Olav Kyrre. From the house of Hardrada and notorious for maintaining a long period of peace.

Oskilgetinn: Viking insult for being born out of wedlock, bastard.

Ostmen: Vikings living in Ireland, meaning men from the east.

Petrichor: Pleasant smell when it rains after a long period without rain.

Runes: Runes were an ancient alphabet and were used in Norway up till the 15th century.

Seidr / Seidmadr: Magical practice that focused on seeing and shaping the future. Seidr is the title given to women and seidmadr for men.

Tik: Viking insult meaning female dog

Valhalla: The Hall of the Slain who live blissfully, training and feasting daily, and lead by Oden. The slain also prepare to fight by Oden's side in Ragnarök.

Hel: Afterlife for those who did not die honorably and lead by Loki's daughter, Hel.

Valkyrja / Valkyrie: Chooser of the slain sent by Oden to choose who goes to Valhalla

VIKING DAYS OF THE WEEK

Sun's Day: Sunday

Moon's Day: Monday

Tyr's Day: Tuesday, named after Odin's son Tyr who is the god of war and justice.

Odin's Day: Wednesday, named after Odin who is the god of war and death and King of Asgard.

Thor's Day: Thursday, named after Odin's son Thor who is the god of the sky, thunder and fertility.

Frigg's Day: Friday, named after Frigg or Friia who is the wife of Odin and the goddess of marriage.

Saturn's Day: Saturday

ABOUT THE AUTHOR

R. Adrian Kolosso is by no means a historian, native of Norway nor a Viking; as neat as that would have been. Any factual errors are completely his own. This is a work of fiction.

Halfdan Saga, Battle of Edge Keep is R. Adrian Kolosso's first book to be published and hopefully the first book of a series. As this is being read he in the works of writing more fiction stories. He hopes that you enjoyed reading his book. It took a team of wonderful people to make this story come to life, along with avid readers such as yourself. Thank you.